BROKEN GOD

APRIL GAISFORD

FOR MY SPARKLY EMMALINE

This book is for all the ladies out there that want to join a motorcycle club. Or the ones that got swept away with BikeTok and now have a helmet kink.

Content and Triggers

Broken God contains many tropes and triggers. Please read with discretion; this list is not all inclusive.

Possible Triggers:

Violence, murder, sexual assault (off page, past tense, of children and adults), kidnapping, domestic violence, human trafficking, drug and alcohol use, divorce

Tropes:

Best friend's little sister, outlaw motorcycle club, unrequited love, FFM, why choose/non monogamy, height difference, grumpy/sunshine, BDSM

Definitions

Throughout the book, you will find a few terms that are specific to motorcycle romances. I have included a couple here, but if I have missed any, please feel free to reach out to me on social media!

Cut: the vest members in the club wear to show their allegiance. The vest is usually leather, contains a large club patch on the back, name tags and designations on the front.

Church: a meeting room specifically for the group. Little or no other business is conducted in the room. It is large enough to fit all members of the club

Contents

Moros, god of doom

Moros is the son of Nyx, the goddess of the night, and Erebos, the god of Doom.

He is the god of doom. An adjective attributed to him is "hateful."

Moros has the ability to make mortals foresee their death. He is the one to drive people to perdition.

Moros is called "the inevitable" and is as relentless as the Erinyes, the goddesses of vengeance. He is known for chasing his victim all the way into the Underworld.

Moros is associated with suffering that often comes when a mortal meets their doom.

He has no temples in Ancient Greece. His name is only spoken to pray he never comes.

Chrissy

Greecetravelideas.com, 2021

(Edited from original text)

Steel Warriors

Steel Warriors began in Pennsylvania, USA, as a group of men who supported the rights of minors during the strikes in the 1930s. The men would gather at strikes to support their neighbors. It was a bloody and gallant time for the group. When the workers gained their rights and the large-scale strikes slowed to a trickle, the group of men continued to gather. They began riding motorcycles as the popularity of the vehicle rose. The group officially became a motorcycle club in the 1960s.

In the 1990s, a member named Richard Meyers wanted more power and money from the club. The board members were content with their club and denied Richard's request to start new business ventures and take a seat on the board. In the late 2000s, Richard left Pennsylvania to open his own chapter in Texas. He made himself president of the San Antonio chapter. He established business with street gangs and the cartel. He soon had everything he desired: money, power, and more.

Texts from Tori

Tori:

I'm coming to stay with you.

Won't have service while I'm traveling.

See you soon.

Tyler:

Fuck yeah! (Undelivered)

PROLOGUE

ALEKS

"I'M GOING TO FIND her," Tyler types furiously on his phone. He's said this before. It's been three weeks since his younger sister, Tori, said she was coming to visit. We haven't seen her in 18 years. Tyler keeps in touch with her over the phone. Facetime, texts, and an unnatural number of videos about animals or farting or farting animals. He shows me most of them.

"Where would you start?"

My voice is deep and gruff. It's the first thing I've said all morning. Even that is too many words. I sip my dark coffee, watching Tyler pound his fingers on the phone.

"I don't fucking know, but it's been three weeks, Aleks. Where the fuck is she?"

I don't know. I don't know where she is for the first time since I met her as a kid.

"Are you going to call your parents?" Tyler's groan is all the response I need. He won't call them. Not yet. Maybe not ever.

I'm facing the doors to the restaurant. It's my spot. I can see the entire space from here. The doors open, shrouding someone in the bright midday sun. A small woman stands there, looking around the restaurant. The early morning sunshine prevents me from seeing her face, but I don't need to.

My life isn't a fucking romance novel. Sapph tells me about all the books she reads—the breaths people hold. The unrequited lover getting a happy ending. The bad guys getting the girls. The drama of younger sisters falling for their brother's best friend. All the fucking romance tropes. She reads those damn books and tells me because I don't tell her to shut up.

That isn't my life. I'm not a book boyfriend. I don't get the girl. I don't get the happy ending.

But I know Tori. Even unable to see her. My breath hitches as the small woman walks through the doors. This isn't a romance novel, but it's hard to fucking breathe.

"She's here."

Chapter One

VIC

I ran away from my life. I ran from my home, my family, my job.

I packed a small backpack and left all my electronics behind. I gathered some cash and took buses, trains, and cabs until I reached San Antonio.

I'm on the lam, on the run, attempting to hide, which is damn stupid. I'm a nurse, not someone who goes on the lam.

And yet, here I am, walking into a biker bar I've never been to. I'm not even positive this is the right bar. Tyler never told me the name of the bar his motorcycle club owns. I searched Google and came up with three possible bars. The club has a surprisingly small digital footprint, which bodes well for me.

I open the doors to Dionysus. The name surprised me; a biker bar named after a Greek god seems pretentious. I'm shocked that the area matches its name, not its owners. The bar looks clean, not overly dark. Various tables cover the floor: bar-height tables and booths are scattered around. Exposed brick is on three walls with industrial features. LED signs that look like old-school neon signs hang behind the bar. All the bottles of liquor are stored below, out of sight. I hope that's for aesthetics and not stereotypical shootouts. Couches fill one corner with large

TVs, a few gaming systems, and a couple of pool tables. Edison lights, which are my favorite, hang from the ceiling in gorgeous designs. Dionysus would approve.

I'm adjusting to the light differences when a large body slams into me. A small yip escapes as I'm swept off the floor and spun through the air. Tyler has his arms around me. I haven't seen him in forever, but I still know him. I relax against him as he stops spinning. He's rambling he missed me; he's angry I haven't texted. Where the hell have I been?

Me? I'm just fighting back tears. I don't want to cry right now. I squeeze him tightly, realizing he's very different from the last time I saw him. He left home at 18 to join a motorcycle club. I was 13. My parents all but disowned him. He is the black sheep of our family. They don't like that I stayed in touch with him, but I didn't give a shit. Tyler is my person. We talk regularly, but we don't see each other. At all. That's a whole different story.

My feet land on the ground. My senses adjust to everything. Once my head stops spinning, I get a good look at Tyler. He's still taller than me and beefier than he used to be. His shoulders are broad, not the skinny teenage shape they were when I watched him ride off on his shitty bike. He has a beard that reaches his collarbone. It's tinted red. The sides of his head are shaved, but the blonde hair on top has some length. He took after our mother while I inherited my father's genes. I look nothing like Tyler: short stature, long wavy brown hair, dark eyes. We have the same nose, but that's about it. He's still babbling when a beast walks up to our sides.

"Tor, you remember…"

"Aleks." Whoa, my voice did not need to be that breathy. Holy hell, this man.

"Tori." Was my name on his lips just as breathy? Am I projecting that? Probably.

Before me stands a man, if you can call him that; he's over six feet tall, towering over my short five foot four and a half inches. The nurses always add that extra half-inch at my yearly checks; I might as well own it. His arms cross over his chest, each bicep as big as my head. His long blonde hair spills over his shoulders. He has broad, muscular shoulders that I am definitely not drooling over. My gaze trails down his body. His dark T-shirt fits perfectly. Was it tailored? T-shirts don't fit anyone that well. The dark denim jeans are the kind that would look better on my floor.

Well, my mind is officially in the gutter. No man has the right to fill out jeans that way. He wears dark combat boots. My eyes scroll back up, observing his cut. President. His tag says "Moros." That's interesting. I knew he was the president. He has the look for it. His jaw is covered in scruff, enough to hide the skin below, but not much longer. Like Tyler, the sides of his head are shaved, but the top is long. It hangs down over his shoulders. It's thick and full, and I want to run my fingers through it. His tongue darts across his luscious lips, and my eyes track the movement. What do those lips taste like? That tongue? How good would it feel on my cunt?

"Vic," I mumble, holding my hand out.

Should I shake his hand? Can I hug him? Please, god, let me hug him. Will he scoop me up like Tyler did? Fuck, I hope so. I want to wrap my body around him and climb him like a tree. I finally reach his eyes. Holy shit, they are blue. Piercing blue. Icy blue. Lustful blue. Burning blue. He glances down at my hand, then back up.

"He doesn't like to be touched, Tor," Tyler explains quietly by my side. I forgot he was there.

"Vic," I repeat with more confidence and drop my hand.

"What?" Aleks's voice ruins my panties, not that they stand a chance. Of course, his voice is deep. What else could it be when you look like a demi-god?

"My name." I'm still mesmerized. I've never met someone that looks like him. Sure, I've seen actors and models, but never in person, never this close. I drop my head to stare straight in front of me. My gaze is eye level with his chest. I want to sink my teeth into the skin beneath his arms, in the skin beside his nipples. Will he moan if I bite them? Will he make me kiss the hurt after, forcing my head against his chest?

"Your name?"

The world around us is gone. It's only this man: his body, his voice, my lust. Shit, I have never had it this bad. I want to lick his chest, taste his dick, see what makes him lose control. My eyes roam his body, and he watches. His gaze doesn't tear away from my own. He is watching me ogle him, and I can't stop it. He probably gets this all the time. Scratch that. He definitely gets this all the time. Anybody with eyes would look at him like this. Holy hell, it's so hot in this bar.

I cough, trying to clear my head. His lips curve up into a knowing smirk.

"Yeah. My name," I blink a few times, tearing my eyes away from Aleks. How long was I staring at him? Tyler is oblivious, just watching with giant puppy dog eyes. He's so happy to see me. I am, too. I'm glad to be done traveling. "I go by Vic now." Tyler shrugs casually. "You and Tyler were the only ones to call me Tori. I've been Victoria since college. It's time for a change," I explain.

"Got it. Vic. What the hell took you so long? I almost called Cathy!" Cathy, our mom. He never talks to her. Never. Before I can answer, a shrill voice yells from the corner, growing closer with each word.

"Clint," the woman whines, "you never greet me like that! Who is this?" Jealousy oozes from this woman.

"Destiny, this is Vic, my baby sister." A red-haired woman walks up to Tyler's side, wedging into his grip. His hesitation doesn't stop him from wrapping his arm around her. She doesn't notice his discomfort. She looks me up and down with contempt.

"Oh, Vicky," she says to me, then looks back to Tyler. "You've never mentioned her before."

"It's Vic," Aleks leaves no room for argument. Destiny huffs, turning her attention back on me.

"Yeah, I have. I just called her Tori before." Destiny opens her mouth to say something else. It's going to be stupid. I've only known her for about eight seconds, but I can already tell she's a bitch. What does Tyler see in her?

"Wait, did you call him Clint?" I interrupt.

That's when I notice his cut. He has a Vice President patch on one side. "Clint" is written on his name tag. His name is not Clint, not even his middle name. In no way could his name be associated with Clint. There must be a story here. His face shrivels with embarrassment.

"We use nicknames on our cuts and when we're out to maintain some anonymity," Aleks explains. That's why his says "Moros." Is Moros his last name? I've never heard anyone use his last name.

"Why Clint?"

Aleks has that smirk on his face again. God, his face is beautiful like that. I wonder what a genuine smile looks like. What does lust look like? Does he tip his head back when he orgasms? Can I get him in a position where he can't move his head, and I can watch pleasure ripple over his features?

Aleks turns to Tyler, whose hand is dragging across his face.

"Oh, I don't even know this story! Tell me, Clint." Yeah, I don't like her.

"No," 'Clint' groans. Destiny turns to Aleks.

"You tell me, Mor," she chirps. His scowl deepens. This is his regular face; the deep lines of a frequent frown are visible beneath his beard.

"It's not my place to tell," he mutters.

Destiny pouts, stomping her foot. I've never been to a biker bar. I've read motorcycle club romances and watched all of Sons of Anarchy. I'm pretty sure that makes me practically an expert on the subject. My sarcasm hasn't faded in the past few weeks of travel, even in my head. If the stories in media are anything like real life, I should be able to find someone to tell me this story. I scan the room, looking for an accomplice in my mission.

A group of young guys hang around the pool tables. A few have cuts without all the badges. They are probably prospects. They won't tell the VP's embarrassing story. Some stragglers hang around the tables, looking tired and hung over—reg-ular club members, but not the type to share secrets. A group of women in tight clothing gather near the prospects and other men. Assuming they even know, I doubt I can get it out of them.

Then I see it. A table in the corner with six older men. All fat with decades of alcohol and greasy food. Gray hair and wrinkled skin from a lifetime of hardships. If I know anything about biker clubs, and I do because I'm clearly a media expert, they will tell me the story. Without saying anything, I turn and walk in their direction. Tyler asks what I'm doing, but halfway through his question, realization dawns. He curses and groans but doesn't try to stop me. I want to look back to see their faces, but I can't. I need to see this through.

"Morning, men," I greet the table. They all turn their attention to me. A couple of the men look amused, while others look angry over the interruption. I clear my throat, trying to keep my wits. "Your VP over there," I point back to Tyler, "I'm told he goes by Clint, but no one will tell me why. Would one of you?" I lean down, pressing my hands on the table. They are close enough together that my breasts shove out of my v-neck shirt. My breasts are small, so pushing my arms together makes them appear larger. Using my breasts is easy. As one, they glance down at my chest, up at me, then over to Tyler. They all burst out in laughter, startling me with the sudden loud noise. I stand up, glancing back at Tyler. His ears are dark red now. His cheeks never blushed, but his ears always gave away his embarrassment.

As the laughter dies down, one of the old bikers points at the man to my left. "You wanna do the honors, Joe?"

According to his cut, the man beside me, Joe, glares at the other man. "I'm not telling that fucking story," Joe barks. A hint of amusement twinkles in his eyes. This stirs another round of laughter from the table.

"Several years ago," one of the other men starts, "before he became VP, we were volunteering at a church." Well, that's not how I thought this story would begin. "Ole Clint went missing for a while, along with Joe's 19-year-old daughter. We found Clinton near the pulpit, getting the Monica Lewinsky treatment." The table explodes with laughter again. Joe tries to act angry, but he eventually starts chuckling. I join this time, amused with this story of my brother.

It doesn't surprise me at all. When the presidential scandal broke in the 90s, our parents had to explain it many times to Tyler, much to their disappointment. They hated having to explain oral sex to their young son, but he didn't see the problem with it. Tyler loved the idea of being in a position of power and getting a blowjob somewhere inappropriate. The nickname fits him completely, even if the club doesn't know his childhood obsession.

I turn and walk back to Tyler, Destiny, and Aleks. Tyler is both annoyed and joyful. Destiny is annoyed and angry that I got the story before she did, and she's jealous that he was with someone else. Aleks has a slight smile on his face. It doesn't reach his eyes. A full smile would be devastating on his face. I walk up, patting Tyler's shoulder.

"Good ole Clint," I tease. He swats my hand away, and we both giggle. Destiny huffs, stomping her feet. She demands I tell her the story. Instead, I turn to grab my backpack. It fell to the floor when Tyler scooped me up. I don't see it, though. It was right here. As panic rises, I scan the area for the bag containing everything I have. All my cash is in that bag, the few outfits I brought, and my only pair of sneakers. I am wearing sandals now. I need that bag!

"I had it taken to your room," Aleks's voice sounds behind me. I whip around to see him. He nods toward a door in the back corner, behind the pool tables. "We set it up when you texted." An underlying question lingers on his words. Where have I been for the past three weeks? I'm not answering that.

"Oh, thank you." I want to tell them I can stay in a hotel. I don't have access to income right now, and a hotel would drain my cash in a few days. If the room is set up, I'll stay there. Anything else can be sorted out later.

"You showed up on the perfect night," Tyler starts, untangling himself from Destiny. "Shirley is grilling tonight for a party. It's always the best!" He is so excited. He was always easy to please as a teen. I'm glad to see he is still like that. It's been eighteen years since I last saw him, and the time is glaringly obvious as I take him in now. I hate that we haven't been able to see each other. With him disgraced from my family, we haven't had the chance to get together.

He tells me Shirley is Joe's wife, basically the mom of the club. Stepping away from Destiny, he wraps his arm around my shoulder and leads me through the bar. He points and waves at a few men, telling me who they are. None of that information sticks. Maybe one day, but not today. I'm tapped out on taking in new information. We reach a door with a touchpad. Tyler explains it leads to the rooms for the members and you need a card to access it. He tells me I have my own now and pats his pockets.

Aleks reaches over my shoulder, holding out a card. One side has the club logo, and the other is blank. Tyler thanks him as he grabs the card. I glance at Aleks in time to see him roll his eyes. I try to fight the laughter, but I'm not entirely successful. Tyler can't keep up with anything. I'm surprised they trusted him with his keycard. Tyler scans the card, hands it to me, and guides me through the halls. Destiny doesn't follow, thankfully, but neither does Aleks. I'm less thankful for that.

Tyler shows me the elevator and stairs. He takes me to the second floor and points down, explaining where the board members stay. Only a few older members who haven't moved out have rooms on this floor. The bottom floor is for the club whores and guests. Patched members and a select other few get the third floor, which is where my room is.

He leads me to the end of the hallway on the third floor. The exit is at the end, with my room on the right. The exit leads down to the garage. His and Aleks's rooms are directly below mine. He scans the keycard on the touchpad beside the door and waves me inside. My bag is sitting on the bed, waiting for me. A sigh of relief falls from my lips.

The room is simple. Blue walls with a single window surround a full-size bed. It has a metal frame and a grey comforter, simple but nice. A dresser with a mirror is beside the main door. Two other doors are in the room. Tyler points to one, telling me it's a closet and the other is a bathroom. I share a Jack and Jill bathroom with Sapph, another woman. She's on a mission and will return in a few days. I didn't think they let women in the club. I'll ask about that later.

Tyler asks what I need. What do I need? Everything. Nothing. I settle for a shower and a nap. If there will be a party tonight, I need to rest and freshen up before that. He nods but grabs my shoulders, drawing my attention to him.

"I'm so fucking glad you are here, sis."

I smile at him, glad to be here, too. I wish I weren't running from family. I wish I didn't feel the need to. Honestly, I wish for many things at this moment, but none of them will happen. He hugs me tightly and leaves the room. I rummage through my bag with only three outfits. One is still clean; I'll need to wash the others soon. My cash and sneakers are at the bottom, along with the few sentimental possessions I couldn't leave. I glance around the room, debating where to put all my things. I chuckle at myself; it's not like I have a lot of things.

I collapse on the bed. I want to take a shower first, but exhaustion consumes me. I don't realize how tired I am until my body settles onto the comfortable bed. It may not even be comfortable under normal conditions, but it feels like a fluffy cloud right now. I'm asleep before I know what's happening.

CHAPTER TWO

ALEKS

She's mine. She's fucking mine.

Tyler would kill me if he knew what I thought about his baby sister. The things I want to do to her would break her. She's so tiny. I've towered over people since I was a teen. No one has ever made me feel like a giant like she does. I could grab her ass and pin her hands above her head without any effort. Her ass... Tyler is going to kill me.

Her hips are wide, perfectly round. She's not a tiny woman like some of the drugged-out club whores. No, Vic is a woman who has curves and a full figure. I want to drag my hands over her skin, spend all day touching her, strolling my fingers over her curves. Find out how soft she is. I need to know what sounds she makes when my lips suck her nipple.

I throw back another shot. I've been at the bar since Tyler led her to her room. Knowing she's in there, taking a shower, stripping her clothes off, rubbing hands over her sides... shit. I slam the empty glass down, motioning for a refill. My jeans are tight and wildly uncomfortable right now. I should go rub one out. She's coming to the party tonight, and if she wears Daisy Dukes again, I'll be hard all night. Her hips in those shorts should be illegal. So thick.

Vic is different from other women. She makes me want things I have never wanted before. I don't like touching people during sex. I don't like touching people at all. Sex is a form of release. With Vic, it will be a work of art, a life changing experience. No, I can't think like that. I don't get to have her. She's my best friend's little sister. I'm broken beyond repair, and she deserves better.

The burn of the second shot does nothing to steer my mind away from Vic. Someone slides into the seat beside me. I don't even need to look. It's her. I can feel it. My dick can feel it. I glance over and give her a nod. She smiles weakly, nervous about something. She nibbles on her lip, drawing my attention there. My cock is going to get chafed against the denim. Don't touch it. Don't touch your dick in front of her.

She's still wearing the shorts and v-neck top she had on earlier. Her hair is rumpled, and her eyes look sleepy. The bartender asks what she wants. She orders a soda, not familiar with the club. Everyone is already drinking, and most will be drunk before the hour ends. She doesn't look at me, taking in the LED signs behind the bar.

I study her profile. The delicate lines of her jaw, her cheeks rounded with age. Her wary eyes don't go unnoticed. For all intents and purposes, she has a good life. Married to a state senator. Master's degree in nursing. No kids, lovely suburban house. Good health, no outstanding debt. Nothing on paper is concerning, but her eyes tell a different story. Something dark lingers there. Something that drove her to leave her perfect suburban home to stay at a biker bar. It's not a dirty bar, but it's no place for someone like her.

I've been keeping tabs on her since Tyler and I left Pennsylvania. Even before then, I did what I could to watch over her. I was a teenage boy living with demons and limited resources at my disposal. I checked in on her when I could and snuck away at other times to see her on the playground at school. She was ten the first time I met her. I was fifteen. It wasn't love or lust, but I had a deep desire to protect her and keep her safe. Some deep internal part of my psyche knew. I don't know what it knew, but I couldn't leave her alone. When Tyler and I moved from

Pennsylvania to Texas, I got updates from him about her. I started social media accounts to follow her, creating more as she did.

My ability to watch over her has advanced from Myspace to more lucrative means. She doesn't know. I still follow her on social media under fake accounts. I track her bank accounts and tap into her home security system. That is surprisingly easy for such a wealthy household. I don't invade her privacy. I only check in enough to know what she is up to. If there is anything I can't access, I have a guy who can. I know as much about her as anyone who lives 1500 miles away and doesn't directly speak to her can. I've wanted to call her myself. Hear her voice over the phone. Tyler occasionally includes me on his Facetime calls with her. Like always, I give a few grunts, and that's all I can muster. I don't like talking to people. The less I say, the better.

"Hi," her voice is soft—not meek, just not loud. I can say 'hi,' but instead, I nod.

"Um, do you have a maintenance person that works here?" Confusion sweeps over my face.

"No. We call one." She nods her head, turning away from me. I shift to face her more, but not enough to expose my raging boner. "Why?"

"Oh, well, it's..." She starts as if she will make some excuse. Then, she steels herself. Her shoulders rise slightly, not noticeably, but it's hard to miss when I'm staring intently. I need to snap out of it. I can't fuck her. "The shower in my room doesn't work. It spurted a few times and rattled, but nothing happened." I process this, trying to remember the last time someone used it. Sapph has been with another chapter for a while, maybe a month? The room has been unoccupied since then. I glance at the clock. It's late afternoon. The plumber would come out if I called him now, but what if I didn't?

"It's too late to call him now. I'll call tomorrow." Tomorrow is Saturday. He probably won't work then, especially if I don't call. "You can use my shower." Problem solved. We don't even need a plumber.

"Oh, no. I don't want to bother you. I'll go use Tyler's." She edges off her seat to leave. Nope. Don't like that.

"Trust me, you don't want to use that one. Tyler may be in his late 30s, but he's still a bachelor. Even our cleaning crew won't go into his room." She grimaces, wrinkling her nose in a way that has my cock leaking precum. While I want her in my room, I don't think I could get her there without everyone seeing the outline of my rock-hard erection. "Besides, he's in there with Destiny." I roll my eyes at her. I can't stand that woman. Vic chuckles beside me.

"You don't like her?"

I bring my drink to my lips and give an affirming nod to her question. It's an understatement. The brown liquid stings on the way down, not hitting as hard as earlier.

"What does he see in her?"

"She's got a good pussy." Vic blanches beside me.

"Oh, gross," her hand moves to swat me, but she catches herself. She waves her hand in the air instead. Fuck. I'm done for. Is this real? This overwhelming, unable to breathe, need to be near her, desire to keep her feeling. She didn't touch me. I hate being touched. She remembered that. Half the whores have been slammed against walls for trying to grab me. Repeatedly. Some bitches just never learn.

"I don't want to hear about her pussy or his dick. No, thank you." My lips curve up at the corners. This is the closest thing I have to a smile. This is also the most I've smiled since I was a young child. My life isn't happy. I don't have many reasons to smile. She changes that for me. Silence settles, both lost in our thoughts. Before we say anything, Lucy, my bar manager, walks up.

"Mor, we need to get another bartender on staff. I can't keep running with the whores filling in. The ones that help are the worst." She inclines her head toward the group of women in the corner, already climbing over the men.

"I can do it!" Vic's sudden words catch us off guard. "Not permanently, but I can help until you find someone else." I eye her suspiciously. She traveled for three weeks on a trip that should have taken two days, less if she flew. She showed up with a small backpack and is now looking for temporary work. Nothing about this makes sense.

"Do you know how to make drinks?" Lucy asks. Vic snaps her fingers and points at Lucy.

"No," I snort at her answer. "But I can read and count and carry drinks. So that counts for something, right? You don't need to give me a paycheck or anything. I'll work for tips."

"Well, fuck me. You're hired," Lucy reaches out to give Vic a high five—both grin from ear to ear.

"You'll get paid, but we can do cash if you prefer," I insist. Vic smiles at me. My cock was almost soft again. It's not now. The image of her curved lips tinted a blushing pink is forever burned into my memory. I want to replace every memory with that one.

"Okay. Can we go shower now?" My brain misfires. Visions of us in the shower, covered in soap suds, my hands on her body... "You said I could shower in your room? I need you to show me where it is." Right. I need to take her there. I nod, hoping the glaze over my eyes looks more like alcohol than lust for my best friend's little sister. I down the rest of my drink, waiting for her to turn before adjusting myself. It's obvious what I'm doing, but I can't walk through the bar without shifting.

I follow her to the rooms, watching her ass sway. Hell, at this rate, I'm going to need a chastity cage. I've never used one, but I can't have a hard-on every time I'm near her. I end up behind her on the stairs. The distance puts her ass directly in front of my face. It's even better up close. Those shorts were made for her. Are they painted on? They are so tight. I wonder what they feel like coming off. They'll need to be peeled off her skin. My fingers would need to glide across her hips as I drag the material away from her waist.

She stops at the landing for my floor and turns to me. I meet her eyes. She knows I am staring. She knows what I am thinking. She doesn't glance down at my hips. She knows what she'll find there. Vic tries to hide her smile. Even biting her lip doesn't stop her smile or the slight pink shading her cheeks. She says she will grab her things and will be right back. I wait by the door, trying to think of anything but the fact that she'll be naked in my room in a few minutes. The only thought that fills my mind is her showering. I've never been so consumed by something that wasn't traumatic.

When she's back, I lead her into my room. I head straight for the bathroom but realize she has stopped in the doorway. She stares around my room, marveling at my space. It's not what she expected. The walls are white with grey undertones. When the light hits it just right, it looks stone grey. The ceiling is dark grey, drawing the grey undertones from the walls. The floor is dark hardwood, with a large, colorful rug filling most of the space. I don't care for cold floors, and I don't want carpet permanently installed. A few pieces of artwork hang on the walls. The bed is rumpled. I never make it when I wake up. The room is light and clean, a perfect place to relax. With all the shit we go through, I need a clean space to decompress. Her attention finally draws back to me.

"I didn't think you'd have such a nice room."

I glance around the room with her, trying to see what she does. If she believes me to be the ruthless biker president, this room would be out of place. I'll show her who I am and why this room makes sense. I shouldn't. I should stay away. She doesn't need me: someone who is broken and damaged.

I have nothing to say, like always. I turn and walk to the bathroom. I've stayed in this room for the past five years. I remodeled it completely when I moved in. I debated not taking this room, but this room is the largest in the complex. It's hard to beat having a four-person shower. I've never had another person in there; the space is all mine. Vic is the first person to use this shower other than me. Her gasp tells me she'll like it.

She stands in the doorway, hands over her mouth, eyes wide as she scans the bathroom. White subway tiles cover the walls' bottom half and the entire shower, while the top half is painted teal. A few framed pictures hang on the wall between industrial light fixtures. The massive shower is in the corner, with a towel warming rack. I designed this space for myself; it's calming and easy to clean. What's better than that?

I explain which nozzles do what. It's not complicated. Vic could quickly figure it out on her own. She watches me curiously. I'm her new interest now that she has seen my room. I show her where the towels are and how to use the warming rack and ask if she needs anything. When she hesitates, I do, too. Does she want me to stay? No, I'm reading that wrong. She wouldn't want me to, but I can't leave. I finally ask if she knows how to get to the backyard. Her eyes pinch shut in confusion, and she slowly says, "No."

I huff a laugh at her and tell her to find me in the bar when she finishes. I head to her room to check out the shower. I have no intention of fixing it for Vic. If it keeps her in my room, that shower will stay 'broken.' Sapph turns the water off every time she leaves. Vic doesn't know that and doesn't need to. I'll tell her the plumber doesn't have much availability. They are always so busy, especially when it's fixing a shower, that I don't want to fix. So busy.

Vic's room is a standard member room. It's plain compared to mine, but she can decorate it if she stays long enough. She hasn't said how long she's staying. I hope it's a while. It took her three weeks to get here, and she just took a part-time job in my bar. Surely, that means she'll stay. I don't want to ask. I don't want to know if she's leaving, and I'll have to wait another eighteen years to see her. I won't let her go. She's here. She's mine.

She only had a backpack with her. Maybe she has another suitcase in a hotel room, but I have a feeling she doesn't. She left a few things on the bed. I lift the clothes, but that's all: no devices, books, magazines, or anything else. Unable to stop, I grab her shirt and bring it to my nose. I inhale deeply, absorbing her scent. It's crisp, like the ocean, but something else too. I fist her shirt tightly, cock growing in my pants. Goddammit. I can't even use my shower or room to masturbate in. I palm my cock over my jeans.

I lock the door to Vic's bedroom and sit on the bed beside her pile of clothes. I tug my dick free and pull on it. It's still leaking from before. Fuck, I have it bad for her. Shirt in one hand, dick in the other, I think of that sweet little ass walking up the stairs, swaying perfectly. She's so perfect. I bet she would feel so tight around my cock. I wonder if that damn husband of hers ever fucked her properly. I bet she makes the sweetest noises, moaning and gasping as I thrust deep inside her.

I squeeze my dick harder. I have her on the bed with her feet on my shoulder. She's so short they rest against my collarbone, not long enough to reach any higher. Her hands squeeze her breasts, driving her wild with desire. My balls tighten with my orgasm. I imagine her cunt squeezing me tightly as she yells through her climax. I would pull out and spurt my semen all over her exposed cunt and belly. My orgasm tears through me suddenly. Instinctively, I use my other hand to catch my release.

Her shirt is still in my hand.

Her shirt is now covered in my jizz.

Fuck.

I use her shirt to clean myself. It's already dirty; I might as well use it. Fuck, what a stupid mistake. What the hell am I supposed to do now? "Oh, hi, Vic. Here's your shirt. Sorry about the jizz. Yeah, your shower is broken, and you'll have to use mine. Then you can wear your clothes with my jizz on them." Jesus.

I stare for a minute around the room. My mind is hazy with alcohol and post-orgasm fog. With the semen-covered shirt in my hand, I check the shower. It does exactly what she said: spurts and sputters, then groans. I turn off the knobs and reach to rub my face. I remember the cum-soaked shirt before I do and sigh. Back in her room, I grab all her clothes. I'll wash them. That's a nice thing, right? What the fuck am I doing?

I'm sitting at the bar when she walks up beside me. She looks anxious and unsure. I've had another double and feel like shit. This alcohol is not helping anything.

"Um, hi," she starts, glancing around. "Did someone go into my room?"

"Yeah, I did." That didn't clear anything up for her. "I was checking your shower." She nods but doesn't look convinced.

"Did you take my clothes?" Ah, I haven't told her.

"Yeah. I washed them. I'll put them in the dryer later." Her face still hasn't changed, scrunched with confusion.

"Oh. Thanks." Was that a question? It wasn't clear.

I throw back my drink and lead her through the rooms again. Our garage is at the back of the restaurant. Above the garage is our backyard, a massive pool, chairs, grills, a fire pit, and a yard with fake grass. It has privacy fencing to block the view from other buildings. Buildings in this area are low, but we don't want to be on display. The backyard is only accessible through the rooms. We don't get unexpected guests here, only the restaurant is open to the public.

Vic walks behind me quietly, not saying anything. She has on tight jeans with a worn band tee. It looks worn from use, not like it was made that way. It must be several years old. I lead her over to a stack of coolers and grab a beer for her. She tentatively takes it, sipping it as she looks around. Her clothes aren't out of place here, but she seems like she is. She's probably more comfortable in a snooty black-tie affair with Prosecco and snails or something. Tyler yells at her from across the yard then joins us. He rambles for a few minutes, then tugs her away to introduce her to others. I lean against the short outdoor bar, drinking my beer.

"She's pretty cute," Lucy says beside me. I glance at my bar manager. Her hair is neon pink, styled with hair ties to look like a mohawk. It's a good look for her. I grunt at her statement, not in the mood for conversation. "So, you gonna fuck her?" I give her a side-eyed glare that causes Lucy to chuckle. She shrugs and starts to walk away. "Okay, but if you don't, someone else will. It's been a while since we've had fresh blood." She waves in Vic's direction.

Tyler has abandoned Vic. Destiny is arguing with Tyler. She's always starting some shit. Vic is more comfortable now. She's chatting with Rio and a couple of others. Her smile is bright as she animatedly tells a story to the men. They want her. Even from across the yard, I can see the lust in their gazes. The fucking passes they make over her body are audacious. My blood boils, and my teeth clench. I collapse into my favorite chair near the fire pit, watching the party.

Shirley eventually brings food out, and everyone starts eating. Vic sits with Tyler, Destiny, Rio, and Lucy. She looks comfortable there. I lose myself, staring at the fire. These gatherings are always hit or miss for me. Some nights, my demons run wild, and all I can do is sit and dissociate as they keep me in a chokehold. I can enjoy the party, be near people, and swim on other nights. Tonight is different. I'm dissociating, staring into the fire, oblivious to everything around me, but my demons aren't out. Just a small woman with a thick brown bun at the top of her head and sinfully tight jeans.

Chapter Three

ALEKS

"Here, this is for you."

Vic holds a plate of food for me. I don't know how long I've been sitting here, lost in my mind. I take the plate from her, noting how she holds the opposite side so there's no chance of an accidental brush of our fingers. The plate is loaded with my favorite foods. It does look delicious; Shirley knows how to throw a party. Did Vic guess what I would like?

"Shirley told me what you like to eat." I huff a laugh. She must be able to read my mind. She holds out a fork and plops in the seat beside me. "How often does she put on these events?"

"About once a month, give or take."

"That's a lot. Do people help her?" Vic's eyebrows lift, impressed with the party occurring around us. A few dozen people fill the yard: members, prospects, whores, a few kids from older members.

"Some of the whores will, but Shirley does most of it," I reply, and Vic grunts unsatisfactorily.

"That doesn't seem fair."

I shrug in response and dive into the food. Shirley has organized and cooked for these parties for as long as I can remember. She doesn't work outside of the club. I've never asked if she liked it, but I assume she does since she keeps putting them on. She and Joe have a daughter, but she left the area and works at some corporate job in Portland. I'm glad she got away from us. Shirley still organizes all our volunteer opportunities and parties.

Vic sits quietly beside me while I eat. She has a beer she sips occasionally, but she isn't drunk. I can't help but wonder what drove her here. Is she leaving her husband? He's a piece of shit, in my opinion, but she did marry him. She must like something about him. He's a conservative Republican; does she hold those same views? She hasn't said anything to Tyler about her marriage or her political beliefs. They talk about her job but not much more about her personal life.

After a while, she questions how long the parties last. They can easily go until morning before people clear out. She mutters a curse and says she's going to bed. She's not used to the late hours. As she rises, she grabs my empty plate and heads to the racks where we leave them. It is awkward to have someone do that for me. Typically, I hold it until I have to pee or get another drink. Sometimes one of the whores will come over and take it, thinking it will grant them some favor. I don't think Vic is doing that. She's just a thoughtful person, or maybe whipped by her husband.

She walks back and hands me a glass with a double shot. I stare at it, confused about what is happening. I'm not familiar with this level of kindness. Is she doing this because we gave her a room? Does she think she owes me? She doesn't. Do I need to tell her that? I don't want her to feel obligated to wait on me.

"I noticed yours was empty," she points at my drink with a soft smile. "Thought you could use another." My face is pinched with uncertainty.

"You didn't have to do that."

She shrugs, "I know, but you didn't have to let me use your shower or wash my clothes."

I did have to do those things, but I'm not about to tell her I masturbated into her shirt. Or that I wanted the image of her naked in my room. I nod at her, and she walks away. I retain enough control not to watch her leave. I feel that control slipping, though. She will be my downfall, my weakness. For the first time in my life, I want that.

Tyler sits in the chair beside me, and Destiny climbs into his lap. She's thankfully subdued with alcohol or drugs. Whatever Tyler gets from her, Destiny gets drugs and alcohol. Tyler looks happy, but I think that's because his sister is here. He isn't usually this content. He glances around the backyard.

"Did she go inside?" I don't need to ask who.

"Yeah, went to bed," I tell him.

He nods, and Destiny snores softly against his chest. I turn back to the fire, wondering about Vic's actions. "Did she say anything about why she's here or how long she's staying?"

"No," Tyler shakes his head regretfully. "I haven't asked. Don't want to know if there's an end date." I share his sentiments. I want to know what drove her here, but if she's leaving... I won't entertain that idea. She can't leave.

The party eventually dies down, and I go to bed. I sleep for a few hours, like always. Nightmare-filled sleep is just not worth it. Tonight, the visions stay away. It's not overly restful, but it is silent. It's unusual for me. I never get peaceful sleep. I wake up early and head down to the bar. Several people are passed out in the seating area. They collapsed wherever they were when the drugs took over. I step over them and walk up to the bar. Shirley is behind it this morning. She leaves after serving the food at the parties and comes in early to clean up. She passes me a mug of coffee and moves about cleaning sticky surfaces.

"Do you like doing this, Shirley?" I ask, my voice gravelly with sleep.

"Hm? Oh, yes. I like having something to do. The house is quiet. I think Joe is here somewhere anyway." She waves her hand around the area, unsure where her husband is.

"Would you tell me if you need help or don't want to do it?"

She pauses, "Yes."

I give her a skeptical glare. "No, you wouldn't." She shrugs but returns to cleaning. I need to do something about that. What should I do? We have custodians that clean and chefs to cook. I could pay to cater the parties. Would that offend her? Before I can devise a plan, someone slides in next to me.

"Good morning," Vic chirps with every bit of brightness I would expect from a morning person. I hate it. I love it. I want her to dial it back. I want it every morning of my life. Should I be this conflicted? With much better social skills than me, Shirley brings Vic a mug of coffee and greets her warmly.

"Thank you," Vic's voice is filled with appreciation. She is genuinely grateful for a mug of coffee. I marvel at the happiness shining across her face. "Weird question, do you have a public transit map?"

"A fucking what?" It slips out before I can stop it. That control from last night is gone. Vic looks startled while Shirley puts her hands on her hips angrily.

"A public transit map or schedule? For buses or trains or whatever?" Vic explains weakly. What the fuck is she talking about? It's too goddamned early for this.

"I don't have one," Shirley answers quickly. "Our public transportation is not great. We don't have a bus stop out here. Once you get closer to the city, there are more stops." Vic nods.

"Do you have a number for a cab? And maybe a phone I can use?" Shirley searches the bar. What is she looking for? The fucking yellow pages? What is this, 1998?

"Where the hell are you going? Take a fucking Uber."

"Aleksander!" Shirley's use of my full name catches me off guard. She's the closest thing to a mother I have ever had, but she doesn't reprimand me. Never mind the fact that I'm the goddamn president of this club. What the hell is happening? Did I wake up in the Twilight Zone? Has the simulation failed?

Shirley glares at me while Vic looks stunned. Her face fades to embarrassment. Fuck. I thought I could make it longer than 24 hours before fucking things up with her. That's probably a record. Call Guinness. I'm a damned fool. I rub my hand down my face, sighing heavily.

"I'm sorry, Vic. I'm just," I pause. What am I? Confused? Hungover? Trying to figure out why the simulation has failed this early? "Why do you need a cab and a phone? Where is your phone?"

"I need to go to the store to grab a few things. Another outfit or two and some shampoo. I didn't want to bother anyone, and Tyler isn't up yet." She didn't tell me about her phone. I'll push that later. I sip my coffee. Shirley returns to searching for whatever she thinks will help.

"I'll give you a ride," I tell her.

"Oh, no. You don't have to. I'll wait for Tyler. It's not a big deal." She waves her hand in front of me as she drinks her coffee.

"I didn't ask," I don't mean for my voice to sound menacing, but I couldn't stop it for anything.

Shirley claps her hands together. "Well, perfect. Have fun, you two! I'm heading out back to clean." With that, she disappears, leaving me alone with Vic. She is wearing jeans and the shirt I washed for her. I left the clothes outside her room, not wanting to enter while she was asleep. Well, I did want to enter, but I won't invade her space like a creep—not yet, anyway.

The only thing I can think about is my cum on her shirt. Her sweet ocean scent mixed with the musky smell of my jizz. My dick stirs to life, and I'm in danger. I can't have a boner if I'm taking her around town. I haven't had this many random erections since I was thirteen. This is wild. She does this to me. I can't stand it, but I want more.

"You don't have to. I can wait for Tyler."

"Aren't you training with Lucy at 3 today?" Vic nods. "Tyler won't be up before then." She curses, looking down at her coffee. "Go get your purse or whatever, and I'll meet you in the garage." She nods sullenly but does as she's told. Good girl. I grab an extra helmet from our storage area and head to my bike to wait for her.

She enters the garage a few minutes later, bagless but wearing her sneakers instead of her sandals. She spots me and smiles, lighting up the entire fucking garage. Most of the lights are off, but her smile is radiant. She's the most beautiful person I have ever seen. I don't know how anyone can be that happy in the morning. I want to find out her secret.

"Oh," she starts when I hold a helmet out for her to take. "I thought we would take a car. I need to buy a lot." She eyes my bike. It's matte black with a backseat and saddle bags. It's the one I use for longer trips. I wouldn't normally take it around town, but we'll need the space.

"It's got room." She hesitantly takes the helmet, watching me. I don't know what she's waiting for. I give her a confused look.

"I'm waiting for you to slap it and tell me how much that bad boy can hold. You know, like the car salesman meme?" The playful glint in her eyes is adorable. I know the meme she is talking about. I may act like a caveman, but I'm not one. I have the internet; I see the memes. I deadpan stare at her, secretly amused with her. She eventually shrugs and pulls on the helmet. I tug mine on and climb onto the bike.

Vic holds her hands out to grab my shoulders but hesitates. She draws them back, unsure how to get on the bike without touching me. She won't be able to. I know that, and she knows that. I hold my hand up for her, flicking my fingers so she'll take it. She gets the hint and climbs on the bike behind me. Her body is small and warm. She shifts, trying to stay away from me. That won't work while we're riding. I tug her arms around my cut. I tell her to hold on, but she's still tense behind me. She grips my cut, trying to keep her hands off my chest.

I want her to touch me. I've never wanted that from anyone. I like that her legs are pressed against mine. Her front is against my back. She can't see over my shoulders. Her head and shoulders lean awkwardly away from me. Fuck, I hope she relaxes against me soon. Not just to make the ride better but because I want her there.

I start the bike, the roar of the engine filling the garage. I click the button to raise the door, and we drive into the bright morning sun. I groan against the shining light, and Vic's arms tighten across my chest. That feels good, damn good. I keep my mind clear as we drive through the empty roads. It's not early, and most people are already at work, leaving the streets mostly empty.

I swerve between the lanes. Vic clenches me tightly with every new movement. Tyler and I took her for rides when we were younger, not frequently because her parents were scared little bitches. It's probably been a long time since she was on a bike. I park in front of Aphrodite, a boutique, and she visibly relaxes behind me. She hops off as soon as I kill the engine. She glances up at the store and freezes.

"Aleks," she starts cautiously. "I can't afford this. I just wanted to go somewhere cheap." She fiddles with the helmet, debating putting it back on. She didn't specify where she wanted to go, but I didn't ask. I knew I would bring her to this store eventually. I climb off the bike and take her helmet, depositing both on the bike.

"Don't worry about it," I state as I walk toward the door. Vic calls my name as she rushes to catch up. She reaches out to stop me but doesn't.

"I can't buy anything here, and it doesn't look like the type of place that would have my size." She eyes the door suspiciously as if it might attack her.

"Do you trust me?" I turn to face her, crossing my arms over my chest. She tracks the movement, taking in my biceps and chest before looking up at me.

"No." At least she's honest.

"Well, start." Without waiting for a response, I open the door and walk in. I don't hold it for her because she won't enter before me. I nod at the cashier, who greets me. The young girl instantly rushes over, swooning at me. They always do, but this one is new. Vic finally walks in behind me with a huff. Her arms are crossed over her chest, and dissatisfaction covers her face.

"What can I help you with, honey?" Ugh, I hate those endearing names. I glare at her. She flinches but holds her ground. She's got some guts; that's good.

"My girl needs some clothes." I step to the side so Vic is visible. My large body blocked her completely. Vic huffs at my answer while the cashier glares jealously.

"I can handle myself, thank you." Vic's words are angry, but she acknowledges the cashier.

"Okay," the cashier starts slowly. "Just let me know if you need anything, hun." She gives me a cheesy grin then sashays to the register purely for my benefit. I'm not impressed at all. Vic hasn't moved from her spot behind me. I wave my arm for her to walk through the shop. She huffs but walks around the racks. She plucks a tag and balks.

"Aleks," she says sadly. I step close to her and lean down. My words are soft near her ear.

"Pick out ten outfits, try them on for me, and I'll buy them."

"Absolutely not," she leans closer to me, absorbing the warmth of my body to fend off the chill of the air conditioner.

"It's non-negotiable. You're my guest. Tyler would kill me if he knew I wasn't taking care of you." Honestly, Tyler wouldn't care if I didn't spend hundreds of dollars on clothes for his little sister, but Vic seems to buy it.

"Three outfits," she counters. My lips curl up again, and I lean in closer. Her hair brushes against my cheek. It smells like the ocean, crisp and salty, with a hint of coconut.

"I said non-negotiable."

"I'm not letting you spend that much on me," she turns to face me but realizes how close I am and stops. She fiddles with the shirts before her and sighs, out of her comfort zone. Does her worthless husband not take her shopping? She makes good money with her job but still deserves to be doted on. "Four," she tries again, "and some underwear." She pauses but quickly adds, "That I won't try on in front of you." I chuckle; it's an odd feeling when I'm completely sober. I stand up, and she turns to look at me. An ache is in her eyes that I can't define. My face falls at her expression.

"Fine, but you need boots, too. Those," I motion at Vic's sneakers, "are inefficient for working at the bar and riding." She sighs, her shoulders drooping. She doesn't argue with me. "Pick out more than four outfits to try on, and we'll narrow it down." She groans, rolling her head back in frustration.

"You're really fucking demanding, you know that?" She crosses her arms in the most adorable fucking move I have ever seen.

"I am president of a biker club. You don't get that by asking nicely."

Vic huffs at me again but turns to walk through the racks. I walk to the back, near the fitting rooms. A few loungers are positioned back there, and I sit, watching her move around. She flits from rack to rack. She glances at me, huffs, rolls her eyes, and moves to the next rack. I watch her calmly for a moment before a memory crashes into me.

I'm sixteen years old, sitting in the passenger seat of a beat-up car. Eric parked at the convenience store to run in for condoms and lube, if I'm lucky. He's one of the nicer men in the club. I don't put up much of a fight with him. I don't go with him willingly, but I don't have many options either. Eric will bring me a candy bar and a soda for after. It's the only thing to look forward to.

I stare out the window, depressed and lonely. I have Tyler, but he doesn't know what happens behind closed doors. No one does. No one asks questions, either. Why would they? Legally, Richard is my guardian. Don't guardians have time alone with their kids? Why would that be suspicious? No one questions the soundproofing in his room, either. He's head of a biker gang. He needs the soundproofing for meetings so no one knows what goes on behind closed doors. And no one *knows what goes on except me. And I don't talk.*

It's spring in Pennsylvania. The snow is starting to melt, and wildlife is returning to the area. Squirrels scurry around in search of food. Large birds fly overhead, ready for warmer weather. Trees have tiny green buds, the first signs of life in the area. Little brown birds are in the parking lot. They hop around, pecking at the ground. One taps at an abandoned food wrapper. They flit from spot to spot, jumping under cars and fluttering to the cart return. They bounce back and forth in search of something.

The drab skies of Pennsylvania fade to the well-lit store I'm sitting in. The birds dissolve from my vision, leaving Vic. She seems to hop from rack to rack. She's not actually hopping. She's huffing, but the rise and fall of her shoulders is reminiscent of those little birds. She's flitting around the store in search of outfits that I will buy for her. She walks to me, not amused at all. I watch as she grows larger. She broke me from a flashback. I'm not spiraling as she stops in front of me. I usually need drugs or copious amounts of alcohol to slow the spiral, but my head is clear now.

"Bird," my voice is weak. It's a whisper, a plea for her.

"What?" Bewilderment etches her perfect face.

"I called you bird."

"Why?" Her face twists with disbelief. A smirk spreads across my face.

"You won't like the answer." She rolls her eyes, but before she can respond, the cashier walks over.

"Aww, bird, what a sweet nickname. You're so romantic." She looks at me with 'fuck me' eyes. It happens all the time. It doesn't bother me anymore, but Vic is not immune. She glares daggers at the other woman. If looks could kill, the cashier would be dead. Vic is jealous, and it's so fucking cute.

"Thanks, Cherry," Vic makes a point of looking at her name tag. "I'm just going to try on these outfits now." She motions behind her and walks into the fitting room. Cherry's lips purse together, and she returns to the counter, leaving us alone.

Vic comes out a moment later in tight black jeans with rips. She has a plain white shirt on, and her bright blue bra shows through it. Fuck, it's hot. I look her up and down and bite my lip to counteract the arousal coursing through my veins.

"Okay, this one is good." She knows exactly what I'm thinking. I'm glad she trusts my opinion. She goes back into the room and comes out a few moments later. This time, she has on a dress. It fits like a fucking glove. Her hips are accentuated by her smaller waist. Even her small breasts look larger. Is she wearing a push-up bra, or am I imagining things? It's probably both.

Her grin is electric as desire coats my face; she says nothing. She tries on several more outfits while I remain silent. I debate offering to hold the outfit she wants so I can hide my bulging dick. The last outfit is a pair of ripped shorts and a tight tank top. She's removed her bra, and her nipples peak through the material. My gaze is fixed on them, and I lick my lips, wondering what they taste like. Are they as soft as I imagine? How pink are they? Will she squirm when I suck them?

I don't notice her walking to me until she bends over. She leans close to my ear. I can smell her, feel her warmth, feel her breath on my cheek. I long for our skin to touch, but she doesn't move closer. She whispers near my ear. Her words are deep and sensual, and I want more.

"If you would have told me you would stare at me like I'm the only girl in the world, I would have agreed much sooner." She blows against my skin, what would have been a kiss. Goosebumps spread like wildfire over my entire body. I shiver despite the warmth. Does she want me as much as I want her? Could she be with me? She is the only girl in the world. I will always stare at her like that.

"Okay. I know what I want," Vic straightens. She looks completely normal, as if she didn't just force my cock into a permanent erection. I'll never go soft again with just those few words. I can't let her off that easy. My brain doesn't work, though. I need to say something. I can't sit here like a love-struck boy with his first boner.

"Boots." Fuck, that's embarrassing.

CHAPTER FOUR

VIC

I HAVE NEVER SEEN so much lust pointed at me in my life. I've had friends that looked at each other or crushes like that. I've never been on the receiving end. It is undeniable, though. Aleks wants me. Bad. And I want him, too. Gods, do I want to fuck him.

He doesn't like to be touched. How would that work? Would he restrain my arms? I haven't done that before, but pretty sure I could get down with that. My sex life has been so vanilla; ice cream seems exciting. Missionary. Every time for the past– gods, what was it? Nine, ten years. I haven't had decent sex in ten fucking years. I hate my life.

I pick out a pair of boots without Aleks's help. I select the outfits that got the most significant reaction from him. If he's paying, might as well give him what he wants. We walk to the register, where I put all my things down for Cherry to scan. In my previous life, I didn't really have women I despised. Sure, a lot of them were clowns, but most were intelligent enough to not be so brazen. Here, the women are fucking fearless. Especially when it comes to Aleks. I can't really blame them. I would fawn over any other man that looks like him. But Aleks, he's mine.

No. No, he's not. I can't claim him. He's my brother's best friend. He's president of an outlaw biker club. He's nearly a foot taller than me. I'm a nurse in a conservative household. He's wrong for me in every sense. None of that seems to matter to him. I wonder how far he will let things go. Tyler doesn't realize the feelings Aleks and I have. Tyler can be so dense sometimes.

I fiddle with some items at the register. I really don't want to hear the total for these items. It will not be cheap. Cherry scans each item slowly. She flutters her eyelashes at Aleks, but he doesn't notice. He's watching her grab each item, remembering what I looked like wearing it. I shift my feet, letting my thighs rub together. It's not enough pressure, but it's something. He tracks the movement but returns his gaze to the clothing. Cherry finally reads the total, and I cringe. I can't afford this with the money I have. I hate that he talked me into this. I didn't come here for them to take care of me. I can handle myself.

Aleks and Cherry engage in a brief, awkward stare-off. I watch, also feeling uncomfortable. Finally, Cherry speaks up.

"How do you want to pay?" Aleks looks slighted.

"Ring it out as cash and add the receipt to the binder." Cherry and I have matching faces now. What is Aleks talking about? "Are you new?"

"Yes," Cherry looks incredulous, crossing her arms over her chest.

"This is my shop. I pay out of profits. It's in," he leans over the counter, looking beneath it, "that binder." He points to a thin three-ring binder directly under the register. Cherry is full of disbelief as she pulls out the binder. A write-up with Aleks's photo in the back explains everything he told her. She angrily follows the directions, then the realization hits her. He's the owner. That means he's loaded. She picks up her flirting from before, but it's exaggerated now. I roll my eyes, waiting for her to bag everything up.

Aleks owns a boutique. I haven't considered his wealth. The club does well; their compound is excellent. It doesn't exude money. It's more subtle than that, but they would need lots of money to pay for what they have. I wonder what other secrets Aleks has. A restaurant, a boutique, what else? His businesses are random. Maybe a gas station? A pottery shop? I hide a snicker at the thought of that. He's far too big to handle delicate pottery.

We finally leave the store, an extra receipt in the bag with her phone number on the back. In case Aleks needs anything at all from her. I am miffed about the whole interaction. The cost makes me uncomfortable. I want to punch Cherry in her stupid face. The only thing that makes any of this worth it is the look on Aleks's face when I tried on clothes. I could get used to that, preferably in a less hostile environment. I only watch as he tucks the items into the saddlebags on his bike. I realize too late that I could have helped him.

He holds out his hand for me to climb on again. It's warm and calloused and completely covers mine. He tugs my arms around his chest without hesitation. I hold onto him as he weaves in and out of traffic. Maybe his touch aversion is only triggered in certain situations. I should ask him about that. Lord knows I want to touch that man. I won't without permission, but fuck I want to.

Aleks drives to an outdoor strip mall and stops in front of a Sephora. A local coffee shop is set up next to it. I almost bounce off his bike, giddy to get coffee. In my plan this morning, I wanted to stop for coffee. It's a luxury I've denied myself on this trip. I've been drinking gas station coffee or whatever the bus station had available, which usually wasn't much and definitely wasn't good. The shop looks cute, and a chalkboard display tells me they have what I want. An outdoor seating area has small tables, giant umbrellas, and string lights running around the area. They aren't on now, but they will be adorable when they are. Without waiting, I walk toward the coffee shop.

"I thought you could get the rest of what you need before coffee," Aleks says from his bike.

"What?" I look around, unsure what he means. I need shampoo. I don't see a Walmart around here. He nods at the store beside the coffee shop, Sephora. That's an interesting assumption. I've never been inside one. I only wear a little makeup, and what I get is always cheap.

"I don't...Aleks, do I look like I go to Sephora?" I didn't even put on lip gloss today. My face is bare; my hair is in a messy bun, and I mean messy. I'm pretty sure I have some acne from traveling the way I did for so long. Not to mention, I don't want to spend my money at Sephora. I'm on a tight budget. Coffee is my splurge of the day. Aleks doesn't listen to me. He walks into the store, holding the door for me. Dammit.

I glance around the store. Maybe I can get the shampoo and conditioner I need and get out. Aleks tags along behind me, looking at everything. I cringe when I see the cost of the products I want. These are so much more than what I am used to paying. Another woman walks up, speaking to Aleks and ignoring me. She offers help. He refuses, not particularly kindly. I try to suppress the jealousy over a man I shouldn't want and can't claim. I hesitantly look for a shampoo that will work for me. I grab each bottle gingerly, worried it will explode, and suck my wallet away from me.

"I'll pay for it."

I startle at Aleks's words in my ears. I didn't notice him walk up behind me. I am focused on the label of the bottle I'm holding. I take a deep breath, settling my racing heart. I place the bottle back on the shelf. It would work, but I can't bring myself to get one that expensive.

"You own this store too?" My snark is undeniable. I don't mean to be so argumentative. I'm uncomfortable with him spending such large amounts on me.

"No, but I can afford it."

Without asking, he grabs the bottle I was looking at and the matching condi-tioner. He gives an expectant look. I sigh, resigned to living in my personal hell. I've spent so long buying my luxuries that I don't know how to let someone else spend money on me. He follows me to the body wash section. I stare at the bottles, overwhelmed by the options. He picks one up, opens it to sniff, then holds it to me. I sniff, realizing it's close to the one I already use. Did he see my bottle when I showered in his room? I don't think he could have. He's been close several times; he may be good at recognizing scents.

He asks if I want anything else, encouraging me to pick out whatever. Do I let him buy me more things? I would like a different shade of lip gloss. It's nice to have options sometimes. I've only got one color with me. It's my favorite dark pink matte tube. It's moisturizing but still matte. I could find something comparable here. He notices my hesitation and tells me to go get it. Fine, I'll let him buy the damn lip gloss.

He follows me again like a little dog waiting for a treat. Does he want a treat? Is he buying me all these things so I will suck his dick or something? I would have done that for free. An uncomfortable feeling creeps through me now. Is he trying to buy me? Again, I'm frozen in front of the lipstick, but not with indecision this time.

"What are you thinking?" Aleks doesn't startle me, even though I'm unaware of him. I'm so lost in my own thoughts today. I need another nap.

"Is this...do I owe you for all of this?"

He looks offended by my question. I'm unsure if his reaction makes me feel better or not. He assures me he is just trying to do something nice for me. He holds up a tube of shiny red lipstick, and I roll my eyes at him. He teases me as we look through several different colors and styles. I relax with him. I'm so wound up from everything that has happened over the past month. I need to relax a bit. Working tonight then resting afterward will help.

We check out, and he pays with a card this time. At the coffee shop, I insist on paying. He lets me without arguing. I wait for our drinks while he packs the bags on his bike. He's so big and surly; I would never expect him to be so nice.

We settle into a table near the back. It overlooks a park where a few kids play. It's quiet, blocked from the traffic on the main road. We sit quietly. He's never been one for talking. At this moment, I don't mind it. If he's always quiet, I will be awkward around him at some point. Small birds bounce around the ground and pick at cookie crumbs and rocks.

"Why did you call me 'bird'?" Aleks is just as lost in thought as I am. He glances at me blankly before answering.

"You remind me of these little birds." I laugh loudly, looking down at the birds. I can see why he would say that. I was stomping around the boutique. I probably looked like these tiny birds to him. Something in my chest clicked when he called me that the first time. I've never had a nickname like that. It felt right. I don't mind if he calls me that.

"Why are you here?" Aleks asks. I know what he's asking. I'm not ready to give him that answer. I want more time before I have to share that information.

"You insisted on bringing me shopping." I offer in response. "Does your touch aversion have exceptions?" He is unsatisfied with my answer and my attempt to change the subject.

"I don't know. How long will you be here?" This is the worst game of twenty questions ever. What's next? My most embarrassing memory? A recount of my first period? Probably my first sexual encounter; that was a doozy.

"I don't know. Do you want me to leave?" It's not an answer to his question, nor a complete topic change.

"No. I don't want to wake up to find you gone." His statement is soft but firm. Fear rings in his voice. For a moment, I wonder if he knows how I left Pennsylvania. He couldn't possibly know I took as little as possible and caught a bus out of town in the middle of the day without a word to anyone but Tyler. He couldn't. I shake my head.

"I'll tell you if I need to leave."

We both sit quietly while we finish our drinks. I usually nurse mine, but I gulp it down since I can't take it back with me. The ride back to the compound is shrouded in discomfort. We don't say anything when he parks in front of Dionysus. He helps me unload the bags, but I take them all from him. I give a short thanks and head to my room to unload everything.

That was more awkward than I planned. I want Aleks so much. He wants me, too, but it's a bad idea for many reasons. I put him out of my mind and focus on getting ready for my first shift. In the bar, Lucy explains where the tables are and how the ordering system works. It doesn't matter what name the whores give for their drinks; I can put whatever I want in them. Except tequila. The women can't have tequila. Once, Lucy served tequila sunrises all night and found various clothing items around the bar for the next week. She didn't know where all the clothes came from, so she just burned them.

The shift goes surprisingly easy. I get lots of tips because I'm new. I have on a pair of Daisy Dukes with a tight tank top. I conveniently forgot my bra, and it is surprisingly cold in the bar. The ice I continuously run over my neck certainly isn't the problem. No, I would never keep my nipples hard for good tips. I'm a sweet girl who just happens to know how to make money quickly. Lucy laughed when she first saw me with ice but commended me. I make great money.

Aleks and Tyler take turns glaring at me, the men, and anyone who gets too close to me. I love the possessiveness. Tyler was more aloof when we were teens, but he missed all my early dating and crushes. I serve them a few times. Aleks tries to give me a big tip, but I refuse to take any more money from him. At the end of my shift, we shut down the bar and help the cooks clear the kitchen. The main room will stay open for club members, but they are on their own for drinks. Lucy tells me most of them will move to the backyard for the rest of the night and invites me out with her.

I change my clothes, wearing a looser, but still fitted tee. My bra is still missing. Damn thing is always gone when I need it. I chuckle at my own thoughts. The bra is tucked away with all my other intimates; I hate wearing it. In the backyard, I find Lucy and grab a beer. We chat for a few minutes, and she explains the lay of the land. I soon join some of the people dancing. Pop music is playing, and I'm happy to lose myself for a while. I'm still astounded by the space out here. The pool, dance area, bar, lounging places– it's a massive space, and it's all above a garage. It oozes money.

Rio comes up to dance with me. He's quickly becoming one of my favorite members. He's funny and doesn't act like he wants to fuck me. That's a nice change from everyone staring at me like they've never seen a woman. We move together, laughing when we collide, having a great time. Eventually, he leaves to get another drink. I walk to the edge of the pool and sit. I kick my sandals off and lower my feet into the water, savoring the incredible sensation.

I'm resting with my head tipped back, watching the sky. Some stars peek through, but light pollution blocks most of them. Stupid lights. I want to go out into bumfuck nowhere one day and just lay in a field staring at all the stars. I'm completely lost in daydreaming of grass fields and thousands of stars when someone nudges my knee. I look down to see Aleks. His hair is wet from swimming, slicked back, hanging on his shoulders.

He isn't wearing a shirt. Why would he be; he is swimming. I can see his chest, his very muscular, tattooed chest. My mouth waters at the sight. I would drag my fingers across him, pinch his nipple, trace the ink on his skin. His chest is more ink than skin and more muscle than ink. I didn't think something like that was possible, but he has muscles for days. Not weightlifting muscles for show, but hard-earned from calisthenics and life. The corner of his lips turns up while I ogle him.

"Grab my cut; there's a case in the inside pocket." He nods his head toward the bench behind me. I didn't realize I sat so close to his spot. I lean back to grab it. It's a bit further than I can comfortably reach. I stretch my leg out to balance myself. Aleks grabs my calf, pressing my leg down to anchor me. Even in the water, his calloused hand feels warm on my skin. That would feel so good over my entire body. I take a deep breath, trying to settle my raging cunt. I finally grab the tin and hold it out to him.

"Open it," he tells me. I pop it open, finding a few joints and a lighter inside.

"Light one for me." It's not a request. I haven't smoked in a while. I got some edibles a while back but haven't gotten a chance to take them. Between work and other aspects of my life, it's frowned upon for me to consume, but here, nothing stops me. No one will say anything. No one will drug test me. I could get high and stay high. I don't know when or if I'll return to Pennsylvania. I suppose I'll need to at some point. Fuck, I don't want to think about that right now.

With that thought, I light the joint. To hell with Pennsylvania, I'm here to relax, or at least not be there. I cough as the smoke enters me. I hold the joint out to Aleks, waving the smoke away with my other hand. He watches with a playful glint in his eyes. Even without a smile, his face is captivating like this. The thought passes through my mind again: he would be devastatingly beautiful with an authentic smile.

"My hands are wet. Hold it for me." He lifts his hands out of the water, showing me drips that splash into the pool. I eye him dubiously and take another hit. His eyebrow raises at me.

"It's puff, puff, pass, buddy," I cough out, a laugh smothered between the choking sounds. He shakes his head and moves closer to me. His chest rubs against my leg. His hard, warm chest. My pussy tingles at the touch. Hell, I'm really hard up if a simple brush on my calf heats me like this.

I hold the joint out awkwardly as his lips move near. I'm laser-focused on his lips as they wrap around the joint. I loosen my grip while he pulls on it. My fingers graze over his lips and scruff. His lips are soft, contrasting with the prickly hairs covering his face. His beard is short, not quite long enough to really be soft.

His eyes are on me while I take the joint back from him. I've never experienced such intimacy from smoking. It was always a playful or relaxed event. This is something else. He takes another hit, again with me mesmerized and him watching me. We take turns like this until the joint is gone.

Aleks turns his back and leans against the wall. One arm props on the edge while the other drapes across my legs. His ribs are pressed against my calf, and the touch burns. Is my breathing regular? The joint is kicking in, and I don't know what's normal anymore. We sit in silence for hours. Or maybe it's minutes. It's probably 32 minutes exactly. Time doesn't exist anymore. I watch people dance and drink, and my mind is quiet. Aleks's body is warm. His wet hair lays on his back. I grab a small clump, twirling it in my fingers. It's soft, not just from the water. It feels like it's always soft. I caress the strands between my fingers, wildly impressed with the feel of this hair.

He turns to look at me. Oh shit, I'm touching him, or rather, his hair. With his body against me and the weed, I lost all sense of control. I drop his hair and place my hand on my lap. I mutter a weak apology. Aleks looks back over the pool.

"I don't mind."

I want to say something else. I want to ask him what he means, why I can touch him, but no one else can. I want to tell him how good his body feels against my leg, that he should touch me more. I want to tell him so many things, but every thought fades to nothing before it fully forms. Instead, I relax with his side pressed against me. I return to his hair, twirling and rubbing it like it's a comfort item. I'm like a child with their favorite blanket, touching and enjoying.

I don't know how long we stay like that. It's pleasant and calm. The sounds of the party are muted in the background. Clouds roll through the sky, only noticeable because they block some stars or the moon. It's the perfect way to end the night. Eventually, someone yells at Aleks. He pushes away from me, but his hand squeezes my knee before he dives under the water to swim over to them. I watch his body glide through the pool. He could be a mermaid. Merman? Would he still have a cock? An image of a merman swimming through the water with a blue and green tail pops into my mind. He has a penis dangling in the currents. The image of a merman with a flopping cock sticking out sends me into a fit of giggles.

The giggles are hard to stop. They always were when I got high when I was young. I try to reel them in but decide not to. Maybe if some of the men think I'm crazy, they won't lust after me. No, that's not right. Based on the whores around the compound, crazy is their type. I eventually calm down. It's time to go to bed. I grab the towel from Aleks's chair and dry my feet. His towel is so plush that it could be a cloud. Maybe I'm just really high. Then again, after shopping with Aleks, he seems like a man who enjoys luxurious things. I can get down with that.

Chapter Five

ALEKS

She's so soft. So warm.

I can't think of anything else. Another club is constantly causing problems for us, but I find it hard to give a fuck. I just think about Vic. The club, cartel, and drugs all take a backseat to her. I need to touch her. I want to fuck her. I want to possess her. I want her to think about me the way I think about her. She does sometimes, but she still sees me as her brother's best friend or maybe the guy she knew when she was a kid. She doesn't see me as hers. I don't know how to change that.

A soft knock sounds from my bedroom door. It can only be one person. Tyler bangs and yells at me. No one else knocks. They send Tyler or text if they need something. I've punched a few too many people for interrupting my personal time for anyone to consider knocking. She doesn't know that, but I wouldn't hurt her.

I open the door quickly and lean against the door frame. I scan Vic up and down as she raises her head to look at me. I love the height difference; towering over her makes me feel powerful. I can protect her from here. She's so tiny and needs to be protected.

"You don't have to knock."

"Oh," she bites her lip, shifting on her feet. She's fucking adorable when she's uncomfortable. "I thought all the doors were locked." She's trying not to look me up and down. I'm preparing to go down to the gym. I have on basketball shorts and no shirt. I put socks on but was interrupted before I got to my shoes. It's the best interruption.

"They are," I agree. "I had your card keyed to my room."

It is a bold move, but her shower is not working for some mysterious reason, and the damn plumber is busy. So, so busy. She bites her lip harder this time. My hand twitches to pull it free. She speaks before I get the chance.

"I just need to shower." Her eyes meet mine, fire and determination glaring at me. I smirk and step aside. She walks through my room like she owns the place, finding her confidence. I watch her round ass walk into my bathroom. With a sigh, I sit on my bed and check my phone. The shower starts, but it sounds louder than it should. I look up and find Vic left the door cracked.

The door is cracked open.

Did she forget to shut it all the way? Is it an invitation? My breathing increases at the thought. My dick hardens in my shorts. I close my eyes, trying to push the thoughts of her away. She's my best friend's little sister. She's married, or at least she was last time I checked. I should ask her, but it's not a deterrent for me. The shower door opens and closes with a soft clunk. Fuck, she's naked a few feet away from me, and the door separating us isn't even closed.

She starts singing some soft ballad. Vic will never be a pop star, but she's not terrible, either. I chuckle as she sings a few bars, then switches to a different song. My dick is at full mast now. I'm like a fucking teenager with all these uncontrollable boners. I scrub my face, unsure how to handle this. I could go back to her room and masturbate into her dirty clothes. Fuck, I bet I could find some panties she wore.

Jesus, I'm a fucking creep.

I rub myself through the shorts. If I go to Vic's room, I'd have to walk in these shorts for everyone to see, and that's damn embarrassing. I continue to palm my dick through my shorts, torn with indecision. I don't know how long she takes to shower. Could I finish before she gets out? At this rate, I could finish in three hard pumps.

Vic's singing stops. Would she hear me through the shower? The jets can be pretty loud. By this time, I'm all but fucking my hand. A soft humming sound comes from the bathroom. Oh no, it sounds like she fell. I better go check. Her body is so smooth and perfect that falling in the shower would hurt. She is definitely moaning in pain and needs to be helped.

I'm fucking delusional.

I'll just peek in and see if she needs me.

I press the door back slowly. Vic's in the shower, her side toward me. One hand is braced on the wall. Her other hand is between her legs. Holy shit. Her head is tipped back, eyes closed, and lips pressed tightly together. She's touching herself in my shower. My cock jerks at that.

In proper creep form, I step into the bathroom. I fist myself this time, stroking up and down. With her eyes closed, she doesn't see me move in. I drop my shorts, stepping out of them and toeing off my socks as I walk closer. I'm not overly quiet, but she doesn't notice. I stand just outside of the shower, watching her. Her fingers glide over her entrance, slipping inside, then back out to rub. The glass walls of the shower are fogging. I can't see her well. I push the door open quietly and step inside. She still hasn't noticed me. Maybe I'll become an assassin. I've been stalking online for years, so why not step up?

My little bird makes that soft humming sound again. I try to match her fingers' pace, but she switches techniques. I commit every little movement to memory. I'm going to touch her like that. I want to make her feel as good as she does. Vic deserves to feel that.

Vic's breathing hitches. Her body jerks several times. She's coming. She's in the throes of her orgasm. Her mouth is open in a silent scream, breast heaving with quick breaths. She's so fucking beautiful. My member leaks at the sight of her.

Her cheeks are flushed. She settles down, a soft smile spreading across her lips. I take a step to her. I'm not close enough to come yet.

"Do it again."

She yells, jolts back, and slams into the wall behind her. Her hand goes to her chest as she yells a string of curses that would impress any of the men downstairs. Her face settles in recognition; then, she looks down at my shaft. She watches me stroke it a time or two. I'm not going fast right now. I want to watch her touch herself again until we can come together. The need to come in front of her is overwhelming. I've wanted it but haven't been so consumed with it.

"Do it again," I grit out. My hand tightens around my dick, almost punishing. She notices the grip, eyes widening. Her eyes meet mine after slowly trailing up my body. She looks at me like she wants to eat me whole. Many people find me attractive and tell me so, but Vic's is the only opinion I care about.

As if moving of its own accord, her hand strokes her breasts then glides down her stomach. I want to touch her so badly, but right now, I need to come. My cock aches with the stiffness. My eyes track her fingers, finding the apex of her thighs and then disappearing inside her pretty cunt. It could be my dick, but I'm a sick, depraved bastard. Vic needs to see what she does to me.

I increase the speed of my shaft. I won't last long. Vic lifts her leg and props her foot on the bench built into the shower. The new position gives me a better view of her tight pussy. I take a step closer to her. The height difference makes it harder to see her cunt, but the way she looks up at me... Shit, even the most celibate would cave to that. Her hand moves faster, matching my pace. Despite staring up at me, she matches my strokes. Her eyes burn with lust and determination. My little bird isn't scared of being a deviant. I fucking love it.

I take another step closer. The tip of my cock brushes against her soft belly and jerks in response. My balls tighten, tingles of the impending orgasm rolling through my body. I brace one hand on the wall beside her head. I give a few more pumps. Without a word, I come all over her stomach. I close my eyes for a brief moment but open them to watch my release land on her. The white fluid hits her stomach, rolling down her body in multiple streams. Surprise tints her face but is overtaken by her orgasm. She doesn't hold back her sounds this time, moaning loudly. Her back arches, leaning closer to me. She's so goddamned gorgeous.

I drop my forehead to hers as we both calm our breathing. Vic drops her hands to her side, trying not to touch me after that. All the other girls try to touch. They want to cuddle or massage or some shit I do not want. Not Vic. She gives me the space I need. The space I find myself not wanting. After a moment, we both breathe normally. What do I do now? Usually, I toss a wipe at the chick and tell them to get out. I won't do that to Vic.

I scour my mind, searching for the correct answer. I'm in enough subReddits about sex that I should know this. Aftercare. That's what they call it. They clean up their partners and offer them water and a blanket. Someone mentioned chocolate. I don't keep chocolate in the shower. What a stupid thought. Of course, there's no chocolate in the goddamned shower. I finally step back. She watches me intently, face void of emotions. I grab her loofa and the new body wash I bought her.

I wash Vic's body gingerly, ensuring I get all my jizz off her. She doesn't say anything, only turns so I can get her back. I move her into the water to rinse her off. This feels awkward as shit. She's never going to let me touch her again. Before my anxiety takes over, I kiss her forehead and climb out of the shower. She says nothing as I dry off and walk back into the bedroom.

I'm a damn idiot.

I sit on the edge of my bed, scroll through Reddit, and search for any answer that won't make this any worse. Water, food, blankets, cuddles. That's what is most recommended. She hasn't turned off the shower yet. Does this situation even require aftercare? Is it just good practice? Why the hell am I so incompetent? The answer to the last question is obvious, but I don't want to go down that path. My demons have been quiet since she entered the room. They usually are when she's around. I want them to stay that way.

Vic spends several minutes in the bathroom. She carries her bag and doesn't acknowledge me when she walks out. Gods, this is stupid. I clear my throat, preparing myself to make this whole situation worse.

"Hey." Solid start, Aleks. Solid fucking start.

She turns to look at me. My body settles under her gaze. She isn't showing any emotions, but she isn't running either. That's a good sign, I think.

"I'm going to get a pizza and watch a movie. You want to stay?" That's the exact opposite of what I was going to do, but she doesn't know that. She thinks for a moment and shrugs. The relief that leaves my body is almost palpable. She settles on the bed. She slides closer to me but still far enough away to not touch. Conflicting feelings swamp my body: gratefulness that Vic willingly gives me space but a deep desire for her to not do that. I send off a text to ask the kitchen to bring up a pizza. I've watched her long enough to know what kind she prefers. Like I said, I'm a creep.

"Do you want to watch "23 Dresses"?"

"What?" She looks perplexed at my question.

"That movie about the bride." The edges of her eyes tighten, trying to figure out what I'm talking about. I don't actually know what her favorite movie is. She shares her accounts with her husband. I can't tell which movies are hers or his. Romcoms are viewed a lot. Realization creeps across her face.

"You mean "27 Dresses" with Katherine Heigl?" She bursts into laughter. I'm not surprised I got the name wrong. I don't watch romcoms. She settles down and shakes her head. "No. I don't want to watch that. You can pick the movie." I give her a skeptical look. I don't think she will enjoy what I pick. "What? You don't think I would like the 1983 slasher cult classic Sleepaway Camp?" Now, it's my turn to chuckle. I shake my head at her but consider her. That's a very specific reference. Is she into slashers? That could bode well for me.

I spilt the difference and start Scary Movie. I pass Vic a bottle of water, and she takes a sip. She seems more relaxed now. A prospect shows up with our pizza after a bit. She does an excited little dance when she realizes it's her favorite. Her shoulders shimmy as she grabs a slice. It's like a mating dance some bird in a documentary would do. She's everything to me.

•••

She fell asleep halfway through the movie. I pulled one of my blankets over her. After the movie went off, I fucked around on my phone for a while. It's nearly dinner time now. I would love nothing more than to sit here with her while she sleeps. She's been trying to get on our sleep schedule, and a long nap will throw that off.

"Hey, little bird," I whisper, not wanting to startle her. She groans and stretches her arms above her head. Her shirt isn't tight, but it falls against her breasts, outlining them nicely. The urge to wrap my lips around her nipple is strong. I blink to clear my head. "It's almost dinner time. We should go down." She nods, sits up, and looks around the room. She rubs her eyes and apologizes for falling asleep. I shrug it off and get up to get dressed.

"I should go change." Her shirt and shorts aren't inappropriate for the bar, not compared to what some of the whores wear. I do appreciate her conservativeness. I have no desire to punch half my men for staring at her. "I'll meet you down there?" My heart skips a beat at her suggestion.

What the fuck was that? I nod, and she leaves my room. I rub my face, trying to figure out who I am. A man that doesn't know what the hell is happening. A delusional creep that masturbates and comes on his best friend's little sister. A motorcycle club president that couldn't give a shit about the club right now. Yeah, that all tracks.

I join Tyler at our booth, nodding at a few men as I walk by. Destiny is already sitting with him. They are huddled together, whispering about some bullshit she's concocted. Destiny better have a damn pussy of gold because she's fucking terrible. He's the only one who doesn't see it. I slide into my seat, and they look up at me. Tyler gives me a curious look.

"You look weird, Pres."

"Thanks," I mutter. Fucking dick.

"Nah, it's like content and stressed simultaneously," Tyler explains. It's an accurate assessment.

"Oh yeah. I can see that," Destiny chirps. I suppress the urge to punch her. I'm not above beating a woman, but Tyler's my best friend. I reign it in for him.

"You worried about tomorrow?" Tomorrow, we meet with the club president, who is causing us many problems. They have been interrogating our women and prospects, harassing the clients at our legitimate businesses. We're pretty sure they're fucking with some of our bikes when members are around town, but we can't prove that. I shrug in response to that.

"What's tomorrow?" That voice soothes my soul. Vic is searching the area, looking for a chair to steal. She's not sitting at the end of the table. I stand and motion her to the empty spot beside me in the booth. She slides in happily. Destiny's jaw opens while Tyler eyes me warily. Vic settles, unaware of what I've done. No one has ever sat beside me. No one, even before I was president. When I was VP, I sat at a separate table near the other leaders so I wouldn't have to be that close to them. No woman has ever sat with me in any capacity.

"Well?" Vic looks at us expectantly. Tyler is the one to answer.

"We're meeting with another club that's been causing problems." Vic glances at me, then Tyler. Worry tints her eyes, but she doesn't need to worry. We've done this before. I shift my leg, pressing against hers. She doesn't pull back from me. The contact brings a comfort I've not felt before. I am really fucking damaged if simply resting my leg against her comforts me, but I knew that already.

One of the servers comes over and gets our orders. Tyler, Destiny, and I know the menu and don't need to see it. Vic isn't as familiar with it and copies Tyler's order. Destiny tries to chat with Vic about some celebrity scandal. Vic is friendly but clearly has no idea what she is talking about. My little bird isn't interested in Hollywood gossip.

After our plates are cleared from dinner and we have fresh beers, we relax in the booth. Tyler and I typically sit here for a few hours before going elsewhere. The backyard, gym, garage, our rooms, wherever the mood strikes. My phone chimes with a text message. It's the VP of the other club reminding me about tomorrow. I show Tyler, who rolls his eyes. I lean back in the booth, respond to it, then stay on my phone. Destiny starts some petty argument with Tyler, and the two of them leave. Vic leans back and glances over at me.

"Is that…"

"Don't say that out loud," I interrupt her before she finishes her statement. I glance around conspiratorially, and she giggles. Fuck, that sound goes straight to my cock. "I pretend to work while I scroll here. Everyone thinks I'm dedicated, but I'm just reading about cast iron pans on Reddit," I whisper close to her ear. She laughs loud and carefree. She covers her face, and I hate it. I can't hide the tick of my mouth as I watch her. She deserves more laughter. She eventually settles in the booth, resting her head back. Her neck is exposed. I stare at it, imagining what it tastes like. The feel of my lips against her neck consumes me. What would she sound like if I sucked there?

"Tell me about these subReddits you follow," Vic sits up to look at my phone. I hold it over for her to see. My arm closest to her drops to my lap. As we talk, I inch my hand over and over and over. My fingers trace her knee. She wears tight jeans tonight, and the fabric is rough against her. My hand settles on her knee. I stroke the inside of her knee, where her calf ends. She doesn't seem to respond but doesn't push me away, either. We scroll through posts about cast iron, gardening, people asking if they are assholes, and porn. I swipe quickly past the porn. She grunts a time or two but doesn't say anything. She insists I stop at every Am I The Asshole post so she can read it. Sometimes, we discuss them, others we agree, and that's that. It's the best way to spend the evening.

I wake up the next morning in bed alone, much to my chagrin. My sleep was riddled with the same nightmares it always is. Bodies thrusting and sweating. Pain and grunts. I roll onto my side, trying to clear the visions in my head. Nightmares, memories, demons, it's all the same at this point. Sapph once told me romance novels always claim a tormented man sleeps better when his fated girl is with him. It sounds like utter bullshit, but I'm not against trying it. Vic didn't run when I made her masturbate with me. I'll convince her to sleep in my bed one night. Even if I don't sleep better, I could wake up to her face.

I grab a hoodie and my cut. We're meeting the other club on the outskirts of town. It's a bit of a ride, but that's one of the few things that make this life worth it. That and beating men to a pulp. That's fun. We ride our bikes out of the garage and fall into formation on the road. Tyler rides beside me, and others pair up behind us. We aren't taking everyone, but we have about ten men with us. This meeting is meant to be a conversation, but they rarely end without violence. I could do without that today.

My men chatter on the Bluetooth connecting our helmets. They are extra chatty today. Most are talking about who they fucked last night. Typically, the Bluetooth feature is used for directions, updates, breaks needed, or other emergencies. Today's path is familiar, and all the other stuff is unnecessary. I switch my speakers off; Tyler will signal if anything is wrong.

The silence heightens the feel of the road. The bike rumbles beneath me, exuding power and the only calm I get outside of Vic. Riding has been my release since I got my first bike. It was the only way to clear my head once I could ride alone. Traffic clears before I take a trip down the dark alleys of my memories. I open the throttle and pull away from the pack, racing away from my demons. The hot air of San Antonio doesn't bother me as my bike roars down the road. Power thrums through my veins. My mind briefly clears, as close to nirvana as I can get.

I slow down when we near the meeting point. The other men weren't far behind me. They never are; Tyler has learned I want the peace of riding alone. I don't go out alone often, so they fall back for me to get the semblance of a solo ride. We turn on the side road, creeping down the dirt path. Large boulders block the view of the road, and the other gang is already here. They rise from their bikes and form a straight line while we park and dismount. We don't shake hands. There are no pleasantries here.

"Heard you got a new piece of ass in your club. Little tiny brunette," the president of the Longhorn Devils pipes. I don't bother learning his name. Chances are he'll be dead within a year or today if he keeps pushing his luck.

"You could borrow some whores if you're lacking." He glares at my response. I stand with my arms over my chest, waiting for him to respond.

"Nah, I'll just take that little new one."

"We haven't broken her in yet. Don't want to give you something you can't handle." Tyler shifts his weight at my words. It's the only sign of discomfort. The other president laughs, and his men join in. I hate this stupid banter. I've tried to skip it in the past. Getting straight to the point always ends in a fight. Sometimes, the banter will lead to a less violent ending.

"Let's cut this short. I don't wanna be out in Satan's asshole all day." The heat isn't even unbearable yet. It's still early enough in the morning that the sun isn't scorching the earth. "I want the cartel run."

"I want a private jet," I respond. I have no intention of giving him our cartel run. It's dangerous working for the cartel. We've lost more than a few good men, but the money is unparalleled. We have a good rapport with the cartel, and they leave us alone for the most part. We only transport the product. The Longhorn Devils distribute. A middleman runs between us. We give him the drugs; he provides the drugs to the other club. Sure, it would be easier to cut him out, but I fucking hate working with the Longhorn Devils.

"Give me the run."

"It's not mine to give," I shrug nonchalantly. This was what he wanted to talk about when they arranged the meeting. I had stupidly hoped it would be something else. He's wanted to take the run and sell the drugs. The Longhorn Devils had the run to start with but fucked it up royally. We had an in with the cartel and got the run. They agreed to let the Devils continue to sell, as we wanted nothing to do with that. It's worked for a couple of years.

Suddenly, all his men pull knives. The banter didn't work this time. Oh well. I charge at the president, not giving a fuck about his knife. It's not my first fistfight with weapons.

Chapter Six

VIC

"Hey! You want to go to town with us?" Lucy calls as I walk into the restaurant. She and Shirley move around the bar and kitchen, checking cabinets and shelves. They are taking inventory of what they have or still need.

"Hell yeah!" I fist pump the air, glad to get out for a bit. I love this compound. There are many things to do, but getting away for a bit will be nice. Working at the bar is fun, and I make killer tips. Or rather, my tits and hard nipples earn me killer tips. Worth it. The pool and backyard are so relaxing but get noisy and crowded. I've made a few new friends. Rio is my new best friend. He is hilarious and sweet but refuses to tell me why they call him Rio. It must be a good story. I just need to find the right person to weasel it out of.

"Shirley is prepping for tonight's anniversary party and forgot a few things. We will hit a few stores and grab what we need."

"That sounds excellent," I reply. "What's the anniversary?"

"For Mor taking over as president." It's still weird hearing him called Mor. Most men call him that, but Tyler and I still call him Aleks. I should ask him what he wants me to call him. Tyler didn't introduce him as Mor. I interrupted before he said his name. He's Aleks to me. He hasn't corrected me.

We load into a massive SUV and leave the compound. A prospect follows us on his bike. I didn't expect that, but I guess I should have. We first stop at a liquor store, grabbing only a few specific beverages. Lucy informs me the bar provides most of the alcohol, but Aleks and Tyler prefer a specific one the bar doesn't stock. Perks of the job. I spot my favorite beer in the store and ask if I can get it. My favorite lager is made in Pennsylvania but is expanding to other cities. It's one of the few things I miss about the state. At the next stop, Shirley picks out some specific items, more things she prefers that the restaurant doesn't carry.

Lucy drives through a coffee shop, and I nearly moan at the site. Nothing compares to getting a sugary drink from a coffee shop. The bar has a creamer I like, but it's not the same.

"Do you have a dress for tonight?" Lucy asks while we wait for our drinks to be made. I shake my head. "What about a swimsuit?" Another shake as my drink is passed to me.

"Oh, we should go to Aphrodite!" Shirley swoons. I whine over my drink, not the sound I want to make over my favorite beverage.

"It's so expensive, though," I tell them. The clothes are great, and they have many pieces in my style. I barely made it through Aleks buying the clothes for me. I can't bring myself to pay that much. I name a couple of other stores that are cheaper but still have decent clothes.

"Nonsense," Shirley chirps. "We'll put it on Aleks's account. He doesn't mind paying for it." She notices the incredulous look on my face. "Are you really going to deny a lonely old woman like me a girls' shopping trip?" I groan and roll my eyes, and Lucy laughs at us.

"Shirley, you're fucking ruthless. Fine." They gossip about some of the prospects. I listen, trying to commit some of the information to memory. I don't know how long I'll stay here, but I want to get to know everyone better.

Cherry isn't at the shop this time. A woman older than me taps on the screen behind the counter. The chime alerts her that we've entered, and she greets Shirley warmly. Relief settles, knowing I don't have to deal with Cherry. Hopefully, this woman's familiarity with Shirley means there won't be any awkwardness at the register. As those two chat, I walk around the shop, looking at dresses and swimsuits. I select a couple to try on and head to the back. Lucy takes a call and walks out of the shop. Shirley tells me to let her see the outfits I try on.

I don't show her the swimsuits, but I show her a few dresses. The third one I try on is the one she likes best.

"You should get this one. Aleks will love it." I turn in front of the mirror, trying to see my backside.

"Aleks will?" I know why she thinks he would care, but I hope I'm wrong. I don't particularly want people to think I showed up and instantly started fucking the president. I don't know how many people know our history. Not that there is much to speak of, but there's enough.

"Yes. I see the way he looks at you, hun." She winks at me, and I fight back the cringe. I glide the material over my stomach, smoothing it down. I do look stunning in the dress. It's a yellow dress with a loose skirt. The halter neck has a broad collar. The back is cut out with lace straps that fall across my shoulders and end at the side of my hips. The body hints at modesty, but the cutout gives it an edgy feel. It stops on my upper thighs, just a hair longer than indecent. I could never wear something like this back in Pennsylvania. I don't care what Aleks thinks; I want this dress for me. "He's never looked at anyone the way he looks at you. He touches you more than he touches anyone."

"It's trauma, isn't it? His reason for not touching." I've seen enough victims in the ER to recognize his response. It's not a recent trauma for him, but certainly one he hasn't healed from. Shirley hums at me, not wanting to say anything. I can respect that. That would be a violation of his privacy. He wouldn't tolerate someone sharing his secrets.

"How long has he been president?" I ask, offering to change the subject. I don't want to put her in an awkward position.

"Five years, but Richard and his board members spent a long time grooming Aleks." Her choice of words is odd to me.

"For the presidency?" I ask softly, worried the truth is more sinister than that. Her use of the word "grooming" could go one of two ways. I hope she isn't hinting at what I think she is.

"Aleks never liked any of them. He claimed it was politics. He has changed a lot of their ways. Richard spent a lot of time alone with Aleks," she pauses thoughtfully, staring into her memories, searching for the right words. "People don't turn out like Aleks overnight." Her words are soft and sad.

Is she implying the previous board abused him? My mind reels at that thought. He was with Richard in Pennsylvania; they were part of the club there. If I remember correctly, Richard left to join the San Antonio chapter. That's why Aleks and Tyler left when they were 18. But if Richard was abusing Aleks, why did he go with them? That doesn't make sense. Before I can ask anything else, Lucy walks back in.

"Damn, girl," she drawls. "Hot!" She nods toward me, causing both Shirley and me to giggle. I remove the dress and grab the clothes I am getting. Somehow, the other two don't pick out anything, and I'm the only one who buys clothes. I try to pay for them, but Shirley insists. The cashier agrees, and the cost is added to Aleks's account.

Back at the compound, we unload the items we bought. After storing my clothes and changing into the dress, I help Shirley and Lucy prepare for tonight. A couple of the other bartenders will be there so Lucy can attend the celebration. We're moving things around in the bar when the roar of motorcycles fills the room.

"Boys are back," Lucy tells me. The men start walking in with black eyes and bloody knuckles. Shock spreads through me at the sight. I've seen some shit in the ER, but I didn't expect a meeting to end like this. It is an outlaw biker club. I probably should have seen this coming. Tyler walks in, laughing with one of the men. A cut above his eyebrow made the side of his face bloody. It's likely not a bad cut, as head injuries tend to bleed more. I rush around the bar and up to him.

"Holy hell, Tyler. Let me look." He rolls his eyes but doesn't stop me. We step over to the side. Sure enough, the cut isn't bad. Aleks storms by, heading to his office in the back. I don't get a chance to look at him.

"You could use a butterfly bandage. Do you have a first aid kit?" I ask, looking at the already bruising cut.

"Yeah, in Aleks's office. You need to look at him. I think he got stabbed." My heart stops. Stabbed? I take a deep breath. He walked past me, so he's not dead. That doesn't mean a stab wound won't kill him. Recalling my ability to stay calm in a crisis, I tell Tyler to lead the way. Aleks is already in his office with a tumbler of whiskey on his desk beside the first aid kit. He doesn't look terrible, but it's clear he's in pain.

"Tyler, sit here. I'll look at Aleks, then help you."

"Help him first," Aleks says gruffly, taking a long drink. I consider arguing, but it would be futile and a waste of time. This could be dangerous depending on where and how deep the stab wound is. I clean Tyler's forehead and place a butterfly bandage over the cut, one will do. I toss the supplies in the trash and turn to Aleks. Tyler walks to get a drink from the bar behind Aleks's desk. Not advisable, but he won't listen. I don't waste my breath.

The sleeve on Aleks's hoodie is ripped. I can see the cut beneath. I can't tell how deep it is, but it will need stitches. The first aid kit has the supplies I need. It won't take me long if Aleks will let me. Tyler starts rambling about what happened, but I don't hear him. Aleks is meeting my gaze, waiting for me to say something. Shirley's words bang around in my mind. They groomed him.

"Oh, hell, Aleks. Let her look at that cut. You can't stitch it yourself, and I'll be damned if I do it with an actual nurse in the room." Aleks glances behind me at Tyler. "I'll fucking spit in it." Aleks looks back at me and nods. I slide the first aid kit across the desk as I round it. Aleks sits up to shrug off his cut and hoodie. He has on a dirt-covered, sweaty grey shirt. I lean over to look at the wound. It's not awful, but it needs to be cleaned and stitched. He won't die from it.

"What the fuck are you wearing, Tor?" Tyler practically yells from behind me, where he is sitting on the couch with his drink. I forgot I put on the dress. Aleks responds before I can say anything.

"Vic," he grits out to correct Tyler. I can hear the pain in his voice, but I still love the sound of my name from him.

"Sorry, Vic. But seriously, I can see half of your fucking ass." I roll my eyes but squat down instead of bending over. I'm now conscious of the length of the dress. I use a water bottle to rinse the wound first, then spray it with antiseptic.

"Lucy and Shirley took me with them today, and we stopped at Aphrodite." I keep my touch as light as possible. I don't want to irritate him any more than necessary. "I didn't bring any dresses or a swimsuit. So, I got some." Aleks watches me as I talk, but I keep my eyes on his arm. I don't want to stitch up his elbow or something. Tyler grunts behind me. He rolls his eyes, drinking more whiskey.

"Did you put it on my account?" Aleks's voice is rough. He sounds terrible: angry and hurt, but something else. Intrigued, maybe. I nod to him.

"Oh, so we're paying for you now?" Tyler jokes from behind me. A playful grin covers his face, and I stick out my tongue at him.

"I don't know why you say "now," like you two haven't been sending me money in sneaky ways since you left." Aleks looks away from me at that comment.

I don't know for sure if it was them. It's not like I have some millionaire uncle or anyone to give me copious amounts of cash. Nothing ever showed up as cash. It was more subtle. I'd go to pay my college tuition to find it was already paid. A large medical bill was covered once. Other small bills, nothing obvious. At first, I thought it was my parents, but they denied it. I thought it might be my husband, but he complained about paying for dinner. I never asked him. They always did an excellent job of staying anonymous, but once the sender had an address in Texas. That was when I put it together.

"I didn't pay for shit," Tyler spouts, finishing off his drink. I look up to Aleks, but he refuses to meet my gaze. He has been the one paying for me for almost two decades. Probably longer. Even as a teen, sometimes I'd find cash in my room. I assumed I was forgetful, but maybe it was Aleks paying for me in his own way. After the shower scene, I wouldn't be surprised to learn he snuck into my room and dropped cash. I just hope he wasn't masturbating. That would be weird. I was a kid then. He was a teen, but a five-year gap is huge at that age.

I open my mouth to speak to him when a shrill voice sounds in the hallway. Destiny is shrieking, looking for Tyler. He groans behind me, and Aleks sighs heavily. Before I can ask Tyler why he is still with her, she is in the office in hysterics. She shrieks over his bloodied face, calling him baby names, fretting over him unnecessarily. It's a small cut, not something to freak out about.

"Get out," Aleks commands through gritted teeth. Destiny looks between him and me but has the sense to listen. Thank gods for small miracles. I finish bandaging Aleks's cut, then prop against his desk and face him. His office is small, with built-in shelves on the wall behind his desk. A large gun safe stands beside his desk. A couple of chairs face the desk, with a sofa along the side wall. Two pictures that match the ones in his bedroom hang above the couch. On the other wall are photos of the club in various places.

Aleks leans forward, and his head brushes my stomach. He props his arms on his knees, hands dangerously close to my thighs. My skin tingles at the closeness. A slight flick of his hand, and he would be touching me. Nothing else matters when he is this close—not the money or Tyler's stupid girlfriend. My troubles from Pennsylvania are long gone; even his trauma isn't a problem.

"Can I touch you?" My words are barely more than a whisper. I didn't intend my words to be that soft, but anything louder would feel too loud. It's a quiet, intimate moment. Nothing about this should be intimate. We're just in his office. It's not like this is a first date or anything. Being this close to him is something special, though. I can feel it in my bones. Aleks is fucking extraordinary.

He nods softly, and I let my fingers slide into his hair. It's dirty from his ride and fight, but it would be so soft when clean. It's unfair that he should have such soft hair. I wonder what he does to take care of it. Probably nothing, I'm sure.

I haven't inspected his shower products. I've been too distracted by the glorious shower heads. Yes, plural.

Before my mind escapes down a random track, Aleks slides close enough that his head presses against my stomach. His fingers brush against my thigh. Tingles shoot from my thigh up my hips, through my stomach, through my chest. I want to keep my breathing steady so he doesn't feel the change, but I can't.

I massage his scalp resting against my stomach. His fingers glide up and down the outside of my thigh, from my knee to the hem of my dress. He doesn't drift higher than that. This slight touch sends more shivers through my body. It's been a long time since I've been touched like this. Wes rarely touched me. I wasn't wholly touch starved. I had friends to hug and saw my mother occasionally. But intimately, I've had nothing for years now. It feels so good.

"I want to fuck you," Aleks says against my stomach. Fuck, I want that too. I want that badly. I didn't mean to leave the bathroom door open yesterday. It was genuinely an accident. I wasn't upset when he walked in, though. I am upset that he only masturbated in front of me, but it was hot as hell. I'd gladly do that again, but I want him inside me. I want to feel his thrust, his power, his massive dick filling me. He's so big.

"I want to fuck you, to claim you, to make you mine." It's a serious claim. As much as I want Aleks, do I want a serious relationship? I just ran away from one. Do I want to jump into another? With anyone else, that answer would be no. With Aleks? Have we not been in a distant relationship this whole time? Him sending me money, watching through social media, and whatever other hacks he found. Occasionally chatting on video or phone calls.

"That's a lot of words, Mr. Moros," I tease. A small attempt to diffuse some of the heat. I don't know if I can commit to someone claiming me. There's no real reason to say no, but I haven't been here that long. I shouldn't say yes right away. His head turns under my hands, and he nips my side. I jerk at the ticklish feeling, twisting away from his. A few squeaky giggles burst from me. His hands tighten on my thighs, keeping me in place. His rough, calloused hands hold my smooth thighs. My skin burns under his touch, wanting more.

Before lust takes over, I realize he is laughing too. Aleks is laughing. I turn his face toward mine, hoping to see a genuine smile. It's not as bright as I would like, but his face is exquisite. I trace over his jaw, dancing along his beard. The corners of his lips are still tipped up, but they slowly drop as I touch him. I reach his lips. My thumb brushes against his bottom lip, following the edge. My nail catches the corner, and I feel his breath hitch. His eyes burn with desire.

"Your face is exquisite," I whisper.

I lean in, wanting to press my lips to his. I want to feel how soft his touch is. Will he kiss me gently? Roughly, to claim me? Will I set the pace? Will I try to claim him with my kiss? He rises to meet me, pulling his chair closer. I am in between his legs in this slow, passionate moment. Time has ceased to exist; it always happens with Aleks. He is the only person in the world. This inevitable kiss is all that matters right now.

"Hey, Pres! They are..." a man interrupts. "Shit, sorry."

And just like that, the spell is broken. Aleks leans back to look around me, and I fumble with the first aid kit, putting it all away. Why does this feel so scandalous? We are both adults. We can make our own choices. It shouldn't matter that I'm married legally. Or that he is my brother's best friend. Or that he has known me since I was ten. Those things aren't significant.

Except Tyler doesn't know. He probably wouldn't be mad but wouldn't be happy about us not telling him. The age thing would be creepy if Aleks tried this when I was ten, but I'm 31. I can make that call for myself. As for the marriage, it was over a long time ago. It's just a legality at this point. I'm here now and can do what I want. Including fuck the president of an outlaw biker gang.

"What, Harpo?" Aleks barks out at the man. A tall, muscular man stands in the doorway, staring out into the hallway. He refuses to look at us. We aren't indecent. We weren't even doing anything scandalous. I don't know why he is acting like that. Surely, he has seen worse than two people about to kiss in this compound. Hell, I've seen worse in the short time I've been here.

"Shirley is looking for you. She wants to start the party." Aleks grunts again, back to his caveman ways. Harpo walks off, and Aleks stands. It's easy to forget our height difference when he's sitting. He towers over me. Between his height and his muscles, he looks like he could toss me like a ragdoll. I stare up at him, wondering what it would be like to wrap my arms around his shoulders and tug him down to me. I would kiss him gently, then roughly, then pepper kisses across his cheek and bite his jaw.

Aleks smirks, able to read every thought I have. My cheeks burn. Lust? Embarrassment? Both? He informs me he needs to change and will meet me out there. He kisses my forehead, just barely bending to reach it. Then walks off.

He kissed my forehead. A fucking forehead kiss! What am I, five? Why did he kiss my forehead? Why not properly kiss me? He said he wanted to claim me. Then went and kissed my fucking forehead. Okay, now I want him to claim me. I want to feel his passion, his desire. I want to burn for him. I don't want a goddamned forehead kiss!

Chapter Seven

ALEKS

I hate this night. The rest of the club appreciates the big celebration. They go all out and decorate; nobody mourns the loss of Richard. I'm the only one that thinks of him tonight. He fills my mind like a heavy fog, and I can't see anything else. I fall into a pit of darkness and let demons roam free tonight. It's the only night I don't try to fight them.

The party gets started as I take my seat by the fire pit. It's been five years since I became president. Five celebrations. Everyone knows to leave me alone. At the first celebration, I lost my shit, fought a couple of prospects, and broke a couple of my fingers. Shirley asked if I wanted to stop the celebrations, but it was apparent how much she enjoyed putting them together. Everyone had a good time. Even the prospects I beat were grinning. I told her no. The following year, everyone avoided me as I sulked in my chair. It's been the same every year since. Members keep the new people away from me. They drink and celebrate while I drink and suffer alone. I stay until morning when everyone is gone or passed out, then I go inside and sleep a couple of hours. After that, it's business as usual.

I don't bother with tumblers or chasers. I have my bottle of liquor, Richard's favorite. It's a fucking terrible drink. Some call it self-harm to drink the beverage of my tormentor. I don't know what else to do. This compound is riddled with memories of him, memories of trauma related to him.

I was so young when I met Richard. I was in the care of other men before him. They weren't kind, but compared to Richard, they were saints. He met me at thirteen and brought me to his house. It stunk of stale cigarettes and sex. Some days, I long for the simplicity of the first days in his house. It wasn't so bad in the beginning. It was a couple of months before the gentle touches started, the soft caresses, the loving feeling I hadn't experienced before. It was easy to misconstrue his intent as a young, broken boy.

I fall deeper into the memories, watching them as if they were movies on the television. It's easier to remove myself from the memories and pretend it wasn't me for a few minutes. I'm just watching some dark cult fiction. If only it were that simple. If only it had been fiction—the touches, the grabbing, the damage.

The image of Eric taking me to the convenience store plays. This isn't a normal memory. Usually, Richard is the focus, but I can't get the memory of the parking lot out of my mind. I can feel the cool glass against my forehead. The dread of what's to come engulfs me. The little birds flit around the parking lot, so free and joyful. Bright little yellow birds. No, that's not right. They were brown, not yellow. Why are they yellow now?

The present overtakes my vision. She's there. Across the yard, dancing with Rio, Tyler, and Destiny. She's laughing and bouncing and bright. Her eyes meet mine as she raises her arms in the air. She tips her head back, enjoying the music. She's so light and carefree. I watch her for several minutes. She isn't beckoning me to come to her. She isn't trying to pull me from my melancholy. She's enjoying herself and still consuming every bit of my mind.

I look back at the fire in front of me. The flames lick through the air. Tiny embers burst and float to the ground. Red fades to orange, then to grey smoke. The memories start to creep back in. The flames sway, dancing through the wood with their hands raised in the sky. No, not hands. That's still my bird. I take another long pull of the bitter alcohol. The burn distracts the movement of the fire, pulling the memories back to the forefront.

Richard is standing in his office, tugging on his belt. Richard is in his bedroom, buttoning his shirt up. Vic is in my shower, touching the apex of her thighs. The fire dances, hands raised to the air. Another long pull of the harsh liquor. Richard pushes my chest against the wall. He presses behind me. He whispers what a pretty boy I am. Vic tells me my face is exquisite. No one has ever described me as exquisite. Beautiful, pretty, sexy, handsome, but never exquisite.

A log cracks in front of me. Music plays quietly in the background. The liquor doesn't burn anymore. The fire doesn't put off any more heat. The string lights around the yard blur in the background. The chair is hard against my back. No one is near me. I'm alone physically, but the memories keep me company.

Something cold and hard nudges my hand.

"Looks like you're empty." It's another bottle of liquor. A small hand holds the neck, extending it out. I take it, realizing my other bottle is indeed empty. I twist the cap. The crack of the seal breaking reverberates through my mind. I've heard that sound so often, bent over a bed, desk, chair, or couch.

Another nudge on my arm.

"Thought you might like a chaser. It's my favorite." A beer bottle. Another memory stirs, but Richard isn't in it. Who is that? It was a lifetime ago. In Pennsylvania, a biker has this bottle. He laughs loudly. He was always so happy. What was his name? Billy? Joe? Kevin? It doesn't matter. He played cards with me and taught me how to play blackjack. He'd bet quarters or candy bars, whatever he had. He knew I didn't have anything to bet. He would "loan" me a bag of Skittles or a roll of coins. We'd play late into the evening before Richard took me.

A chair creaks beside me. Laboriously, I turn my head. My little bird. My bright yellow, flitting bird. She's settled beside me. She's on my shoulder, keeping me company. No, she's in the chair beside me. She watches the fire. The flames dance in the dark.

"I'll take it if you don't want it." Her words are soft. What is she talking about? What will she take? She can't have my memories. They are too dark for her. She's too bright. It will ruin her. I will ruin her. She notices my confusion and nods to the bottle in my hand. Right, the beer. I bring it to my lips, taking a long pull. It's good, better than I remember. It tastes like poker and Starbursts and coins.

I forgo the second bottle of sorrow for the lightness of the beer. Another one appears in my hand. I don't question its appearance. I just drink. My mind swirls with memories and alcohol. Birds hop around my vision. A hand leans near me. A small hand. Not mine, not Richard's. I stare off past the fire. The string lights sway in the slight breeze. My mind is quiet. Still. Not settled, but no longer plagued with demons. The night air is crisp. The sounds of the party have died down.

"Want me to take her inside?"

Rio comes into view. He motions beside me. Vic is in the chair. Her hand is extended along the arm, reaching for me but not touching or expecting. She's offering support without asking. I've never been supported like that. Not quietly, without pretense. Her head rests on her arm, eyes closed. She fell asleep beside me. She is keeping me company without demands. She's just there. A pain in my chest worries me. Is this a heart attack? No, it's something different.

I shake my head at Rio. I don't want him to take her way. Her presence is comforting. My anniversary wallows are always dark, sad, and morose. Other memories filtered in tonight. Better memories. It was her. She brought brightness to my misery. Rio leaves but returns a few minutes later with a blanket. He drapes it over her and nods to me before walking away.

I look around the backyard. A couple is fucking in one corner. A few people sway drunkenly on the dance floor. A couple of people sit in the shallow end of the pool. Most have returned inside. I have respect here. They give me the space I want. They don't question my demands; they follow my commands. They respect me. Is it because of my ruthlessness?

Five years ago, Richard challenged me. His board had been replaced due to the death of the previous members. He was losing his grip. Whispers of me taking over could be heard at any time. I didn't want to. I didn't want to be in charge while Richard was still alive. He became frantic, wild, unpredictable. Everyone questioned him. I never said anything. I remained silent. Questions over his decisions became louder, entered church, spoken to his face. Every time someone asked why, he turned to me. He suspected me. He thought I was organizing a mutiny. I did no such thing but did nothing to stop it either.

He demanded we fight. Joe was considered a neutral party on either side of this situation—not that there were sides. Richard was paranoid. Joe said we should fight until one of us tapped. The winner would be president. Richard wasn't in bad shape but was nearly twenty years older than me. I was 31 and in better shape than him. The gym was my refuge.

We squared off, and I knew how this would end. Richard would never tap. I had to kill him. This was the end of everything. My demons took over. By the end of the fight, I knelt on his chest, strangling him. Maybe the crowd cheered. Maybe they were silent. I only heard static. I was pulled off him. His lifeless eyes stared up at the sky. It should have felt better than it did. Little relief came. The party continued. Life continued.

I became president. Silent. Moros, god of death and pain. Did they respect me because of my violence? My ruthlessness? Richard wasn't the first or the last man I killed. Did they respect me because my decisions were just? Good for the club? I don't know. Maybe it doesn't matter.

The sky around us is dark. Stars are bright in the sky, the stars that can be seen anyway. The sun will be out soon. The party is over. Vic lets out a sigh beside me. She'll be sore in the morning in that position. Without any further thought, I scoop her up. A sting pulls in my bicep from my stab wound, but I don't care. She doesn't wake. Her arms wrap around my shoulders, and she nestles against my chest. She's small in my arms, warm and content. I carry her to my room and gently place her on the bed.

She's still in her dress. I unbutton the neck, not wanting her to feel strangled in her sleep. I touch her exposed back; she's soft. A shiver rolls through her body. I pull back and tuck her into my sheets. I pull off my clothes and slide into the bed beside her.

Damaged men in romance novels sleep when their girl is beside them. That's what Sapph told me. The men only sleep a few hours, like me. Then, their girl winds up in their bed unwittingly, and both sleep soundly all night. That's how all the good romance novels go.

My life isn't a fucking romance novel.

I sleep like shit. Alcohol swirls through my veins, leaving me restless. I sleep for a few hours, like usual. I rise, dress in clean clothes, and leave my room. Vic is sleeping peacefully in my bed. She doesn't need me to wake her because I cannot sleep in one position for more than half an hour.

In the kitchen, Shirley is back, cleaning up from last night. I offer to help, but she waves me away. She hands me a mug of coffee. She doesn't ask how I slept. She knows. She knows everything. She's never said anything to me. She doesn't treat me differently than anyone else, but she watches me. At first, I thought she was worried about me having a mental breakdown. That's always a possibility. Now, she watches for signs of life beyond my demons, any spark she can latch onto.

"Vic is beautiful." Seems she's found her spark. I grunt at her, sipping the dark coffee. The heat and bold flavor push back the rest of the alcohol in my veins. My head pounds with the looming hangover. Some greasy food will help that. Shirley is already working on that. We've done this dance before; she knows exactly what I need. I treasure her for that.

"She could be good for you, Aleks. You deserve that." I scoff at her comments and shake my head. I don't deserve good. Shirley looks like she will say more when soft steps pad into the kitchen. Vic walks in wearing baggy sweatpants, a crop top that shows the tiniest sliver of skin when she moves, fuzzy socks in a pair of slides, and a messy bun on top of her head. I never knew a person could be so adorable and sexy at the same time.

Vic greets Shirley warmly, accepting a mug of coffee. She adds her creamer and leans against the counter beside me. She stares into her mug, blowing to cool it down. Shirley waves to get my attention. Then, she dramatically motions for me to put my arm around her. It would be hilarious if it weren't awkward. Shirley knows more about this stuff than I do. I take her advice and move closer to Vic. I wrap my arm around her. She straightens, glances at Shirley then up to me. She stares for a moment.

"Can I lean into you?"

Yes. Yes, she can always lean into me. She can touch me without asking. She can kiss me, hold my hand, grab my arm. Whatever she wants, she can do it to me. I want her touch. I don't want her to ask every time, but fuck. When she asks, I want her even more. I've never had someone respect my boundaries the way she does. I manage a nod then she nuzzles into my chest. She keeps both hands on her mug, but her body is pressed against mine. I rest my hand on her ribs, eyes fixed on her. Vic chats with Shirley for several minutes while she cooks.

When she's done, Shirley hands us each a plate loaded with eggs, bacon, potatoes, and toast. She's a godsend. We thank her and take our regular booth in the dining area. We eat in silence—a calm silence. It's not expectant or awkward. There's no undertone of needing discussion—just quiet. Maybe Shirley is right. Perhaps she is good for me.

The next few days pass in a blur. The club is quiet as we sleep off the party. The anniversary celebration always takes a few days to recover from. People move slowly on autopilot, still hungover or even drunk. I don't get any moments alone with Vic. She showers when I'm out. Tyler, Lucy, or Rio are always around. Vic enjoys spending time with them. As much as I want her to myself, I'm glad she has other people here.

Sapph will be back in a couple of days. Sapph is one of my favorite people in the club. We can't patch her in because of her vagina. It's a stupid fucking rule. I brought it up before when I was still VP when she first came around. The idea was shot down. Sapph said she didn't mind and didn't want me to cause problems. I let it go, but maybe I should revisit it. She's the only person besides Tyler I will spend time with alone. We don't do it frequently but will every now and then.

I've never had the desire to fuck Sapph, and she's never tried to come on to me. We respect each other too much for that. It's a platonic relationship that I value deeply.

I'm lifting weights in the gym. I have a few pulled out around me. I press the bar above my chest, letting the burn of the weight ground me. This is the heaviest I've lifted before; the challenge feels good. I drop the bar on the rack. The doors to the gym open and close, barely audible over grunge music blasting through the speakers. I glance up and see Vic staring at me. She's in bike shorts and a sports bra with sneakers. She shouldn't be allowed to walk around like that. I fight the urge to adjust my dick in my shorts. I've masturbated enough in the past few days that I shouldn't have erections like this.

She watches me for a moment, then walks toward me. I grab the remote and lower the volume in the room. A dull ringing clears after a minute. I sip my water as she finally reaches me.

"Did you know there's a guy tied up down the hall?"

"Yep," I respond. "He's the one that stabbed me." We brought him in yesterday and roughed him up a good bit. He's tied up for now. Only the gym and that room are here in the basement. That door should have been locked. I was the last one there; did I forget to lock it? I shouldn't slip like that.

"Will you kill him?" she asks tentatively, and I consider her question.

"Probably not. He only stabbed me." She nods and looks around the gym. "Want to join me?" I wave my hand around the stations I have set up. I've never let a woman in my circuits. Occasionally, I'll work with the other members, but I prefer to work alone.

"I can't lift that much. I'm going to hit the treadmill for a while," Vic waves behind her at the machines. Not the response I want, but fair enough. I hold my phone out to her, and her eyes crinkle in confusion.

"You can change the music," I say, increasing the volume to the earsplitting level it was before. A wicked grin covers her face. She takes my phone and walks to the treadmill. I didn't intend for her to take it, but it's not like I'll use it. She starts the treadmill, still fumbling with the phone. I didn't expect this to be a difficult task. Finally, the song stops, and a new one starts.

It's Britney fucking Spears.

That's why she took my phone. So, I couldn't change it back. Jokes on her; I can work out to anything. She starts running, and fuck, my cock jerks again. These basketball shorts will do nothing to hide a throbbing erection. I rip my shirt off, scrub my face, and toss it aside. I lean back and thrust the bar up, praying the blood surges to my muscles and not my aching dick.

The song changes to Adele, and I push harder. This is the song she sang in my shower. I have to rack the bar. My chest is screaming. The metal clangs as the heavy bar settles. Vic is behind me on the treadmill. I can see her in the mirror. She runs, arms pounding, legs flexing, muscles rippling. Her short legs look so strong. The shorts accentuate her ass. Her small breasts still manage to bounce in the bra. Her skin glistens with sweat. It reminds me of when she was in the shower when she touched herself.

She stops the treadmill. She hasn't been on that long. Is that all she wanted? She stalks in my direction. She can see my dick tenting my shorts; it's not subtle. I groan, rubbing my hands over my face. She stops at the end of my bench, between my legs. Her eyes flick between mine and my cock. After a minute, she drops to her knees. Am I breathing hard because of the exercise or because she is reaching for my shorts?

Vic reaches slowly for my waistband, watching for signs to stop. I don't give her any as she tugs the material back. My dick springs free, fully erect for her. Her small fingers touch the head of my dick, her touch unlike anything I have ever felt. She traces the tip, dragging her finger over the hole. I groan, and Vic wraps her fingers around my girth. My cock jerks in her hand since no one else has touched it in years. She leans in, pressing her lips together to kiss the tip. Demons flare in my mind. I can't stay focused on her. I can't let her suck me. I can't let the memories take over.

I grab her hand, which is still wrapped around my base, and tug before her lips touch me. She looks up at me. She's so fucking sweet. As if she can read my mind, she stands without a word. Vic kicks her shoes off and slides her shorts down. I've seen her naked before but watching her remove her clothes is a different sort of seeing. It's intentional and just for me.

She steps over my legs, eyes on mine the whole time. When she is straddling me, she looks down, lines my cock up with her entrance, and slides back and forth. The excessive amount of wetness from her lower lips coats my dick. Fuck, she's so wet and warm. She slides down, encasing me with her pussy. My hands reach for her hips. My eyes shut as her warm, tight cunt surrounds me. We both stay still, adjusting to the new sensation. She shifts ever so slightly.

Vic rips her bra off and leans forward. She grabs the bar behind my head and lifts her hips. She drops down again, and the feeling is overwhelming. I've dreamed of this for so long; it doesn't feel real. She moves faster over my lap, and I strain not to burst. I slide my hand along her rib and grab her breast. I drag my thumb over her nipple, and she groans. She shifts her hips in a different direction, and stars dance through my vision. I won't last long at this rate.

Both her breasts are in my hands now. I lean in, wrapping my mouth around one nipple. She moans loudly, thrusting her hips harder. It feels exquisite. I wonder if she still thinks I'm exquisite.

"Don't stop," she mumbles. I don't. I won't. I never will.

I circle her nipple with my tongue. Her movements become more erratic. My balls tighten with my growing climax. I'm going to come inside her. Fuck, I'm not wearing a condom. I haven't fucked anyone in a while, and I'm clean.

"I had a vasectomy and was recently tested," I tell her, so she doesn't worry about pregnancy. She must not be concerned about it, but I want her to know.

"I can't get pregnant, and I'm clean," she mumbles through quick breaths. "Come with me." Her hand lands on mine over her breast. She squeezes tightly, and I squeeze tighter. She clenches around my cock, and I explode inside her. This is heaven. The way she clenches around me, the way my hot release burns inside her. She doesn't lift up, only grinds against my hips, moaning loudly. Her body jerks in ecstasy. I look at her face, wanting to see her now. I've envisioned it before and want to see it. Her mouth is open in a soft o, and her eyes shut tight, better than when she masturbated in my shower. They flutter open halfway, and a small smile fills her face. She leans in to rest against my chest.

Vic rests above my heart. The thudding feels louder than usual. I wrap my arms around her, our bodies slick with sweat. She takes several deep breaths to calm her body. I hold her close, not wanting to let her go. She's perfect, and I need to keep her here in my arms. I kiss her forehead, and she chuckles.

"You and the fucking forehead kisses," she mumbles. She rises to look at me, but the gym door opens and closes. She's naked on my chest, and I panic. I roll off the bench to the floor. Foam mats line the floor; the fall won't hurt her. I put my arms out to brace myself and not collapse on her.

"Shit, Pres," Harpo starts. "Sorry." I glance in the mirror at him. He's turned away with his hand covering his eyes. Vic groans beneath me and rolls her head into my arm. She mutters a curse as her hand lifts to the back of her head. A small spot of red blood tints her brown hair. What the fuck happened? Her forehead is pressed against my wrist as she cups her head. I glance around for anything to press against, but only sweaty clothes are nearby.

"Go get a first aid kit," I bark at Harpo, and he turns to grab one. While his back is to us, I grab my discarded shirt and lift her to tug it on. She sits up but sways. I hold her shoulders as Harpo comes over. He holds the box out, but his face is still turned away, cheeks-stained red. Vic is covered; why is he acting like that?

"Fucking help me," I demand.

"Okay, but," Harpo starts, then points down with his other hand. My soft cock is still hanging out of the waistband of my shorts, surrounded by a wet spot. I tuck it back in. If there was any doubt about what we had been doing, it's gone now.

"Shit, sorry. Give me some gauze," I say.

Harpo helps me with the cut on Vic's head. When I flipped us over, I didn't realize how close the hand weights were. She hit the edge of one of the dumbbells I used in my circuit. The bleeding eventually stops, and she isn't swaying anymore. She said it's not a concussion and that she was dizzy from the sudden shift. Harpo goes to the machines on the other side of the gym. It's big enough that we have space but not privacy.

She leaves in my shirt with her shorts and shoes back on. I can't even manage to fuck her right. How can I expect her to want to be with me if I can't even do that? I don't know how to have a relationship with her. Shirley was wrong. I'm not right for Vic.

CHAPTER EIGHT

VIC

ALEKS HAS AVOIDED ME since the gym incident. He felt so good inside me. It's not just that I haven't had decent sex in years, but Aleks is entirely different. He's eager and desperate and big. Shit, I want to do that again, but he seems hesitant. Slamming my head into his weights really did a number on him. It wasn't a bad cut and totally worth the sex. It upset him, though. He acts like I'm fragile now.

I'm sitting in the booth with him, Tyler, and Destiny. Meals are the only time I've seen him. He hides in his room or office. The guys have gone out on their bikes a few times. They didn't return beaten up, but they were gone for hours. I didn't ask what they were doing. I don't want to know. The guy in the basement, now gone, was enough for me.

Tonight is my last shift in the bar. I'm still trying to figure out what to do after. I have a nice nest egg, but I probably need to devise a game plan. I've been here for a few weeks and gone from Pennsylvania nearly twice as long. I'm a bit surprised Wesley hasn't shown up in the bar. I don't know what to do about any of this. Everything feels more convoluted now than it did when I got here. I guess I can't just run from my problems. That doesn't mean I'm going to run back to them.

Lucy walks over to the table. "Hey, ya'll," she greets. She turns toward Aleks and me. "The new bartender just called and wants to start tonight. I told him that was fine, and he'll cover your shift. So, you're officially off the hook!" She grins at me, and I try to mimic her enthusiasm. It's not about the money but what I will do with my time. I've never had free time. Even on vacations, there was an itinerary. Weekends have chores or events. There is always something to do.

"Yay!" Destiny cheers, clapping her hands. "Let's go on a double date!" Tyler's face scrunches together.

"Those two aren't dating," he states like it's the most obvious thing. He's not wrong. We just fucked once and masturbated in front of each other. And have fantastic chemistry, but that's not dating. Neither Aleks nor I say anything.

"Ugh, fine. A group dinner. Let's just go," Destiny eggs on. "Let's go somewhere fancy." Tyler and Aleks groan in such unison I almost think it was only one of them. I smile at the synchrony of their actions. Tyler rubs his face and asks what's fancy.

"Applebee's!" Destiny nearly yells. My eyebrows knit in confusion. Is she serious right now? "You know, like the song?" She starts humming and dancing to a song only she can hear.

"Oh, I think you mean trashy. Pretty sure the song is trashy like Applebee's." Destiny's mouth drops open at my correction. Tyler laughs loudly along with Aleks beside me, and I steal a quick glance. I was right. His face is ethereal when he smiles. I stare in awe for a moment until Aleks looks at me.

"Where do you want to go?" His beauty stuns me for a moment. I have to force my mind to think. I finally look away from him, needing to not stare at his godlike face.

"Um, maybe Tex-Mex or barbecue?" Aleks and Tyler discuss a few places while Destiny pouts. They settle on a restaurant and ask how long we'll need to get ready. I tell them I only need fifteen minutes. Aleks stands up, agreeing to meet back here in fifteen. Destiny instantly starts arguing. She claims she needs more than fifteen minutes to get ready for a date. She needs more than fifteen minutes to get ready for anything, but I don't say that. I walk away as she screeches behind me.

I debate a dress but will need more layers if we ride their bikes. I'm not comfortable riding with exposed skin. I settle on black skinny jeans with a few rips and a white top with a bright pink bra underneath that is visible through the shirt. I slip on my boots and grab a jacket. It's not cold, but I want layers on the bike. I spritz some saltwater spray in my hair to liven up my waves, slap on some mascara and tinted lip balm, and I'm good to go. Fifteen minutes, right on the dot.

I meet the guys in the bar. They are waiting closer to the door, chatting idly. I love how comfortable they are around each other. I'm glad they have each other, especially after all this time. Aleks really is like a brother, which is weird since I fucked him and want to again. Thankfully, he's not my brother.

We wait a few more minutes for Destiny to arrive, and Tyler yells at her across the bar. They start bickering over how long she took. At this point, I wonder if he likes fighting with her. He groans and complains and never seems happy about it. I can't fathom why he would stay with her otherwise. Maybe they fight and have good makeup sex.

Aleks hands me a helmet, and we head for their bikes. He helps me on and pulls my arms around his waist. I love being pressed against him like this. The wind blows around us as Tyler and Aleks weave through traffic. I don't watch ahead because it makes me nervous. They are good drivers, but that does little to soothe my anxiety when they split the lane to pass. My hands tighten several times, and a chuckle rumbles in Aleks's chest. That makes my pussy clench. Damn, I want to fuck him again.

Aleks has his hair down tonight, and the ends whip through the air. They smack against my face shield. I'm worried they'll get stuck. I reach up nervously. I haven't let go of him while riding before. I usually cling to him for dear life. I slide his hair around to his other shoulder, adjusting it under his cut so it will stay. My hair flies behind me, but no one is back there. Aleks tilts his head slightly, but that's the only acknowledgment I get.

We arrive at a Tex-Mex restaurant with outdoor seating. The air is warm and humid but not uncomfortable. We take a seat on the patio, and Destiny instantly starts up some random ass conversation. I don't bother to listen. I rarely know what she's talking about. Dinner is so good. I enjoy the food at Dionysus. The compound has a smaller kitchen area where we can make food, but I haven't had much variety since getting here.

Tyler and Destiny leave to go to the bathroom. If they're going for a quickie, I'm glad they didn't say that. I watch the clouds move across the sky, thinking about how much I like it here. I love being around Aleks and Tyler. Even the other members are fantastic. I miss working in the ER. You never really knew what would come through the doors. I miss the challenge, energy, and camaraderie. The club has that feeling of belonging, but I'm not really part of it. They protect me, but I'm not part of the club, more of an outsider.

A motion on my side draws my attention. Aleks is braiding his hair. It's a loose braid, straight down the middle. I can't tell what's more mesmerizing: watching his fingers deftly gather hair and twist it together or watching his hair pull back from his exquisite face. Damn, he's so pretty. His piercing blue eyes shine under barely visible eyebrows. His hair is so light it's almost translucent. His beard has a hint of brown to it, short but full. My fingers twitch to rake through his scruff.

He pulls a hair tie from his cut pocket. I'm transfixed on him. Shamelessly staring as his beauty transforms. I don't think that's possible. Just a different sort. I can't even describe it. He's fucking perfect. He was hot when we were younger, but I was so young I didn't register it. I meet his eyes. He's staring at me with an intensity I've only seen a few times. When we masturbated. When I fucked him in the gym. Will he go to the bathroom with me for a quickie? Shit, I should have worn a dress. Easier access and all.

He leans forward to say something. My breath hitches, but Destiny's voice pierces the air as they walk to the table. He leans back, and my stupid heart lurches. What was he going to say? He can whisper it in my ear. Oh, his breath against my ear, warm and gentle against my sensitive skin...

"Well, well, well," a loud voice sounds behind me. "If it isn't the two fearless leaders of Steel Warriors. Just the men we want to see." Two men walk up to our table. They have cuts, but it's for a different club. One man's patches tell me his name is Lloyd, and he's the president of Longhorn Devils. The other man is Walker, and he's the treasurer. Lloyd is older, maybe five years or more than Tyler. The other guy looks to be the same age. Lloyd likes beer, if his gut hanging over his pants tells me anything.

Aleks and Tyler look at them indifferently, and neither says a word. Based on the little knowledge that fills my motorcycle club expertise, this doesn't seem like a typical interaction. Typically, a battle of wits occurs before a fight. Oh god, I hope they don't have guns. Would they shoot? We're in a public area with kids. Does that matter to them? Does that matter to Tyler and Aleks? I hope so, but I don't know for sure. Do outlaw motorcycle clubs have a code of morals?

"Look at this pretty little new thing," Walker says beside me. Standing to the right of Lloyd, he's closer to me and staring at me like I'm a Little Debbie cake. A shiver of disgust rolls down my body. I scrunch my face to show my disgust but don't say anything. The whole table remains silent.

"You know, Mor, maybe I'll take her instead of the deal." Walker reaches like he will stroke my face. I swat my hand in the air like I'm shooing away a fly.

"And what would you do? That beard looks like it has more bugs than a dead cow, and no one is ever satisfied with three inches." I turn my back to him and see Tyler and Destiny snicker. Aleks is glaring at the man, watching his every move. Walker takes a step closer. Aleks tenses, ready to fight.

"Didn't anyone tell you not to turn your back on a threat?"

"Sure, but I don't see one." That's the line that triggers Walker. He grabs a fistful of my hair. The exact spot where I hit my head in the gym. The cut is healed, but it's sensitive. This isn't the first time I've had my hair grabbed by a man. One hand flies to his wrist, but my other balls into a fist. Aleks rises with his fist clenched, too. As if we planned this, I elbow Walker in the groin while Aleks breaks his nose. He falls away quickly. The sudden release of hair causes my head to surge forward, and I collide with Aleks's stomach. His hard, muscled stomach. On instinct, his hand wraps around my head, holding the spot where my hair was pulled. The pressure is nice against the ache.

Walker lays on the ground, moaning and rolling around. Tyler is standing with his hand on his gun, holstered on his hip. People around us stare and mumble. Lloyd takes in the scene, then grabs Walker to leave. He shouts that this isn't over. I can't see because I'm still held against Aleks's stomach. I'm not complaining, though. I like it here. It's hard and warm and smells like leather and man, and is that vanilla? I take a deep breath, trying to commit the scent to memory. I'm going to masturbate to that later.

Aleks tips my head back, looking down at me. I've looked up at him since I arrived, but something about this angle is profound. He asks if I'm okay. I manage a nod; my mouth is surprisingly dry. My panties are decidedly not. What does it say about me that I just elbowed a man in the groin while Aleks punched him, and I'm so turned on?

Destiny whines about being scared and wanting to leave. Tyler agrees we should probably go. Aleks finally steps back from me. I take a deep breath, trying to tear my gaze from him. It's so damn hard. I shake my head to clear it. Tyler asks if I'm okay, and I tell him I am. We clear the table and get on the bikes.

We're all wearing Bluetooth helmets. Aleks bought a bunch for the club a while ago. It must have cost a pretty penny. According to the interwebs, these bad boys aren't cheap. Aleks tells Destiny to keep her fucking mouth shut while we ride. He wants the line clear for him and Tyler. I hold tight to Aleks as we swerve through traffic, still not watching the road. I wonder if I'll get used to that at some point.

After several minutes of riding, Tyler announces we have a tail. Aleks says at least three are behind us. They discuss the best action and settle on a highway with fewer people. They have some morals if they don't want to cause wrecks or endanger others. The exit is coming up in a few minutes, and they make some aggressive maneuvers to try to lose them before that. It's unsuccessful, but I manage not to scream into the microphone. So, I consider that a win.

"Can you shoot?" Aleks asks, turning his head slightly to indicate he's talking to me.

"Hell, no! She's not shooting at them!" Tyler yells into the connection. I wince at the loudness.

"I'm not a marksman or anything, but I know how to pull the trigger." Without another word, Aleks shifts and passes a handgun to me. I've been to the range a few times. Just enough to know I can hit my target about a third of the time while I'm standing still and aiming. Loosening my grip on his chest, I take it from him.

"If they start shooting, return fire. It's not about hitting them but pushing them back." Right. Shoot to scare. I can do that. Tyler groans, but he and Aleks talk through a plan. They are going to split the two lanes of the highway. The goal is to split the three men up to make it easier to take them down. That's not the same as scaring them, but I suppose that part isn't my job. Tyler guns it, and Destiny shrieks in my ears. Yep, that's loud as fuck.

As they suspected, one of the bikers pulls around to chase Tyler. My heart starts racing. We're really in the middle of a chase. Tonight was supposed to be a date night. I was just ogling Aleks for braiding his hair. Now I have a gun in my hand with the instructions to shoot it. I had no plans of being involved in their club stuff. Guess I am now.

A gunshot fires, and sparks fly a few feet in front of us, off to the side. It's much too close for my comfort. Aleks holds steady and doesn't react at all to being fired at. How often does something like this happen? What would it take to be so steady on a bike while being fired at? Is he really that good at controlling his emotions? I cling tighter to him, then remember my task. Shoot to scare. I reach behind me and pull the trigger. The recoil catches me off guard, and I nearly drop the damn thing.

Aleks squeezes my knee reassuringly. One of the men behind us swerves at my shot but recovers quickly. They are gaining on us. Shit, my heart is beating out of my chest. I start sending thoughts and prayers to every god I can think of. I don't think Eros or Loki really care about this moment. It's not like I believe in prayer, but it distracts me from the gut-clenching fear of being chased by a rival motorcycle gang. Oh, sweet, 6 pound, 8 ounce, newborn Jesus, wrapped in gold swaddling, please let us live, or whatever Ricky Bobby said. That sends a chuckle through my tightening chest. You just can't beat Ricky Bobby.

"I don't know what to do with my hands," I mutter into my helmet, quoting one of my favorite lines from the most random movie at this moment.

"What?" Aleks responds. The confusion in his voice is unmistakable.

"Shake and bake, baby!" Tyler yells. A smile grows on my face as my confidence grows. The number of times Tyler and I video called just to watch some random Will Ferrell movie together is almost embarrassing. None of my friends will watch it with me. So, I would call Tyler but trying to start a movie at the same time while on a video call is surprisingly hard.

Adrenaline pumps through my body. I turn slightly to get a better sight line. I wrap my fingers around Aleks's shirt for a better grip. He grabs my knee, holding me in place. I raise the gun and aim at the men. My accuracy is usually about 30 percent at the range. Not great, but I'm content with it. I'm hoping to just scare them with a bullet near their head. Maybe a mirror, if I'm lucky. I pull the trigger.

The man's head snaps back as a stream of blood spurts from his neck. Oh shit, I actually hit him! He loses control of his bike. It wobbles to the left, then right, then tips and hits the ground in front of the other biker. I'm frozen as I watch the other man fly off his bike, landing face-first with his arms over his head on the asphalt in front of his motorcycle. Both men stay still on the road. My breathing stops.

A tap on my knee draws my attention. Loud voices sound through my helmet. I can't make out the words. Air returns to my lungs in tiny, quick breaths. I just killed at least one man, possibly two. Holy fuck.

"Bird, give me the gun." I can hear Aleks. Chatter still sounds through the speakers that I can't make out. I turn around, wrapping my arm around Aleks. I don't intentionally hand him the gun, but with it pressed against his chest, he takes it from me. In a blur I can't process, he catches up with Tyler and takes out his tail. A phone trills through my mind. Aleks is talking to someone. I recognize the voice. It's Harpo. Aleks is telling the club what happened. He didn't say I killed them. Just that three are down on the highway. It's like watching a movie.

"Going silent," Aleks's voice is soft and comforting. Destiny's voice disappears, and I thank my lord and savior, Dolly Parton, for that one. I hold onto Aleks's chest, trying to breathe. It's hard in this helmet. I'm not claustrophobic, but it feels tight in here. Aleks drapes his arm over mine on his chest. The image of the wreck plays in my mind over and over. I haven't seen a motorcycle wreck in person, let alone caused one. Many victims of crashes have come through the ER, each as gruesome as the last. Images of motorcycle crash victims roll through my head. So many died in the ER, under my hands while I gave chest compressions. Knowing I just did that to two people...

At the compound, Aleks and Tyler pull into the garage and back their bikes into their spots. Destiny is off and running inside. Chicken. My brain is a mess—somewhere between present and total breakdown. I pull the helmet off, taking a deep breath. Aleks holds his hand out for me. I swing my leg off and twist to walk away. Before I do, Tyler grabs my arm, and I'm transported through time to eighteen years ago.

Tyler and Aleks came by the house on a Saturday morning while Mom and Dad were out buying groceries. They wouldn't stop by while Mom and Dad were at home. Dad disapproved of the bikes, and Mom was always disappointed in their life choices. But I loved them and was always asking to go out with them. Of course, my parents said no. So, anytime my brother and his best friend showed up, it was a special event.

It was about a month before my thirteenth birthday, and they said they wanted to celebrate early. That was not a problem; I'm always down for celebrating. They took me out with them for the whole day. Cell phones weren't as prominent as they are now. We didn't have to worry about Mom or Dad calling every thirty seconds, demanding to bring me home.

I rode with Aleks because Tyler's bike was too small for me. We cruised through the hills of western Pennsylvania, went to breakfast, and stopped at a festival in town. We played a few games, and Aleks won a stuffed hippo for me. A hippo I still have. Wesley tried to throw it away one time, and I lost my shit. I climbed in the dumpster to fish it out, then slept in the guest room wrapped around the hippo. I never told Wesley where it came from, and he never touched it again. The hippo is one of the only things that wasn't a necessity that I brought when I left Pennsylvania.

We ate at my favorite restaurant. They took me to a different restaurant for ice cream cones that are so big it's larger than your head. When they finally took me back home, I climbed off Aleks's bike using his shoulder instead of his hand. He didn't have a touch aversion then. Tyler grabbed my arm the same way he holds it now. Back then, they said goodbye and hugged me. The hug wasn't unexpected from Tyler, but Aleks never hugged me. I knew something was wrong but didn't ask what. We had such a good day. I didn't want to ruin it. Neither did they. Aleks kissed my forehead. It was my first forehead kiss from him. Stupid forehead kisses.

They left for San Antonio the next day, and I didn't see them for eighteen years.

Tonight, Tyler tugs me away from Aleks and into his arms. He whispers fears of losing me and anger that I took the gun from Aleks. I stand awkwardly in his arms, fighting away tears. When he lets me go, he grabs my neck on both sides and shakes me lightly.

"Don't do that shit again." We both chuckle as he finally releases me. Aleks leads me inside to store our helmets. Tyler wanders off to find Destiny.

"Stay with me tonight," Aleks says. It's not really a question, but not really a demand either. I nod, but I want to stop by my room first. I change into a shirt and pajama shorts sans underwear. I grab my hippo and remove it from my bag for the first time since I arrived. Aleks stands near the bed in his room, fiddling with his phone when I walk in. His shoes are off, and his braid is gone, leaving his hair over his shoulders. Overwhelming arousal courses through my body. He looks at me, then spots the hippo in my arm.

"You kept it." Again, not a question, not a statement. I shake my head and take a couple steps toward him. For the first time, he holds his arms out for me. I run and jump, not wanting to settle for a hug, and toss the hippo onto the bed. Aleks catches me easily as emotions take over my body. I bury my face in his neck. He wraps one arm around my ass, the other on my back. Without thinking, I kiss his neck several times, and he groans.

"Fuck me," I whisper. "Fuck me hard." He takes the invitation and crashes into the wall beside the bed. The impact of the wall causes me to moan as I grind my hips against him. In his arms, my hips land around his waist. I nibble on his neck as he grinds up into my core. I moan louder, trying to shimmy down. Both of his hands are on my ass, squeezing, feeling, claiming. The tightness feels so good, distracting me from everything that has happened. And shit, there's so much of it.

I suck on his neck, finding a spot that drives him wild. He thrusts into me roughly with a groan that I can feel. My breasts rub against his cut. The patches provide the perfect amount of friction. The leather on my breast, his fingers near my ass, his beard against my face, I could come just from those sensations. I grind my hips against his waist, and he hisses out a breath.

"I'm not wearing underwear," I whisper between breaths and kisses to his neck. "Slide the shorts aside and fuck me." He slips his fingers under my shorts, reaching my uncovered core. He curses when his fingers glide over my wet lips. I grind my hips against him, wanting more of that touch. He reaches beneath me, unbuttoning his pants to pull his cock out. If I could move without falling, I'd sink onto him. He holds me. I shuffle down his body as he adjusts his grip.

I lace my fingers together behind Aleks's neck. He may have welcomed me into his arms, but that doesn't mean he wants me fondling him. He slams into me all the way to the hilt. I moan loudly at the sensation. He feels so good inside me. His hands on my ass grip tightly. I love the pressure and want more pain. I want to mingle pleasure with the pain. Before I can ask him for that, he pulls back and slams into me again.

His pace is brutal, claiming, as desperate as my own need. Because of our size difference, his mouth is against my forehead. I swear to god, I'm going to start wearing platform shoes just so he has no excuse for fucking forehead kisses. I want to scream in anger, pleasure, fear, heartache, lust. I drop my hands, wrapping around his back. I cling to his body, letting his cut give that delicious friction. Fuck, I'm so close.

Pulling myself against Aleks's chest instead of the wall changes the position he's entering me. His jeans rub against my clit. The new angle doesn't seem to bother him at all. He pounds inside me with a glorious rhythm. My fingers clench against the patch on the back of his cut as my body tenses. He curses, and the sound of his voice is all it takes. I cry out as an orgasm crashes through my body. It's a mind-shattering orgasm, and I barely register Aleks coming with me. He holds me securely as I tense and jerk against him.

Aleks drops his forehead against mine as our breathing settles. I calm down, nearly falling asleep in his arms. The tension and emotions from the evening are too much for me to handle any longer. He tucks me in bed, hands me the hippo, and tucks it under the covers. I smile at the gentle motion. Just before I fall asleep. He presses his lips against my forehead.

Another goddamned forehead kiss.

This motherfucker....

Chapter Nine

VIC

I'VE SPENT EVERY NIGHT since the shooting incident in Aleks's room. Sometimes he fucks me. Sometimes, he fingers me while rubbing himself. He comes on my stomach, and I fucking love it so much. Seeing him release on my stomach is oddly empowering. I did that to him. He came because of me.

But I still only get fucking forehead kisses. Every time. Aleks fucks me, comes on me, gives me an orgasm, then gently kisses my fucking forehead. I love the gentleness of it, but goddammit, I want an actual fucking kiss.

The days are dull. I have nothing to do. Sometimes, I'll read. I've spent a lot of time by the pool. I'm going to blow through all my savings in sunscreen. I'm not risking skin cancer, but what the hell am I supposed to do every day? One day, I even went down and helped wash dishes in the kitchen for free. Ugh, I need a job or something.

Something warm on my cunt draws me away from my half-awake state. A tongue licks straight up my core. A beard offers extra sensations. I twist, giving Aleks better access. I hum at the delightful feeling. He hasn't done this yet. He continues licking up and down, never touching my clit, not even slipping inside. It's like he's never done this before. I wiggle again, hoping he will shift his technique.

He seems to get the hint, and his tongue flicks faster but still just up and down. Does this work on the other women? Maybe they just fake it around him because it's Aleks, the president, the fucking god. His tongue is doing nothing for me. I shift again, trying to at least get his tongue near my clit. Then his teeth clamp around one of my lips.

"Oh, Jesus, fuck." I push his head back, not even concerned with his touch boundary. Teeth on my labia are a hard pass. "No teeth."

"Sorry," he mumbles. "Should I stop?"

Aleks looks sad at his question. His eyes, just above my pubic bone, are everything. Even when sad, they arouse.

"No, just," I pause. My mind is still shrouded with arousal and pain I didn't want. I don't want to tell him he is bad, but I need him to change his technique. "Can I show you what I like?" He nods his head, excitement dancing in his eyes.

I shift to sit up a bit and slide my hand down to my pussy. Aleks tracks the movement with burning intensity, the stare I love so much. I rub my finger up and down my wet slit, then slip it just inside. Only a knuckle deep. I thrust in and out a few times, then draw it out. I slide it up to my clit and bring my other hand down. I part myself and make a show of rubbing my clit. Pleasure courses through my body, and I tip my head back at the feeling.

Aleks moves in, licks up and down my opening, and then dips in. I mutter approval as he mimics the motions I just showed him. I typically want fingers in the mix, too, but we'll work up to that. Then his tongue swirls my clit, and I curse. I force my head forward to watch him. His eyes meet mine. His mouth is wrapped around me. His hair falls over his cheeks like a curtain, blocking the view from the side, and I nearly orgasm just from the way he looks.

"S..suck," I whisper. He follows my command, and I moan loudly. He pops off my clit, then does it again. That's what sends me over the edge. My body jerks, and he continues to suck. He slips his lips off but circles it again. Gods, it feels so good. I grind against him. Despite my orgasm, my body is writhing, building up for a second one.

"Fingers," I mutter. I'm not great at talking during sex. That ability ceases to exist when I'm in the throes of passion. I hold two fingers up and curl them back and forth. Thank gods Aleks is smart. Two fingers are instantly inside me, copying the motion I just showed. I grab the back of his head, drawing him back to my clit. Like the good student he is, he swirls his tongue around my clit. Such a fast learner.

The second orgasm is more intense than the first. My body lifts off the bed, and I scream. I'm generally not a screamer, but I also don't usually get two orgasms. The fingers, the tongue, the scruff, the way he looks at me, it's the perfect storm. Choked gasps fall out of me as I come down from my orgasm. His fingers stop but stay inside me. He does not take his mouth off my clit. It quickly changes from pleasure to pain. Part of me wants him to keep going, to find my limit of pain, but I get the impression he wouldn't like learning I am in pain.

I push Aleks back, muttering to stop. Uncontrollable giggles erupt from my chest. He slides up to my side, and I twist into his chest. I prop my leg over his hips. My over-sensitized clit needs a break. I keep my hands against my face. Aleks wraps his arms around my body, holding me close.

Then gives me a fucking forehead kiss.

"Aleks," I say softly. He grunts, the only sign he heard me. "Do you not like kissing?" His arms tense around me. "You don't have to answer that," I backtrack quickly. I wish he would, but I don't want to make him uncomfortable. He has a lot of trauma he hasn't dealt with. I don't want to drag it up if he isn't ready. I pull my leg back to give him space, but he catches my thigh with his hand and tugs my leg back around him. Maybe I'm the exception to his aversions. Warmth spreads through my already heated body.

"I'm not used to kissing," he responds.

"You don't kiss the women you fuck?"

"No. That's just for release." Hmm, that's interesting. I didn't peg him as the boyfriend type, but it's been eighteen years. Surely, he dated someone.

"What about girlfriends? Did you kiss them?

"I haven't had girlfriends." His words are tight. He doesn't want to admit that. He wants to tell me but doesn't like his own responses. I'm not sure how to process this information. I've been married for almost ten years. I dated as a teen. Even Tyler has had a few girlfriends since then. I'm lost in my thoughts, and Aleks's voice pulls me back.

"Do you want me to kiss you?"

"No," I start but quickly correct myself. "I mean, yes, but not if it makes you uncomfortable."

He grabs my chin and tips it up. My heart beats faster. I stare at his lips. They look so soft. Will he be out of practice like he was at eating pussy? Will I get to show him what I like? I flatten my hands against his chest. His heart pounds under my palm. Is he nervous? Excited? I'm excited. Maybe I should be more nervous. Will this change things? What if he doesn't like kissing? I can go without kisses, I think. For him, I will.

Before he even moves, a fist bangs on his door.

"Mor!" Tyler screams from the other side. I don't think I have ever hated my brother so much. "I know you're in there. We all heard your whore screaming. Nice." I can hear the smirk on his face. He doesn't know it's me. He would be so pissed. Not only for Aleks being the one to fuck me but for hearing his little sister orgasm.

"Come on, Mor! Sapph will be here soon!"

Sapph. The mystery woman that lives in the other half of my room. I know little about her. They talk about her a lot and clearly like her. Has Aleks fucked her? Did she get forehead kisses from him? He said he hasn't been in a relationship, but what is he doing with me? Jealousy eats through me. I'm not a jealous person, but I can't fight the unease rising in my stomach.

Aleks climbs out of the bed, grabbing his clothes. So much for those soft lips.

"I'll go distract Tyler, and you can come out in a bit so he doesn't realize you're the 'screaming whore.'" His Tyler impression is spot on. I giggle at him as he pulls on his cut. I want to see him in a clown costume just to see if anything can make him less beautiful. If the image in my head holds up, it won't change his beauty. He walks over and kisses my forehead. Again. I stifle the sigh as he leaves.

Aleks and Tyler are chatting by the booth, not sitting. Destiny follows behind me as we walk into the restaurant. They are waiting for us before they sit in the booth. Destiny rushes around me to Tyler like she didn't see him just a few minutes ago. Aleks turns and looks at me. His gaze is neutral, hiding what we just did in his room. Not letting on that I am his "screaming whore."

Before I get the chance to sit down, a woman walks into the restaurant and yells, "I'm back, bitches!" Everyone cheers, holding up beers that would be unacceptable anywhere else in the morning. She heads straight to our booth.

Holy hell, she's gorgeous. She has long black hair, a heart-shaped face, and medium-brown skin. She looks like a goddess, tall and muscular. She has an air of confidence. She knows her own worth. I bet if she wore a gold dress, she would glow. As it is, she wears black skinny jeans and boots similar to my own. Her leather jacket is grey, and she has a shirt with the club's patch. I didn't know the club had logoed gear.

She walks toward us like she's on a runway, a deadly, dangerous runway. She could kill a man with a flick of her wrist and not think twice. I bet she has, and that's so damn hot. She walks to Tyler, and they cheer, wrapping each other in a hug. Now I'm jealous of my brother hugging a woman. A totally different jealousy than I felt about Aleks and Sapph this morning.

Holy shit. This is Sapph. This is the woman they've been talking about. I'm standing here, not breathing because I'm fucking attracted to her. I want to taste her. Wrap my legs around her body as I lose myself in her. Fuck. If I had known leaving my husband and traveling to San Antonio would lead me straight to this level of attraction, I would have done it sooner.

She turns to Aleks and holds her fist out. Aleks raises his hand, but before they connect, she jerks her hand back in an explosion, sound effects and all. I didn't think she could get any more attractive. She doesn't touch him and has a special handshake with him. Damn, she's perfect. I haven't wanted anyone other than Aleks this much. Is it this club? Do they have a special potion to make them gods? Is that why they named it after a god? Is it because there are so many already here?

"And who is this gorgeous woman?" She's looking at me. She just called me gorgeous. She holds her hand out to take mine, and I place my hand in hers. Sapph's is rough with callouses from handling tools and weapons. She brings my hand to her lips and kisses it. Her brown eyes focus on mine. They are so full of depth. I could stare at them forever and never run out of things to look at.

"Vic," I giggle out. I fucking giggle. I'm not an adult. I'm a teenager with a crush.

"Oh, you didn't tell me about her." She speaks to Aleks but stares at me. My breathing is shallow. She doesn't let go of my hand. I'm lost in her eyes. Her hair drapes over her face and frames the edge of my vision. Her face is clean and smooth, and I want to touch it. With my fingers, my mouth, my cunt. I want to wrap her legs around my face and see what she tastes like. Heat rises through my chest. My cheeks burn with the blush coating them.

"It's Tori, my sister," Tyler draws my attention from her. "She goes by Vic now. Vic, this is Sapph. She's your new roomie." Yes, she fucking is. "Come on, let's sit. You've got to tell us what you've been up to!"

Sapph finally releases my hand. It chills instantly at the loss of her touch. I want that back. I want that on my body. My breasts, my waist, my ass, everywhere. She turns away from me to grab a chair and breaks my focus. Aleks steps sideways as my surroundings come back. He is watching me, and my blush renews. Does he know what I am thinking? Shit, will he be mad about that?

I slide into the booth, and Aleks sits next to me. Sapph pulls a chair up to the end of the table and starts talking with Tyler. I can't focus on her story. I'm drowned in arousal and worry and desire and fear. Aleks doesn't press his leg against mine like normal. He knows I want her. He saw it in my eyes. I still want him. I don't want to lose him. I don't know Sapph well enough to pick her over him. I don't think I could choose anyone over him. It would be Sapph if it were anyone, though.

Maybe she'll be an ass or something. Perhaps she's not even gay. It's not like she has a sign or said anything. This feels like Alanis Morissette's song, "Meeting the man of my dreams then meeting his beautiful wife." Ironically, I'm with my brother's best friend, but I'm equally attracted to his best friend.

I press my thigh against Aleks's. He doesn't respond. He's listening intently to Sapph as she recounts her mission. I try to focus, but I'm so lost in my own head. He doesn't talk to Sapph anymore than anyone else. Is he mad because he likes her? He knows I want her, but maybe he does too. I'm totally down for a three-way. She looks like she knows how to pleasure someone, whether it's a man or a woman.

"You still got that Harley? I'm surprised it made it back in one piece. How often does that thing break?" Tyler laughs, and Sapph sneers playfully in response. Aleks has a soft smile on his face. He doesn't give any attention to me. He looks genuinely happy that she is back, just a bit reserved. My heart cracks just a little.

My thoughts reel. If he doesn't want me, I could go back to Pennsylvania. I've been gone for nearly two months now. I should go back and deal with things. I really don't want to. I want to stay here with Tyler and all the other friends I've made. Lucy and Rio. And Aleks. Gods, I don't want to leave him.

"You got a Gold Wing yet? We all know your old ass is ready for an old man's recliner."

"I've been begging him to get one of those!" Destiny chimes in. Tyler groans as Aleks and Sapph laugh. I can't decide who is prettier when they laugh. For a moment, I dream of what it would be like to have them both. Aleks fucking me from behind while I go down on Sapph. Sapph in a gold bikini, glowing in the string lights around the pool while Aleks and I lounge on the edge, smoking. Riding down the road. I'd ride with Aleks on the way to a date, then home with

Sapph. I don't know what kind of bike she has. Maybe we would just go to a park, and Aleks would rest under a tree while I lean against him. Sapph would have her head in my lap while I stroke her hair.

Harpo yells at Aleks across the bar. He's standing near Aleks's office and waves him over. Aleks rises to leave and squeezes my knee quickly before he gets up. He doesn't look at me. I watch his back as he walks through the bar and into his office. My breathing is shallow. A desire to cry over this situation tingles in my throat. I don't have Aleks. Or Sapph, for that matter. It's not like I could really lose them.

Sapph slaps her thighs and says she's going to unpack. I offer to go with her, since I'm her roommate. I should probably tell her about the shower, too. I follow her like a damn puppy. I've got it bad for two people. This is ridiculous. It's not like having some unrealistic celebrity crush. No, this is real and difficult and a complete mindfuck.

Sapph tells me to walk through her room, and I follow her. Her luggage is already on her bed, and she pulls things out. She chats about her trip, and I listen intently, taking in her story this time. I ask a few questions to show I'm involved and definitely not focused on her breasts. Her jacket is hung over a chair, and the logoed shirt has rips all over it. I can see her smooth skin. I can see my lips on it.

"I'm going to shower, then chill for a bit. You wanna stay with me?"

"Yeah, but the shower doesn't work. Aleks called a plumber a few weeks ago, but they've been swamped." Her smirk has a twinkle of delight in it. Her whole face lights up.

"Is that so?" I nod my head and hum a confirmation. She glances at me and walks into the bathroom. I follow her out of sheer curiosity. She steps beside the shower, reaching down to something I can't see. She searches for a minute, then stands up. Sapph reaches the shower and turns the nozzle. It sputters for a moment, then water sprays out. My eyes go wide.

"I turned the valve off before I left to avoid any leaks. It does get a leak occasionally," she shrugs, eyeing me suspiciously. "Aleks knows that. Where have you been showering?"

"In Aleks's room," my voice is barely a whisper. He knew. No plumber is that busy. Even if they are, dozens of plumbers would be available. He didn't get a plumber or fix the valve because he wanted me in his room. I huff a laugh. "I guess I can shower in here now." My voice is breathy. More than I meant for it to be. I didn't mean to imply I would shower with her, but based on how she looks at me, that's what she thinks.

"I'll wait for you," I say, pointing toward my room, indicating that she can shower alone.

"Why don't you wait in my room? You can start some music. Pick any," she winks and pulls her shirt over her head. Her brown skin is covered in bold tattoos. Birds, a dragon, a sword, a mermaid, and a couple of pinup girls all over her skin and arms. I didn't notice the ones on her arms before or didn't register what they were. She reaches for the clasp on her bra, and I force my feet to move.

She has a speaker on a dresser beneath a mounted TV. I press the button to turn on the device. It doesn't turn on, and I think for a moment. I check the power cords. If she shuts the water off, she's probably the type to unplug devices. Sure enough, it is unplugged. Once it's on, I remember I don't have a phone. Maybe she'll have a streaming app on her TV.

I decide to search for a remote. It's not snooping; I just need the remote. Sapph probably has it somewhere. It's not on the dresser or the desk. She seems like the type who would put it in a drawer. I check the desk drawers and nightstand but don't find any remotes. I'm still definitely not snooping. I open the top drawer of the dresser. It makes sense to keep the remote closest to the device. The drawer glides out easily, and I freeze.

A few remotes are here, but they are not for the TV. Dozens of sex toys are neatly organized in the drawer. Dildos and vibrators, and butt plugs of varying sizes line one side. Masks, gags, and ropes are stacked between the dildos and other devices. Floggers, paddles, and crops sit side by side. Clamps with and without chains are organized in small bins. A larger box has wooden clothes pins. A metal pinwheel that looks startlingly sharp sits near the bottom.

A long double-ended dildo rests beside a strap-on harness. Does that mean she is gay? Or at least bisexual? Maybe she just likes to peg men, but why the double-ended dildo? Does that work for a hetero couple? I reach into the drawer and glide my fingers over the toys. As suspected, the pinwheel is sharp. I can't help but wonder what that would feel like. Restrained, gagged, and blindfolded when this rolls across my skin.

I pick up the pinwheel and roll it over my finger, noting every little prick. Where would Sapph use this? Would it go on my clit? Is that even what it is for? Jesus, would I want that? Yes. I don't have to think about that one. I've wanted to explore pain and pleasure for a long time. The wall thuds beside me, causing me to jump and look up. Sapph stares at me curiously.

I stop breathing, frozen in place like a deer caught in headlights. I hold the pinwheel in one hand, the other resting on the drawer, ready to grab more things. Oh hell. My face burns. I bite my lip, hoping for a distraction, but it only makes my panties wetter. Sapph takes a step forward. Her thumb tugs my lip from my teeth, and she stares at them momentarily.

She pulls the pinwheel from my hand and grabs me with her other hand. Slowly, she lightly presses the pinwheel into my wrist, then rolls it up the inside of my forearm. Goosebumps spread across my flesh in eager anticipation. I want more. Her grin grows, covering her entire face. I can't make my face move at all.

Sapph replaces the pinwheel and shuts the drawer with her elbow, still holding my hand. She reaches behind me to grab her phone—not the drawer full of toys. Without letting me go, she pulls me to the bed, settles us against the headboard, and starts some music. She drops my hand but sits close enough that I can feel the warmth from her body. Or maybe that's mine. I don't even know at this point.

"Are you a lesbian?" The question bubbles out before I can stop it. That's so inappropriate, but I have to know. If I'm going to keep lusting after her, I need to know there isn't a shot. I can go back to Aleks and daydream until the crush is over. She hasn't given me enough information to be sure I can't have her.

"Yes. Are you?"

"Mm, bisexual." It's been a long time since I've admitted that. When Wesley proposed to me, I stopped telling anyone. When I commented on attractive women, he would scold me. I soon learned to keep those thoughts to myself. He's not here, though. Nothing to stop me from sleeping with women. Well, except Aleks.

"And Mor?" Sapph asks. A moment passes before I realize she means Aleks. I haven't gotten used to his nickname.

"He's..." What is he? "Tyler's best friend," I answer. It's not a lie, but it's not the answer she wants. I don't know how to answer that. She nods, seeming to understand my situation.

"Are you into BDSM?" She juts her chin toward the drawer.

"I've never done it," my voice is soft, almost meek. I haven't had a conversation like this before.

"Would you?"

"Yes." The breathy response is easy.

"What about monogamy? Are you a "one partner" kind of girl?" Her question catches me off guard.

"I've never given it much thought," I answer. Could I be with more than one person? It might depend on who the people are. I'm pretty sure I would do anything to have both Aleks and Sapph. I get lost in my thoughts, searching my soul to find answers to questions I've never asked.

Her face contorts into a gorgeous grin. She looks at the drawer, consumed by her thoughts. I can't remember what music she chose at this point. We sit silently for a while. She invites me to go to the club when her playlist ends. I nod enthusiastically. That's definitely something I want. I just need to let Tyler and Aleks know. They do not like it when I go off without telling them. They haven't stopped me and don't try to, but I respect them enough to let them know.

Sapph tells me she plans to leave in an hour and to meet her in the parking lot in front of the bar, and she'll give me a ride. I practically bounce from her room. I need to find Tyler. Or Aleks. Whoever comes first. Maybe even Shirley or Lucy if I can't find the other two fast enough. I want to get ready, to put on something hot and sexy. I want to impress Sapph.

I search for a while but can't find anyone. Even Shirley and Lucy aren't around. I settle on getting ready, then look for them again. Worst case, I leave a note on their doors or something. I should consider getting some kind of phone, even if it's just a cheap one from Walmart. I slip into high-waisted skinny jeans and a green cropped spaghetti strap top. A strip of my stomach always shows, but it will be cooler if we dance at the club. I have some booties with nice heels that are perfect. I put on my usual mascara and tinted lip balm and add eyeliner. I twist a few braids to secure the back, keeping my hair out of my face. Perfect. I look hot as hell.

It strikes me how different I look from a few months ago. I was forced to be so conservative in Pennsylvania. Wearing what I want now is exhilarating; I love how I look. I was pretty in my modest dresses and kitten heels before, but I'm a fucking bombshell now. I turn in the mirror a few times, admiring my own ass in these shoes. Finally, I head out to find Aleks or Tyler or someone.

I'm so excited. I'm going to a club. I look fucking fantastic. I feel amazing. I hope to get to know Sapph better tonight. Maybe she'll tell me more about what she likes to do in the bedroom. Maybe she'll kiss me. Damn, I didn't realize how badly I just want to be kissed. It's like I'm sixteen again. I want lips against mine.

Aleks is coming up from the basement when I walk down the hall. I am heading toward his office when he walks up. He doesn't see me. I bounce to him, lost in the thrill of what's to come. I grab his elbow to get his attention, momentarily forgetting his touch aversion. It all happens so fast. A hand is around my throat. I'm slammed against the wall.

My world comes crashing down. He knows. He found out what I did. He's going to kill me this time, I know. I have to fight.

"I can undo it! I swear! Please!"

Chapter Ten

ALEKS

Vic is attracted to Sapph. I can see it in her fucking eyes. She looks at me the same way. She wants me; she's said that. Has she? I rack my memory, trying to remember if she actually said that. She hasn't pushed me away. She sleeps in my room. She still has the hippo I gave her years ago. Is that the same as wanting to be with me? She could just want sex, but she could get that with anyone.

Vic presses her thigh against mine in the booth. I give her space. If she wants Sapph, can I let her go? I can't look at her right now. I can't watch her lust after my friend. Sapph is a lesbian. She could take Vic if she wants. I've seen her game. She could easily steal her from me. I can't compete with Sapph. Would Vic want to be with a woman? Would she stare at her like that if she were straight?

Tyler and Sapph are teasing each other like always. The normality is almost suffocating. How can things be the same and so different? Vic is on my side. Her leg pressed against mine. I want her. I need her. Sapph is on my other side. Does she want Vic, too? I've seen her look at women the way she looked at Vic. She kissed her hand, and her eyes lingered too long on Vic's. Fuck, they want each other. The noble thing would be to step back and let them have each other. Sapph can give Vic what I can't: a real relationship. Sapph isn't fucked up like me. She has her own issues, but not like mine.

Harpo yells for me across the bar. I'm glad for the reprieve. I need space to think through all of this. I don't know if I should say anything to either of them. Maybe neither will act on it. Sapph can pick up women like it's nothing. Vic is already fucking me. Maybe that will be enough for her. I doubt I can be anything more. Will that be enough for Vic, even though she deserves so much more?

Harpo enters my office before me and closes the door once I'm in. I take a seat in my chair and debate a drink. It's still early, and I want to hit the gym this morning. I'll wait on the drink. I can work out and then drink while I mull over this situation.

Harpo looks stressed. I've never seen him like this. He runs his hands through his hair, paces the room, sits in the chair, and stands again. I'm patient with him, but I didn't come in here to watch him pace. Finally, he settles in his chair but doesn't look at me. His head is down, arms resting on his knees, fingers twisting together. It's odd for Harpo. One of the things I have always respected him for is his ability to remain calm and collected.

"I have to tell you things," he starts, finally looking up at me. It's a quick glance, then he turns away. "I... you won't like it." Well, that's ominous as fuck. At least he didn't ask me not to be angry. Any time someone asks me not to be angry, I go ahead and get angry. Obviously, I'm going to be angry if you start with that.

"I can handle it." Harpo sighs, and concern fills my body. Harpo, the man of secrets and confidentiality, has something to tell me. I'm on high alert now. He's never dug into my past out of respect, but what if he did? Did he stumble on something and wants to let me know? What will he do with that information? Some of it could backfire on me. If he knows why I wanted to kill Richard...

"Fuck," he mutters. "I don't know where to start." He rubs his hands over his head and straightens with resolve. "I have a business partner in Kansas City." The way he says "business partner" indicates it's not an entirely legal business. "She has a warehouse and has had some problems with shipping in this area. I mentioned the club since we have talked about finding other business opportunities. It would work well since she is in fashion, and you have Aphrodite.

"She hired someone else to investigate the club and do all the research I normally do. You know, not wanting me to give a biased opinion. It's a fair deal." Harpo bites his lip, still refusing to make eye contact. He, or someone else, knows my demons. That's what this is about, right? Why else would he need to tell me?

"She wants to talk to you and Clint to present her business plan, but she wants to talk to you privately first." He gives me an expectant glance. I refuse to react. I can speculate why she wants to talk to me, but I won't. His shoulders sag. "Obviously, you have some sort of trauma. A few of us suspect what it is." His words are soft and slow. "I didn't... I've never tried to confirm our suspicions. It's yours to tell or not. But," Harpo stands now, pacing again. His large frame takes up a lot of space in my small office.

"Shit, I know, Mor."

Of course, he fucking does.

"I couldn't help but put two and two together. Suddenly, these pieces clicked. I don't have a full picture, but I know enough. Too much." My jaw ticks as he looks at me. "I'm not going to say anything, but you deserve to know I have that information."

I don't deserve shit. I don't know how to feel about this. I know some of my members suspected this, especially those who have been around for a long time. No one ever said anything to me. That was always fine. I didn't want to tell them, and they didn't ask. It's worked for years. I trust Harpo won't say anything, but I'll be damned if he starts treating me differently now.

"Will it impact your position?"

"No! No," he answers quickly. "I work with all kinds of secrets every day. They don't affect me, but I haven't hidden those secrets from the person if I know them. I haven't...had someone with this level of secrecy before." I suppose it's comforting to know there aren't many people he knows that have a history like mine.

"Do you have any physical proof?" Harpo looks at me and grimaces.

"There's audio."

"How much?"

"I don't know," Harpo's voice is apologetic. "The one I did find is buried in years of data. There wasn't a good system for storing data before I came in."

"Fuck," I can't really do much about it. There's a huge window of time that the file could be from. If it took Harpo this long to come across it, it could be years before anything else surfaces. I'll deal with that shit later. "Fine. As long as your work doesn't change and you keep that shit to yourself, we don't have a problem."

He sags in the chair in relief. Jesus, he was really fucking worried about my reaction to that. How did he think I would react? I rarely let my guard slip. I can usually control my emotions. My past can set me off, but enough time has passed that it's easier to deal with.

"Okay. Catherine wants to call you today. Are you free to talk to her now?" I nod. I have no desire to return to the table and watch Vic and Sapph lust after each other. Not that I want to have conversations about my past, either. A future business deal that takes us away from the cartel would be ideal.

"Wait, does she have physical evidence?" Sorrow is written in Harpo's eyes.

"I don't know." Fuck. I wave my hand at the phone, indicating he can call. I don't know this woman. Harpo trusts her enough to work with her. I better be able to trust her, too. I won't let her leak this information.

Harpo takes my phone and dials on speaker phone. I listen to the trill of the ring. Who is this woman? She has a warehouse and works with Harpo. That's all I know. When did he start working with her? He works with people outside of the club. He was doing that work before he became a prospect. Anyone would be stupid to pass him up. He's phenomenal at his job.

"Marzanna," a woman's voice answers the phone.

"Catherine, it's Harpo."

"Hello, Harpo," her response is friendly and familiar.

"I'm with…" he pauses, glancing at me. He doesn't know which name to give her. "The president of the club."

"Ah, yes. Is this line recorded?" She's direct. She gets points for that.

"Yes, but I shut the recording off." Harpo apologetically shrugs. He explains, "I knew she would want privacy, so I shut the recording off before I came in here. I would have activated it immediately if you decided not to take the call." I nod. I trust Harpo to make the right decisions regarding the club's security. He's never given me a reason not to trust him. "I'll leave." Harpo walks out of the office and closes the door behind him.

"You should take me off speaker," Catherine informs me. Fuck, that's foreboding. I lift the phone and turn off the speaker.

"Harpo said you have a business offer."

"I do, but I want to address a concern first." Catherine doesn't hesitate the way Harpo did. She's confident in her abilities. I wonder what her line of business is. I've never had a warehouse owner speak so boldly. "Do you want to go by Aleksander or Mor?"

"Aleks is fine." If she already knows, there is no point in using my tag name.

"Aleks, I work in the shipping business and have had issues close to the Gulf. Most of my shipments come straight up 35." A lot of illegal business is conducted along Interstate 35. With it running straight across the middle of the country, it's a perfect path for all sorts of business. This offer is becoming more intriguing. I will be disappointed if it's something stupid like tennis balls.

"I want your club to provide protection and possibly a stopping point." That's…interesting. I don't speak, letting her continue. There's no reason she needs to talk to me privately about this. "I had someone other than Harpo dig into you, several other members, and your club. Everything she found is what I am looking for, except for one bit of information." That dread is back. Harpo put the pieces together with the information she had. Why would that be a deterrent for her business?

"I work with a mafia in Spain." That's unexpected. "We ship and process drugs for them. Similar to what you are doing with the cartel." How does she know what we do with the cartel? We've taken significant measures to cover our trails. "A man I believe you know has become my point of contact in Spain." I stop breathing. There is only one man that I know that could be in Spain.

"Isak Calland."

My heart stops. My body is on fire. I fight the demons trying to take over. It's something I repressed even further than what Richard did to me. God, it was buried so deep. Catherine isn't talking. Can she hear my fucking thoughts? Am I talking? I lick my lips, but they are closed. My lips and my mouth are dry. I manage a long inhale.

"I can't pay you," my father's voice pleads. "What if I give you something else?"

"What do you have?" The man's voice is thick with an accent I don't recognize. The floor creaks; my bedroom door squeaks open. Light filters in. I pretend to be asleep. Covers pulled tight. Eyes shut.

"I know it's not just drugs you work with," my father is firm. He knows what he is doing. He doesn't falter in his offer.

I was eight years old. I haven't slept well since that conversation.

"You can understand why I wanted to present this to you before making an official business offer."

"Yes," I croak. Dry, everything is so dry. "What do you know?"

"Everything," she says softly and apologetically. "My hacker found a couple of photos of you as a child with him, but I know the business he is in. I am not in those ventures." She pauses before continuing. "Would you like to know more about what I am going to propose?" I take a deep breath. I need oxygen.

Harpo works with her. Holy shit, is this what Harpo knows? I thought he meant Richard. How could anyone know about this? How could they suspect this? No one knows where I came from before Richard, not even Tyler. I just showed up one day, and everyone was cool with that. No one asked about my history or my parents. I never asked what, or if, Richard told them anything.

"I would like to come out in a week or two to present the business plan to you. If you are comfortable, I can arrange with Harpo." I can barely breathe, let alone think about a business plan. Fuck. I want to scream. I want to hit things. I want to burn this pain away, this pain that has been repressed for so long.

"That's fine," I muster. Do I want to help with this business? I don't know, but I can't think straight with images of my childhood flooding my mind. Catherine said she isn't involved in human trafficking, but what if that changes? I can cancel the meeting if I can't work through my shit.

"I look forward to meeting you, Aleks." I'm glad she didn't say, 'work with you.' That would have been presumptuous. The phone clicks and the dial tone blares through my head. I place the phone down gently. I grab the tumbler beside the phone and hurl it across the room. It hits the opposite wall and shatters. That was my favorite tumbler.

My mind is overwhelmed with the past. I can't fucking think. I can't fucking breathe. I grab my headphones and trudge toward the gym. What the fuck else am I supposed to do? I can't, won't, sit here and wallow, but I can't move on either. Not with these flashbacks reeling like a goddamned movie.

I pull on my headphones and hit play. I turn the volume all the way up, and Britney fucking Spears blares through my mind. I'm momentarily frozen by the dominating music Vic likes so much. My demons offer the image of Sapph holding Vic's hand. The way Vic looked at her. The way she looked at Vic. The fucking giggle Vic made when she introduced herself. I've gotten that giggle from her, but I had to fucking work for it.

I switch the music quickly, needing something else to drown out my thoughts. It's not as effective as I want. Combined with pounding the punching bag, the demons are harder to hear. I can't see where my punches land. I can only see my stupid ass father. Always broke, always high, always asking for shit. I can see the men he let in the house. The one that took me away. Or bought me, I suppose. Like I'm some damned toy at the store. I've never let myself consider that reality. My life in exchange for my father's debt.

That man, Isak, treated me better than my father. I got three meals a day. Baths were regular. He even let me stay in school for a while. I never graduated high school. I didn't make it that far. You don't get that luxury when you live the way I did. That man, the one that took me in exchange for my father's debt, he didn't touch me. Not a single finger. He told me things. Things no child should ever hear in that context. He was the first person that confirmed I never wanted children. I didn't want to be around others.

My hands burn from the impact. Sweat pours down my face. My knuckles are split and will be bruised. The pain only dims the memories marginally. The music drowns the sound of the memories. I don't need to hear the conversation my father had with Isak. I can recall every word. When my hands hurt too much, I throw a few more punches. I go to the treadmill, running from the rest of my memories.

My feet pound on the machine. Each step reverberates through my entire body. I stare at the spot across the room. The only wall with nothing on it. No windows, no mirrors, no posters. Just the door and the plain white wall. Better for clearing my mind when there is nothing to stare at.

I run and run. My feet pound and pound. Sweat drips and drips. My legs burn. Everything is soaked. My hair, my face, my shirt. My jeans and boots, which I didn't change out of, are rough against my sweaty body. My muscles scream. Finally, screaming louder than the images.

I climb off the treadmill, not worrying about a cool down. I want to keep the burn as long as possible. I need a shower. And a drink. And more drinks. I need to be so fucking drunk I can't walk straight. I chug a bottle of water, hydrating before my binge. I rub a towel over my face. The rough texture grounds me in the present.

I fling the towel into the laundry cart and make my way upstairs. It's an arduous climb, but I refuse to acknowledge the weakness after the workout. I don't know how long I was down here. I had to restart my playlist at least once. It was more than a couple of hours. I don't normally work out that long, but it's good for bad days. And today is definitely that.

I turn down the hallway that leads past my office. The one I have been forced into so many times. The one Richard would grab me and pull me into. What if my father hadn't been such a shit person? I wouldn't even be here now. I could fucking kiss Vic and let her touch me. I could give her everything she needs. She wouldn't need Sapph for anything. She could be happy with me. If only I didn't have men like my father and Richard in my past.

A hand grabs my arm. Richard grabs me like that. No. I fucking killed Richard. I already killed him once. I spin. I'll kill the motherfucker with my goddamned hand around his throat again. I won't live in his presence anymore. He is dead.

I slam him against the wall, ringing his fucking neck. It's small, but it's been a while since I've held someone's throat in my hand. I only see red. Everything is red. Noises are muted. Flashes of Richard and what he wants flitter through my vision. I hold his throat, squeezing tighter. Hands grip my wrist. They are small and soft.

"I can undo it! I swear! Please!"

That voice. That's Vic. What is she doing here? Richard can't know she is here. He'll take her from me. I squeeze tighter but hear the shouts around me. People are running. Everything is so loud. Something hits my shin. It's sharp and painful against my already worn legs. I glance down. Those boots.

I've seen those boots before. They are Vic's. She bought them from my boutique. The one I bought after I killed Richard. Richard is dead. I'm not holding him in my hand. I look up. Vic is in my hand. She's clawing at me, fear in her eyes. Fuck.

I drop her quickly. She collapses to the floor and covers her head. What have I done? I was so wrapped up in my own past, my own problems, that I just choked the only woman I have ever loved. I take a step back. Shit. Another step. I have ruined everything. Holy hell. Vic looks at me, but her emotions are too jumbled to decipher anything on her face. Her eyes are fogged over in a familiar haze. She's reliving her own traumas right now. What did I do to her?

Before the others reach us, she is up and running. She doesn't look back as she bolts straight out the front door. I don't see where she is going. A fist lands in my face, darkening my vision.

Chapter Eleven

ALEKS

I had my hands around Vic's throat.

That's the only thought as the water pours over my skin. The water is so cold my skin pebbles. Shivers rack my body, but I don't change the temperature. I leave my arm propped against the wall as the water hits me. Each icy drop drives me further into despair.

Tyler punched me. I don't think he broke my nose, but I'll have a black eye. Combined with my bruised knuckle, it doesn't look that different from other altercations. It's so damn different, though. I've choked my fair share of people, including women. I'm not afraid to take down a bitch that deserves it. But Vic...

I yell and pound the tile in the shower. Pain sears through my fist and already bruised knuckles. I slam off the shower. The handle holds up against my rage. It's stronger than I expected. I dry off without looking in the mirror and pull on a shirt and jeans. My cut is spread open on the chair, drying out from the sweat. I need a fucking drink.

I yank open the drawer with all my bottles, causing them to clatter together. I grab a scotch and pour a large helping. I knock it back and reach for a second. As I do, I spot the spray bottle I keep vodka in for cleaning my cut. It's not uncommon to get sweaty in it, though not usually as much as today. I forgo a second drink and decide to clean my cut. It's probably a better use of my time.

I bring it to the rumpled bed. I never make the bed. Vic pulls the covers up, but it's not neat. She quickly tosses them up and leaves it at that. Vic. Despair fills my chest. I flip the cut inside out and lay it on the bed. She was just lying here not long ago. Before I nearly killed her.

I almost fucking killed her.

I grab a tumbler from the shelf, add water, and just a drop of soap for my cut. A rag sits beside Vic's toothbrush in the bathroom. With Sapph back, I wonder if she knows I didn't need a plumber to fix her shower. Sapph always turns the water off before she leaves for an extended period. She travels for a few weeks once or twice a year. This is the longest she has been gone, nearly two months. She kept extending her return date.

I dab the lining of the cut, trying to lose myself in the process. The alcohol tingles in my veins. Not enough to get me drunk, but enough that I can feel it. I want another. And another. And another. But if Vic comes back, I need to apologize to her. When. When, not if. She'll be back. She will. Tyler is still here. She doesn't want to go back to Pennsylvania.

She could still run. She doesn't have to stay here. She's a fucking nurse. She could find work anywhere. I focus on rubbing the arm openings and neck of my cut. Those are always the worst places. My room grows dark with time. It was mid-morning when Sapph first returned. Now it's late evening and dark. Time has passed. Since Sapph returned. Since Vic was attracted to her. Since I spoke with Harpo and Catherine. Since I tried to kill Vic.

I want to convince myself I didn't try to kill her. I tried to kill Richard. But Richard has been dead for five years. I already killed him. I did know that. It didn't stop me from trying to kill him again. Fuck, I can't even function with a simple reminder of my past. Harpo was right to be hesitant to tell me what he knew.

Does Harpo know about Isak? I carefully lay out the cut to let it dry and leave my room. I bang on Harpo's door. He opens it, steps back, and then checks the hallway after I walk in. Looking for Tyler to pop up and try to kill me. Or maybe someone else. Everyone loves Vic, except maybe Destiny. She wouldn't try to hurt Vic but wouldn't defend her either. When Harpo is convinced no one is lurking for the chance to kill me, he shuts the door and locks it.

I sit on his couch, and he grabs a beer for me. I pop it open but don't take a drink. His room is smaller than mine and dark. He works random hours of the day, sleeping between stretches of scouring the internet or whatever he does. Massive screens fill one corner next to a neatly made bed. The screens are blank, showing his multicolored background. It's a swirl design, nothing personal. He doesn't have many personal effects, either. Few of us do.

"What was on that audio?" My voice is gruff from hours of misuse. Screaming, pushing the limits, drinking alcohol.

"Richard in his office...with you. You didn't say anything, but he said your name several times, narrating what he was doing." Goddammit. That fucker could never keep his mouth shut. He had to narrate it as if he wasn't getting what he wanted. His voice still haunts me. I can't put together a solid thought at this point.

"Is the date on the file?" I ask. I need to know what the chances are that there are more clips.

"About the time Richard had the mics installed around the compound. It seems to be early audio. Possibly before they figured out how to shut off the recordings or delete them completely." Harpo sips his beer and does not make eye contact, which is fine. I don't want to look at him during this conversation, either. This is the closest to admitting what happened that I have ever gotten.

"Could you pick out more without listening to them?" Pity fills his gaze at the confirmation that this wasn't an isolated incident. Anyone who knows anything about Richard knows what he did to me wasn't a one-time thing.

"No. There are no unique identifiers from that time. The files have a date stamp. A few have location tags, but not many. Not until I took over. If you had exact dates and times, I could isolate the files. Otherwise, we'd have to listen to them." I sigh heavily. I will not allow Harpo to listen to those files. Knowing things like this are in our system, should we ever need to go through those files for research, I will do it. I won't take the chance of someone else finding it or having to listen to it. I sit quietly, unable to process everything that has happened.

"You want ice for that?" He points at my face, but I shake my head. My face is the least of my concerns. "Was it because of Catherine and me?" His voice is weaker, but I know what he's talking about. I want to tell him no, but I wouldn't have choked Vic without that reminder, would I?

If I stayed at the table with her by my side, the chance of choking her would have been minimal. My reaction to someone grabbing me from behind has never been reasonable. Would that have still happened with Vic? Even without Catherine and Harpo rehashing my worst memories, how would I have reacted if Vic had grabbed my elbow as she did? I've punched people in the past. Slammed them against walls. It's not a common situation, but it has happened enough that I know how I would react. It's always with violence.

Would I have punched her? Slammed her into the wall? Would that be better than holding her six inches off the ground by the throat? Maybe, but still no. Tyler would have punched me either way. I would still feel like shit. A little less, but shit nonetheless.

"Where did she go?" I deflect. I can't answer his question. Yes, it's because of them; no, it's not because of them.

"She jumped on the back of Sapph's bike, and they rode off together. Sapph was expecting her because she already had a helmet for her." Of course, Sapph was taking her somewhere. Why wouldn't she? Vic deserves someone who won't choke her to death.

"Do you know where they went?" Harpo shakes his head.

"No, I haven't tracked her." His eyes meet mine, "Do you want me to?" I shake my head.

"No." I stand up, chugging the rest of the beer. "Thanks." Harpo doesn't say anything else as I leave his room.

The hallways are quiet. It's too early for people to be back from the bar or backyard. The weather is hot, and people will want to swim. I go back into my room and collapse on the bed. I sit there for a moment before my body gives out. I fall over, drained from the past twelve hours. I've dealt with shitty situations before, but nothing has hurt like this.

I can smell Vic on my pillow. Her saltwater spray, that lingering coconut scent. I take a deep breath, inhaling what I can. How long until that scent fades? How long until she leaves?

My phone rings, waking me from a slumber I didn't realize I was in. I drag myself up, grabbing for my phone. Once I find the damn thing, I answer it without looking. My head is pounding. Dehydration and stress make my physical body match my mental state.

"What?" I snap. I don't sleep well. I frequently wake from sleep, but that doesn't make it more tolerable. It's worse because I was asleep and didn't wake up on my own.

"I've lost her." What the fuck is this? I'm disoriented and can't understand what is going on. My room is shrouded in darkness. I don't have a fucking clock in here. Who needs clocks when we have phones and watches? I'm not wearing my watch. I forgot to put it back on earlier. I hold the phone out in front of me. The screen flashes on. It's three a.m., and Sapph is calling me. What did she say? Oh, right.

"Who?" My voice is rougher than when I spoke to Harpo. It sounds like I've been chewing gravel.

"Vic. She came to the bar with me. I went to the bathroom, and she was gone." That wakes me up. "I tried calling Tyler, but he isn't answering. I've been searching for a fucking hour and don't know where she went."

"Shit. Send me the bar address. I'm on my way." I grab a hoodie and my cut. It's not entirely dry, but it will be fine. I step into my boots before I make my way to the garage. I slam on a partial helmet, not opting for the full coverage. If I'm searching for Vic, I want full visibility. I slip on my glasses and drive out toward the address Sapph sent.

Sapph's favorite club is on the other side of the city. It's one of the few gay bars she prefers. Many clubs are closer to the compound, but she doesn't care. She has friends that go to her favorite bar that she'll want to see now that she's back. Despite the clear traffic, it's still a half-hour drive. She rode this way with Vic on her back. Pressed against her body. Did Vic hold her more willingly than she holds me?

Shit, I need to stop for gas. That adds more time to my trip. I'm just trying to get to the bar as quickly as possible. How far could Vic get? Is she walking? Did she take a cab? Will she disappear for three weeks again? Fuck.

I turn on the exit for the club and my phone rings. I pull over at the light, stopping on the sidewalk. I answer the phone quickly without looking. It's Sapph. She found Vic, and I can head back to wallow. God, I hope it is.

"Aleks?" That's not Sapph or Vic. I can't place the voice. It's familiar, but my mind is a fucking mess.

"Yeah?"

"It's Tessa from Bexar." Shit. The county jail. She only calls when someone has been arrested. I'm on good terms with her from years of slipping her cash to release some guy quietly. I let the whores rot or let whoever they are fucking bail them out. I'm not spending my money on them. Tessa and I have an understanding.

"Who is it?" The last thing I need to deal with now is a member that got picked up for some bullshit.

"Hold on," Tessa answers. The phone is shuffled around, then a moment of silence.

"Aleks," her voice is soft. She's scared and nervous.

Vic is at the county jail. Son of a bitch.

"Bird." The relief in my nickname for her is palpable.

"Hi, Tanesha said I could call. She knows who you are."

"I told you, it's Tessa." Tessa's angry response is muted in the background. Vic gasps.

"Oh my god. That was.. oh shit. I'm so sorry, Tessa. That was terrible of me. Fuck." Vic mutters a few more curses and chokes back a sob.

"Bird." No response. I wait, trying to hear what's happening. I can't hear anything.

"Do you want to come get her?" Tessa is back on the phone, sounding irritated.

"Yeah. I'll be there in thirty."

"Good." The call disconnects, and I text Sapph to let her know what's happening. I also message Harpo to ask him to scan the county database and remove any mentions of Vic. He doesn't do that often, but it's a risk I will take for her.

I drive faster than I should to get to the jail. What the fuck did she do? And how did Sapph not realize she was picked up? This is a fucking shit show. How did we wind up here? Things were going well before this morning. I had Vic. She was happy. Tyler didn't hate me. Harpo didn't know shit about me. Well, he did, but not enough that he felt the need to tell me. I could keep my fucking emotions under control.

The wind whips my hair as I fly through the mostly empty streets. I need to secure that better before I get Vic on my bike. My thoughts run wild with everything that has happened. I let them. My bike is one of the few places I'll let my thoughts rage as they demand.

I ease through the county court grounds, parking quietly and heading inside. The less attention I draw to myself, the better. Tessa buzzes me in, and I do a sweep of the area. I can see Vic in a cell far from the front desk. I don't have a good sight, but I still recognize her brown hair. I nod at Tessa as I walk up.

"What did she do?"

"Harassed some cops. They haven't booked her yet." Tessa slides a clipboard for me to sign in on, pushing some of her bright box braids back from her dark, round face. I slip one hand into my cut pocket and pull out some cash. I've done this enough to know the angles to avoid so the cameras don't pick up anything. I clip the cash on as I sign an alias on the paper.

"You need to keep an eye on her. She's got a nasty bruise," Tessa pauses as she scans my face. "Based on your face, I'm guessing you knew that." She has no idea how well I know that. "She one of the girls at your club?" I shake my head in response.

"Tyler's sister." I trust Tessa enough to share that information. She already knows a lot about the club.

She hums at me. "She didn't ask for Tyler. Just you." Tessa nods me over to the cell as that information settles in me. Vic asked to call me—not her brother, not Sapph that she rode into town with, but me. Why would she ask for me?

"Vic," I call out to her when I near the cell. She snaps her head up, wiping her face. She's been crying. Damn, I hope she hasn't been crying since our phone call. She walks to the door, taking me in. Her throat is already starting to bruise. It looks awful, each of my fingers a bold red on her skin. She reaches out for the door as it loudly clicks and slides open. Her hands jerk back, settling against her chest. I hold my hand out for her, but she hesitates. She glances at Tessa, then back to me.

Vic finally puts her hand in mine. I guide her back through the building, nodding thanks to Tessa before we walk toward the door. I lead her to the parking lot where my bike is, holding her hand the whole time. She doesn't pull away from me. That is a fucking miracle. She has every right to hate me now.

"I called her Tanesha. That was racist." Her eyes are far off. Why are her first words to me about Tessa? Did she drink a lot at the bar? Is she still drunk? How will I get her home? Not home. People don't throttle your throat at home.

"Yeah, it was," I respond. Vic glances up at me, her face still neutral but with a hint of surprise in her eyes. The corner of her lips turns up slightly.

"Thanks for being honest with me. Even if it was a bit brutal." She chuckles, looking down at her fingers, which are still tangled with mine. I reach out with my free hand to stroke her arm.

"Hey," I start, but she interrupts me.

"Don't apologize. Just take me back so I can sleep." Her big eyes find mine, "Please?" I nod to her. I'm going to apologize, but I can wait if she wants me to. I hand her the helmet but keep the glasses for myself and climb on the bike.

"Wait, where is your helmet?" She stands beside my bike, not putting on the helmet I just handed her. Stress fills her eyes. I don't want her to be stressed, but I'm not fighting over a damn helmet.

"I was on my way to Sapph when you called. I didn't expect you to need one." Vic takes a step back, holding the helmet out to me.

"Then you take this one. I'll call a cab."

"Vic," I try to hide the anger in my voice. It's a damn challenge. I'm not angry at her, but I can't handle arguing or leaving her here. "Put the helmet on and get on my bike," I manage through gritted teeth. She shakes her head, taking another step and extending her arm further. I sigh. "You are riding back with me. I'm not letting you ride without a helmet. Please put it on so we can go. It's going to rain soon."

The smell of rain fills the air. I don't want to ride in the rain, but I don't have another option. I won't leave my bike here or let her take a cab.

"But then you'll be without one," she sniffles, and her chest rises and falls quickly. I swing off my bike and tug her into my arms. She breaks down as soon as I have her engulfed. She sobs into my chest while I hold her close. I don't know how to comfort someone like this. Whores cry at the club, but I leave or ignore them. I just hold her, not sure what else to do. She sniffles after a couple of moments, settling down.

"Your cut isn't comfortable to cry against," she mutters against the leather. I release her and tug my cut off, draping it on my bike. She tries to protest, but I don't stop. She wraps her arms around her waist. I'm unsure if she is trying to comfort herself or fight off the crisp air. It's not cold, but cooler than it was earlier. She's only wearing a tiny crop top. I unzip my hoodie to more protests and wrap it around her shoulders. A fresh wave of tears streams down her face. I pull her back into my chest, holding her while she cries softly. At least her cries aren't as bad as it was a few minutes ago.

"You're not going to fight me on everything right now." It's not a question or a demand, really. Just a statement. She finally nods. I lean in to kiss her forehead, but she tips her head back, looking up at me.

"If you kiss my fucking forehead right now, I will physically fight you." Her words are solemn, but humor shimmers on her face. I cup her cheek, using my thumb to stroke away the tears. Everything from today is forgotten in this moment. She tilts her head into my hand. Fuck, she's perfect. I care about her so much. I need more of her.

I need to feel her. I need to know that she doesn't hate me, at least not now. If she does in the morning, I'll deal with that then. For now, I want to taste her. I want to feel her lips against mine, the press of her tongue in my mouth. I lean in, and she reaches toward me. I will stop at the first sign of hesitation, but she isn't giving me that.

My lips lightly graze Vic's, the barest of touches. It's better than I imagined. Her lips are soft and sweet. She leads the kiss, guiding me the way she wants. I match her movements, deepening the kiss. Her hand slides up my arm, over my shoulder. I've never been touched so gently. She wraps her fingers around the back of my head and pulls my neck, bringing me against her. Her tongue traces over my lips. Instinctually, I open my mouth, and her tongue swirls around my own.

Blood rushes to my cock. I want more from her, but we're in a parking lot at the county jail. I can't take more tonight. Not after all the shit I've put her through today. I can't get more, but I'm not ending this kiss. She's sweet and demanding and knows precisely what she wants. She moves her lips, and I match her. We adjust to each other smoothly. It's not as awkward as I thought it would be. We work together so well. I have to repair all the damage I did earlier. I need her in my life.

A raindrop hits my shoulder, then another, and another. I break the kiss a bit reluctantly and look up at the sky. Rain falls quick and heavy. I look down at Vic, who is staring past me into the clouds above. She laughs and brings her gaze back to me. She pulls me back to her lips. I squeeze her tighter against me, trying to protect her from the rain. She kisses me deeply, holding me against her like I'll pull away.

Maybe she is still drunk. Maybe her own emotions are too messy for her to make rational decisions. She shouldn't be kissing me. I shouldn't let her. This is ridiculously fucked up, but I'm not going to stop it. I'm too selfish for that. The only thing I'll stop for is her.

This is one of those scenes from the romance books Sapph reads. Kissing in the rain. It's romantic, right? Probably not in the jail parking lot, only hours after I choked her. We'll sort that out later. I'm savoring every bit of her taste in the pouring rain. I'm not letting her go.

Chapter Twelve

VIC

What the fuck?

I can scarcely think of anything else. Nothing makes sense. I thought things were going well. What happened between Aleks going to speak with Harpo and me finding him in the hallway? Is he mad that I am attracted to Sapph? He wouldn't have choked me over that. He's not that kind of man. I've known that kind of man, and it's not Aleks.

At the club, Sapph and I danced and chatted. It was nice to forget Aleks for a bit. I drank enough to forget my neck had his handprint on it. I talked with Sapph for a while, between her friends greeting her. Her name is Runi, but people outside the club call her Ru. She wouldn't tell me why they call her Sapph. Apparently, no one tells their own stories. I still haven't learned Rio's story. Aleks's is based on a Greek god; it wasn't that hard to figure out.

I told her about my history with Aleks. I avoided my dating life and what I've been doing with Aleks. I didn't mention why I came to Texas, but I shared about my job back in Pennsylvania. Our conversation quickly turned sexual. We spent a solid hour discussing what she is into and what I want to try. I have great chemistry with her. Nothing happened outside of a few not-so-innocent arm brushes.

At one point, she went off to the bathroom. While I waited, I realized I needed to pee, too. I didn't see where she went, so I walked toward the bathroom. I found a bathroom, but it wasn't until I came out of the stall that I realized it was the men's room. A man at the urinal eyed me, but I just washed my hands and left like I knew what I was doing.

Outside of the bathroom, I had no idea where I was. I was drunk enough to be lost but not blackout. I wandered around, looking for the bar seats Sapph and I had been in. Somehow, I wound up outside. I walked for a minute but couldn't remember where the door to the bar was. I think Sapph took us in through a side door, and I was on the main street. I spotted a couple of cops and asked them for help.

They weren't much help. To be fair, I didn't have enough information to give them. After a minute or two, I gave up on my pursuit, and the fucking alcohol destroyed any bit of self-preservation I had. I asked the cops how many people they had murdered, then continued to ask. I questioned their personal rap sheets. They did not like that. I tried to lighten the insult by talking about the flawed justice system. My mind thought justifying their behaviors would help.

It did not. They asked for my ID, but I didn't take it. Sapph told me I wouldn't need it to get in and that she could buy the drinks. I didn't explain why I didn't want to take it, and she didn't question me. The cops weren't so understanding. They threw me in the back of their car and drove off. I couldn't really fight. I didn't have a phone or wallet. I had already spent the cash I took with me on drinks.

By the time Tessa let me talk to Aleks, my mind was a mess of fear, anger, pain, and alcohol. I've always known I have some internalized racism. It's hard to grow up in a privileged community without developing some biases. I'm aware of my own shortcomings and work to change them. Under normal circumstances, I can recognize my microaggressions and stop them. I was not in normal circumstances last night. I feel fucking terrible about calling her the wrong name. I wanted to beg her for forgiveness. Tell her I'm not a horrible person. But none of that would have helped. She doesn't owe me forgiveness. She doesn't need to know I'm not always terrible. I apologized and will not make that mistake again.

Kissing Aleks was amazing, but it was probably a mistake. What shit timing. I shouldn't have kissed him only hours after he choked me. Well, at least under those circumstances. I would probably enjoy being choked during sex, but not in anger, when he was filled with rage and murder. I recognized that look; it's familiar enough to me.

I told him I needed to sleep in my room at the compound. I couldn't be trusted with my actions. Sapph was already in her room and heard me come in. She rushed over and wrapped me in a tight hug. When she pulled back, she looked me up and down, then gasped at my neck. She immediately freaked out, and I had to explain what happened. She hadn't noticed the bruising in the dim lighting of the bar. Just as I wrapped up my story, someone knocked on the door. Sapph answered it. She immediately began cursing, but Aleks stopped her. He handed something to her and left.

Sapph turned back to me with my hippo in her hands. I broke down. I couldn't hold my shit together any longer. She caught me before I hit the floor. I sobbed and wheezed and shook. She lifted me onto the bed, handed me the hippo, and walked into her room. She returned with a weighted blanket and wrapped it around me. She rubbed my shoulders and cheeks while I cried until I fell asleep. I woke alone when the sun began to peak through the window.

This is all probably a sign that I need to figure my shit out. Am I staying here? Am I going back to Pennsylvania? Is there a third option? I could just run again. I didn't bring my passport, so I'm stuck in the States. Where would I want to go though? I've always been interested in the Pacific Northwest. I could start there. I don't really want to leave Tyler and the club. Running has only landed me here. I can't do that again.

I head to the restaurant and sit at our regular table. No one else is up. I rub my hands over my eyes, trying to wake up. I need coffee and painkillers. Maybe I'll drink early today. I could pass out again. It wouldn't be a good rest, but it would pass the time.

"Vic," a hand grabs my arm. Tyler draws out my name as he tugs me out of the booth. He wraps me tightly in his arms. I breathe deeply, trying not to cry. He releases me after a moment.

"You got arrested? What the hell did you do?" He holds my arms as he looks me up and down. I'm still in Aleks's hoodie. I didn't sleep in it but pulled it back on when I left my room. I have on shorts, but they're barely visible. The bar is always chilly in the morning when people aren't around, and the AC swirls through the space. The hoodie also has the benefit of covering some of my throat without being as obvious as a scarf or turtleneck. Not that I have, either.

Tyler notices my neck and tugs the hood off my head. He twists my chin from side to side, looking at the damage. I wince in pain at the movement. Then he growls at the person behind me. Tyler literally growls. I don't know how long Aleks has been there.

We haven't talked since he picked me up at the jail. I went straight to my room, and neither of us said anything when he brought the hippo. Fuck, I was in jail. My name will show in the arrest records. Wesley will see it. He will be monitoring those. He has before with other people. Did I give Tessa the address for the bar? Did Aleks? Did she just know? Hell, they'll press charges, and I'll have to go to court. I start spiraling. This is bad, so bad.

"Bird," Aleks starts, but Tyler interrupts him.

"Don't fucking talk to her." I turn in Tyler's arms just enough to see Aleks. Concern etched into his features. Fear and regret, too. It slows my spiral, bringing me back to the present.

"Can we sit?" I motion to the table and take a step to slide into the booth. Without thinking, I move to the side with Aleks. Tyler grabs my arm and pulls me to his side of the table. I don't argue. I'm too worn out for that. I stare at my hands on the table while Aleks and Tyler sit. I look up to say something, but Shirley walks up with coffee for us.

"Do you want anything to eat?" Her voice is somber. The tension is radiating from the table. I shake my head. Aleks tells her to bring me something. I don't argue. I should eat. I wrap my fingers around the warm mug. I open my mouth to ask a question when Destiny walks up.

"Clint," she whines, "where am I supposed to sit?" He glares at her.

"You're supposed to sit your ass on the curb. I told you last night we're done." Well, that's interesting. I'm glad he's done with her, but the timing is suspicious. I hope it doesn't have anything to do with all this other shit going on. She tries to argue with Tyler, but Aleks speaks up.

"You can either leave, or we will make you leave." He doesn't even look at her. His threat is laced with promised violence. Tyler casts him an angry look, but I don't think it's because he threatened Destiny. Tyler is just livid at Aleks. Destiny finally leaves, going out the front door. I hope that's the last time I see her. Now, I can start talking.

"Can you guys, or your club or whatever, erase arrest records?"

"What the fuck, Vic?" Tyler spurts.

"They didn't book you. You aren't in the system," Aleks answers. My shoulders sag with relief. That's one less thing I have to worry about. Wesley won't know my location. "Vic," Aleks starts. Tyler sends him another death glare, but it doesn't stop him. "I'm so sorry." His words are soft. I get the feeling these aren't in his everyday vocabulary. I nod to him.

"I know," I pause and glance at Tyler. He's about to kill me. "I'm sorry for grabbing your arm."

"Fuck, Tor. Vic. Fuck," Tyler curses. I turn to him to explain.

"It's a trigger for Aleks. Surely you know that. I shouldn't have grabbed him, and he shouldn't have choked me. It's just a fucking shit situation." Aleks stares at me with a blank face. He is totally unreadable. Tyler glares at both of us. He doesn't know what to say. Shirley walks up with a plate of toast and hands it to me. I take a small bite, but it hurts to swallow.

"Why are you so cavalier about being choked?" Tyler manages.

"It's not the first time my life has been threatened like that," I shrug. "And Aleks didn't do it with malicious intent toward me."

"What do you mean it's not the first time?" Oh, that was a slip I didn't want to make. I chew on my lip and fiddle with my untouched coffee. I can't escape this conversation. Tyler has me blocked in. I can't crawl under the table. Their legs take up too much space, and they would grab me before I got anywhere. Could I jump over the seat? What are the chances this window isn't tempered and would shatter easily?

"Victoria," Tyler's voice is demanding.

"I came here for a reason," I whisper. I can't muster more than that.

"Wesley." His name from Aleks isn't a question. Hatred simmers beneath the word. Tyler glances between Aleks and me, cursing under his breath. "You said you can undo it yesterday. What can you undo?"

I don't remember what I said. Adrenaline was coursing through my veins. After I grabbed Aleks's arm, everything was blurry until I was riding down the highway with Sapph. I know what I feared, though.

"I had my tubes removed a couple of years ago, not that I can really undo that.. He's wanted a kid since we got married," I supply without elaborating. I wanted kids when I was younger. After the way Wesley treated me, I knew I didn't want them. I didn't want to risk having them with him. Even if I did manage to get away from him, I have no desire to be a parent anymore. The silence stretches between us.

"So, I don't get to be an uncle?" Tyler asks lightly to break the tension.

"Nope," I reply with a sad smile. Aleks watches with a blank face.

"Did you bring your driver's license?" Aleks asks randomly. I shake my head. "You ran with no license, phone, or credit cards. You're hiding from him." I nod, finally taking a sip of my coffee. I can't look at either of them now. Tyler looks between Aleks and me, piecing together the situation. Tyler jumps up from the booth.

"I'll kill him. I'm going to fucking kill him." I grab Tyler's arm. I can't pull him back into the booth, but the touch makes him pause.

"This is why I didn't tell you," I hiss. Tyler tenses. "You can't kill him. He's a state senator. Not particularly famous, but high profile enough you can't get away with killing him."

"Watch me," Tyler seethes. I tug on his arm. He relents and sits back in the booth. "We'll make it look like an accident. He can fall down the stairs or something. Wait," his face lights with a realization. "Cathy said you fell down the stairs a couple of years ago," he gives me a questioning look.

"I did," I nod. "I just had some help falling." That fall landed me in the hospital for two days. Tyler's fist slams on the table. Aleks has been surprisingly quiet through all of this. I don't know what he is thinking.

"Why are you so quiet?" Tyler spits at Aleks. "Gonna find Wesley and start a 'beat up Vic' club?" I flinch at his words. Tyler doesn't notice, but Aleks does. He glares at Tyler, who realizes what he did. He mutters an apology. I shuffle in my seat. I want to crawl into bed and cry. For about eight days. At least eight, maybe more. This is so uncomfortable and painful.

"What do you need?" Aleks's soft voice brings the tears I've been fighting off. The first one falls, and I swipe it away with the hoodie sleeve.

"Wesley won't give me a divorce. So maybe an abandoned castle in Europe with unlimited food?" I try to joke, but it falls flat.

"You aren't leaving this club," Tyler states plainly. A small drop of relief settles in my chest. I knew I could stay here. Hearing it out loud from one of them just makes it more real. More tears trickle down my face. I try to swipe them with the sleeves. Tyler pulls me into a hug, and a sob rolls through my body. He whispers assurances against my head. They'll take care of me. When I pull away, he announces he will talk to Harpo and leaves the booth. Aleks is still watching with his expressionless face. I hate it.

"Come with me," he says, rising from the booth. I want to argue. I shouldn't go with him, but he doesn't leave any room for argument. Curiosity gets the best of me, and I follow him to his office. He opens a safe and takes out a phone still in the box. He holds it out, and I take it.

"Vic, I..." he starts, but I interrupt him.

"I need time, Aleks." He drops his hand after I take the phone. Without anything else, I turn and walk away. I'm so fragile right now. Anything could break me. I could make a choice that will only cause more problems. I need to be by myself for a bit. I need to heal from recent events. I need a lot of things, but I really need space.

CHAPTER THIRTEEN

ALEKS

I GAVE VIC A phone before she left my office. I have plenty of burner phones, but also nicer phones. Shit breaks, and I don't want to deal with the damn sales associates at the store. Harpo can fix many of our phones, but not all of them. She has mine and Tyler's numbers and a few others she has added. Most importantly, we can track her. I threatened to implant a tracking device if she lost the phone.

She hasn't spent any time alone with me in ten days. I want to say it doesn't hurt, but I'm not a liar. It fucking sucks. The bruises on her neck are an array of blue, green, and yellow. My face is like a light rainbow of bruising. Tyler watches us cautiously but hasn't said anything else. I don't know if there is anything that can make this situation better.

Vic is more comfortable around Sapph. They spend time together in the afternoons, then join us for dinner. Vic enjoys having her phone back and people to text. I have received at least 500 messages from her in ten days. Most are memes or videos. Sometimes, she'll send a text, usually a joke or something stupid. I don't know how she has any time because she is doing the same thing with Tyler and Sapph. She doesn't send messages when we are together. How she can send the sheer volume of messages within only a few hours is a mystery.

Harpo set the meeting with Catherine for today. She wanted to come in quickly to get things moving. I've barely regained control from her last meeting. I don't want to deal with this one. It could be good for the club, but I don't know what that will mean for me. I've sacrificed so much for this club. Is there a limit to how much I can give?

Harpo waves at us from across the bar. Catherine has arrived. Tyler and Sapph move to the door. I reluctantly climb from the seat.

"Aleks," Vic's voice is soft, concerned. I sink next to her in our booth, glad for any excuse to not walk over there. She sat by Tyler until yesterday. He noticed when she sat on my side but didn't say anything. I was too consumed with relief and hope to comment. "Hey," she holds her hand, palm up, on her knee. I angle my back to the bar, something I never do, and place my hand in hers. "Come find me after the meeting." Her request isn't sexual or worried. She wants to help me. I squeeze her hand. I want to kiss her, hug her, hold her. I don't. Instead, I rise from the table and walk across the bar.

Vic follows close, standing just behind me when we stop. I can feel her warmth on the back of my bicep. She's so close. Two women walk into the bar and are greeted by Harpo. A tall, skinny woman older than me shakes his hand formally. Her dark bob looks stark against her white leather jacket and jeans. I get the feeling that she doesn't usually wear jeans. She has an air of professionalism.

The woman beside her is shorter, about the same height as Vic, but she's younger. Two different colored braids frame her round face. She also wears jeans and a leather jacket, but hers are far more colorful than the other woman's. Her jeans are bright red, and the jacket is a complementing tan, covered with pins and patches. Her boots are yellow. She stands out with her colorful outfit. Vic is known to wear colorful items, but this woman is brighter. I dig it. She has her own style.

Both women hold helmets in their hands, which is unexpected. Did they ride bikes? They look about as much a biker as Vic does. She can play the part, but it's not natural for her. Harpo offers to take their helmets, and I call for a prospect to store them. I glance in the parking lot for a different bike. Before I spot it, Harpo starts with introductions.

He points to Catherine, the taller, older woman. She nods at me and shakes Tyler's hand. The younger woman is named Jo. She reaches out to me. Before I can say anything, Vic steps in front of me, blocking Jo and taking her hand. She leans in and whispers something. Jo's round eyes widen, and she turns to glare at Catherine.

"You didn't tell me that," she mumbles, not quietly and through gritted teeth. Catherine just gives her an exasperated look.

"Welcome to Dionysus, home of Steel Warriors, San Antonio chapter." Tyler offers them a drink. Catherine says she doesn't need a drink, but Jo insists. Vic and Sapph lead her to the bar, chatting animatedly with her. It would be nice to have women around that aren't just after biker dick. Men don't banter and giggle the way women do. It's adorable watching the three of them at the bar. They are so happy and full of light.

"She's far better at socializing than I am," Catherine speaks from my side, eyes focused on Jo. I recognize that look. It's the same one I have for Vic. Harpo mentioned Catherine and Jo are dating. I grunt in solidarity. Their relationship has similar dynamics to ours. I think Sapph mentioned something similar in her romance books. Grumpy and sunshine, that's what she calls it. Shit, I need to find something else to talk with her about. I know far too much about books I've never read.

Vic laughs at something Jo says, tipping her head back. Her neck stretches long, and her brown hair falls down her back. She left it down today. I watch her elongated neck, but I spot Sapph staring at the same spot. The bruises are apparent in her position. Suddenly, all the bullshit crashes back in.

Catherine and Jo are not like Vic and me. We have to deal with Sapph and Tyler and being completely different people. With drinks in hand, the three women walk back to us. Each carries extra tumblers, offering them to us. Sapph hands me a drink while Vic passes one to Tyler. I don't like that she is avoiding me. Logically, her giving the drink to her brother makes sense, but I'll be damned if I'm happy about it.

Tyler leads the way to my office, with Catherine and Jo behind him. Jo chats with him about the bar, but I don't engage.

"Hey," Vic whispers from my side. "I'm serious. Come find me." She's so sweet. I don't deserve her. I brush my fingers over her cheek and push some hair back from her shoulder. I want to kiss her. Right here, in front of everyone. It's not even about them. I just want Vic. I don't deserve her. I let my hand fall as Vic steps away.

I walk into the office last. Catherine and Jo sit in chairs facing the desk. Harpo, Sapph, and Tyler are sitting on the couch. Catherine takes in the tension radiating off my body. Tyler whispers to Harpo while Sapph listens in.

I reach my chair, settle in, and look to Catherine to start the meeting. She has a briefcase in her hands. I don't know where that came from. She taps her fingers against the leather case, looking at me momentarily. She's wondering where to start, how much I told them, and how much Harpo told everyone. I only told Tyler she has a business proposition. I couldn't bring myself to repeat the rest.

"I want your club to provide protection for some of my shipments. They are being attacked in this region, and I need more protection to ensure deliveries." Harpo remains silent, staring at his hands. Tyler looks intrigued. Sapph is indifferent.

"We can do protection. That's not a problem," Tyler answers, not asking any further questions. Catherine taps her briefcase again, watching me for another moment. This is not an enjoyable situation. Tyler is comfortable taking the lead while I observe. Still, I'm an ass for not saying anything about this to any of them.

Catherine pulls out some papers and passes them around. Each of us gets our own copy. The room is silent for a moment while we look at the paper. It's a standard business contract detailing shipments and expectations.

"Marzanna is a fashion business, correct?" Sapph asks. Her voice is stern. It almost distracts me from everything. Almost. Jo calmly responds with confirmation. That doesn't seem like a normal response for her. It doesn't fit the brief signs of her character I've seen. I get the feeling that she is ordinarily bubbly and excited.

"Why are clothing shipments being targeted?" Sapph's putting the pieces together.

"We ship more than just clothes," Catherine answers smoothly. She has been in this business long enough to be comfortable with her answers. It's not something that happens quickly, not for regular people.

"Drugs," Sapph says bluntly.

"Yes, our containers are easily modified to bring in drugs mostly undetected," Catherine explains.

"So, you just want muscle?" Tyler prompts. "That's not a big issue."

"It's more than that," Harpo says softly. Sapph and Tyler look at him with matching, confused expressions. "The business comes from a mafia in Spain." I cringe at that reminder. I take a deep breath. I can't spiral out of control.

"Your boutique will be a good front for shipping. We'll throw in some of our pieces if you are interested." It's my turn to nod. I don't particularly care what we carry in the store, but if it presents a less suspicious image, I'll approve it.

"Why do you want me?" Sapph asks from the couch. I stare at Catherine, unsure why she requested Sapph to join us. She hasn't given me any reason to think she needs to be involved.

"Having women involved in this business venture will make it look less suspicious. We can name you as a manager or fashion buyer," Jo explains.

"We work with this mafia and the cartel you are already in business with," Catherine speaks, breaking the quiet. "Both will process half their product in your warehouse to move to dealers in the area. The rest will change vehicles before they come to us. You will get a cut of their sales, and I will pay you for your help with the other shipments. We want an escort for some of the shipments. Here's a map of where we are being hit the hardest. We want you to start before that point."

Jo passes out a map with a few points marked. Some are further out than others, spread between the gulf and the border.

"When would this start?" Tyler asks.

"After your club approves it, we'll take some time to set up your facilities. Once that is complete, we'll start with the next shipment," Jo explains. I find it surprising how involved Jo is. From what Harpo has mentioned about the two, Jo only started with Catherine in the past year or two. I would do everything to keep Vic out of our business.

"Who is attacking your shipments?" Tyler questions.

"We're not sure," Catherine answers. "We suspect either a rival gang or perhaps the other motorcycle club, the Longhorn Devils." Of course, they would be involved. Fucking pain in my ass.

"Will you be around for a few days?" I ask, speaking for the first time. Catherine nods.

"Yes, we can stay longer if needed."

"We'll present it to the club tomorrow and vote in three days. We're having a party tonight and an ice cream social fundraiser in two days that you are invited to attend." Jo's eyes brighten and she practically vibrates in her seat. Her moods switch quickly. Probably necessary to maintain any semblance of normality in this line of work. Before leaving the room, Catherine hands each of us a file. I place mine on the desk, planning to look later. It's likely just a business contract.

"How will the club feel?" Sapph asks. I shrug. I don't honestly know. Harpo, Tyler, and Sapph chat about the club briefly. I find myself staring at the photo of Tyler, Vic, and me when we were young. Things were simpler then. A muttered curse draws my attention. Tyler is stalking out of the room with the file clenched tight in his hands. Sapph is staring at hers with teary eyes. What the fuck is in this file?

I flip mine open. A death certificate is on top. I scan quickly, realizing it's my father's. The bastard died a couple of years after I was taken. Probably an overdose.

Behind the certificate is a write-up that Harpo usually gives us about someone we are tracking. It's information about Isak.

The door opens and closes as Harpo and Sapph leave. I grab a drink from the shelf behind me, needing to silence my brain. It isn't as bad as last time. I wasn't caught entirely off guard today. It's not information I want to address, but I won't kill anyone, either. Not today. The door opens again, and I turn to find Vic crossing the room.

She walks around the desk and glances at the papers Catherine gave me. She pushes them aside to see better, then tucks them in the folder neatly. Then she hops on the desk and sits on top of them. I snort at her actions. I wonder if she understands what those papers are and who they represent. She just stares at me for a moment.

"You let me touch you." I nod at her, but it wasn't a question. "Do you just need to see it before I do?" I haven't considered that an option before, but it does help. When I can see her move toward me, it's easier to silence the demons. I nod again. A soft smile grows on her face. "I want to tell Tyler."

I give her a confused look. Tell Tyler what? That she can touch me? He won't care whether she can touch me or not. Her smile widens at my bewilderment.

"I've missed you," her words are soft. She places her feet on the armrests of my chair, and her knees spread. I inhale quickly at the sight of her bare pussy in front of me. Damn. She leans forward, grabs my tumbler, and drinks the rest. She places the empty glass on the desk and slowly moves her hand to my chin. She grabs me, holding my attention on her. It's intense, more intense than anything I have experienced.

"I've missed you so fucking much, Aleks," she speaks in barely a whisper, lips inches from mine. My knuckles are white against the arms of my chair, not touching her feet. Her bare feet. When did she take off her shoes? Why is that my concern at this moment? Gods, I've missed her too. I want her in my arms, in my bed. Her body against mine, warm and soft. She kisses the tip of my nose and leans back, sliding her dress over her hips.

"Aleks," she whispers. She's just trying to distract me. That's all this is. I was just given heavy information, and she knows I need a distraction. I can take that. If she's asking for anything more...

"Aleks," she says again, more insistent, deeper, desperate. I don't hesitate this time. I slide in. I graze kisses over her thigh as I slide closer to her core. I'll take whatever she is giving me for any reason at all. I'll give her what she wants, regardless of whether I need it. I can't control myself around her. I won't.

Her hands slide through my hair as she gently tugs me closer. I kiss the curly hair above her core, trimmed neatly in a small triangle. I've never cared what women did with their cunts. I didn't look at it. That's for them. I love this, though. She leans back, giving me better access. I slide my hands over her thighs as I take a lazy lick of her entrance. Her moan is stifled like she's biting her lip. I glance up to find her staring at me with such heat and intensity that I can feel it in my soul. Fuck, she's everything to me.

I slip my tongue in and out of her opening, teasing it the way she likes. The way she showed me. I've never gone down on a woman before her. Thank fuck she showed me what she wanted. That's all I want, to give her exactly what she wants. I vividly remember the way her fingers slid up and down her cunt, showing me exactly what she needs. I remember the sounds she made while I tasted her.

Her chest rises and falls as I make long strokes up and down her. I don't want to rush this. I don't know if she wants a quick fuck, but I'm going to drag this out as long as I can. I swirl her clit, eliciting one of those moans that heats my blood. I wrap my lips around it, sucking lightly. Her hips jerk closer.

The door opens behind her.

"Hey, pres! Cath... shit." Harpo. He must have some spider sense for when we are fucking. This is the third time he's interrupted us. Vic tightens her grip on my head.

"Goddammit, Harpo," Vic calls angrily. "He's occupied at the moment. Say what you need to or shut the fucking door." I smile against her cunt, thrusting my tongue deep inside her. She groans, tipping her head back. "At least come inside and shut the door if you're going to watch." Harpo is as entranced by her as I am. I'll beat his ass for that later. I've got her in my mouth now. I latch onto her clit again, gaining another thrust of her hips.

"Shit, they're staying for the party. We'll, uh, see you out there." The door shuts quickly, and Vic grinds against my face, taking what she wants. I'll give it to her. I slip two fingers inside her, curling against that spot that drives her wild. She moans loudly. I wish I could swallow her sounds and consume them for myself. Gods, she's all I fucking want.

I wrap my arm around her lower back, holding her closer. Her hand holds my head against her tightly. I love the feel of her arm around me, keeping me where she needs me. She owns all of me. I wonder if she realizes that. Feet shuffle outside the door, and muted voices sound. Tyler gives a joyful cheer, and then they fade away. Once it's quiet, I devour her thoroughly.

I lick, suck, thrust, everything she showed me combined with a few things I saw on Reddit. Seems those work for her, too. Reddit is good for more than just gardening advice. I graze my teeth over her clit, lighter than I did last time, and she shudders in my arms. Damn, that's a great feeling. I pull back, rubbing my finger over her clit. I stare at her bare cunt, glistening with arousal. My fingers circle faster, and I lick the length of her opening.

"Shit, don't stop. Don't stop," she mutters, bucking her hips against me. I'm happy to oblige. I lick her up and down languidly. Another tip from Reddit is that when they say, 'don't stop,' it doesn't mean go faster. I keep the exact pace with my tongue and fingers. Her chest heaves, hips rolling against me. Her fingers have a death grip on my hair. I kept it short for years to avoid that feeling, but I'll grow it to my ass if she wants.

She orgasms with a loud yell. Juices spill from her pussy onto the file Catherine gave me. I slip my tongue inside, forgoing the steady stroking she requested. Based on how she falls back on the desk, twisting and arching, that was the right call. I guide her through the orgasm, extending it as much as I can. My cock twitches in my pants, already leaking. Fuck, I love everything about her.

As her breathing slows, I slow my fingers. Her arm is draped over her face, not lifting to look at me. I pull back with a gasp from her. She lifts her head with a sated, lazy smile on her face. She chuckles slightly.

"You need to tell Harpo to stop fucking following us," she laughs, rising to sit in front of me. I can't stop the smile spreading on my face. She has a point. She leans forward, and I think she will kiss me, but she doesn't. She kisses my beard, cheek, chin. She's tasting herself on me. It shouldn't be as hot as it is. I palm my raging erection, needing to adjust to avoid the friction of the jeans. She gives a chaste kiss before leaning back. Confusion knits my eyebrows together. I don't want chaste kisses. I want to devour her. Ah, I understand her disdain for forehead kisses.

She pushes my chest, sliding me back from my desk. I track her movements, resigned to jerk off after she walks out. As much as I want to come inside her, on her, near her, I won't ask for anything. With her eyes trained on mine, she slowly places her hands on my thighs and slides them up. Higher and higher. My heart pounds wildly in my chest.

Giving me every opportunity to stop her, she unbuttons my pants. Nothing could make me stop her, but I'm not prepared for a blow job. Aside from being with Vic, I've never consensually participated in oral. I'm not positive I won't lose my shit if she tries to go that route. Vic wraps her tiny hands around my cock, and my eyes close. I can't keep them open when she feels that good. Her fingers silence my demons. Fuck, I could come just like this. Her lips press against my cheek as my eyes remain closed. She glides her hand up and down. Her grip isn't as tight as I would prefer, but I can work with it.

Before anything happens, she steps back. I open my eyes to see her rip her dress over her head, exposing her bare body. She's been walking around with nothing underneath her thin dress. I growl at her. Anger, lust, desire, and annoyance are all forced into one sound. She steps closer, staring at me the whole time. I take in her body, trim, warm, soft. I can't resist the urge to touch her. I lean forward, but her hand lands on my chest, holding me back.

Vic reaches past me, fiddling with something, then the armrests slide back. She does the same on the other side. I watch with intrigue, unsure why she is fucking with my chair when I want to bury my dick inside her. She climbs into the chair, putting her knees where the armrests were. Ah, that explains it. I slide down just a bit. Her tits are level with my face. I grab one, squeezing it tightly. My other hand rests on her hip.

Moving entirely on her own, Vic grabs my dick and guides it to her entrance, sinking entirely on it. I groan as her cunt wraps me with heat. I press my forehead against her chest, trying to breathe and not bust inside her right away. She takes several deep breaths, then slides up and drops back down quickly. I groan between her breasts, unable to do anything else.

Vic bounces in my lap, sliding her tight pussy against me. Wet from her recent orgasm, it feels like heaven. So warm and slick and perfect. I want to stay wrapped in this feeling forever. Nothing compares to her enveloping me in her warmth until she clenches. Shit, I'm done for.

"If you keep that up," I groan through clenched teeth, "I will come quickly."

"Make me come with you," she mumbles breathlessly, not ceasing her movements. Her head is tipped back, savoring each rise and fall over my cock. Damn, she is gorgeous. I watch her for a moment as her words sink in. How do I make her come with me? We haven't done that. She's always managed it on her own. How did she do it? What do I do to make her come? I don't make women come. I use them for release, nothing more. Not Vic, though.

It finally hits me, and I bring a hand to her pussy, bouncing over my dick. With my hand splayed against her stomach, my thumb strokes her clit, and she moans loudly. Figured it out. I increase the pressure, using the same technique I did when I had her on my lips. She groans louder. Her thrusts become more erratic. A tingle in my spine spreads to my tightening balls.

"Come with me," she mutters. Don't have to tell me twice.

I erupt inside her. My hand tightly grips her hips. I struggle to keep my thumb moving against her clit as my orgasm tears through me. She cries out, collapsing against my chest as her hips jerk over me. Her pussy clenches in the most glorious feeling. Her hands slide to the side of my cheeks, framing my face. She pulls back from my chest and crashes her lips into mine. I wrap my arms around her back, holding her as close as possible. I'm wearing too many clothes for this, still fully dressed while she's entirely naked. It's unfair.

She kisses me desperately, claiming everything I give her. I'll give it all to her. She can have everything. She already has everything. It's all for her. Our bodies settle, and she pulls from the kiss far sooner than I would prefer. She relaxes against my chest again, and I hold her tightly. I'll swap kisses for having her in my arms. I stroke her back, and neither of us says anything as we relax in my chair together.

Chapter Fourteen

Vic

Holy shit. I sneak out of Aleks's office, heading toward the bedrooms. Fucking him is glorious. I want that. I want so much of that. I'd like more of it with both of us completely naked, but I'll take what I can get. Now that I think of it, it's rare that we're both naked. One of us always has on some form of clothing.

I head to my room but pause on the second floor. Screw it. I don't want to be in my room right now. I go to Aleks's. Enough of my things are in his room to shower and change. It's not my full selection, but it will do.

After the shower, I sit on his bed, debating whether to dry my hair. I lie on his pillow, convincing myself I'll only be here for a minute. I won't. I fall asleep. A lot has happened today, and a nap is a good idea if there is a party tonight. I curl up with Aleks's pillow subconsciously, taking in his scent. Leather, mint, vanilla. God, I love it so much.

I want something more than whatever we've been doing the past few weeks. Not more as in a whole committed relationship, but more as in being open about whatever the fuck we're doing. I don't want to hide. Now that I have figured out how to touch Aleks, I want to do that all the time. I don't want to sneak around

Tyler or worry about getting caught leaving his room or office. I want more than his leg pressed against mine. Oh, I want so much more.

Lips surrounded by soft facial hair brush against the side of my forehead. Aleks is back. I crack open my eyes, trying to wake up from my comfortable position. He squats in front of me, pushing my hair from my cheek. It will be a mess when I sit up, but I can deal with that in a few minutes. His eyes are soft and filled with happiness. It's such a rare look for Aleks.

"I like you in my bed," his words are soft. His eyes search the area his fingers touch, marveling at something. I want to say something in return, but he beats me. "If you're going to the party tonight, you should get ready."

He stands and walks to his closet. I can't help but watch as he slips into dark jeans, a grey Henley, and his cut. He pushes the sleeves to his elbows, revealing his forearms covered in colorful ink and muscles. Holy hell, he's pretty. He glances back at me, smirks, then sits on a chair to pull on his boots.

I finally sit up, stretching my arms high above my head. He stares at the arch in my back, the lift of my breasts. I chuckle, dropping my arms by my side. We haven't defined what this is, but our attraction is obvious. I'm surprised Tyler hasn't already figured it out. He can be so dense sometimes.

"You didn't respond to telling Tyler," I remind him. Despite my desire, I won't say anything without Aleks's permission. He ties his boot and drops both feet to the floor. He oozes power in this position. Relaxed in his chair. His long hair is down, framing his face and hiding the shaved sides. His arms rest on the chair, his chest broad, and his thighs and legs so strong. Hell, I want to climb him like a fucking tree. Again.

"What are we telling him?" Oof, that's a good question. I snap my fingers and wave my hands like guns firing.

"Yes," I smile at my response. I love finger guns. His lips curl slightly, but not to a smile. "I'm not sure. That we're fucking? That we're..." I trail off, waving my hands between us. We haven't said anything about what this is.

"What are we, bird?" He asks again. Well, fuck.

"I don't know, Aleks," I sass playfully. "What are we?" I turn his question back to him. Are we dating? Are we friends with benefits? I think we're too close to be fuck buddies. He just stares at me. I sigh, resigned to lead this conversation. He doesn't say much usually; why would he now? Always watching, observing the situation. "I don't think I'm ready to be in a fully committed relationship, but I want you. If that's too selfish," I start, but he stands and walks toward me. He stops directly in front of me. I have to tip my head all the way back to see him. It's so different than when we are just standing. He's so damn big. Being in this position in front of him warms my entire body.

"I am fully committed to you," Aleks says softly, wrapping his fingers around my cheeks. "If you aren't ready for that, I'll take whatever I can get." He leans down and kisses me gently. Well, shit. Pretty sure I love this man. How could I not? He's fucking beautiful. He cares deeply for me and gives me what I want and need. He knows me well.

Tyler bangs on the door, yelling for Aleks to join him. Aleks glances at the door, then back to me. His eyes scan my lips before meeting my gaze.

"Tell Tyler what you want. I'll see you out there." He kisses the tip of my nose, and a shiver runs through my body. The gentleness of it clashes with the very essence of his being. I'm such a damn sucker for a gentle giant, even if it's only for me. He leaves the room to find Tyler yelling something about pussy. I fiddle with my hair, completely lost in thoughts of Aleks, before getting dressed.

Tyler and Aleks are sitting at a picnic table with Catherine and Rio. Jo and Sapph are at the bar. The party is raging around us. Loud music, people chatting and dancing, joints being passed around, giant fans blowing air around the back-yard, trying to cool the space. Summer in San Antonio is nothing like summer in Pennsylvania. I opted for shorts and a loose T-shirt. Anything to keep cool. I approach the table and climb in between Tyler and Aleks. They sit too close for me to fit, but that doesn't stop me.

"Oh, let me just," I grab their shoulders, pushing them far enough apart to weasel between them, "squeeze in here." I sink onto the bench with a huge grin, wiggling my ass between them to get comfortable. Sapph and Jo return with drinks in hand. Sapph passes one to me, and I grin at her. It's hard to be in the same space as her and Aleks.

Aleks and Sapph are so different, but I want them both equally. Aleks said he is fully committed to me, but he doesn't have a problem with me not being ready for that. Would he be mad if I wanted to fuck Sapph too? That would be glorious. The things she could do to me...Nope, I must stop that line of thinking before getting carried away.

Someone says something to Rio, and a thought is triggered. I slap the table, startling everyone.

"I want to know their stories!" My words are louder than they should be, but I continue anyway. "I know Clinton and Mor, fucking moody god," I jerk my thumb at the men by my side, "but I need to know Sapph and Rio." Tyler laughs loudly beside me while the others join in. It's Aleks's chuckles rumbling beside me that catch me off guard. I turn to look at him. His face is covered in delight. Such an unusual expression for him.

"Okay, so," Tyler starts, pointing to Rio. Rio groans, burying his face in his drink. A joint is passed around the table, all of us sharing. I love the comfort of this group. I'm included in this group. My heart swells as Tyler continues. "When this one came here as a prospect, he decided to watch the movie Rio, the kid's movie about the birds?" I nod, familiar with the movie. "He watched in the bar area for everyone to see." Ah, they made fun of him for watching a kid's movie.

"I was watching it with my nieces!" Rio calls in defense. I smile at him, loving his answer. Tyler often did that with me, but we never watched animated movies.

"That's very sweet, Rio," I state. "These guys are just assholes." I tease and elbow both men beside me, gaining another round of laughter.

"And this one," Aleks says, surprising me. I didn't think he would be the type to tell a story. He wouldn't tell me Tyler's story. "Sappho is a poet of the gods. One of the only remaining works is a prayer to Aphrodite to make a woman fall in love with her."

"Oh," I drag out the word. "So, another Greek legend."

"Yeah," Sapph leans back with a cocky grin. "We're both good with women and our tongues."

The table bursts out in laughter, and I grin at Sapph. She's sexy tonight with skin-tight jeans and a halter top. Her arms are covered with ink. I can envision spending hours in bed with her after she fucked me raw with her massive dildo and just tracing her tattoos.

"I like her!" Jo's declaration breaks my trance.

"Hey, here comes Lacey," Tyler announces, wiggling his eyebrows at Aleks. I glance at him, intrigued about who she is. I look back to find a tall blonde woman walking our way. She's in a thin red dress that looks like sin incarnate. Her hair is pulled into a high ponytail, which makes me think it would make a great handle while fucking her from behind. Seriously, I guess I'll change my address to the gutter. She's not even my type. Though I can vividly imagine fucking her from behind. The arch of her back...

Oh. That's why Tyler told Aleks. This must be one of the girls he fucks. That makes sense. She's all ready for him, too. He's never fucked me from behind like that. I wouldn't say no to that kind of brutality. The feel of his hips slamming into mine, my hair wrapped around his hand, the pressure against my head as he pulls me...

"Jesus, Vic. What are you thinking over there? You're practically drooling." Sapph's question barely pulls me from my horny haze. It's as if I didn't just get two orgasms earlier. I meet her gaze with hooded eyes as Lacey finally walks up to the table. The intensity of Sapph's stare is almost overwhelming. If I wasn't already heated, that would do it. I wonder if I can orgasm just from the way she looks at me.

"Lacey," Tyler calls, breaking me from my sex stare-off with Sapph, "surprised we haven't seen more of you around." She steps up to the table, standing between Sapph and Aleks, a little too close to Aleks for my taste.

"Hi, Mor," she says in a sensual voice. Sapph scoffs at her. Guess we hate her, then. I can get on board with that. I don't care that she fucked Aleks, but if Sapph doesn't like her, then I don't either. Aleks tilts his head slightly as we all watch silently. The silence is both anxious and bored. I really love this group of people.

"You know, you don't have to fuck him and leave. You can hang around for a bit," Tyler says. He almost sounds hurt that she wouldn't stick around. Does he think she's the one Aleks has been fucking?

"There's a spot beside Clint," Sapph mutters sardonically, pointing to the end of the table before taking a drink. I chuckle at her. I wonder what this one did that Sapph dislikes her so much. Maybe Sapph pulled a gun on her. The image of Sapph standing with her legs apart, gun aimed lazily at Lacey, pops into my head. Sapph is confident enough that she doesn't need to assume a fighting position. She's that good. Her muscular body, casually poised to take down an opponent...

"I always hang around," Lacey answers, blinking at Aleks with long lashes. He isn't giving her any attention. His shoulders are tense. He's worried about how I will react. I'm not really a jealous person. Well, I don't act on it. I feel the jealousy, but that's about the extent of it. Besides, it would be hypocritical for me to be jealous when I want to fuck Sapph.

"You haven't been lately," Tyler says with disappointment. I wonder if Lacey would be better for him than Destiny, who thankfully hasn't tried to come back.

"I've been in California with my brother. Just got back last night," Lacey responds, finally looking away from Aleks. Jo watches with intrigue at the interaction. I don't blame her. Watching someone else's drama is always more fun than being in it. This isn't dramatic, but I'm excited to see how it plays out.

"No, that's not right. Aleks has been fucking a lot lately. You're the only one he would fuck that frequently," Tyler gives a confused look to the side of Aleks's head. Aleks never talks much, but he usually stays attentive in conversations. This is the most removed I have ever seen Aleks in a conversation, especially one about him.

"Who have you been fucking, Aleks?" Silence.

"Do I need to call Harpo over?" More silence.

Giddiness and anxiety rise in me. Tyler is going to flip his shit in about four seconds. I'm just enjoying the build-up.

"Who?" Tyler's question is softer now. Is he piecing it together? Doesn't matter. I'm about to shatter his world. "We've heard you, man," he pleads.

"Me," my voice is confident, though not overly loud. Aleks stares at the table. Jo gasps as Catherine grabs her hand and pulls her from the table. Jo protests but follows. Catherine doesn't pull her far, just out of hearing distance. Jo maintains a direct line of vision to us though. I throw her a wink, and her delighted smile grows. Rio gets up and walks away awkwardly. Tyler stares with an open mouth at us. Sapph chuckles and wishes Aleks luck but remains in her seat. I give her a wink, too. Lacey gasps at him.

"You found someone new?" The hurt in her voice is undeniable. I almost feel bad for her. Almost. Not enough to do anything or really care.

"My little sister?" Anger laces Tyler's question. "My fucking baby sister that you have known since she was ten?" Tyler stands from the bench, eyes focused on Aleks, looking past me entirely. "How long?"

"Pretty much since I got here. Took a minute to get to the actual fu..." I start.

"Don't you dare finish that sentence," Tyler spits at me. Aleks looks at him now. Tyler's anger at me is enough to draw Aleks from his shame. He doesn't need to be ashamed. We're adults and can do what we want, regardless of Tyler's thoughts. We probably should have told him sooner, but it's too late. Tyler blanches. "I gave you a high five for the whore screaming in your room. Please tell me it wasn't her." The desperation in his eyes makes me cringe. Neither of us says anything.

"Goddammit," Tyler paces with his arms propped on his head. He freezes his steps, turning his attention to me. "He choked you." I nod at him.

"Yeah," I start. I open my mouth to say more, but Aleks touches my leg. Probably a good idea to stop me. I nod at him. The combination of alcohol and cannabis have eradicated my filter. I was going to tell them I would love to be choked consensually, but that would not go over well.

Tyler storms off, and Aleks rises beside me. He kisses my forehead. I don't mind it this time. He says he will talk to him, and I offer a soft smile. That's a good idea. Aleks is a wonderful friend to Tyler. This is probably hard for him. I didn't consider how much it would impact their relationship. I hope Tyler realizes we can make this decision on our own. We didn't get together to spite him.

Lacey glares at me as Aleks follows Tyler. She stalks off to find someone else to talk to. I watch in shock that she doesn't follow Aleks. She seems like the type to follow and offer comfort with her body. Sapph is watching me with intrigue. I slide into Aleks's seat closer to Sapph.

"So, we don't like Lacey?" I ask, sipping my drink.

"Not necessarily," Sapph shrugs. "I just don't like her with Mor. She's too needy. Clint might be good with her." She leans forward, propping her arms on her legs. "Are you and Mor exclusive?"

"We didn't specify that," I respond breathlessly. Sapph chugs her drink with lust-filled eyes focused on me. I finish my drink, too.

"Let's dance," she nods toward the dance floor and offers her hand. I take it as she leads me to the space. We dance together, moving to the beat, bumping into each other. Jo and Rio join us, begging for details. I fill them in with breathless words from dancing. Just dancing. I'm not breathless from my raging arousal. One song bleeds into the next, and the party around us fades to nothing. The warm air is made hotter by the movement of our bodies.

Sapph spins me. Between the alcohol and weed, I crash into her chest with my back. Her hands are on my hips, steadying me. We sway to the beat together. My hands glide over my shorts and shirt, enjoying the touch. Sapph pulls me closer to her. Her breath is hot on my neck. I tilt my head, giving her better access. In this moment, everything else is forgotten. It doesn't matter that Tyler is mad, that Aleks is trying to calm him, that Aleks's ex-fuck is here. It doesn't matter that we aren't alone on the dance floor. The only thing that exists is the closeness of Sapph's body.

"I want to tie you up," she whispers in my ear. The feel of her breath on the shell of my ear is as much the cause of the shivers racing through my hot body as her words. "I will tie your hands above your head," she mutters, guiding my hands into the air. "I would worship your body with pleasure and pain, give you exactly what you want." I can see it in my mind and feel the burn through my body. "I want to spank you, wrap you, put clips on your body, and watch you scream as I rip them off. I want you to beg for me to stop after giving you so many orgasms it hurts. I want you to scream my name because I won't give you an orgasm." Her hands trail my sides. With my eyes closed, every word she says is heightened. I can see it all.

"I'll send you back to Mor, and he can fuck you senseless. You won't be able to walk for a week." I shiver at the image.

"Would he know?" I whisper.

"Yes," her breath is hot against my neck. "I tell my partners about the others. He's never been exclusive." I consider her words. This would be the perfect situation for me. I want them both so badly. They both offer something different. How amazing would it be to have them both?

"Oh, little bird," goosebumps cover every inch of my skin at my nickname. I love it when they call me bird. "The things I would do to you." Sapph presses a small kiss to the spot just behind my ear. It takes every ounce of self-control to force reality back into my mind. I can't moan with this many people around. After I just announced I'm fucking Aleks.

Gods, what am I doing? I'm legally still married. I'm sleeping with my brother's best friend, a god of a man. And I'm attracted to one of his friends. A wave of shame crashes over me until I realize we are all consenting adults. What's really stopping me from doing this? Other people's opinions? The only opinions that matter are Aleks's and Sapph's. Maybe Tyler's, but I won't let it stop me from enjoying my life.

I explored my sexuality in college, but not to the full extent. I met Wesley my sophomore year, and we were immediately monogamous. Nearly thirteen years of only being with him. I got mediocre sex and a handful of orgasms that weren't self-induced. Now that I am away from him, my body is in full slut mode, and I love it. I've known people who had multiple partners, and I was jealous. Wesley would never have considered that. But if Sapph and Aleks weren't monogamous before I showed up...

"You need to talk to Aleks," Sapph mumbles as she pushes me away from her body. Despite the heat of the night, my body feels chilled at the loss of hers. I look forward to find Aleks stalking toward me. Not angrily, but hungrily. The desire in my body quickly switches from Sapph to Aleks. I couldn't survive having them both at the same time. My body would collapse, my brain no longer working due to sheer ecstasy.

Aleks approaches and wraps his hand around the back of my neck. His fingers press into the base of my skull, pulling me into him. His lips crash into mine, and satisfaction overtakes my entire body. This is so perfect. I wrap my arms around his back, pulling him closer. My fingers scratch at his cut to get a better grasp.

His lips are warm and soft and demanding. His tongue pushes into my mouth, not asking for permission. He doesn't need it. He never needs permission. He can have what he wants. I'm practically climbing him to get more. I tug on his back, wrap my leg around his, anything to get more. His fingers squeeze my neck before he releases me and pulls back far sooner than I want. A small grunt escapes at this loss. My eyes flutter open to find Aleks staring at Sapph. I can't read his emotions. Mine are obvious. Between Sapph and Aleks, I'll never function properly again.

"Tyler's not mad, but won't come back out," Aleks looks down at me as he speaks.

"Who's Tyler?" I ask, momentarily forgetting I have a whole-ass brother. Aleks smiles. A genuine smile and my knees are weak. My breath hitches. Looking up at his face is already my favorite angle, but this smile. Devastatingly beautiful. Painters could never capture the sheer beauty of his face. The ethereal glow, the magic of knowing how rare this is, the pleasure of receiving this face. I stare unabashedly, trying to commit every tiny millimeter to memory. I never want to forget this look on his face.

He leans in, the allure thickening the air around me. His warm lips are against my forehead, and I moan. I moan over a goddamned forehead kiss. But gods, if it's not more than I can handle now. Was that joint laced with something? I just had him inside me hours ago, but it's not enough. I want more. I need more of him. He walks away, leaving me staring agape after him.

"Holy hell, Vic," a male voice calls behind me. It's not enough to break me from watching Aleks's ass in those jeans as he walks away. "I figured Aleks was good, but damn." The people around me laugh, and I finally turn to realize I have an entire audience. Rio, Sapph, Jo, Catherine, Lucy, and Shirley are near us. Lacey glares at me from just behind Rio. I take a deep breath, a weak attempt to ground myself in reality. Desire courses through my body, and I just want more.

Chapter Fifteen

ALEKS

VIC IS ADORABLE. SHE is dancing in her shorts and thin shirt with a group of people. Even from across the backyard, I can make out the shape of her breasts. I should be mad, jealous, possessive. Everyone can see her. But I can see her. No one else matters.

Tyler isn't happy that I'm fucking her, but he isn't going to kill me either. He'll get over it soon enough. We don't need to hide anymore. That is worth it. We weren't really hiding before. We just didn't display anything around others. Except for Harpo, but that's his own doing.

The next day, I sit at the head of the table as club members file in. I was destined for this spot for a long time. Richard kept me too close for me to not end up here. I never particularly wanted to lead, but now that I am here, it's not so bad. We can do some fun things, like the ice cream social tomorrow. I've found ways to make the club more profitable. We still work with the cartel. We've been with them for many years. Things aren't as tenuous as they were in the beginning. We've got a good thing going.

I bang the gavel and call the meeting to order when everyone is seated. I briefly describe who Catherine and Jo are and why they are here. I let Harpo explain their offer. He can explain it and answer questions better than I can. I also hate talking. The less I can do, the better. Tyler fills in a lot. I have the power to control the group, but I rarely present the ideas.

I watch everyone's face while Harpo speaks. I gauge their reactions. One member blanches at the thought of working with the mafia. Most look intrigued at the prospect. It could be a good deal. Easy enough. We could probably even drop the cartel run. That would ease tensions with the Longhorn Devils. Fuck, I hate dealing with them. Shutting them up would be a huge benefit.

"You have two days to think this over. We'll vote after the ice cream social," I tell my men when Harpo finishes. They nod and look around at each other. "Anything else?" I ask. Silence settles, but several members nudge and try to inconspicuously convince someone else to speak up. Emphasis on the try. F for effort. This is pathetic.

"Say it or forget it," I grunt and raise the gavel to clack it.

"We gotta know," one of them starts quickly to stall me. He pales when he realizes he has everyone's attention. Rio sits up straight.

"You got an old lady now," he says bluntly. Shit, I didn't mean to claim her as my old lady. I did with that kiss, though. There is no doubt that she is mine. Sapph shifts uncomfortably in the back. She isn't technically a member and can't vote on anything, but her role is vital to the club. She runs a lot of side jobs for us. Since she is a woman, she can get away with things the men can't accomplish as easily. Not everyone respects her the way she deserves, but I do. She gets to sit in on the meetings, so I don't have to repeat everything. Tyler tenses with a scowl on his face.

"Yes, Vic is off limits," I keep my voice neutral and don't add anything else. "If that's all?" I raise the gavel again, daring anyone to say more about that subject. They cower slightly. I don't like to create fear within my ranks. I want them here because they want to be, but I won't let them run over me, either. They don't need to know anything more about Vic than she is mine.

I bang the gavel and end the meeting when no one says anything. Tyler jolts out of the room. He usually will hang around with me to talk about the meeting. I'm not surprised he doesn't want to stick around today. He's barely had twelve hours since he found out I'm fucking his little sister. He didn't even see the kiss last night. He'll come around eventually; it'll just take time.

The members file out of the room while I remain in my seat. I don't have plans for the rest of the evening. I haven't decided whether to smooth things with Tyler or give him more time. This situation is unprecedented. He's never been this angry with me. Sapph saddles up and takes Tyler's seat. She props her elbows on the table.

"I have a proposition for you," she says casually. I raise my eyebrows, curious to hear her out. "I want to fuck Vic." Didn't see that one coming. I blink a few times and try to school the rest of my emotions. I knew she wanted to fuck her, but I didn't think she would act on it. I don't even know how to respond.

"We've shared girls before. I would date them, and you would fuck them. I want that with her." I open my mouth to argue. I'm not just fucking Vic. We haven't said what more we are doing, but it's not just sex with her. I plan to say that to Sapph when she continues. "Roles reversed."

I cock my head to the side, considering. They both want each other. If Sapph is only having sex with her, I would still get what I want. Did I ever want her to be exclusive? I've never been exclusive with anyone. Truth be told, I just want her with me. I never considered anything beyond that. Even now, I'm content with what we have. Will I want more, need more from her? What more could I get? Neither of us wants kids. Neither of us have a desire to be married. She's been monogamous for all her life. Does she still want that? She doesn't want anything serious. Does that mean she's open to a non-monogamous relationship?

"What does she want?" I ask. Sapph shrugs and leans back in her chair. She props her arms behind her head.

"I don't really know. I saw an opportunity to chat with you about it and figured I'd start there. We could call her down now," she suggests. I nod, and she pulls out her phone to text Vic. Many times, Sapph and I have shared girls. I don't like group sex and don't like dating. They would date Sapph. She would take them on dates and whatever dating entails for them. They would come to my office or the gym or wherever to fuck, then go back to Sapph. It would last anywhere from a couple of weeks to a few months.

Vic enters the room and takes it in quickly. Nothing about this room is special. Only one window is behind me. A long table fills the center of the room. Chairs line the table and walls. A large state map is on one wall, and our logo is painted on the other. It's a business room, not a gathering room. Sapph motions to the seat across from her. Vic walks through the room, glancing between the two of us. Sapph didn't tell her why she called her. Sapph doesn't even look at me before she starts talking.

"We have a proposition," I snort at her use of 'we.' It's her proposition. She casts a quick glare at me. "You're already dating him," Sapph motions to me, but Vic's eyes widen. She looks like she will deny it. I don't want to admit how much that look hurts. I know she doesn't want a committed relationship. That doesn't make her denial hurt less.

"Whatever you want to call it," Sapph waves the words away before Vic can say anything. Vic's shoulders relax as she watches Sapph. "I want to fuck you. I'm not really looking for a girlfriend, more of a fuck buddy or friends with benefits," she glances at me before continuing. "I believe I can offer you something Mor won't." I squint at her suggestion, unsure what she means.

"You're interested in BDSM," her words are a question for Vic, and she nods, blushing slightly. I didn't know she was into that. If Vic is, Sapph may be correct about offering something I won't. I've had girls request being tied up or spanked or whatever. I've never been comfortable doing it. I don't like that power dynamic. It's a little too close to my demons' cage. I don't want to let them out.

"I'll let you explore that, then you go back to him for cuddles and kisses." I give Sapph an unimpressed look. I've never been the cuddles and kisses type of guy.

Though, I would for Vic. I find her watching me, looking for any indications of my thoughts. My face is blank.

"Are you okay with this?" Vic's words are soft, unsure.

"Is that what you want?" I question. I'm okay with anything she wants that involves her being with me.

"Answer me first," Vic says sternly. I appreciate her effort to get her answers.

"Sapph and I have done this before. I don't date women. That's usually her role while I fuck them. So, this will be a bit different," I shrug.

"That's not an answer," Vic glares this time. Hell, she's going to make me say yes or no. Am I okay with this? Is it something I want? If Vic genuinely wants more from sex, I can't give that to her. I glance at Sapph. Can I be with Vic, knowing she is sleeping with one of my best friends? Shit, this situation is so messed up. Tyler already hates us. This won't make things any better. Is that reason enough to say no, though? I look back at Vic. She's still staring at me, waiting for a yes or no.

"Yes," I say. "I'm okay with this." Vic remains tense, but relief shows in her eyes.

"Will you be with other women?" She asks Sapph.

"Not right away. Maybe eventually. I'm not looking for much right now." Vic glances between the two of us then leans back in her chair. She crosses her arms. Her demeanor says she is serious. Her eyes tell a different story. She's hopeful, excited, maybe a little cautious. I think she's ready to throw caution to the wind. She's tired of living the way other people demand.

"How will it work?" Sapph briefly considers Vic's question, then glances around the room. I have no idea how to answer that. I don't know how any of this shit works.

"You'll come to me when you want the dirty, kinky stuff and go to him for everything else. I'll take you out for girl's day or whatever. Probably with Shirley and Lucy. But for the most part, our relationship will be more physical." She nods her head at me with a playful smirk. She's about to say something stupid. "Mor will give you all the lovey-dovey boyfriend shit. Flowers and massages and sweet kisses." I roll my eyes. I've never bought flowers in my life.

Vic watches me, assessing my reaction. I'll buy flowers for her—an entire flower shop. If she wants, she can build a greenhouse and have flowers year-round.

"You're okay with this?" She asks me again. I nod. It does work out well. She gets what she wants without either of us being uncomfortable. Sapph knows how to develop a symbiotic relationship. Vic turns to Sapph. "And what about what you want?"

"I just want to fuck you. I'm not interested in an emotional relationship. You'll be with him, and I'll tell you when I want something or when I'm available. Basically, you'll have your relationship with him, a separate relationship with me, and I'll be friends with him. I won't go to him about you. We'll keep things separate." Vic looks between us as she considers. Sapph adds, "And we'll all hang out daily because he's still my best friend." Her voice gets high and squeaky, and she bats her eyelashes at me. I roll my eyes at her, but Sapph just laughs. She's not entirely wrong about being my best friend. I don't know what I would do without her.

"Do you want to know when I'm with her?" Vic asks me confidently. I wonder if this is something she has thought about before. It's not something I've considered. I stare at Vic, trying to decide if I want to know that. It's not. I would be distracted, desperate to know what she is doing, if she is okay. I shake my head. She nods acceptingly. "Would you want to see any marks on my body?"

"What kind of marks?" I ask, startled at her question. I've never asked Sapph what she's into. What she does is her own business. Except now it's Vic's, too. And mine, by extension.

"I want to explore masochism." Vic doesn't break my gaze. Sapph remains quiet during our conversation. It's easy to see how this could work. We each respect the other enough to give space when needed.

"You've been thinking about this a lot?" I ask, but it's obvious.

"More like daydreaming, but yes. I know what I want to try." I glance at Vic's throat, where the slightest yellow still shows the imprints of my fingers. I can't see her injured like that. Before I can speak, Vic turns to Sapph. "That's a no. Is that a problem for you?" Sapph shakes her head.

"No," she answers with a smirk. "I can play without leaving a mark."

I can't believe this is my life right now. What the fuck is happening? The woman I have been in love with for a decade is sitting in my club talking with my best friend about kinky shit. And how that will affect my relationship with her. I get Vic. She wants to be with me. She's here. This isn't some wet dream or fantasy. This is real life. She turns to look at me, and my fucking heart flutters. It's such an unfamiliar feeling that I almost rub my chest.

A knock on the door, then Tyler's head pokes through and breaks the moment.

"You done in here?" He asks, looking at me. Sapph answers first.

"Yeah," she glances between Vic and me. "Let's take it easy to start with and adjust as we need to. This is different; we may need to change things as we go. We need to communicate for this to work." The three of us nod at each other. Excitement dances in Vic's eyes; Sapph's are shrouded in lust. Tyler calls to me to follow him. I rise and step beside Vic. She tips her head back to look up at me. Her face is perfect. Soft and sweet and kissable.

I lean down to kiss her. My fingers trace her neck where the bruising is. A subtle reminder of what I did to her and how I will be better. Her hand strokes my forearm as my lips brush her forehead. I pull back and meet her gaze. This woman is everything to me. I will do anything to make her happy and keep her safe.

"If you're done eye fucking my little sister..." Tyler trails off with a hint of anger in his voice. It's not as prominent as it has been. I hope it means he will forgive me soon. With a final stroke of Vic's cheek, I leave the room and follow Tyler. Without a word, he heads for his bedroom. I don't hang out in his room. It's messy and gross for a man in his mid-30s. I don't say anything.

He grabs clothes off the couch and tosses them near a hamper in the corner. Only a piece or two make it in. The rest fall in chaos on the surrounding floor. His room is nearly as large as mine. It feels smaller because of the empty pizza boxes, half-full trash bags, and more clothes than I realized he owned. I take a seat on the couch he just cleared off. Tyler offers me a beer; I nod as I accept it.

"You fucking love her, don't you?" His words are accusatory, as if I did something wrong. Perhaps he sees it as a betrayal since it's his little sister.

"Yes," I answer honestly.

"Since when?" Tyler sits opposite me on the edge of his unmade bed. I debate how to answer the question. I don't think he will like the truth, but I don't want to lie.

"Her wedding day," I finally tell him. "I didn't admit it until recently, but I knew then." Tyler curses under his breath and rubs his hand over his face. His appearance is at odds with his bedroom. He is clean and well-groomed. He takes care of his beard and wears clean clothes. I don't know where he keeps the clean ones, though.

"What are we going to do about Wes?" Tyler makes a good point. My instinct is to kill him. He doesn't deserve to live. It would be a risk to harm him, but it is worth it, in my opinion. "Road trip to Pennsylvania?" His voice has a hint of amusement, but he is serious. I don't respond. I have no desire to go back. A silence falls between us as we consider our options.

"Aleks," he says after a moment. He rarely uses my real name. Since I got my tag name, that's what he's called me. I brace myself for whatever comes next. "What did Richard do to you?" I can't hide the flinch at his words. We've never talked about Richard. Tyler knew; there's no way he didn't. But we didn't speak of it. I don't respond and stare at the beer bottle in my hand.

"I saw him grab you and drag you off. I convinced myself that's just how he was with you. He was always that way." Tyler hangs his head and props his arms on his knees. "And you choked Vic because she grabbed you the way he did." He pauses, but it wasn't a question. "I should have done something." This is the reason I don't talk about it. I don't want sympathy or pity. I don't want to reflect on how things could have been different.

"It wouldn't have mattered." I was strong enough to fight him by the time I was sixteen. I did several times, but Richard was faster and more experienced. It wasn't worth the effort to fight him. The ending was always the same.

Tyler stands up and chugs his beer. He tosses the bottle at the trash can in the corner. It shatters; a few shards fall to the floor. He cusses again and picks them up. The tension in the air is palpable.

"You're not going to hurt her, are you?" He holds anger in his eyes, but a protective anger.

"No," I respond quickly. I won't do anything to hurt her. Not intentionally, anyway.

"Fine," Tyler says briskly. "I'm going to date Lacey." It sounds like a demand, but I shrug. I never dated her or wanted to. She was just an easy fuck for me.

"Good." My word is quick. Tyler has always carried our conversations. He likes to talk. I like to not speak. It's one of the reasons we work so well together. His shoulders begin to relax. I can see the tension leaving his body. A thought hits me as I watch him calm down.

"Before you relax," I start, and he instantly tenses again. "You should know Vic is fucking Sapph, too."

"What the fucking fuck!" He yells. I don't blame him. It's a wild situation. "If I would have known she would come here and fuck all of my friends, I wouldn't have let her come." We both know that's a lie, but I don't argue with him. He's been trying to get Vic to visit since we moved here. She never could. He still would have wanted her here if Tyler had known she would hook up with Sapph and me. He throws his hands up and collapses on the bed.

"Well, shit," he shakes his head. "What did Catherine give you in the files?" The topic change catches me off guard. Despite having known Tyler for over half my life, his sudden shifts still stun me.

"My father's death certificate," I debate adding the rest. It's not something I want to share with anyone, but this seems like a moment of honesty. After everything with Vic, I don't want to make things worse. "And a man in her mafia,

I know." There, vague enough, I don't have to say more. Tyler considers my words and then glares at me.

"What happened?" I freeze at his question. I've never said the words out loud to anyone. Not even myself. I grind my teeth, struggling with my thoughts about how to tell him. After all this time, he deserves the truth.

"My parents were junkies. My mother overdosed when I was an infant. My father borrowed more than he could afford. I," here I hesitate again. Tyler stares at me expectantly. He isn't piecing this together. I'm going to have to say it. I have to admit what my father did to his child. "I was collateral." My voice is gruff, but the words come out. Tyler doesn't say anything. He sits up with a grunt. He crosses his arms over his chest as the silence becomes oppressive.

"Will you see him?" I stare at him blankly. My father is dead; of course, I won't see him. "The man in the mafia. I assume he's the one that took you to Richard." That's one way to put it.

"I don't think so," I shake my head. "Catherine said he stays in Spain." Tyler's forehead scrunches.

"Where the fuck were you born?" Tyler questions. There's something I haven't thought about in a long time.

"I was born in Norway. My father moved to Spain after my mother died. Isak brought me to Pennsylvania."

"Holy fucking shit," Tyler huffs a laugh. "You don't have an accent." I shrug.

"Never talked much." It's hard to pick up an accent when I'm not around people talking. My mother died when I was young. My father was always high. If he did speak, it was slurred. I barely made it to school before Isak took me.

"I'm a terrible fucking friend. We've known each other for what, twenty-something years? And I've just learned you weren't even born in Pennsylvania." I shrug at Tyler.

"I would've lied before," I tell him honestly. The few times someone asked about my past, I diverted the question or outright lied. Tyler is now the only person to know. Perhaps Catherine, if her hacker, is that good.

"Well, fuck, man," Tyler walks to his mini fridge and grabs another beer. He offers me one, and I take it. Mine is empty now. "I never asked about your history, and you're fucking my baby sister. Guess neither of us is getting the best friend award." I chuckle at him. No, I suppose we aren't. He collapses on the couch beside me. "Wanna call it even and play some video games?" Now, that is an excellent idea.

Chapter Sixteen

VIC

"You really fucking love him, don't you?" Sapph says after Aleks walks out of the meeting room.

I don't love him. I don't really know him. But I do, don't I? I've known him since I was a girl. I've been around him for weeks now. I know him well enough to get his favorite drinks. I know he'll take care of me, no matter what that looks like. I know he'll give everything for me. I know deep down in his core he is a good person. He is damaged but still so good. He loves the people around him. He wants the best for everyone. I do know him, and I do love him.

"Let's go back to my room," Sapph speaks before I answer. A wave of excitement rolls through me. Tyler didn't say what he wanted with Aleks. I hope it takes a while. I want to spend some time with Sapph. She is so gorgeous and can give me what I want. My core heats at the thought of that. I want nothing more than to fuck her right now. I follow her through the bar and to her room.

Once her door closes, Sapph rushes me. Her lips crash into mine as she shoves me against the wall. I groan into the kiss. My hands reach for anything I can get, her shirt, her pants, her back. She takes a step back from me, leaving me panting.

"Let's set some ground rules," her voice is hoarse with lust. Her eyes burn into me, heating my core even further. I bite my lip, trying to suppress a moan. "I prefer the color method for a safe word. Are you familiar with that?" I've read about it before.

"You ask how I'm doing. Green means good; yellow means slow down; red means stop." Sapph nods her head, happy with my answer.

"You can always say the color at any point to stop." I nod that I understand, still breathless and panting. "Do you have any limits that you know of?" I've done a bit of research into BDSM. Not much, but enough to know there are a few things I don't want.

"No degradation. I'm not into embarrassment or waterworks," Sapph shrugs at that. It's not her thing, either. "No marks," I pause, "for now," I add with a playful wink. Sapph's grin is enormous and beautiful. She rivals Aleks with her beauty. In a competition, they would tie for first place, and my panties would be ruined.

"Good," she looks me up and down. "I'll go easy today. Anything you want to start with?" I nibble on my lip, somewhat nervous about asking for what I want. It's such a strange feeling when I haven't been given it in years.

"Bondage, spanking, and," I hesitate briefly. "I want to taste you."

"Oh, little bird," Sapph stalks toward me with predatory intent. It's so hot. She must have turned the heat on because my skin is already flushed. I'm pressed against the wall when she reaches me. Her hands land on the wall on either side of my head. Her own breathing is quick, eyes dilated with lust. "Will you strip for me?"

"Without music?" I ask with a huff. It was meant to be a laugh, but that's all I can manage now.

"Take your shoes off." She motions her head toward my feet and starts some music. I slip out of my booties and wait for further instructions. I didn't particularly want to be a sub: a bottom more than a submissive. But I follow her lead, at least until I am more comfortable. "Strip."

I don't put on a full strip tease. I'm not an exotic dancer. Removing my clothes feels like a chore without trying to dance to music. Sapph doesn't care as her eyes bore into my body. Calculating her next move, lusting after every new exposed bit of skin. I finally stand naked in front of her. She rips off her shirt and jeans, leaving her thong and bra on. She walks to me, and my cheeks heat with arousal. Her hand cups my pussy, and one finger slips inside me. I groan and roll my hips into her hand.

"Holy hell, little bird," she breathes. "I've never had a woman so wet so fast. I haven't even done anything." Before I can respond, she is kissing me. The kiss is insistent. She's setting the tone for the afternoon. Her finger strokes the inside of my slit, teasing and searching. Her palm rubs against my clit broadly, not giving the specific sensation I want. I moan, moving my feet to widen my stance. As soon as I do, Sapph pulls away from me quickly and completely. She leaves me gasping as she walks back to the top drawer where all her toys are. My disappointment quickly shifts to excitement.

Sapph returns with a pair of leather cuffs. She clasps them around my wrists in front of me without a word, then turns back to the drawer. This time, she returns with a pair of nipple clamps in tow. My breath hitches at the sight. She eyes me momentarily, assessing whether my gasp was excitement or hesitation. It was excitement, all excitement. I want this.

Her hand spreads over my breast, rubbing and squeezing. She pinches my nipple then does the same to the other side. My breast tingles beneath her touch. I watch her brown hand slide over my pale skin. Even all the time in the sun hasn't changed my pasty color. I swallow as she leans in to wrap her lips around one nipple. Without thought, I raise my hand to grab her head. I stop when I remember the cuffs banding both hands together. By the time I remember, she has pulled back. I watch as she brings the clamps to my nipple and places the first one on.

It stings for a moment. Sapph asks if it's too tight. The stinging subsides to a dull pressure, and I shake my head. She puts the other on and checks with me again. I give the same answer. She tugs the chain between them, eliciting a gasp from me. The feeling of my nipples being tugged simultaneously is intense. My pussy clenches, wanting so much more. My cheeks heat from blood rushing to them. My entire body is warm.

Sapph steps back and looks up and down my body. I can only imagine what she sees. Flushed cheeks, clamps on my hard nipples, hands cuffed together. Wetness is probably visible on my inner thighs. I want this so badly. My breaths are quick and heavy, anticipatory. She turns back to her drawer and grabs an item. When she faces me, she is holding a black paddle. On one side, the word 'slut' is embossed with red leather.

She steps in front of me and places the paddle on the side of my thigh, just above my knee. We watch as she slides the smooth leather up my leg, over my waist, then across my ribs. She pulls the paddle back then taps it over each breast. It isn't a hit, just a light tap. It's enough to make me bite my lip, a promise of what's to come, a slight tease before the show starts. Now my cunt is leaking on my thighs. I never thought I would be so aroused by the thought of someone hitting me with a paddle.

"Turn around," Sapph instructs in a surprisingly casual voice. I expected some deep, husky voice. She has better control than I do. "Bend over and rest on your elbows. Feet spread apart." I do as she instructs, standing in the exposed position. Cool air brushes against my aching cunt. I take in a deep breath, preparing for what's next. I don't know how I will react to being spanked. I've assumed it will feel good, or at least arousing. Maybe good isn't the right word.

The paddle touches the back of my thigh, just above my knee. I drop my head into my hands, trying to steady my breathing. Sapph drags the leather-covered paddle over my ass and then down the other side. I try to stay still; I really do. The anticipation is too much, and I lean back into the touch. I want more. I don't even know what more is, but I want it. Badly. Sapph chuckles, deep and gravelly, like I would expect. She's aroused, too.

A soft thwack lands on my ass. My breath hitches. It stings. The sting runs straight through my entire body. Tingles cover every inch, inside and out. Somewhere deep inside tightens, aching to be released. I rub my hands over my face. Sapph catches the movement and mumbles about how that won't do. Next thing I know, her entire body is pressed against my back. I groan as she leans over me. One hand glides to my wrist. The other wraps around my waist. I look up and watch her unclasp one of the cuffs. When it's free, the chain between the nipple clamps is tugged. I cry out in surprise at the sensation, that dull ache reaching a new level.

Sapph kisses my spine between my shoulder blades. She guides my hands behind my back. I'm still bent over, an awkward position to hold without the support of my arms. She slides the cuffs above my elbows and tightens them. My arms are pinned together against my back. I can wrap my forearms behind me or leave them at my sides. I can't use them for support anymore.

"You can hold yourself up or rest on your face," Sapph explains. "How are you feeling?"

"Good," I say breathlessly, then remember her system. "Green."

"Perfect. Tell me if it gets too intense. I'll go light on you today." I can hear the smirk in her voice. She smacks my ass harder this time. The blood rushes to the area. It's not terribly painful, but I wasn't expecting the sensation. It hurts and feels so good at the same time. I've never felt anything like this.

"Should I," I start with a shaky breath, "should I count?" My breaths come out in heavy pants.

"No, this isn't a punishment," Sapph says and hits the other side of my ass. It's harder, causing me to jolt forward into her bed. She has a homemade quilt on her mattress. The rough texture of the cotton combined with the thick seams rub against my clamped nipples. It's a delicious pain. She proceeds to hit me several more times. Hard smacks are intermingled with softer ones. I try to count them in my head but quickly lose count. My mind is swarmed with pleasure and pain. It's exquisitely erotic.

Sapph pauses and rubs my ass. The pressure against my stinging skin is delectable. I moan under her ministrations. I moan, low and long. She chuckles behind me, her hands moving closer to my soaked core. She asks how I'm doing.

"So, so green," I mumble. Sapph traces my ass, then finally reaches my core. Her finger easily slides through my entrance. Her middle finger taps my throbbing clit, and I scream. I didn't realize how close I was to coming. Seriously, another tap or two could set me off. I wiggle back to her, trying to get more of that touch. When she pulls away from me, I whimper. I could cry at the loss of her touch. The paddle touches the inside of my knees. Sapph instructs me to spread my legs wider and rubs my ass.

She smacks each of my ass cheeks harder than any previous strike. As I cry out, the paddle hits a third time, directly on my cunt. It wasn't a brutal hit, but it was enough to throw me off entirely. My knees buckle. If it weren't for already being on the bed, I would have collapsed with that. I slide down just enough for the nipple clamps to pull tighter. I groan desperately. I need something. What do I need? More? Less? To come?

Sapph is pressed against my ass, stroking my sore cheeks. My core clenches around the emptiness. That ache deep inside is more intense than anything I have ever felt. Nothing compares to this. My brain is foggy; I can only think in pain and pleasure now. Sapph grabs my ponytail and jerks me up. More pain, more pleasure. I nearly sob at the sensation. Her lips hover next to mine, but she doesn't kiss me.

"Stand up," she says. I shift, taking tiny steps on shaky legs to bring them closer together. My legs feel weak, tingly, almost out of control. I manage to stand up straight. She still holds my hair tightly. It's hard to see. My vision is clouded over with lust, with need. She turns me to face her. Sapph keeps her hands on my body, aware of my instability. She tugs on the chain, and I release a low groan.

With her hand still in my hair, her other finds my clit and massages lazily. My eyes flutter shut. Then Sapph kisses me. I groan into her lips. I try to find some semblance of control over my body to kiss her back. My attempt is sloppy and weak, but she doesn't seem to mind. The touch on my clit draws me closer and closer to release. My insides clench, ready to explode with ecstasy. Just as I reach the cliff of free fall, her hand is gone. I grunt and whine and jerk to get her back. I was so close! So fucking close.

"I'm going to give you a little break, bird," she explains.

"A break?" I cry. I don't want a break. I want more! I want release! I want to come! I want nothing more than that. I've never wanted anything as badly as I want an orgasm right now. A break?! No, I don't want a break!

"What color are you?"

Part of me wants to say 'yellow' or even 'red'. I want to come, but I don't really want to stop. The part of me that wants to say those colors pales in comparison to the part of me that wants this to keep going.

"Green," I whimper, desperate and excited.

"Good," she says as she grabs my elbows. "Sit on the floor, back against the bed."

Sapph guides me to the floor and into the position she wants. My elbows are still pinned by my ribs. I can move my forearms to the side but can't reach my opening. Before I know what is happening, Sapph stands in front of me. She props one leg on the bed. It takes me a moment to realize she has removed her thong. Her exposed pussy is directly in front of my face. I stare at the beautiful display. Her dark, curly hair surrounds brown lips. Moisture coats the inner lips, displaying her own arousal. I lick my lips, wanting to lean into her.

She does a small hop with her foot on the floor. Now her cunt is close enough that I can smell it. It smells like sex and arousal and everything I want. I don't ask or wait for approval. How could I with her this close? I lean in and lick her lips. She's the perfect height for me to reach her. I slip my tongue between her lips, teasing the opening, tasting her sex. It tastes like heaven. It's sweet enough to make me forget my sore ass.

I want to use my arm and my hands. I want to touch Sapph, but I can't move my arms. I groan and kiss her opening. My tongue explores, searching for her clit.

I find it, and she exhales quickly. I suck it between my lips. I pop off and flick it with the tip of my tongue.

"Yes, do that," Sapph whispers. I look up as she twists around. Something brushes against my chin. Sapph has a vibrator in her hand. She's reaching around her ass to fuck herself with it. I suck her clit between my lips as she slides the vibrator in and out of her pussy. I scrape my teeth against her clit. Sapph nearly tumbles over me, cussing at me for that. She starts to thrust against my face, so I don't think I did anything wrong. I suck her clit into my mouth again and flick my tongue against it. She rips the vibrator out of her body and grabs the back of my head roughly.

I stick my tongue out as she grinds against me. Her pussy clenches over my tongue with her orgasm. Her juices spill down my throat as she moves over my face. I lick as much as I can, entirely at her mercy. She jerks me back just as quickly as she pulled me into her. Her face is on mine, kissing and tasting herself on me.

The nipple clamps tug against my breast. I open my mouth in a gasp, and Sapph's tongue invades my mouth. My own cunt leaks all over her hard floor. I'm distantly glad she doesn't have a rug. This mess will be easier to clean on hard floors. She finally steps away from me, releasing my hair. My scalp tingles when she pulls my hair so hard. My body is swirling with sensations. Pain, arousal, desire, need.

Sapph grabs my elbow and the chain between my breasts. She pulls both, guiding me to stand. I whimper as shivers cover my entire body.

"Color?" Sapph asks. Her eyes are hooded, cheeks flushed with her orgasm.

"Green," I whisper, unable to form a complete sentence.

"Do you want to come on your back or your knees?"

"Knees," I say without thinking. I don't even consider it. My body knows what I want and bypasses all thoughts to answer.

"On the bed," Sapph nods. I turn and get into position awkwardly with my arms still pinned at my sides. As soon as I am, the paddle connects sharply with my exposed ass again. I cry out as a vibrator slides inside my aching opening. My yell changes to a loud groan. She slowly fucks me with the vibrating toy while spanking my ass. I'm so close. Deep inside my body, that growing ache expands like a balloon. It's about to pop.

She pulls the vibrator out and presses it directly against my clit. I instantly explode. My body quakes. Bursts of bright light explode behind my eyes. In my eyes? I don't know if they are open or closed. I can't see anything. My body is weightless. It shakes. I can feel it, and I can't. I'm overwhelmed and sated. I'm soaring and falling and soaring again. I've fallen down a waterfall. I'm drifting through a lazy river. I'm climbing a rainbow and then falling down a fluffy cloud.

Hands touch my body, wherever it is. Words are whispered in the distance. My arms are free, spread wide. I'm Jack Dawson, flying on the prow of a ship. A soft wrap covers my shoulder. Water dances across my face. Rose whispers how beautiful I am. No, not Rose. Sapph. I'm in her bed, covered with a blanket. She is rubbing my face with a wet cloth.

Holy fuck. I've never had an orgasm like that. Did I die? Was I dead? Am I dead now? Sapph chuckles next to me and kisses the side of my face. She comes into vision. The fog around me clears. She's saying something, but I can't hear her. She holds me in her arms, and I sigh. I've never felt like this. So calm. So quiet. So content.

After several minutes, Sapph offers me water with a straw. I barely need to move to sip. She puts the bottle down, and her arms stroke my body. It brings me back to reality. I look up at her with a sappy grin on my face. I know it looks ridiculous, but I really don't care.

"How are you now?" Sapph's voice is soft with a hint of a smile.

"Green," I whisper.

CHAPTER SEVENTEEN

VIC

Sapph let me rest and then helped me shower. The unequivocal calm I felt after my time with her is surreal. I've never felt anything so sublime. My muscles are relaxed, and my mind is quiet. I could walk through a serene meadow in the soft morning sun and wouldn't know the difference.

As it stands, I am walking into the restaurant, searching for Aleks. When I last saw him, Aleks went off with Tyler. I could use some food right now, and I hope they are in the restaurant. If not, I'll grab dinner and just go to bed. Nothing sounds as perfect as that.

Aleks is at the table with Tyler. They are chatting like normal. I hope this means they have forgiven each other. I don't want to be the cause of tension between them. They are good together. Tyler makes a joke, laughing loudly at himself. Aleks chuckles across from him, a slight grin spreading across his face. I love that look on him. Beneath the scruff on his jaw, he is lovely. Surprisingly gentle features that have been hardened by life. His long hair is down tonight, covering the shaved sides of his head. I love it when he leaves his hair down.

I walk up to the table, and Aleks climbs out of the booth before I say anything. I watch as he slides in next to me. I have such different feelings for him and Sapph.

With Sapph, it's almost entirely sexual. I enjoy spending time with her, but it's not the same as Aleks. I want to claim his body and soul. I want to know him better than anyone and be with him when no one else gets to. Be the person he goes to.

Aleks places his palm on my thigh, and I lean into his arm. I feel his lips against the top of my head, and Tyler groans but doesn't say anything. I close my eyes, savoring the warmth of Aleks's body. I sigh, more content than I have been in a while. The calm in my body, combined with Aleks's warmth, is almost too much. I could sleep just like this.

"Sapph, too?"

Tyler's question rudely draws me back to reality. I lazily open my eyes and glance at him. I give a slight nod. Tyler huffs in response but doesn't say anything else. Fine by me, I just want to sit here quietly. Tyler starts to ask a question when Lacey walks up. She glares at Aleks and me, but Tyler stands. She slides into the booth across from me. Curiosity rouses me from my drowsy state. I give a questioning look at Tyler, but he just shrugs.

The table feels rather tense now. No one is talking. It's not unexpected from Aleks, but Tyler always has something to say. He glances around awkwardly while Lacey just stares at us.

"Where is Sapph?" Tyler asks. Sapph can always be counted on to start a conversation. Usually, Tyler can, but he must be in a mood tonight.

"She's sleeping," I explain. I lean against Aleks's arm, ready to do the same thing. I'd prefer to be in a bed, but I just want to be near Aleks. Tyler grumbles something across the table, but I don't catch it.

"You can't sleep now, bird," Aleks says quietly. That doesn't sound correct. If we'll be up until three am like usual, I can take a quick nap in this booth. I give him a doubtful look. "We have to get up early for the ice cream social. So, we'll need to sleep earlier than normal."

I groan and pull myself away from him. If I lounge against him, I will fall asleep. If we are getting up early, I can't sleep now. His comment is enough to break the awkward tension at the table. The three of them discuss the event tomorrow. A few last-minute plans are discussed amidst stories of past years. I try to listen but drift back to that cloudy space in my mind.

We eat dinner and spend a couple of hours chatting in the booth. Lacey isn't terrible now that she isn't glaring at me. She does seem good for Tyler. She's strong-willed and not nearly as needy as Destiny. I'll give her the benefit of the doubt. Sapph said she likes Lacey when she isn't up Aleks's ass. I can probably like her too.

Bright light suddenly fills the restaurant. The lights are typically dim during dinner and after hours. They all come on for the last call before the restaurant closes, but we're still several hours away from closing. I and many other club members groan at the bright intrusion. Tyler and Aleks rise from the booth to face the people in the restaurant.

"Hey, fuck heads!" Tyler shouts. I gasp and look around at the patrons. Why would he yell that in the restaurant? There are frequently families here. No one really censors themselves, but it's always toned down when nonclub members are around. I realize as I scan the area that only club members and whores are in here. They must have closed the restaurant early tonight.

"The bar is closing early," Aleks starts. His loud voice shocks me. He appears even larger than usual from my spot behind him in the booth. He's already a big man, over six feet and muscular. Addressing the crowd with a booming voice is intense. I've never heard him so loud. "You will not show up drunk in the morning. Everyone needs to be in place by ten a.m. and sober. I will not tolerate drunk and hung-over assholes around the kids. You'll be on grunt duties for a month if you are."

Several men raise their glasses in salute. Lucy and Shirley shut down the bar and lock it. I have no doubts that most people have more alcohol in their rooms. However, I get the impression that they won't take it too far tonight. They respect Aleks and Tyler in a way I wouldn't expect for an outlaw motorcycle gang. The two are good men and deserve that respect. It's nice to see others recognize it, too.

Aleks takes my hand and leads me to his room. Tyler and Lacey stay in the restaurant, whispering together in the booth. He looks happy stroking her arm, brushing hair from her face. I hope he is happy with her. He enjoyed the drama from Destiny, but having a calmer woman will be good for him.

Aleks heads for the shower, and I get ready for bed. I remove my clothes and grab one of his shirts. I slip into the bed and make myself comfortable in the sheets. I'm almost asleep when he comes out. He stands over me, fiddling with stuff on his nightstand.

"You're on my side of the bed," he states plainly.

"So observant," I tease. Aleks doesn't say anything; he just stares at me. "I have a reason, you know." He raises an eyebrow. Sometimes, these one-sided conversations can be fun. "Get in, and I'll show you," I tap the spot beside me. He walks to the other side of the bed and slides beneath the sheets. He doesn't move any closer to me; he stays on the other side.

"Oh," I start. "I didn't realize you hate me." His head jerks toward me.

"What?"

"You're way over there," I motion my hand to the distance between us. "Obviously, you hate me," I tease, keeping my voice light. He harrumphs and slides closer to me. I meet him in the middle and settle on his chest. I sigh contentedly, glad to finally fall asleep. I close my eyes, letting the darkness claim me.

"Why?" His chest grumbles with the word beneath my face.

"Hmm?" I turn my face toward his, no longer comprehending things. I'm in sleep mode.

"Why do you need to be on my side?"

"This," I whisper. My fingers tap his chest where his heart is. "I like to hear it while I sleep." His heart doesn't literally skip a beat, but I do hear his breath hitch. I slide my arm over his ribs to hold him tightly. I kiss the spot I just tapped. "It's mine, Aleks," I say softly. His arms tighten around me. I shift just enough to kiss his cheek. "Good night," I mutter and settle against his chest. The soft thumps under my ear lull me into a peaceful slumber.

I wake the next morning pressed into Aleks's chest. He rolled onto his side at some point, and I'm not upset about it. I nuzzle into his pecs as his hand slides down my spine. The touch sends a wave of goosebumps over my body. I tilt my face toward him, and he leans in to kiss me. Just before our lips meet, Tyler bangs on the door.

"Come on, fuck face! You're going to be late."

It's official: I hate my brother.

Aleks's chest rumbles around me. I snuggle in tighter, not wanting to leave this comfortable nest of skin and muscles. He kisses my forehead. Maybe it's some secret mission he's on to see how many forehead kisses he can squeeze in before I throat-punch him. He shifts to climb out of bed, but I grab his face. I pull him into a searing kiss. He may be going for a Guinness record of forehead kisses, but I'll be damned if I don't get passionate tongue fucking kisses too.

I sigh into the kiss then Aleks pulls away from me. I watch as he climbs out of bed. His smooth muscles ripple as he walks through the room. His ass is shaped perfectly, as if a Greek sculptor molded him from marble. I stare as he slips into dark jeans, a dark shirt, and his cut. He smirks when he catches me staring. I'm not embarrassed; this beautiful man is a god that deserves ogling.

"You can sleep longer. We'll be setting up for an hour or so," Aleks says as he pulls on his boots. I sit up to stretch, raising my arms over my head. He watches the material drape over my breasts. I don't hide the grin I get from watching him ogle me. It's empowering to know he appreciates my body as much as I appreciate his.

"I'll get up now. I can help," I offer, searching for clothes in his closet. I don't have my own space in here. I just hijacked sections of the closet for my stuff. I settle on a tank top and denim shorts. I slip into low-top canvas sneakers and head to the parking lot.

The transformation is astounding. Men are setting up pop-up canopies. A handful line the entrance to the parking lot. Several more form a row perpendicular to the first. Shirley and Lucy are hanging signs on tables that have already been set up. More people bring out tables and chairs. Three more canopies are set at the end of a course on the far side of the parking lot. Cones mark off paths around the parking lot. I watch for a moment more, stunned by the display. Men in leather vests work happily while Shirley titters back and forth.

I find Lucy and ask how I can help. She has me set up chairs at all the canopies. Once the canopies are in place, a few bikes are brought out. Three go to the paths laid out. One goes under a canopy with a canvas tied to the back of it. It has the club logo on it. I spot Aleks and Tyler chatting there. Aleks is considering something. His arm is crossed over his chest, the other stroking his jaw. Fuck, he's pretty.

Another bike is carried out and placed beside the canopy with the logo banner. It's partially disassembled. I need to track someone down to tell me what this is for. I'm excited to see how this plays out. Tyler yells at a few people then they crowd around. I'm close enough that I can hear. He's setting them up in guard positions around the compound. A few at the garage doors, a couple inside to cover the doors that lead upstairs. Lucy will stay inside at the bar to serve nonalcoholic drinks and guide people to the bathroom. Harpo will be surveilling the cameras.

Before I can stop Tyler or Aleks, they both walk away, dealing with another issue. Sapph appears at the disassembled bike. She greets me with a warm smile. She's holding a wrench and taps her other palm with it. Images of her holding the paddle the same way fill my brain. My cheeks flush at the thought.

"Hi," I say breathily. She gives me a knowing smirk before greeting me. "Um," I try to clear the lust fog quickly, "what is all this for?" She scans the area before stepping beside me.

"This," she motions to the bike behind her, "will be for the kids to tinker with. Pretend they can fix it. Those," she points across the parking lot to the paths. Several of the men are carrying a variety of helmets to the tables. "Those will be for rides. A few of us will let the kids ride our bikes with us around those paths. Different courses for different ages." My mind is whirling, but she continues before I ask a question. "That is where Shirley will greet everyone, hand out ice cream, and collect any donations." She waves at the table directly across from the entrance. Coolers are being carried out and placed under the canopies.

"This is for the board members. It's a photo op. Kids can sit on the bike and take pictures alone or with the board members. Mor is pretty popular there. We ask for donations, but it's not required. All the money goes to the schools. For supplies, furniture, books, whatever the school needs." Sapph pauses thoughtfully, "We bought these little coding robots for the elementary school last year. We got pictures of these tiny kids coding bumble bee-shaped robots."

My mind is spinning a million miles a minute. This setup is fantastic and thoughtful. It's such a fun opportunity for kids, and it's a charity event. My heart squeezes, and tears sting my eyes. I love events like this.

Wes would attend charity galas with other government officials. I hated those parties. They weren't about the charities. Half the time, the attendees didn't know which charity they were donating to. No, those parties were for clout, for showing off their money, for buying thousand-dollar seats. I was forced to attend the galas, but this isn't like those. It's clear who this is for. It's for the kids, about the kids, set up for the kids.

A couple of bouncy houses are being inflated near the riding tracks. I wonder if it was all Shirley's idea. Aleks said she plans most of these events. I need to tell her how amazing it is. Sapph walks behind me and brushes close to whisper in my ear.

"All of this was Aleks's idea. Shirley just made it happen."

My eyes widen with shock. Sapph knew what I was thinking. But Aleks. He planned all of this. I turn to watch Sapph walk to one of the paths. Her hips swish, and I can no longer remember if she always walks that way or if it's a show for me. It doesn't matter. It's hot as hell either way. She moseys to the tent with a purple bike. It's the two-seater she took me to the club on a while back. She's going to be giving kids a ride on that bike. I'm going to orgasm just watching it. The thought of her being kind and friendly, and with kids no less! I may not want kids, but there is still something so primitive, so desirable about seeing people be kind to them.

I spot Aleks and Tyler laughing at the booth beside me. I approach them as my mind still reels with everything. I step beside Aleks, and he wraps his arm around my waist. Tyler watches us but shows no reaction.

"If you want something to do," Aleks starts, "Shirley could use help passing out ice cream. It'll be swamped in about thirty minutes." I nod at him, glad to have something to do instead of standing here lusting after him and Sapph. Aleks reaches up and pushes a strand of hair back from my face. I pulled it up into a high bun to keep it back, but some strands always fall. "Have fun, bird," he says with a kiss on my head. As I walk away, I hear Tyler chide Aleks.

"I can't believe my baby sister is the one that whipped you." A soft thud of a fist connecting with a chest precedes Tyler's laugh. I roll my eyes and take a spot at one of the coolers. People begin to trickle into the parking lot. Families with kids of all ages come through. As Aleks said, things really pick up after about thirty minutes. I watch families stroll by, taking ice cream, popsicles, and water bottles. Jars for cash are filling up. Others scan QR codes to donate virtually.

Kids giggle, laugh, cry, and scream as they walk by the bikes. I sneak quick glances at Aleks between handing out ice cream sandwiches. He stands near the motorcycle and steps in to take photos with kids who want him there. Sometimes, he stands behind them with his arms crossed and a menacing stare on his face. Those are older kids, about nine or ten, who also put on a tough face. I chuckle at the image. But the one that really gets me is the younger kids.

Kids about five or six years old walk up to him. He lifts them onto his bike and leans close to them with a grin. My ovaries clench every time he does that. I can't imagine it's pleasant for him, but he does it all the same. He doesn't look like dad of the year or anything, but he's trying. The families don't realize how special that is, how they get a version of Aleks that so few people see. My heart beats a little faster in my chest.

Sapph is by her bike. She helps a girl of about twelve pull a helmet on her head. Sapph instructs her on how to hold on and lean. Sapph is so expressive. She moves exaggeratedly with each prompt. The girl nods at each instruction. Sapph climbs on the bike first, then helps the girl on. She eases the motorcycle through the course. The second time, she goes a bit faster and leans more. She speeds down the short straight away in the course. It's not long enough to get any real speed, but enough to give the kids a bit of a jolt. When she stops, the girl climbs off and cheers excitedly to her friends.

I'm not overly emotional, but I can't stop the lump forming in my throat. Seeing this club, this outlaw gang of surly bikers with a lousy reputation, put on a display of kindness and gentleness with the kids makes me feel all the things.

I hand out ice cream sandwiches until I run out and carry the cooler inside. The chill of the AC makes me shiver. I didn't realize how hot it was outside. Or maybe that's just me. Watching Aleks and Sapph with those kids got me fifty shades of hot. Lucy offers me a drink and I accept. I lean against the bar, giving my feet a rest. Despite working in the ER, I've been out of it for a while, and my feet are hurting. These shoes don't really help either.

Aleks walks in and smiles at me. Yeah, it's not just the summer heat in San Antonio. He takes water from Lucy and sips it.

"You," I start, unsure if I can speak to him without sobbing with joy or humping him. "You did all of this? It was your idea?" He nods and opens his mouth to speak when Tyler walks in.

"Oh, Mister President," he sings out. "You're being summoned!" Aleks shakes his head, downs his water, and turns to walk out. He stops and turns back to me. He kisses my cheek.

"See you out there, bird." Be still my heart. I nibble on my lip to keep from giggling like a schoolgirl.

When I go back outside, Sapph has handed her bike over to another member. She is at the disassembled bike, showing kids how to work on the motorcycle. I'm no mechanic and have no clue what she is doing, but the kids eat it up. Once

Sapph is there, several more girls walk over to participate. It's then that her role dawns on me. She draws the girls to the bikes. She represents the girls who want to do things like this. It's one thing to be offered the chance, but to see another woman doing it is more enticing.

There goes that damn fluttering again. I realize I'm staring when a man walks up beside me.

"It's a pretty great sight," Rio says. "This is the reason I joined this club. My parents were disappointed in my choice to be here, but Mor and Sapph make this place different." I smile up at him. Sapph glances up from her spot. She's kneeling beside a couple of teenage girls, showing them different parts of the engine. She winks at me, causing my cheeks to turn bright red. They were already pink with the heat.

I linger near Aleks's tent while the final families trickle out. People are tearing down the other tents and tables, putting things away. The restaurant will be closed to the public for the rest of the day to give everyone a break. The cooks are preparing for a big party tonight. Shirley deserves a break after everything she did.

The last family leaves and Aleks turns to face me. I smile softly at him. This man has such a rugged exterior. He has been through so much in his life, so many bad things. Yet he is still kind and soft-hearted. My chest tightens as I see him. I want to make him feel as good as he is. Before I say anything, he leads me inside the club. I can't help staring at him with heart eyes.

He stops in the restaurant to speak to a few of his men. I linger close, not hearing anything he says. I hold his arm, rubbing his bicep. His big, muscular bicep. I glide my hand over his back. His smooth, muscular back. The one I could hold onto as he fucks me against the wall. Or the shower. Just before I stroke his shoulders, thinking of my legs hanging over them, Sapph walks up to us. The other men walk away.

"What are you two up to?" She glances between us.

"Probably a shower, then out to the backyard. You?" Aleks speaks easily. He's in a good mood. Seeing all the families seems to cheer him up. He wouldn't like it regularly, but I'm sure these occasional events are good for him.

"You're going to shower? Just shower?" The disbelief in Sapph's voice is palpable. Aleks nods, oblivious to her intent. "You know she's horny as fuck, right?" He looks down at me and searches my face. His hair is braided today. As much as I love to run my fingers to it, something about how it frames his face speaks to my soul. If my soul is located in my vagina. I bite my lip, a weak attempt to quell the rising desire in my core.

Sapph's hands cuff my ears, blocking the sound out. I can hear her talking but can't make out the words. My eyes go wide. She's telling Aleks what to do to me. She knows where my boundaries are, but that doesn't mean she won't tell him something that will push his limits. He shows no reaction to her words. His eyes bounce between me and Sapph.

"No," I start in mock fear, "you don't have to listen to what she says. We don't have to do that." I grab his forearm; a wide grin spreads across my face. "It's not necessary. We can do something different." Sapph's hand gently pushes my head, and then Aleks's hand is on my mouth. She told him to silence me, and he did it! I stare at him in shock.

I could lick him, but he probably wouldn't react to that. I could bite him, but he wouldn't appreciate that. Instead, I decide on a different approach. I kiss his palm. His eyes dart to mine, and I kiss him again. His thumb strokes my cheek as Sapph releases me.

"And that's how you torture her."

His face remains blank. I hate that he is so good at hiding his emotions. His hand slides to the back of my neck, and he tells me to follow him. Shivers cover my entire body. If he didn't tug me, I wouldn't have moved, frozen with anticipation. My breathing is quick as we walk to his room. His hand on my neck is so possessive, so domineering. For anyone else, I would fight it. Not Aleks, though. I won't fight him.

In his room, he releases me and walks to the bed. He empties his pockets but doesn't say anything. I stand by the door awkwardly, unsure what to do. His eyes stay focused on what he is doing.

"What did she tell you?" He finally glances at me but doesn't say anything as he removes his watch. I walk to him while he rubs his wrist.

"We should shower," his voice is tense, not casual or sensual like I would expect.

"Did she upset you?"

"I don't like having power over you." He doesn't look at me as he speaks. Sapph would know he doesn't want to hurt me or do anything physical like that. She probably didn't expect his issues with power dynamics. That's her kink. She would have told him how to control me to get the best experience for both of us. That would work for her, but not Aleks.

I help him slide his cut off, fold it, and drop it on the bed. I rub his arms soothingly. It's not the same touch I used earlier to feel him. It's less erotic and more calming.

"Let me make you feel good," I whisper and slide my hands to the waist of his pants. Once they are unbuttoned, I drop to my knees and reach for the zipper. Before I grab it, he takes a step back. I look up to find him turning away from me. He doesn't like this position, but I don't think it's about the power dynamic. I stand slowly and step toward him. He doesn't stop me.

My hands move slowly to his waist. He still doesn't react, so I continue slowly. Any hint of pain or fear, and I'll stop this. I touch his waist, rubbing my fingers just above the hem of his pants softly. I press my lips against his chest in the same spot I kissed him last night.

"Do you ever let someone else take care of you?" By the way he looks away, I know the answer is no. I knew it before I asked, but asking is the easiest way to show my intent without spelling it out awkwardly. I pull the hem of his shirt up. He helps me remove it. I'm too short to pull it over his head, let alone his raised arms.

"Sit," I motion to the chair in his room. He walks over without question or argument. I kick my shoes off and approach him slowly. My next move is risky but will pay off in the end. I kneel at his feet, not close to the chair. I'm as far away as I can be while still being able to reach him. I unlace one boot slowly and remove it. He helps get his foot out, and I take his sock off, too. I do the same with the other boot. He still shows no reaction. I inch closer to him.

"What you did today," my voice is soft, "was amazing. You gave those kids something special." I rub my hands over his calves and knees. I massage his thighs but don't reach any higher. "You are always thinking of other people. I want to show you what it feels like when someone thinks of you." I slide my hands up higher. I watch him, but he shows no emotional reaction. His cheeks turn pink, and his eyes dilate. My fingers hook into the waist of his boxer briefs and jeans. I tug gently. He'll need to help get them off.

His hips rise. A battle rages in his eyes, but he wants to let me do this. I pull his jeans down slowly, brushing my fingers along his legs. I remove his feet gently and set the pants aside. I caress his legs softly. His cock is already half hard, but I don't reach for it yet. I rub his thighs and wrap my arms around his waist. I tug on his back, sliding him down just enough to give me a better angle.

"Keep your eyes on me," I command gently. He doesn't look away from me.

My lips press gently against his foreskin. A heavy breath leaves his chest. I don't know the specifics of his past with oral. He has denied me before. There is some trauma there. He is trying, though. I swirl my tongue around the tip and lift it enough to slide my lips around it. My eyes flutter shut, breaking my gaze with him. It's hard to do this without my hands when he is only half hard, but I make the effort. I trace his back with my fingers, offering comfort.

I take more of him into my mouth and suck. He hisses as his dick hardens in my mouth. The shift from semi to fully erect gives my mouth time to adjust to his size. He's large, and I haven't done this in a long time. I swirl my tongue around the bottom, ensuring it is wet enough. I look up at him as I slowly slide up and down his length. He is still watching me. His pupils are blown with arousal. I take that as encouragement and stroke him fast.

I relax my throat when he hits the back. Some men enjoy the sound of gagging and choking. Aleks won't like that. I do my best to remain silent. My lips glide down him gently, and then I tuck them around my teeth as I pull back. I'm no dick-sucking expert, but I've seen enough videos from people that are. I don't remember everything they did, but I remember enough.

Aleks brings his hand to my cheek. His thumb strokes my lips as I bob over his cock slowly. He stares stoically as I suck him long and hard. One of my hands slides from his back to between his thighs. I cup his balls and gently squeeze. He groans but doesn't break his gaze.

Between my fingers on his testicles and the long, sucking strokes, it isn't long before he is muttering about his release. I take him deeper and suck harder. I wrap my other hand around his cock. My thumb presses into the base, massaging near his sack. That's all it takes for him to come. I swallow him as deeply as I can, letting his cum spurt straight down my throat. I lick and suck everything from him as he groans. His head tips back. His fingers stay on my face and stroke my cheek slowly as he comes down from his high.

A brief moment of disbelief passes over me. I just sucked Aleks's dick, and it was glorious. My neglected pussy clenches erratically in my soaked panties. I need to attend to her, but I don't want to move my face from Aleks's lap. I'm so comfortable here.

Chapter Eighteen

ALEKS

Silence.

Vic rests her head on my thigh. Her arm is wrapped around my calf, and her other hand is on my thigh, caressing gently.

Silence.

My hand glides to the back of her head, tangling in her hair. My other hand is perched on the arm of the chair. I am naked while Vic is still fully dressed on her knees in front of me.

Slowly, my thoughts return to me. I have never felt such calm before. My mind was completely silent. Not even drugs, alcohol, or sleep can achieve that level of quiet. It was pure nirvana. She did that for me.

I look down at her. Vic's cheeks are rosy, and she watches her fingers trace a bird tattoo on my thigh. I want to say something to her, to explain what she just gave me. But what do I say? "Thanks for a great blow job"? No, that's stupid and doesn't encompass what she just did.

"We should shower now," her soft voice breaks my thoughts.

Vic rises; her warm body leaves me cool. She holds her hand out for me. Despite my thoughts returning, I'm not functioning at full capacity. The smirk on her face means she knows that, too. She grabs my hand and tugs. I finally rise and follow her to the bathroom.

I want to give her so much more than I am. She deserves everything. Vic deserves the world. I can't even stand from a fucking chair after a blow job. How can I give her what she needs? I'm not good enough for her.

"Hey," she steps in front of me. Her shirt is off, and her shorts are unbuttoned. She slides her hand up my chest to the back of my neck. She tugs softly, pulling me down to her. Her lips press against mine in a perfectly chaste kiss. I'm not one for chaste kisses or any kisses, really, but she likes kisses. She deserves all of them, all the time.

"Get in and start the shower," she says when she pulls back from me. All I can manage is a nod. I step into the shower and turn the water on. I want to leave it cold, but she won't like that. Vic deserves a warm shower. I set the water to warm and stand under the spray before it reaches temperature, letting the cold shock my senses.

I'm being ridiculous. Vic's told me before that I am what she wants. I don't get to decide what she deserves. I don't really believe that, though. Not deep down. I want her to have more. I want to give her more, but I can't. I'm too damaged for her, too ruined, too broken.

I don't hear Vic walk in. The shower muffles her movements. She whispers my name, drawing my attention to her. When I look, she tugs my arm, pulling me out of the spray. She has a sudsy loofah in her hands and begins washing my body. I can only stare, frozen with disbelief. No one has ever washed me before.

It feels awkward at first, knowing she is cleaning my body. The glide of her hands with the texture of the loofa settles me. She washes my chest and then rises on her tiptoes to clean my shoulders. A small wave of happiness rattles through me. Vic is so small beside me. She cleans my back, down my ass, then one leg and the other.

When she rises, she stands before me and offers me the loofah. I stare for a moment, trying to process what she wants. Once it hits, I take the loofa and wash her. There is something so intimate about this action. My thoughts of not being worthy are pushed back. I clean her in the same pattern she cleaned me: chest, shoulders, back, ass, legs. She takes the loofa, rinses it, and puts it away.

"Kneel." Her finger points to the floor in front of me.

"What?" I don't want to be on my knees in front of someone. I've done that before, unwillingly. It's not something I do at all now.

"Do you trust me?" The thought of when I first asked her outside the boutique fills my mind. She said no to me then, but I trust her.

"Yes," I barely whisper.

"Then on your knees."

My breathing is ragged, but I comply. I don't know what she has planned. I can't think of anything. My demons are raging in my mind, a stark contrast to the calm I felt just a few minutes ago. The tile of the shower is hard on my knees. I try to focus on that.

"Give me your hands."

I don't question her and hold my hands out instantly. She takes them and places them on her hips. I squeeze the soft skin beneath my fingers. Her curves are unlike anything I've held before. No other woman compares to her. No other person. Her hand catches my chin and tips my face up. Her face is gentle. Vic leans down and kisses my forehead. I understand her disdain for a forehead kiss, but I won't stop.

She pulls my face into her stomach. I close my eyes and savor the feel of her skin against my face. She shifts around, but I stay focused on her waist. I squeeze her hips again. Everything about her calms my mind. It's not as silent as earlier, but my mind is still. Vic's fingers sink into my hair and massage my scalp. The scent of my shampoo fills the shower.

She is washing my hair. I nearly groan as her fingers move over my head. She's gentle and firm. She knows exactly what I need right now. This has never been a position I am comfortable in, and she knows that. She is changing that, rewriting my past. I want to be here for her. Can I give her this? Can I give up this much of myself every time she asks? I have so far. Will there be a day I can't? How will she react then?

Vic rinses my hair and adds conditioner. It's her conditioner, as I don't usually use any. My hair products are a two-in-1. She's repeatedly expressed how jealous she is of my hair and my hair care routine. Once the conditioner is in, she tugs my arms, and I stand before her. Without a word, she hands me her shampoo bottle and turns her back to me.

I wash her hair the way she just washed mine. She doesn't suppress her moans, though. I use my thumbs to rub the base of her head, and her body shivers in front of me. I can't stop my smile from her reaction. I rinse and add the conditioner.

"You should rinse the conditioner out of your hair now," she tells me.

"You won't do it for me?" I try for a playful voice, but it sounds like all my other sentences.

"No," she starts, stepping out of the spray. "I know you're, like, really old. And getting up and down from the floor is probably hard for you." She manages the playful tone I was just going for. I smile at her and pinch her side. She squeals, and I rinse my hair out. When I'm done, I notice she is staring at me with this wistful gaze. I give her a questioning look.

"When I first got here," she explains, "I thought that if you ever truly smiled, like a pure joy smile, you would be exquisite. I don't see it often, but it takes my breath away every time." That word. She's called me exquisite before.

"You've called me that before."

She gives a soft nod with a noncommittal hum and says we need to get out of the shower. As we dry off, she tells me everything she saw at the ice cream social this morning: her favorite moments, silly things the kids did, and watching other members interact with people. Vic had a great time this morning. Warmth spreads through me, knowing she found that joy in my club.

We walk to the backyard once we are dressed, me in my everyday jeans and a dark shirt, her in shorts and a shirt sans bra. She laces her fingers with mine, still chatting about the event this morning. We meet up with Sapph, Rio, Catherine, and Jo. The latter is animatedly talking about a chubby kid she saw that she fell in love with.

The rest of the club comes out, and music starts playing. The grill is fired up, filling the area with scents of charcoal and cooking meats. Booze and joints make their rounds as the sun begins to set. Vic starts dancing with Sapph and Jo. I find a seat at a table and watch from a distance.

Vic is happy with Sapph. I can see how much fun they have together. When she left Sapph's bed, she was sated and doe-eyed. Sapph could give her everything she needs. She can offer her more than I can. I have no doubts Sapph has her own issues, but none are as intrusive as mine. Vic could be happier with her. Maybe I should step back and let them be together. She doesn't need me.

"Did I ever tell you about Theodore?"

I turn to find Shirley standing beside the bench I am sitting on. My stupor is momentarily broken as I turn my attention to her. Shirley is the closest thing I have to a mother. She knows me as well as Tyler does. I give a slight shake, unsure who she is talking about.

"He was my first husband." I raise my eyebrows at her words. I didn't know she was married to anyone before Joe. As far as I know, they have been together for decades. "I met him when I was 16," she continues. "We were high school sweethearts. I married him as soon as I graduated high school. He was perfect." She sighs and turns her gaze out to the dance floor. I look, too. Vic is dancing with Rio now. Sapph is swaying with Jo.

"He was an accountant, bought a home right after school, owned his car, and had no debts. He played golf on the weekends. Everyone thought we were the dream." She turns back to me, and I meet her gaze. "Do you know what I thought?" I shake my head, not entirely sure where she is going.

"He was fucking boring."

I snort at her response. He sounds boring, but I don't know why she's telling me this. I glance back at Vic and catch her gaze. Her face drops from her joyful expression, but she doesn't stop dancing.

"So, I left him. Hopped on the back of a bike of the first stud I saw and found my own happily ever after. Last I checked, Theodore was on wife number 4 and had two kids that won't talk to him." Something tugs at my brain, some point she is trying to make. I spot Vic walking toward me in my peripheral. Ah, that's Shirley's point.

"Joe's not as fucked up as I am. And he's not the president," I explain calmly.

"No," she starts, "but that doesn't mean you aren't worthy of happiness." Well, fuck. That one hit me right in the feels. Today has been a mindfuck. The high of the ice cream social, the crash of Sapph's instructions to get Vic off, the silence of the blow job, the intensity of the shower. I need more drugs and alcohol.

"Listen," Vic's voice breaks my thoughts. "I know your tag name is Moros because you're all broody and grumpy and murdery," I raise my eyebrow at her last descriptor, but she continues. "But this is supposed to be a happy party." Vic stops in front of me and looks down. "What is all of this?" She waves her hand between Shirley and me, indicating the low mood. Before I can open my mouth, Shirley responds.

"Oh, I was just telling him that we need to make Pitch start showering." Pitch is one of the newest members of the club. He never smells good, but I have no intention of addressing his showering habits. "Ah, I'll make Joe do it." Shirley walks off and yells at her husband.

Vic pushes my shoulders back and climbs into my lap. I make room for her as she drapes her arms around my neck. She doesn't say anything; she just settles against me. After a moment, I wrap my arms around her small body. It's warm in the summer heat. My dark jeans don't help the heat, nor do all the people in the space. I don't let her go, though.

We sit like that for a while: her in my lap, me holding her in my arms. I watch the party over her head. Everyone is happy, dancing, eating, drinking, or chatting. This is my usual position. I typically sit off to the side by myself and watch everything else. I don't get to be happy like they are. I am intrinsically broken.

Vic is like the others, always with other people. I don't know why she's here with me now.

"What are you doing?" I ask gruffly.

"Being a weighted blanket."

"What?" I look down at her, utterly confused about her comment.

"Weighted blankets help with anxiety. I don't have a blanket. Even though I weigh more than a weighted blanket should, I can still do the job." I give her a slight squeeze. I don't have anxiety. I was just stressed about being with her. I don't want to mess things up with her. I want Vic to be happy, and I don't know if I can do that for her. I can't give her what she needs. Oh, I hear it now. Damn.

I sit with the realization that she could recognize my problems before I could. I cannot quell the thought that she deserves better than me. Vic needs someone less troubled and more stable. She should be with someone who can take care of her.

"Want to go inside?" Her question is soft, pulling me from my thoughts.

"Do you want to?"

"I want to be where you are," Vic mumbles against my chest.

I think I'm having a heart attack. That's what this clenching feeling in my chest is. I'm dying. Those are pretty good words to end my life on. Warmth spreads, doing nothing to convince me that I'm not having a heart attack. Vic wants to be around me. Shit, I want that too. I glance at her to ask where she wants to be, but I don't have to ask. She wants to be with the others, dancing and laughing in the yard.

"You wanna get a drink and dance?" I offer. Her eyebrows raise in surprise. The corner of my lips tips up, not a full smile.

"Really?" A huge grin spreads across her face as I nod. I understand what she means about looking exquisite with a smile. She's radiant. She smiles a lot, certainly more than I do. That doesn't diminish the beauty of each one, though. Every smile is perfect and beaming. She's out of my lap and grabbing my hand before I can respond.

She tugs me to the bar and pours us each a shot. She clinks our glasses together, tosses hers back, then tugs me to the dance area. Everyone is out there: Sapph, Rio, Lucy, Tyler, and Lacey. Jo even managed to drag Catherine out. Catherine isn't stiff, but she isn't comfortable either.

Vic steps in front of me and starts dancing. I've never danced before; I've always watched. My movements are awkward and off-beat. I keep my hand on Vic's waist and try to match her movements. I look more uncomfortable than Catherine, but I'm trying. Vic doesn't seem to mind.

We dance through several songs. Vic stays with me the whole time. I assumed she would move off with Sapph or Rio, but she didn't. I blame my uneven breathing on the dancing. It's not a hitch in my breath over the thought of my girl.

"Okay," Vic announces with her hands raised in the air. "We're going inside." Some of our friends boo, but Vic just tugs me inside to my room. I follow her. I would follow her to the ends of the earth. This woman is everything to me. I wish I could be everything for her.

I plop down on the bed and place my knees on my elbows in my room. Vic removes her shoes then steps in front of me. Her hand rubs my shoulder, and I press my head into her stomach. Her touch is so comforting. I love having her hands on me.

"Tell me what you are thinking."

"I don't know how to love you," I say. The words are out of my mouth before I can stop them. I didn't want to admit that to Vic. I freeze, barely breathing. Her fingers trace my jaw and lift my face to hers. A soft, knowing smile is on her face.

"You love me?"

I open my mouth to respond but don't know what to say. I do love her. I didn't plan on telling her that, not now. I want her to make decisions based on her own desires. Vic hasn't said she's staying here. She won't return to Pennsylvania, but she could go somewhere else for a better life. She could return to her job, be safe, and settle down. I could even send her money with her knowledge, not that she'll need it with the divorce. I don't want her choices clouded with my feelings.

She steps closer, forcing me to sit up. She moves her leg as if to straddle me, but I don't want her on top right now. I grab her sides and thrust her over my shoulder. She squeals at the sudden movement. As soon as her back hits the bed, I twist and land on top of her. She giggles and cups the side of my face. The sudden change suppresses any thoughts of love or wishes. I can focus on her instead. I bury my face in her neck and grind against her hips. Her giggles change to a moan.

"If you keep that up," she mumbles breathily, "I'm going to come dry-humping you like a teenager." To emphasize her point, her hips roll against mine. I suddenly remember she has been worked up all day and wouldn't let me relieve her. I slip my hands between us, caressing her wet core.

"Is that what you want?" I growl into her neck. She groans loudly and wiggles to get pressure where she wants it.

"Fuck," she drags out the word. "No, I want you inside me," she pants. I don't need to be told twice. I lean back and rip my shirt over my head. She does the same thing and quickly clambers out of her shorts. I take my pants off with the same speed. I cover her with my body once we are both naked.

Instead of sliding into her like we both want, I kiss her. I press my lips against hers gently. She pauses before settling into the kiss. She didn't expect that. I haven't kissed her much while we fuck. It's usually just that, fucking. Tonight feels different. I want to give her something else. Her arms wrap around my shoulders, and she sighs into the kiss. She doesn't move beneath me, content to just kiss. Our lips move together, separate, then our tongues brush.

This moment is soft and sweet. I've never experienced anything like it. Vic is something else entirely. She drags her fingers over my scalp, and I moan. The sensation of her nails against my head is overwhelming. It feels so damn good. Vic rolls her hips into mine.

"Please fuck me," she begs. I shift just enough to slip my hand between us. I guide my tip to her entrance and notch it inside. Her face settles briefly, then scrunches in confusion. I'm not fucking her like usual. I won't pound into her, not this time. This isn't just about getting off.

"Aleks," she croons, and I slide inside her. Once I reach the hilt, she moans, "Gods, you're so big." I didn't need a boost to my ego, but I'll take it. I slide back out and commend myself on my control. I could've already busted inside her for how good she feels. I'm going to take this slowly, or at least slower. I glide in and out of her wet cunt smoothly. She chants my name and drags her fingers over my back. The sensation of being touched, being in this position where she's close enough to touch, is uncanny.

Her pussy clenches around me. It's a good thing she's close to orgasm because that tightening could be my undoing. She mutters my name, occasionally throwing in a 'please.' I don't change anything. I keep my steady pace. Her legs wrap around my waist, and she digs her heels into my ass. She is angled differently now. It feels so deep. I sink inside, and she grinds against my pelvis. I lean over her small torso to hold her tightly against my chest. Her orgasm crashes through her as she continues grinding against me, drawing out her pleasure. Her tightening cunt pushes me off the edge. Hot semen spurts deep inside her. I groan into her neck and breathe heavily.

Vic wraps her arms around my shoulders to keep me close. I don't pull back. I prop my elbows along her sides to keep my weight off her, but my face stays buried in her neck. Our breathing slowly settles. She runs her fingers through my hair and over my back.

"I love you, too," she whispers against my ear. I lean back to look at her. She meets my gaze with a smirk. "As much as I enjoy making love to you," she sings out 'making love' in a swoony voice, "you still have to fuck me against a wall. You're not getting out of that."

This fucking woman.

Chapter Nineteen

VIC

Five days ago, I told Aleks I love him, and he made love to me. So cheesy.

Four days ago, the club voted to work with Catherine and the mafia.

Three days ago, the ice cream social was on the front page of a prominent local newspaper.

Two days ago, Tyler officially made Lacey his old lady, which seems fast, but I don't exactly have room to talk.

Yesterday, the club set an introductory meeting with the mafia.

Today, Aleks is at the meeting, and Sapph currently has me tied spread eagle on her bed. With Aleks busy, now is the perfect time to get in a kinky session. Sapph is not holding back today. She is standing at her dresser, digging through all her supplies. I wasn't surprised to learn she has straps mounted to the bed. Of course, she would. I give a little tug of my wrist to see how much wiggle room I have. It's not much.

Sapph glances over her shoulder at me with a menacing grin. My core tingles at that look. She loosely braided her hair down her back. I don't know what it is about her and Aleks braiding their hair that does it for me, but holy hell. I love the way their braids fall down their back. It usually means something fun and exciting is about to happen.

Sapph finally turns to me with a small bin and a spool of thread. She places the items on the nightstand. The bin has wooden clothespins inside. My whole body tingles with excitement. We did spanking last time. Sapph was not kidding about showing me all kinds of things.

"I'm going easy on you today, but I won't always." Oh, the promise sends shivers through my body. She grabs a clothespin and the thread. She tells me what she is planning as she loops the thread through the spring on the pin. "These clothes pins are a bit looser than normal. My beginner pins," she winks and clacks the pin several times. "They sting then go kind of dull. I'll leave them on for a few minutes, then rip them off." She shows me by tugging on the thread and pulling the pin from her hand.

My breathing hitches at the thought. Sapph licks two of her fingers and reaches between my legs. The action is so fucking erotic. I bite my lip, lift my head, and watch her hand slide between my thighs. She circles around my clit, and I fight back a groan. I'm nearly panting by the time she spreads me open. Instead of plunging inside me, she grabs a clothespin with her other hand. Confusion spreads through me. I thought the pins would go on my nipples or arms. Why is she holding it near my cunt?

An answer comes to my silent question when she clamps it on my labia. I gasp at the feeling. It's unlike anything I have ever experienced. It tingles as moisture builds around it. Sapph threads another pin and places it on my other labia. She drags her finger over my opening between the pins then circles my clit. My breathing is erratic, but a wide grin spreads over my face.

Sapph glances at me and smiles. She grabs another clip, threads it then places it on the soft skin near my belly button. My pussy is clenching now. The sting from the new pin, the constant ache of the others, and the teasing are all-consuming. I can barely string a complete thought together. Another pin is clamped to the opposite side of my belly button. Her fingers swirl through my opening then over my clit again. I mumble something. Maybe a plea for more. It's unintelligible to my own ears.

Sapph leans close and kisses my cheek. "How are you doing, little bird?" We went over the color safe word system before she tied me down. I can see green in my vision, but my tongue feels heavy.

"Green," I finally muster.

"Good," Sapph croons and swirls my clit again. I thrust my hips at her, wanting more. The movement shifts the pins and sends a fresh wave of pain across my skin. "Just four more," she whispers with another kiss on my cheek. She places two more pins near my ribs with another swirl of my clit. This time, her fingers dip inside me, and the moan is so guttural I sound feral. I have never made a sound like that, and I love it so much.

Fingers twist over my nipples, and I open my eyes to look down at them. Sapph leans in to wrap her lips around one nipple. She flicks her tongue against it in a glorious feeling. I watch her move to the other side and don't see her hand until the pin is clamped on my nipple. I yelp at the unexpected sensation. As the pain hits one nipple, Sapph's tongue is on the other. Pain and pleasure blend in my mind, confusing every one of my senses. It's great. It's painful. I want to come. I want to cry.

The other pin is placed on my other nipple, but I expect it this time. It isn't as intense, but it still hurts so good. I glance down at my body. My hips are rolling up and down; pins sit at various angles over my body; my chest rises and falls with uneven breaths. It's so damn hot. Sapph flicks the tip of one of the pins near my belly button. A sardonic giggle escapes me at the tingling sensation. She asks for a color. It's easier to tell her green this time.

"Gods, little bird," Sapph says from the end of the bed. "You are so fucking beautiful like this. Can I take a picture?" I've never had a picture taken of me in a compromising position. Sure, I've taken a picture of my boobs to send to Wes once or twice. I've thought about doing it for Aleks but wasn't sure how he would react. The way Sapph stares at me makes me want to see what she sees. I tell her to take the picture. She snaps a couple with her phone but puts it down without showing me.

She shuffles around in her drawer for a moment. My body settles into the mix of lust and aches. I like being in this headspace. The arousal clouding my thoughts. The pain rips through the arousal. The perfect blend of the two. When she walks over, she has a smooth vibrator in her hand. She presses it against my clit, and I savor the feeling in every inch of my body. She slips it down and into my core. I groan at the feeling. It's not a massive toy and doesn't fill me, but man, oh man, it feels glorious though.

The toy is thrust in and out of me several times. My orgasm is building. It's going to be a big one; I can feel it. My mind clouds with pleasure. I'm right on the edge, and several things happen rapidly. Sapph pulls the toy out of me, increases the volume, and presses it directly to my clit. She also grabs the string and rips the pins from my body. All eight pins fly away from my skin, and blood rushes back to those spots.

I die. I'm dead. I'm having an out of body experience. This is what happens when you die. You float above your body as you watch your final breaths. My body is tight, convulsing with the most intense orgasm ever. My arms and legs are pulling against the straps. It's a good thing they are there. Or my body would be on the ceiling too. Sapph's grin is both intense and maniacal. I've never seen that look on her face.

I'm screaming. Literally screaming. I barely yell with orgasms. This isn't an orgasm. No, this is my death and journey into heaven. If heaven is shrouded in pleasure and sex. The toy stops vibrating against my clit but remains in place. The screaming stops, and I settle back on the bed. My body convulses randomly with the aftershocks of the deadly orgasm. Sapph's hand caresses my body, but I can't see anything.

Some quiet part in the back of my brain registers the straps being removed. I'm still floating in the clouds. A soft cloth slides over my body. It's cool against my burning skin. Lips press against each spot the pins were, except for my labia.

That's a good thing because my entire core is over-sensitive. I'm rolled onto my side, and a heavy blanket drapes over my shoulders. Sapph moves around the room for a few minutes, but my eyes remain shut. I'm soaking up the last bit of pleasure as sleep tries to claim my body.

"You are so perfect, little bird," Sapph whispers as she kisses my forehead. She climbs in bed with me and pulls me against her chest. Her hand rubs soothingly over my back as I finally succumb to the exhaustion.

Sapph woke me after a few hours. She helped me shower, and we chatted about the morning. Tiny red dots cover my body from the pins, but they don't hurt. They'll fade soon. After the shower, we dressed in comfy clothes. I pulled on a pair of joggers and a loose v-neck shirt. We aren't going anywhere for the rest of the day. I may even skip out on the backyard and just chill inside and watch a movie. I wonder if I could convince Aleks to let us all hang out in his room. Mine and Sapph's rooms aren't big enough for more than two or three people. I'd love to have Sapph, Rio, Tyler, and even Lacey join us. She's grown on me lately.

I slide into the booth, and Aleks sits next to me. He takes my hand and laces our fingers together. I grin up at him, unbelievably happy with my life right now. As much as I miss working in the ER, I don't miss long shifts. Being here with Tyler and Aleks has been better than I ever thought it would be. I wish I had visited sooner. I wasted so much time in Pennsylvania. I was unhappy in my marriage, with my family. The only good thing was my job.

The reminder of my marriage has me cringing internally. It's something I need to deal with soon. I've been gone for over three months. I'm honestly a little surprised Wes hasn't turned up yet. Even my mother hasn't called Tyler. I suppose whatever lie Wes has fed them about my whereabouts is enough to appease my parents. If he filed a missing persons report, I would have been found.

I'm not exactly hidden. I haven't used any of my credit cards or online accounts. I made new social media accounts for the sole purpose of doom-scrolling when Aleks gave me the phone. It was a pain in the ass to rework the algorithms to my liking, but it wasn't like I had much else going on. Aleks and Harpo assured me the little trip to the police station wouldn't show up. But none of that means I can't be found.

Chatter is light as we sit at the table. Tyler talks about their meeting with the mafia this morning. Apparently, it went well. The men they will be working with don't seem terrible as far as men in organized crime go. They are hopeful that this venture will be good for the club. Getting everything in place will still take a few weeks, but it's a start.

The door to the restaurant opens, and two men walk in together. I don't typically pay attention to people walking in. It's not like I know anyone, and I wouldn't recognize a threat. Something draws my attention to the door. This is a threat I recognize—one that most people here won't recognize. My body tenses as I try to convince myself I'm seeing things. This can't be real.

Wesley is walking toward the bar where Lucy is cleaning.

I can't breathe. There isn't enough air in here. He's here. This is real. The other man is his best friend. His campaign manager. I'd recognize Silas anywhere. He was the only person other than Wes to visit me in the hospital when I was in the ICU. Wes prevented my parents from visiting me. Silas came in to ensure I wouldn't say anything about what led me to the ICU. Wes is violent in his own ways, but Silas is downright terrifying. He does martial arts training in his free time and looks like a menacing warrior.

Wes is dressed in khakis and a polo shirt. He looks so out of place in this crowd. The restaurant is open, and plenty of nonclub members occupy the space. Most of them are not upper class. Wes has his blonde hair perfectly styled, and I feel underdressed. I'm not even with Wes, but the harassment I received for the past decade is hard to overcome.

"Vic," Sapph's voice draws me back to the table. She, Aleks, and Tyler are staring at me with concern. I must have spaced out for a minute. The way she said my name didn't sound like the first time. Aleks squeezes my hand, and I have to tell them. I try to swallow, but my mouth is so dry.

"It's him," I whisper.

Sapph and Tyler look confused. Aleks stares at me for a second, then turns to the bar where I was just staring. Alarm bells go off in my mind. I don't want him to look. I don't want to face this reality. Terror floods my body once again.

Wes was unpredictable at the best of times. Since I've been gone for three months, I have no idea how he will react. Becoming a widower will gain him the sympathy vote, but it's not an election year for him. He really wanted kids, but would he keep me around for that? He could find someone willing. Is it just about his control over me? Is that why he keeps me around?

Aleks rises from the table at the same time Tyler recognizes Wes. Tyler cusses and stands up. Aleks walks calmly toward the bar, like a true predator, trying to lure their prey into a false calm. Tyler stalks, looking every bit the predator with a target. Shit shit shit. I clamber out of the booth, and Sapph grabs my arm. I quickly explain that Wes is here. She doesn't know everything about him, but she knows enough.

My men finally stop in front of Wes. Lucy tells him these are the owners, and she steps away. Not out of earshot, but enough to not be directly involved. Wes clearly doesn't recognize Tyler. He wouldn't. I didn't have any current pictures of Tyler. The only pictures I had were of him as a teenager. I stay behind Aleks, not ready to be seen yet.

"I am looking for someone," Wes says. He holds up the newspaper with the ice cream social on the front page. The largest picture is of Tyler, Lacey, Shirley, and me. We are standing with some kids near one of the bikes. I didn't realize the photographer was working for the paper. I would have asked to not be in the photo. I don't know how Wes got a copy of a San Antonio newspaper, but I'm not surprised either. He has a lot of connections. I've probably met some of the state senators. They don't work together, but many form relationships, hoping to climb the ladder.

Wes points to my image on the page and explains. "My wife went missing three months ago. I have been searching everywhere for her. I believe she may be local. She has a brother in the area. This is her, and this is your bar, no?" He looks at Tyler, realizing he is the man from the photo. "Do you know where my Victoria is?"

Wes sounds desperate and sincere, but we all know he's not. He's also fucking clueless. The tension radiating off these men is palpable. You could cut it with a butter knife. I glance around quickly. All the members are watching this interaction. They know something is up and await any sign that they should help. I love that they have Aleks and Tyler's backs without question, but this isn't a fight for them.

I release Sapph's hand. I had been squeezing it subconsciously. I square my shoulders. This isn't a battle for the club to face. This is mine to deal with, and it's time. It's time, I tell myself. I've hidden enough. I need to end this. I whisper to Sapph to keep the men back. I don't think they will act in a restaurant full of people, but I can't be certain.

Before anything else can be said, I step between Aleks and Tyler. There is enough room between the three of them that I am just out of arms reach for all of them. An emotion that I can't quite place flashes through Wes's eyes. It's not a good emotion, but it's there and gone before I can pinpoint it. His face becomes a mask of relief; it's clear to everyone that it's fake.

"Oh, baby! There you are," Wes steps toward me with his arms stretched out. I don't want him to touch me. Nobody wants that. I honestly doubt Wes actually wants that. Here we are, though. Wes keeps talking about how he missed me and how worried he was. He pulls me into his arms. I don't fight him, but I don't welcome him either.

He begins peppering my face with kisses. Time slows as I watch him move in for a regular kiss. Fuck. Both Aleks and Sapph are standing behind me, watching another man kiss me. I close my eyes, unable to face any of this.

"Let's take this," Aleks starts, but Wes's lips land on mine. It's a brutal kiss, demanding and unkind. A slight hitch in Aleks's words is the only indication this bothers him. "To my office," he finishes with gritted teeth. Wes doesn't stop. His tongue pushes against my lips. My body is tense, and it's hard to breathe. Disgust and terror fog my mind from any rational thought.

Hands wrap around my ribs, and I'm forced back from Wes. Tyler has his hands on Wes's shoulders as I'm pulled back into Aleks's chest. I can't stop the sigh of relief as my arms wrap around my middle. Silas steps closer to Tyler, who quickly drops his hands. Wes is pissed; he glares at Tyler for a moment. Tyler tells him this is a family restaurant; we should do this in private. Wes collects himself and allows Tyler to lead them into the office. Silas follows, and Sapph walks around Aleks and me. She kisses the side of my head then stomps into the office.

"I can't do this," I mumble out. Aleks spins me around to face him. Instinctively, my hands land on his chest. He cups my face and tips it up to look at him. He's large enough that he could wrap around my entire body and hide me from the world. He kisses my cheek.

"We're going in there. You'll ask for the divorce, and he'll give it. Then you'll be done." A kiss on my other cheek. "You already have the paperwork from Catherine. You can do this." I want to shake my head, but Aleks kisses my lips. It's the complete opposite of Wes's kiss. It's gentle, reassuring, and brief. He pulls back and stares for a moment. His thumb strokes my cheek. "I love you." My eyes go wide at his confession.

I know Aleks loves me. He's all but said it. But he hasn't said it. It's not the best timing, but shit. It is really helpful. I press my forehead to his chest and take a long breath. His leather scent is strong with his cut so close. His presence is grounding. I can do this. I have him, Tyler, and Sapph. I can get through this with them at my back.

I step back, and Aleks follows me into his office. The four people sit awkwardly in the room. Wes is sitting in one chair facing the desk. Tyler took the other chair and positioned it closer to the desk to face Wes. Silas is on one couch with Sapph on the other. Her arms are crossed over her chest, and she glares at Silas. I would typically never bet against Silas, but I wouldn't be surprised if Sapph could take him.

For all his emotions displayed earlier, Wes looks as cool as a cucumber. He could be sitting down for a beer with the guys. Tyler has his elbows on his knees and glares directly at Wes, who is impervious to his gaze. I walk behind Tyler and take a spot by Aleks's chair. Aleks sits at the desk and pulls a file out of his drawer.

He kept the divorce papers Catherine had drawn up for me in his drawer. She gave all of us some sort of paperwork. Aleks got information about his past. Tyler got information about a savings account our parents started when he was young. It's entirely in his name, and they hid it from him. He's been working to access the funds for the sheer pleasure of tormenting our parents. He doesn't need the money, but he is taking it. Sapph received information about her grandparents in India.

No one has said anything, and it's starting to feel awkward. Guess I'll start this meeting.

"I want a divorce."

"No," Wes responds. Aleks tenses beside me while Tyler huffs a laugh and settles back in his chair. I want to ask why. I want to know why he keeps me around, but he won't tell me. He never has. Instead, I step by Aleks and open the file. I pull the top pages out and hold them out for Wes.

"This one gives you everything. The house, bank accounts, all of it. I want nothing but for you to sign it."

"Vic," Tyler says in a warning tone. I don't acknowledge him and keep my focus directed at Wes. I really don't care about any of it. I took what I needed when I left. Everything else is just fluff. I have enough here. This would allow me to settle in here, find a job, get a driver's license, build a life.

"Vic," Wes says as he looks at Tyler. He says the word as if trying it out. He turns back to me. "You go by Vic now? Victoria is too good for you? The life I built for us, for you, is too good? You would rather live here with these people?" He waves his arm around as if to make a point. His disdain for them is obvious. I thrust the papers toward him silently.

"No," Wes says again.

Tyler snatches the papers from my hand. He rips them in half, then again. He throws the quartered papers in the air over Wes. Silas jumps up, but Wes just watches calmly. I hate that he can be so calm, that he thinks he can win this. Well, two can play that game.

"You are coming back to Pennsylvania with me."

"No," I say with the same inflection he used. I open the file again and pull the top papers. "This splits everything 50/50. It's all been appraised. You can buy out my half with the total in the back." I don't know how Catherine came up with this information, but I could kiss her. I wonder if Harpo had anything to do with this. A lawyer's name is on these forms, but I don't know who it is. Catherine doesn't seem the type to make up something like that. She clearly has connections and knows how to use them.

Wes just stares at the papers. I knew he wouldn't give in, but I still hoped. I shouldn't have, but I couldn't help it.

"You know, you haven't introduced me to your friends. I assume you're sleeping with one of these men," Wes looks between Aleks and Tyler. I suppress a sigh and wave my hand around the room.

"Wes, this is Mor, Clint, and back there is Sapph. The guy on the couch," I say to my people, "is Silas. He's Wes's bff and bodyguard." Silas huffs but doesn't argue. He may not officially be a bodyguard, but that is his role today.

"Where's Tyler? I thought you'd run straight to him." I don't respond and shake the papers to get him to take them. When he doesn't I pass them to Tyler, who proceeds to rip them again. I'm glad Aleks, Sapph, and Tyler are giving me space to do this without leaving me alone with him.

Aleks's fingers brush my leg, then move to the desk. He slides the last set of divorce papers aside. Catherine included a few photos of Wes fucking other women. There are images of him with four different women of various ages; the youngest was seventeen. It's enough for a conviction if we could get her on board, but I don't want it to get to that. If she wants to press charges, she can. I just want a divorce.

Aleks slides the last photo aside to reveal a few more I haven't seen. I glance at him, recognizing the foyer of Wes's house. I look at Wes briefly, then shuffle the images to get a better look. The first image is Wes storming up the stairs while I stand in the bedroom doorway. It's not really meaningful until I check the date stamp. It's the day I landed in the ICU. The following image shows Wes standing before me on the landing, clearly angry and yelling. The last photo shows his hands on me.

"I have all of the footage," Aleks explains quietly. As if today hasn't been a total mindfuck, it just keeps adding on. Aleks has actual footage of what Wes did to me. Wes had the cameras installed for security purposes; he used them to spy on me. Apparently, Aleks also used them to spy on me.

I need to sit down. My legs feel weak. I try to take deep breaths; fear trying to take over my mind. I look at Sapph; she's still laser-focused on Silas. Tyler is watching me but glances at Wes intermittently. Aleks is staring at me. Resolve sets in as I take a deep breath. I've been through so much. I survived the ICU, survived Wes. I traveled halfway across the country with only cash to pay. I took out those two men on the bikes. I even handled Aleks's demons and only got picked up by the cops once. Okay, that last one may not prove how awesome I am, but it still stands.

"I am taking everything." I hold the divorce papers up for Wes to see. I don't offer them to him. Instead, I place them back on the desk and lift the photo of the first woman. Wes doesn't react. I put it on top of the desk and go through the rest of the images. He watches with indifferent amusement until I get to the last one.

"Did you know she's only 17?" Wes's eyes go wide, but I continue. "I have her driver's license, and this photo is time-stamped." I point to the corner where it is. "I can get the original footage that isn't tampered with to prove it." His eyes show concern, but his body is still relaxed. I tap the last images Aleks added, considering my options.

"I think," I start, glancing at Aleks and Tyler, "I should take you to meet Tyler." Tyler's eyes crinkle in confusion. It's not like we had plans with code names or anything. That would have been pretty cool. 'Meet Tyler' could have been code for beating him. 'Meet Aleks' would definitely be his death. Alas, we did not make cool code names.

I lean down and whisper to Aleks to get back up, then round the desk with the file in tow. I don't doubt that Aleks, Tyler, and Sapph could handle the two men, but it would be a fight. If Wes and Silas are outnumbered by a lot, things might go a bit smoother on my side. I tell Wes and Silas to follow me. I lead them down the stairs to the basement, where only two rooms are located.

"Tyler doesn't like to be bothered," I explain, leading them into the sound-proofed room across from the gym.

Chapter Twenty

ALEKS

I don't know what Vic plans, but I'll follow her anywhere. I send a text to Harpo and ask him to round up a few men. Vic walks to the door of our hidden room in the basement. We haven't had anyone there in a couple of months. The last guy was the one who stabbed me. The room has been empty since.

Vic swipes her card on the door, and it unlocks. Suddenly, I remember I was suppose to tell Harpo to remove that access from her card. When she first arrived, I told him to give her my access. I meant just to my room, but he took it as the rooms I have access to, which is all of them. I realized that after she fucked me in the gym, but I forgot about it. I'm not upset that I forgot about it right now. Watching her lead them down here is fantastic.

The room looks like a small closet with shelves holding cleaning supplies. Brooms, mops, and buckets are in the corner, and racks of towels and spray bottles are on the opposite shelves. The last time she was in here, the hidden doors were open. We don't typically leave them open; we keep them shut to keep the room a secret. I step in front of her, unlatch the door, and push it back.

"Tyler likes his privacy," Vic calmly explains to Wes.

She pushes the walls back and leads us into the dark room. Harpo, Rio, and a couple of other men file in behind us. I flip the lights on and expose the white room. Wes, Silas, and Vic stand in the middle. The rest of us form a semicircle in front of the door. The large room is empty in the center, but chairs line the walls. A table in the back corner holds several weapons, and a shelf above it contains several chemicals. We're not unfamiliar with torture here.

The door closes with a soft thunk. Wes and Silas look at it and realize how many people are here now.

"What is this, Victoria?" Wes demands.

Vic nods at Tyler and Sapph, who are standing closest to Silas. They grab him and tug him backward. He's caught off guard and is easily restrained. Rio walks over with straps, and they strap him to a chair. Wes silently watches the whole thing unfold. Vic shuffles some papers rather loudly. There isn't much noise in the room. A few grunts from Silas, but the documents shouldn't sound so loud. Vic is rustling more than she needs to. She pulls out one of the photos I made for her.

I didn't have these before Catherine gave her the file. I didn't know they existed. I had access to her security system since they installed it, but I didn't use it frequently. Occasionally, I would check in just to see her, mostly when she hadn't called Tyler in a while. When she landed in the ICU, Cathy told Tyler she had an accident, and we assumed it was a car wreck.

When Vic mentioned the abuse, I had Harpo dig these up. I didn't realize how much was recorded from the event. Wes tried to delete them and did from his local drive. He didn't delete them from the cloud storage, though. Vic finally pulls out the first photo, the innocent one.

"Check the time stamp. Ring any bells?" Wes looks but doesn't react. Vic tosses it carelessly to the floor. Sapph picks it up and shows Tyler. He hasn't pieced it together yet.

"This one?" She holds up the image of Wes stalking up the stairs while she stands in a doorway. Wes still doesn't show any signs of recognition. Instead of throwing it on the floor, she hands it to Sapph. Tyler checks the date and glances at me with a questioning look. I give a single nod, and his face turns red with anger.

Vic glances around at all the men in the room. Her fingers drum on the file as she looks back to Wes.

"You have a choice now," she states calmly. It's more than I would have given him. "You can sign these papers giving me everything. I won't release the photos I have. We," she motions around the room, "will come to deal with the estate. Then you and I will be done." Wes looks down at the papers and then back to Vic. He doesn't know what she holds in her hand. However, I'm not sure Wes would accept her offer even if he did know. He doesn't seem like the type to back down.

"And if I don't?" Wes's voice hints at anger, but his body doesn't show it. He is still relaxed.

"Then, I'll take out this last photo and pass it around," she waves her hand to my men. I'm glad she trusts them to do what needs to be done and to have her back. They do. We all have her back. She's one of us whether she knows it or not. "And I'll take a seat in," she points to a chair off to the side, "that chair." She offers a menacing smile and waits. It only takes a moment for Wes to adjust his posture, readying for a fight.

Vic nods, pulls the photo out of the file, and hands it to Harpo, who stands beside me. I don't need to see it. I know what it is. It clearly shows Wes shoving Vic down the stairs. Even without the sequence of photos, there's no mistaking what is happening in this one. Harpo passes it without looking; he printed it for me. He flexes his fingers and rolls his neck, preparing for a fight. To his credit, Wes looks alarmed now.

Each of the men looks at the photo and recognition dawns. They pass it and shake out their muscles. As the photo reaches Tyler and Sapph, Vic takes the seat she pointed to earlier. She crosses her legs and watches with intrigued boredom. She could be watching an episode of some talk show.

"Oh, fuck no," Sapph mutters as she charges at Wes. The crunch of her fist connecting with his nose is all it takes to break the hold everyone had. All at once, Tyler, Harpo, and Rio are on Wes. The other two men stay back by Silas. He winds up with a black eye and several gut shots, but he doesn't break free of his restraints.

"Don't kill him, please," Vic croons. She glances to where I am standing, watching this all unfold. I move to sit beside her and wrap my arm around her. "You don't want to get a hit in?" She looks up at me.

"Maybe later," I kiss her forehead, and she settles in to watch the show. I've been so concerned she didn't belong here. But here she is, watching a man receive a well-deserved beating. We just need some popcorn and could be a regular couple at the theater.

After a few minutes, Vic rises and calls for them to stop. The four of them step back from Wes. His face is covered in blood, and he is breathing heavily. To his credit, he is still standing. Harpo grabs a chair and pulls him down.

"Who has a pen?" Vic asks and looks at everyone in the room. Tyler pulls one from his cut. "Thank you, Tyler. Oh, by the way," she says to Wes, "this is my brother." Wes glances at Tyler but drops his head. "Okay, now you need to sign." Vic holds the paper in front of him but pulls it back. "Oh, this won't do." She hands the file and pen to me, then walks to the corner where all the liquids are.

"Yes, this is what I need," she says, grabs a bottle and a couple of rags, and walks back. "I don't want you to get any blood on the papers. That would be concerning. Lean your head back and close your eyes. This is just water." It is absolutely not water. The bottles are labeled well, and we have store-bought bottled water. Water is not in the container like she has.

Vic opens the bottle and pours it over his face. Wes's screams fill the room at the same time as the scent of rubbing alcohol.

"You bitch!" Wes screams.

"Yes, yes. You poor thing," Vic says as she wipes his face off. He grunts and twists to get away from her, but she continues her pursuit to clean him up. It's honestly a little terrifying. I've seen Sapph do some violent shit, but she always has a dangerous edge to her. Maybe I'm deluded in thinking Vic doesn't have a violent side; in thinking she is innocent. Glancing at the other men shows they are also shocked at her behavior. Rio looks outright terrified of her right now. Tyler looks impressed.

Vic cleans Wes's hands then takes the papers from me. "It ends here, Wes," she tells him, holding the papers out to him again. "Make your choice." He glares at her. One eye is already swelling. Blood is oozing down his face from multiple cuts. He finally snatches the papers from her and signs his name in several spots. Vic watches to ensure he is using his signature. Rio steps up and pulls something out of his pocket. He tells us he's a notary and notarizes the papers. Sapph and I laugh at the thoroughness of this situation.

Once the papers are signed, Vic tucks them under her arm and looks at me. Now, we do what we do best.

"Take their phones and valuables. Rough up their clothes. You know the routine," I say. My men jump into action. Sapph tugs Vic to the side and keeps her arm around her shoulders. Vic stares at the papers with disbelief. It's finally over for her. "Load them up in their car. Take them out and dump them somewhere. Make it look like a carjacking. Give the phones to Harpo."

My men jump into action and drag Wes and Silas out of the basement. Tyler and Sapph go with them to help, Vic and I are alone in the room. She drops the papers on a chair and stands in front of me.

"Now would be a good time for you to fuck me against the wall," she says confidently.

"Fuck, you're beautiful, bird." I grin down at her, utterly impressed with the small woman standing before me. Her hair is pulled back into a ponytail, still damp from an earlier shower. Her low v-neck shirt leaves little to the imagination. That's something I'm getting used to. I don't like the way others look at her, but I get to see it too.

I grab her and lift her up. Her legs wrap around my waist, and her lips crash against mine. She shifts up my body to get higher on me. I turn around to press her against the wall but spin faster than I intend. She slams against the wall. Before I can apologize, she cries out.

"Yes, fuck. Please. More of that." Well, can't argue with that.

I press my hips against her, and she groans into my mouth. She rolls her hips into mine, causing my dick to harden. I'd bet anything she's already wet for me. I cup her ass cheeks the way she likes, and they sway in my hands.

"Too many clothes," she mutters against my lip. I drop her to the floor, and she rips her shirt over her head. Her tits are perfect, not overly large, but her nipples are peaked. I grab my cut to pull it off, but her hands catch my wrist. "Leave it," she mutters. She drops her hands to the button on my jeans. She pushes them down my waist with my boxer briefs. My cock springs free, and Vic licks her lip. Ever since that life-changing blow job, she gave me last week, I've wanted to try that again. She wraps her small hand around my cock and pulls so tightly I see stars. I groan out a curse. She releases me, much to my chagrin, and pushes her pants down. She steps out of them and looks up at me.

"Fuck me against this wall, Mr. Moros," she says.

I lift her up and shove her against the wall again. Her eyes burn with lust. My dick slides to her opening as if it has a mind of its own. It knows where home is and doesn't need to be told how to get there. As I suspected, she is dripping wet. I breathe heavily and shift my hips. My cock traces her opening to gather moisture.

She groans, and I finally thrust deep inside her. She yells and wraps her arms around my neck tightly. I pull out and slam in repeatedly. She mutters praises and pleas. I can't believe this is real. She just had her ex-husband beaten by the club. We're fucking in a room with his blood splattered on the floor. She's a fucking goddess. I doubted whether she belongs here, but I shouldn't have. She is one of us.

The tell-tell tingle at the base of my spine tells me I won't last much longer. I squeeze Vic's ass tightly and readjust my grip on her. I free one hand and squeeze her tit. One of her hands holds my neck while the other grabs my bicep. Her nails sink into the back of my arm, and I curse.

"I'm going to come," I tell her.

"Yes, come inside me," she cries. "Fill me up so I am dripping with your cum for the rest of the night." I've never been one for dirty talk, but the image she paints pushes me over the edge. I bust inside her with shaky jerks. Her hand slide between us, and she rubs her clit until she clenches around me. The delay between my orgasm and hers is perfectly timed to drag mine out even further.

I hold her in my arms as our breathing settles. Her forehead rests against my chest. Even holding her in my arms, her torso isn't long enough to hit my shoulders while I fuck her. She's so tiny compared to me. A soft chuckle comes from her as the door to the room clicks open.

"Hey, Pres, just wanted to...shit," Harpo's voice freezes. Vic leans sideways to peek around my body.

"You know, Harpo, if you want to join, you can just ask. You don't have to keep hinting." Her smile is downright devious.

"I'm not...that's not...I..." Harpo stutters. Vic slides down from my arms. I tug my pants up, realizing Harpo has a full view of my ass. He did see my penis the last time we were in the basement. This man really has some spider sense for Vic and I fucking. Vic grabs her clothes casually and tugs them on, as if another man isn't in the room with us. Once her shirt is on, Harpo speaks.

"Um, they left with Wes and Silas. Tyler and Sapph followed to bring our guys back."

"Good," I say.

"I'm not feeling up for another round," Vic says to Harpo, "but if you wanna check in later tonight, I may be up for it."

"Vic," I warn, unimpressed with her comment. Harpo is as red as I have ever seen him. He mumbles an apology, and Vic tells him she's just teasing. I hope she is. I am okay with what she does with Sapph, but I'm not ready to share her with more people. If that's what she wants, I'll accept it, just not yet.

Vic and I clean up the room. It's a quick process since it wasn't that dirty. Harpo left to deal with the men's phones and get the divorce papers to Catherine. We head back to the bar for a few drinks, and Vic tells me she just wants to chill and watch movies for the rest of the night. It sounds like an excellent plan to me.

In the past couple of weeks since Wes's visit, Vic has been getting her life back. She is working with Catherine's lawyers to get the divorce finalized. Since Wes already signed the papers that Rio notarized, there hasn't been much to do. Instead of going to Pennsylvania, Vic decided to offer Wes a buy-out option. He can pay her a lump sum for everything and be done with it. He has tried to argue the value, but Catherine's paperwork is solid. I didn't ask how involved Harpo was with it.

Harpo has helped Vic get copies of her important papers. She left them all behind to seem less conspicuous. Traveling without any kind of identification was a risk, but she made it all the way here. Today, I am taking her to get her new driver's license.

Vic walks into the garage wearing a loose button-down top and tight black jeans. Her hair is down in the loose waves she's fond of. She spent at least an hour getting ready. I'm not surprised to see her incredulous look when she spots me by the bike. I don't take the other vehicles we have. She stops in front of me and crosses her arms.

"I'm not getting on there." I just stare at her. "I don't want to look wind-blown and rumpled on my license, Aleks." I love the way she says my name. I have no intention of getting in the SUV. She still can't drive and hasn't gotten her debit card in the mail. I gave her mine, but I doubt she'll use it. She pops one hip out to the side and puts her hands on her hips.

"Aleks," she whines. I hold out the partial helmet for her. I did think of that. This one will do less damage to her hair, I think. I don't care what my hair looks like after a ride. I've never actually looked. She snatches the helmet from my hand. "Fine, but you owe me."

"I figured as much," I reply as I help her secure the helmet. I kiss the tip of her nose as she glares at me. I can't stop the smirk from spreading. She's so damn adorable. I climb on my bike, and Vic doesn't hesitate. She grabs my shoulders and slides on behind me. I sigh a breath of relief over how different things are now than when she arrived. Her hands slide over my hips as I leave the garage.

When she first got here, she was so hesitant and respectful, which secured my feelings for her. I knew she would be like that, but having her kindness directed at me was a game-changer. It didn't take long for me to want more. I always want more from her. I want everything she will give me. I doubt whether I can give her everything she wants. I hope Sapph fills any voids I leave behind.

I stop that line of thought. I've spent enough time wallowing recently, and Vic has called me out repeatedly for it. I'm perfectly content wallowing; it's my base emotion at this point. Vic asked me specifically to take her out today. She wants to spend time away from the club and everyone else. I don't need to wallow while we're out.

I wait with her at the DMV. She tells me I don't need to wait and could ride my bike around. I'd rather be with her, though. I'll get time to ride later. It's nice to sit beside her and do domestic bullshit. I can hold her hand while she chatters on about...something. I should probably listen to a bit of it. Just as I tune in, her number is called.

After the DMV, where she used my address but I don't focus on that, we hop on the bike. She doesn't ask where we are going. When I stop in front of the little hipster coffee shop with outdoor seating, she squeals and nearly falls off my bike from excitement. In line to order, her shoulders shimmy as she studies the menu.

She orders some sugary drink, and I just ask for a water. She teases me for being basic, but coffee isn't my drink. I guide her outside after our order comes up. She spots an empty swing with an umbrella and makes a beeline for it. I follow her, surprised it's empty. Vic tries to push the swing, but my long legs stop it from moving much. She huffs at my chuckle, and I push the swing. I was going to, but watching her attempt was fun.

Vic rests her head against my shoulder and sips her drink. After a moment, she fans herself. "When does it get cold around here?"

"It doesn't," I tell her. It may feel cold to locals, but it's nothing like Pennsylvania.

"Ugh," she groans, "does it ever cool off?"

"Around Christmas."

She rolls her head back then ticks off her fingers. "That's more than three months away." Thinking of how long she has been here catches me off guard. The whole summer has gone by. It'll be fall soon, or what passes for fall in San Antonio.

We sit in silence for several minutes. I ponder the past few months Vic has been in Texas. The swing sways gently. It's comfortable in this spot despite the mid-day heat. We will need to leave soon. She wore jeans for the bike ride and will want shorts or a dress soon.

"Have you ever thought about therapy?" Her question catches me off guard. It came out of nowhere. I'm here thinking about the weather and how long she's been here, and she's thinking about me in therapy. My mind finally stops spinning enough for me to answer.

"Not really," I explain. "I'm involved in too many illegal activities to see anyone who's a mandated reporter."

"It's not like you have to tell them about the illegal activities. You could talk through other stuff or ask for tips to deal with it." I give her a skeptical look.

"Even the stuff I need help with is illegal."

"So, you know you need help." I'll keep that incredulous look on my face for this whole conversation. I'm not entirely sure what prompted this. I know I need help. I've known that since I was in Pennsylvania. It's not like I can walk into a therapist's office and lay everything out. Trying to tiptoe around the illegal activities wouldn't work since so much of my life is illegal.

"I can't stand to be touched. I hate talking to people, and" I raise my hand to her jaw and speak softly, "I fucking choked you. Yes, I need help." She tilts her head into my touch.

"I'm sorry. I was just thinking," Vic pauses, nibbling on her lip. I tug it down and wait for her to finish her sentence. "I just want you to be happy." I kiss her forehead. The answer to that is easy. I may never pass for normal or healthy, but who needs that?

I kiss her forehead and whisper against her skin just for her to hear.

"I am."

CHAPTER TWENTY-ONE

VIC

I DROPPED THE TOPIC of therapy with Aleks. He would benefit from it—hell, the entire club would benefit from it. He has a point about the mandated reporter. I was surprised when he told me he was happy. I feel like I'm dragging him out of depressive episodes a lot for someone who is happy. Maybe that's what makes him happy—that he can be dragged out of a depressive episode. I do see glimpses of joy in him. I just wish he had more.

We're standing near the bar. Sapph, Tyler, and Aleks, along with several other club members, are going to do club shit tonight. I don't keep up with what they are doing, just when they are gone. I enjoy the occasional murder or torture, but I'm not sure about knowing everything. Harpo walks up, but I don't remember anyone mentioning him going tonight.

"Are you going with them, Harpo?" I ask.

"No," he replies, "I'm going to the movies." Oh, I love going to the movies. I haven't been in such a long time.

"Oh, that sounds fun! What are you going to see?" I don't even know what's out now. I have been so out of touch with anything outside of the club.

"They are doing a double feature of Top Gun. I haven't seen the second, but the first is classic Tom Cruise. Hard to beat that. What are you doing?" I was too young to see Top Gun when it was in theaters. It would be cool to see it now. I'll have to check the times and see if I can get someone to take me one day.

"I don't know," I shrug. "I'll probably read for a bit, then masturbate until they get back." Sapph snorts, and Aleks glares at me. I didn't realize they were listening. Harpo is beet red. I probably shouldn't tease him like that, but as often as he has walked in on us, I can't pass it up.

"Goddammit, Vic," Tyler scowls at me. "I don't want to hear about your sex life. It's bad enough you're fucking my best friend."

"I'm dating him, thank you very much," I correct. We all chuckle, and then I turn back to Harpo. "Your night sounds more fun. I hope you enjoy the movie!"

"Do you wanna come with me?" Hell, yes, I do. He looks to Aleks behind me, and I turn in time to see him nod. What the fuck? I don't need permission from Aleks to go to the movies with a friend. I glare between the two.

"I'm taking my bike," Harpo says, but it doesn't clear up much for me. I glance back to Aleks, and then it hits me. Some guys get incensed about their girls riding someone else's bike. I've ridden with several other people since I've been here. Sapph and Tyler have taken me places. That may be different now that I think about it. Still, I can ride on whoever's bike I want.

"Yes, I'd love to go," I finally answer, giving up my fierce female internal dialogue. We say our goodbyes and head to the garage. Riding with Harpo is different than anyone else. He is shorter than Aleks but more muscular. I thought Aleks was ripped, but Harpo is like a bodybuilder. I hold onto him the way I do with Tyler. With Sapph and Aleks, there is always sexual tension. And, of course, I start thinking about sex while holding onto this solid muscle. Maybe I need therapy for my sex-addled mind.

Harpo insists on buying the tickets at the theater, so I insist on buying popcorn and drinks. Harpo clearly got the better end of that deal. Hopefully, my money from Wes will come in soon. I'll need all of it to pay for all this popcorn. I snort at my own joke, then have to explain it to Harpo because I didn't say it out loud. He looks concerned initially, but I assure him it's just a joke about the price. He calms down and laughs with me.

We settle into the middle of the theater. It's relatively empty, and we got here early. I shift in my seat so I'm closer to him.

"So, Harpo," I start, forcing myself not to grab a handful of popcorn while talking. "You're cut says Crates on your name tag, but everyone calls you Harpo. Is Harpo your real name? If so, will you please tell me the story of Crates?" I'm still pissed no one will tell me their own tag name stories.

"No," he starts, and my annoyance rises, but he continues. "Harpocrates is the god of silence, secrets, and confidentiality. Harpo is my cover name. I use Crates," he pronounces it the way I did, like a wooden box instead of the way it is in the Greek name, "as my tag, so it's not directly linked."

"Does anyone in the club know your real name?" I ask curiously. I'm not positive most club members know each other's birth names.

"No," he tells me. "Maybe Mor," he adds.

"Does that bother you?" I change up my nickname frequently. Victoria is just asking for multiple nicknames and personalities. I occasionally like being called Victoria or Tori. Harpo just shrugs.

"Will you tell me your real name?"

Before he can respond, the lights dim, and the opening credits start playing. I sit back and take the popcorn bucket from Harpo, forgetting about his name. I hold it in my lap, eating the buttery goodness by the handful. Harpo grabs a few pieces every now and then. We watch Tom Cruise be his cocky, unapologetic self.

The popcorn is gone by the movie's end, and I need to pee. I didn't want to miss any of the classic 80s movie, even though I own it. It's not the same as seeing it on the big screen.

"Are we staying for the second?" I say to Harpo, scooting to the edge of my seat to make a beeline to the toilet. He checks his phone and asks if I want to.

"Sure, I haven't seen it, but I need to pee." He chuckles and tells me to go. He stays to guard our seats. After the bathroom, I grab another small popcorn and some candy. I don't know what Harpo likes or if he would even eat candy. I return to my seat as the opening credits start for Top Gun: Maverick. I offer candy and popcorn to Harpo. He takes a couple of pieces of candy and then leans close.

"Noah."

"Hmm?" I ask, eyes focused on the jets zooming across the screen.

"My name."

"Oh, nice to meet you, Noah," I bump him with my shoulder and settle in to watch the movie.

When it ends, we walk quietly toward the parking lot, disposing of all our garbage on the way. I check my phone at his bike, but no one has messaged me. Whatever they were doing is still going on. Aleks usually texts me when he is heading back. Sapph starts sending dirty messages when she's free.

"Hey," I say to Harpo as I secure my helmet. "Wanna go get ice cream or something? The rest of them aren't back yet." He hesitates momentarily, so I quickly add, "We don't have to. It was just an idea. We can head back to the club."

"I know this great local place with many flavors and toppings." It's a statement, but he says it as a question. I grin at him and nod. I climb on and wrap my arms around Harpo. In another time, I would have been interested in Harpo. He's a great guy, cute, and has muscles for days. I would definitely have sex with him. Despite realizing I am polyamorous and being with two people, I don't think I could handle another person at this time. Come to think of it, I don't know Harpo's dating status or orientation.

He's embarrassed by sex, or at least by Aleks and me having sex. My mind stays focused on Harpo's sex life as we arrive at the ice cream shop. I wonder if he is good at sex. Maybe he has a small dick because of the muscles. That's a thing, right? No, that's just when they take steroids. Harpo doesn't give small dick energy. Is he a virgin? That could explain his awkwardness, but he's my age. How could he make it to thirty looking like he does without having sex?

We order ice cream and sit at a table near the back. I consider Harpo as we eat our ice cream. He's attractive: clean-shaven, tattooed, and with short dark hair. He looks like a nice gym guy, like someone you could trust to hold your drink in a bar and beat up the person who tries to mess with it.

"You got a girlfriend, Noah?" I ask with a smirk, but quickly add, "Or boyfriend?" He gives a small smile, and I wonder how long it's been since someone has used his name.

"No," he answers simply and eats his ice cream.

"Why not? You're a great guy." His cheeks flush, adding to his adorably innocent look.

"Umm," he starts as I realize that may be too personal. While he's seen me naked on multiple occasions and knows far more about me than nearly anyone else, he may not be as comfortable sharing his personal details.

"You don't have to answer that. I'm just being nosy," I say quickly and try to change the subject. "Do you like sports?" It's weak. I know little about sports and could not talk long about it, especially if we're talking about specific teams. *Oh, yeah, those Pittsburgh Steelers played with a ball so well. They did that thing with the properly shaped ball expertly.* That's all I've got.

"It's okay," he chuckles lightly. "I just haven't talked to anyone about it in a long time. I'm a demisexual bisexual."

"Oh," I say, taking a moment to remember what a demi is. Those are the people who need an emotional connection to feel physical attraction. "Is it hard to date someone while you're in the club?" He nods in response.

"That and I can't exactly let them in my space frequently. They can't stop by unannounced, and I occasionally travel to help a new client."

"Do you want to date?" Now would be the point in my old life where I would start thinking about all the prospects to set him up with. The only openly gay man I know here is Rio, and he already knows him. I can't picture Harpo settling down with one of the whores that hang around.

He opens his mouth to reply when both of our phones buzz. We look down at them and laugh. I open mine to find a group chat started with Aleks, Sapph, Harpo, and me. They are asking where we are and hounding us for not being at the club. Sapph curses Harpo for being the one who tracks us. Aleks just sends a simple "Where are you" without punctuation.

"Guess it's time to go," I laugh and rise. I flip open my camera to selfie mode and crouch beside Harpo. "Hold your ice cream up," I tell him as I position both of us in the frame. His cheeks flush again. If he weren't so cute with flushed cheeks, I would stop giving him a hard time. But taking a selfie with him is hardly embarrassing. I snap a picture of us, adjust a few things, then snap another. Perfect. I send it to the group chat and finish the last couple of bites of my ice cream. Harpo does the same, and we ride back to the club.

I've made a point to spend more time with Harpo. I don't call him Noah when we are with other people, which is always. I don't get alone time with him, not that I need it. He seems like an outsider here. He's a wallflower in the backyard. I make him sit with us and occasionally drag him out for a dance. He'll concede for one or two, then go in for the night. I wonder if he has social anxiety and can't be around other people.

Harpo helped me with the divorce paperwork with Catherine. Wes is still trying to fight it, but I'm not pushing back. The papers are signed. If Wes doesn't pay his portion, it may just turn up during the next election campaign. Maybe it won't. Who knows how things get leaked these days?

I have my driver's license now and am working on securing my nursing license here. I don't want to return to the ER, but I need something to get out of this club frequently. I'll have to stop smoking with everyone, which royally sucks. I suppose it's worth it to get a job. If it's not, I can always do something else. It's not like I have to work now. Aleks has given me access to all his money. Forced it on me is a better phrase for what he did. He gave me one of those phone wallet attachments and put debit cards to his accounts in my name. I told him I would spend all his money, and he dared me. It was a bluff, and he knew it.

We're sitting in the booth now. Aleks and I sit across from Tyler and Lacey like normal. Sapph has a chair pulled up closer to Aleks. He slid closer to me when Sapph settled. His touch affliction has not changed for anyone but me. It's not surprising, but still disappointing. I hoped he would loosen up a bit. Sapph is sitting closer because Harpo pulled a chair up today. He is sitting beside Sapph, close to Tyler.

"We need a bigger table," I tell everyone.

"That's what I've been saying!" Sapph barks out.

"Don't get one on my account," Harpo says. "I won't sit here all the time."

"Boo!" I croon with my hands cupped around my mouth. I like having Harpo around. He completes our little group in my mind. He evens out the sexes, and even numbers are better; no one gets left out. "We just need a round table here instead of the booth. Aleks and Tyler could sit in the back like kings, and the rest of us their lowly peasants." Everyone laughs, even Aleks.

"I'll look into it," he tells me. I beam up at him, and he bends down to kiss me.

"Fine," Tyler exclaims, "but we're setting rules."

"Like what?" I ask.

"No kissing at the table," he says with a playful cheer.

"No, not that!" Lacey scolds. We laugh again as Tyler and Lacey start discussing what rules we should have for the table. Ultimately, nothing is settled.

The restaurant is closed today, and members sit in all the booths. It's a sea of men in leather vests with patches or 'prospect' on the back. Lucy still serves everyone, but she's much more casual about it. Only one cook comes in on these days. I learned from Lucy they get paid extra to come in on days the restaurant is closed. Since they would typically be off, Aleks offers double time, regardless of how many hours they worked that week. There is always a chef in the kitchen.

Explicit music blares through the speakers. It's usually a quieter Top 40 playlist, but not today. I'm not sure who is in charge of the music, but it's not something I care for. It just sounds like a scream. Some days, we go to the backyard after eating, but it's supposed to hit triple digits today. If I want that heat, I'll just climb in the oven. Texas is unnecessarily excessive.

Despite the loud music, the rumble of many motorcycles pulling up to the restaurant is unmistakable. Many of us look around, taking inventory of who is here. Too many members are sitting in this area for it to be our own guys. I don't stop to think about referring to them as 'our own.' Technically, as the president's old lady, I have a right to call them my own, but it feels weird since I have only been here for about four months.

Aleks and Tyler have a silent conversation as the motorcycles cut off outside. The music is lowered substantially. I glance around the room to figure out who was playing it, but there's no way to tell. As I scan, I notice Harpo left our table. I don't know when that happened. The air is tense in the club now.

Aleks gets a text, checks it, and shows it to Tyler. He groans in response and tells someone to open the front doors. They stay locked when the restaurant is closed. Whoever is here must be special to be let in like that. Aleks and Tyler rise from the booth.

"Go to the room," Aleks says to me but turns to the front without waiting for a response. I'm not going to the room. It can't be that much of a threat if they are letting them in the club. The members form a semicircle around Aleks and Tyler. They are about halfway through the restaurant when the doors open.

A large group of men walk in wearing cuts with different patches. I recognize the first two right away. It's the men who attacked us at the restaurant when Aleks and Tyler took Destiny and me out earlier this summer. What were their names? Small Dick and Can't Find a Clit? No, that's not right.

"Lloyd, Walker." Tyler greets. Oh, that's their name. Lloyd and Walker stop inside the restaurant. They are still close to the door but far enough that all their men file in behind them. All the men around Aleks and Tyler have their hands on their weapons. The other club is in a similar posture. A few more of our men fill in the gaps, and I can't see the front anymore. I can still hear everything.

"I hear you got a fancy new deal with the mafia," Can't Find a Clit states. I don't remember which man is which, so I'll use the names I've given them. They're more fitting, anyway.

"It's a wonder you don't wear curlers and a moo-moo with how much you gossip," Tyler responds with snickers from the Steel Warriors. The Long Horn Devils growl and crack their knuckles.

"Selling on the streets is getting more dangerous. We had one guy killed last week and two picked up in the last month," Small Dick tells us like we should be concerned with his men.

"We send our condolences," Tyler says with an utterly somber voice. I'm unsure if he cares or is just that good at this role. Men on both sides grumble, and no one is satisfied with the condolences.

"Look," Small Dick starts, "you got a good thing going with the mafia now. We just want our run back for the cartel, and we'll leave you alone." There's no way that's accurate. I watched all six seasons of Sons of Anarchy. That's not how this works; they'll want more and more until they have it all.

"We also have a good thing going with the cartel. Why would we give that up? You aren't a threat," Tyler explains. It feels like a challenge. Suddenly, I'm nervous and worried I didn't make the right choice by not going to the room. I glance around the restaurant. Harpo is still missing, Lacey took off, and Sapph is standing near Aleks and Tyler. I could sneak behind the guys, but not without drawing attention to myself.

Before I make a decision, a gun is fired. I slide under the table faster than I have moved in a long time. My hands are over my head as more gunshots sound. It's so fucking loud. Tables and chairs are flipped and splintered. Commands are yelled between men on both sides. A couple of bodies hit the floor with grunts and screams as injuries occur. Maybe it's a good thing I'm still down here. They are going to need so much help.

I peek out from my table. Aleks, Tyler, Sapph, and a few others have tables flipped where they were standing. They are using them as cover. I briefly remember someone mentioning that the tables were reinforced. I wonder how long that will hold against gunshots. Bullet holes pepper the walls around the bar. The lovely Edison bulbs are shattered. Glass and wood fragments litter the floor.

Aleks has a bag of guns next to him. I can't hit anyone, but I can help until this ends. I search for a path to Aleks's table. If I stay low enough, I can make it to him to help out. I scan again, spotting men on the other side and where they are shooting. I devise a plan and take a few deep breaths.

This can't last forever, right? It has to end soon. I'll probably make it to Aleks in time to grab a gun and watch the other club run out. I could probably even stay here under the table until that happens. Unfortunately, I don't think it is going to end soon enough.

One of the prospects I don't know takes a bullet right in front of me. He is knocked backward and slides away from me. He groans but pulls himself under one of the tables nearby. I watch the scene unfold with apathy. It's surreal. I don't feel a strong attachment to anything happening at the moment. It's probably just adrenaline, and I'll crash in a couple of hours.

I crawl out from under the table, watching the men firing in my direction. I stay crouched behind tables and make my way toward Aleks. I can't see the bullets, but I can sense them. It's very disorienting. I'm finally about six feet away from Aleks. This is the longest uncovered stretch of my path. I take a few deep breaths and step out. Someone calls my name, and I turn to look. I'm standing, then falling, then everything is black.

CHAPTER TWENTY-TWO

ALEKS

The fucking Long Horn Devils.

I'm so tired of this bullshit. It's been almost a year since they tried to get this run back from us. Nothing happens. It always ends in a fight, but they still return for more. If it wasn't so ridiculous, I would consider ending the entire club at once. I'm confident this will end if we can just take out Lloyd and Walker maybe a couple of the other board members. The new board may want to retaliate.

I aim for Lloyd and Walker. Lloyd is firing back at me, but Walker is aiming at Sapph and Tyler. They can handle their own. I grab another magazine and reload, watching Lloyd for an opening. We keep tactical bags stored under the bar for situations like these. A couple of the men were back there when the firing started and tossed them over.

We don't have shootouts in the restaurant. Since the rest of the club is more secure, this is the most likely place for one. The bags are helpful if we need to get on the road quickly for a situation. Shit is always going down with the cartel. Now, we could be looking at a similar situation with the mafia.

I take a quick scan of my men. I can't hear and am laser-focused on Lloyd and Walker. I try to stay in the moment in case someone needs me, but the noise and yelling are distracting. My men are doing their jobs. A few of them have injuries, but it doesn't look like any are down. It's a good thing Vic is here. She'll be able to help until we get more backup. We have a doctor who works for us. Harpo will have contacted him by now. He'll circle the area until we give him the all-clear.

Vic will be able to help until he gets in. I'll have Harpo grab her from our room when this is over. They can come down together and help with clean up. Harpo watches our security system and calls in backup. He also tracks the police. If they are headed our way, he'll divert them or give us a countdown if he can. Every situation is different. Harpo wanted to fight with us initially, but I wouldn't let him once I saw the value of having him in his room. He's too valuable in other areas to be on the front lines.

A hot, spent shell hits my arm. There is a gap in our line on the side where the shell hit me. I have no idea where it came from. I glance over to find Sapph waving frantically at me. The relief on her face feels exaggerated when I spot her. She uses our signs to signal she'll cover me. I glance at the reinforced table in front of me. It's still solid; I don't need her cover. I scan the Long Horn Devils across from us. My target is still in his position; no one else presents a threat for which I would need to move.

I look back to Sapph, who is very frustrated with me. She finally points to a spot behind me. I have no idea what she is going on about. I glance back to the other club before looking behind me. Then I see what has Sapph so worked up.

About six feet away from me, Vic is lying on the floor. Blood pools around her. I don't know if it's hers. A trail leads away from her body, where one of the men was shot in the leg and moved to cover. But Vic...

She lies flat on her back with her eyes closed. She could be unconscious or dead. I can't tell if she is breathing. I don't know if I'm breathing. She's in the gap of our cover. She could easily be shot. Has she already been hit? Is that why she's lying there?

Another spent shell hits my face this time. I glance back at Sapph as she signs she will cover me. I need to pull Vic behind my table. I watch Sapph stand and fire with a gun in each hand. I grab Vic quickly and carelessly and tug her back to my spot. I know I'm supposed to move her carefully and protect her neck to avoid spinal injuries. But it's Vic.

Sapph clambers over her and kneels by her side. She starts checking on Vic while I sit and watch. I crouch beside her, unable to move. Sapph finally tells me she's alive, just knocked out. She's not shot. Thank fuck.

My fear turns to rage. I nearly lost Vic. I still might. I don't know what's wrong with her. We haven't had a club attack us like this while I've been in charge, and I'll be damned if I let them walk away from this. I twist back and search my tactical bags. There are two flash grenades and two Uzis with extended magazines. I prefer semi-automatic pistols, but this isn't the time for trigger control.

I toss the flash grenades at each end of the Long Horn Devils line. With Uzis in hand and extra mags at my waist, I stand and walk toward the line firing. My mind doesn't register the flashes that burst in the restaurant. Tyler walks on one side of me with an expression equal to mine. He must have seen Vic when I threw the grenades. Rio and Joe are on my other side, advancing on the men in front of us. Bodies of the Long Horn Devils drop like flies until I reach Lloyd and Walker's spot.

Walker is on the ground with a bullet hole in the middle of his forehead. I would be angry, but Lloyd is trying to scramble away. He was shot in the arm and can't hold the gun to protect himself. I step closer and press my boot against the gunshot, pinning him to the ground. He screams, waving his other arm and legs frantically.

This would be when the president says something about protecting his girl or club. Or maybe it is about the other man being weak. Seeing as I'm not one to talk, that isn't something I'll do. Without another word, I point my gun at Lloyd's face and end him. I take a second gut shot just for fun.

A hush falls around the restaurant. I scan the area to take in the damage. A few of my men are down with gunshots. All the men from the other club are dead, save one. Rio steps over and aims his gun at the man's head.

"We need him," I call to Rio. "Someone will need to take these cuts back." Rio holsters his gun and grabs the guy. He zip-ties him to a chair and places him near the front door. He has a perfect view to watch us clean up everything.

"Strip all the cuts off. Lucy," I call out to her. She pops up from behind the bar. "Get a box big enough to hold the cuts. Or multiple if necessary." She rushes off through the kitchen to find boxes. Some of the men are already grabbing cuts. A sickening squelch sounds every time they drop a new body. Fuck, I hate that sound.

I instruct a few members to grab our vans and back them to the dock. There are close to two dozen bodies that need to be dealt with. I own a funeral home with several cremators, but this job is enormous. I'll need cash for that trip. I tell another to start loading bikes on trailers. They don't need to worry about damaging the bikes. The bikes need to be delivered back to the Long Horn Devils Club, and since all the owners are dead, the condition isn't a concern.

People move around the restaurant, completing their tasks. Others begin cleaning and righting tables. It will take a long time to put everything back together, but we don't have any choice. I scan the destruction again as Sapph walks up to me.

"I need to get her to the hospital. She may have a concussion. Doc won't be able to do much for her." Son of a bitch, I almost forgot about her. My mind was in president mode.

"She breathing?" I ask. Obviously, she's fucking breathing. She wouldn't need to go to the hospital if she weren't. Anger and fear burn through me again. Sapph nods, knowing I need the answer to that. "Take the beater. I can't spare an SUV." Sapph turns and rushes to my office for the keys.

We keep several vehicles in the garage for club use: a couple of large work vans, a few SUVs, one truck with an extended cab, and two old worthless cars. They are in good running condition but mostly look like every other car on the road. It's easier to blend in, and we don't worry about cleaning them.

Sapph runs off, and Tyler helps her grab Vic. They leave the restaurant and head for the garage. I stand, frozen, taking in the scene around me. It's surreal. Wood, glass, and spent shells litter the floor. Pools and streaks of blood cover the sealed wood floors. Bodies and men moving the bodies push all the debris around. It's fucking chaos.

Tyler comes back in to help with the cleanup. I'm still standing in the middle of the space, watching everything. Harpo walks up to me; his voice sounds like he's in a bubble at first, but it fades.

"Doc will be here in two minutes. We've moved the worst of our guys to the corner, but several more will need to be looked at." He scans the room before telling me the rest. "A few more bodies are being loaded into the vans, and they'll be ready to go. You sending extra cash with them?" I give a brief nod. "The trailer is being hitched to the truck. I don't know if they can fit all the bikes at once, but they'll head out within the hour."

Without a word, I turn to my office to get the money for the crematorium. I open the safe in my office and pull stacks of cash out. This is going to put a considerable dent in our supply. We have our first run with the mafia next week. That should replenish us, even after everyone's cut. I grab a bag to put the stacks of cash in.

The stacks are in the center of my desk, where Vic likes to sit. Where I've eaten her out. Where she stood when she bravely addressed her ex-husband. Where she stood when she stitched my arm after our last brush with the Long Horn Devils. I hope whoever is left in that club will leave well enough alone. I won't do this again. I need to tell that shithead before we send him back with the cuts. I will end every fucking one of them.

I push Vic from my thoughts. I can't think about her now. There is still work to be done. I get the bag of cash to one of the guys driving a van. The two vans loaded down with bodies take off. Several of my members go with them. They will need a lot of help and time dealing with that mess. With the bodies gone, cleanup has begun. The tables and functioning chairs have been stacked to the side. The damaged furniture is carried out to the dumpsters. I may need an extra pick-up this week. We also need to announce the remodel of the restaurant. Damn, there's so much to do.

The guy from the club whimpers beside me, and I glance down at him. He's terrified and covered in blood. It's hard to say if any is his or not. There's a lot of splatters and drips. I yell at Pitch and Rio to come over. They don't always get along but can complete assignments together. I help them close the boxes with the cuts and grab the guy. The boxes are loaded into the trunk of the last beater. Before I shove the guy into the backseat, I hold him in front of me.

"Tell whoever is in charge now," my voice is deep and menacing, "not to come back here. This stops now. If they want the ashes, have them call Dionysus, and I'll arrange it." I tuck a business card for the restaurant into the pocket of his cut and tap it. He just stares at me with wide eyes. Even if he wanted to respond, we left the duct tape on his mouth.

"Don't piss in the car," I say and shove him in the back seat. Rio and Pitch drive off to deliver the cuts and the last guy. That should be the last we hear from them.

Back inside, my phone rings in my pocket. I'm not sure if I'm more surprised that it's still there or that it is ringing. I answer it, expecting it to be one of my men giving an update on their task.

"They are taking her back for CT scans," Sapph tells me. I take a deep breath. I can't think about Vic. I'll lose my fucking mind, not that it's great to start with. "She's not awake yet; they want to keep her overnight. I told them I'm her girlfriend, so they will update me." Thoughts swirl through my brain, but not a single one is a complete thought. It's all half-formed sentences and images.

"Do you want to come up here?" Sapph's question breaks through the cyclone.

"No," I grunt. "Just text me when she's awake." I hang up before she can respond. I push Vic from my mind and start cleaning with my men.

We work for several hours cleaning glass and blood. Someone comes in with spackle to repair holes in the walls. Décor that was damaged is removed. Overall, it's not as bad as it could have been. It won't be a total remodel. My phone buzzes with a text in my pocket. I don't bother to check it. After a while, Tyler walks up to me.

"I'm going to the hospital. She's awake, and Sapph says they want to release her in the morning."

I nod and wipe sweat from my forehead. A knot loosens in my chest. She's well enough to be released. That's a relief.

"You want to ride with me?" I look at my friend. He's covered in dirt and blood with dark circles under his eyes. He looks worn down. I shake my head.

"I'm gonna finish up here. Let me know when she'll be home. Take a shower before you go." He nods and walks off. I hope Vic considers this to be home. Should she, though? A home shouldn't get you sent to the hospital. At least she isn't in the ICU. Fuck, am I any better than Wes? I didn't throw her down the stairs, but I'm still the reason she is in the hospital. Why was she in the restaurant? I told her to go to the room.

Before that train spirals out of control, I call out to my men to stop for the night. Shower and rest, and we'll work more tomorrow afternoon. I don't want them worn out completely. Most are still running on adrenaline and will crash soon. Many will get drunk or high, and we'll deal with that tomorrow.

I shower in my room, thoughts of Vic filling my head. Her in the shower. She was so beautiful and shocked when I walked in on her masturbating. She rolled with it when I told her to do it again. I'm such a fucking creep, but she didn't stop me. I get out of the shower quickly. I can't stay in here. I get dressed but leave my cut hanging on the hook. I'll need to clean it soon.

I'm going for a ride to clear my head. I don't cross paths with anyone on the way to the garage. I ride through the quiet streets. It's later than I thought. A quick glance at my watch tells me it's early morning; the sun will be up in less than an hour. I take a road out of town and open the throttle. The sound of wind and my tires on the road block everything else out.

I can still see Vic lying on the restaurant floor. She looked like she was sleeping. She was so small. My jaw starts to ache; I've been clenching it all night. The sun rises behind me as I chase the darkness. It's surreal to ride alone. I push faster than I should, seeing how far I can take the bike. My phone buzzes in my pocket, and I slow down. I pull off on the side of the road and climb off my bike. I take a few steps to stretch my legs.

She's being discharged. We'll be home in about an hour.

Tyler's text releases some of my tension. My thoughts are still a cluster fuck. I can't form any complete thought. I'm functioning entirely on autopilot. I check my maps app; I'm about an hour and a half away from the club. Perfect timing. She'll be settled in by the time I get back. I don't know how I'll react when I see her. I've never been in this situation before. I've never cared about anyone the way I care for her.

I don't register any bit of the ride back until I'm backing into my spot in the garage. It's mildly concerning that I road for an hour and a half and don't remember any of it. I take the stairs two at a time and burst into my bedroom. Vic is sitting in the bed. Blankets are pulled up around her waist. Water and a couple of medicine bottles are on the table behind her. She's wearing one of my hoodies. Her skin is pale, making the dark circles more noticeable. Her hair is down, but it's been brushed.

Her eyes meet mine. She doesn't show any emotions as I walk toward her. A whispered voice and feet shuffling let me know other people were in the room, but we're alone now. I sit on the edge of the bed. I can't think of anything to say. I don't know what to do. Can I touch her? Hug her? Do I apologize? Ask what the hell happened?

"Aleks," she whispers.

It breaks something inside me.

Chapter Twenty-Three

VIC

ALEKS COLLAPSES AGAINST MY body. I wrap my arms around his shoulder and hold him as tightly as possible. My body is sore, and my head is still aching. I slipped on something when I turned to see who was calling my name. I hit my head on the floor and ended up with a mild concussion. It would be ridiculous if it didn't hurt so much.

Sapph and Tyler filled me in on what happened. After Aleks went all Tony Montana with his "little friend," he stuck around for cleanup. They didn't mention him again. I know they were talking with him, but I didn't know what, if anything, he was saying to them. I know he's angry or scared, but I'm also worried he's indifferent. I'm afraid this is his breaking point, and I won't be able to help him.

His shoulders shake in my arms. He's crying. I tighten my hold as much as possible and whisper reassurances to him. I'm fine. I'm safe. It's over. He's safe. That's the one that breaks his spell. He sits back to look at me. Tears streak down his exhausted face. He takes me in, scanning up and down my torso. I cup his face and stroke his cheeks with my thumbs. I whisper his name and tug him toward me. He puts up no resistance.

I kiss his lips softly. It takes him a moment, but he settles into the kiss. He pulls away and presses his forehead to mine. He sighs heavily. He brings his hand to the back of my head. I try to suppress the wince, but he can feel that and the bump back there. He jerks back from me. I watch his face for any sign of what he is feeling. Fear shines in his eyes. His eyebrows are knit with worry. The hard line of his mouth shows his anger.

"I was coming to help you," I answer the question he can't seem to form. His whole face shifts to anger.

"I told you to go to the room."

"I know, but I didn't think it was a big deal until it was too late," I watch him. It's not a great excuse. I know that. I should have done what he said and definitely will next time.

"You can't stay here."

"What?" I ask, stunned by his statement, unsure exactly what he means.

"I can't keep you safe," Aleks says through gritted teeth, "if you don't listen to me. If you don't listen, you can't stay here." Is he seriously trying to kick me out? Now? I stare at him, trying to process what he is saying and think of a response. He is scared and hurt. He needs time to calm down and think about this. I'll need to rebuild his trust that I can listen, but I can't do that if he kicks me out.

"I'm not leaving," I say, and he jumps up from the bed.

"I can't do this, Victoria." His use of my full name shocks me. The feeling of being punished flickers through me. I suck in a sharp breath. Aleks is really serious about this. He's pacing around the room, running his hands through his hair. My heart aches to see him like this. Realizing that I am the cause of this nearly cuts me in half.

"Aleks," I say softly. I don't know what to do. We just need to cool down. Give this time, but I don't want time away from him. I want him to hold me, so we know the other is safe. He turns toward the door to leave. I throw the covers back and rush out of bed to his side. I can't let him go. He's stayed away from me for hours. We need to stay together to work through this. His thoughts are too wild to be left alone.

"Please don't leave," I beg, but the door is already opened, and he is storming out.

Aleks silently storms down the hallway. His back is to me, but I know there's a scowl on his face. My heart is breaking into a million pieces. I can feel each little shatter fall to the floor. Blood rushes through my head from standing up so fast. Everything hurts, inside and out. I may be dying this time and not from pleasure. How did things turn to shit this fast? Just twenty-four hours ago, things were great. We were happy together, and everything was right. That's the problem, isn't it? Things were good.

A stunned Harpo stands in the hallway with flowers in his hand. He glances at Aleks and then at me. He looks me up and down and then holds the flowers out to me.

"A few of us got you flowers."

I take the small glass jar from him and thank him. I turn to carry them to the nightstand, but my legs wobble. Harpo has an arm around me in an instant. My eyes flutter with the pain and weakness.

"Sorry," I mutter. "Rose too quickly," I say and wave toward the bed. "I can walk now," I tell him. His grip loosens, but I waver again. Without asking, Harpo scoops me into his arms. I hold the flowers protectively in my arms as he walks to the side of the bed. I lower the flowers to the nightstand and wait for Harpo to sit me down. He is holding me the wrong way to lay me in the bed. My feet will go on the pillow this way. He seems to realize that.

Harpo sits on the bed with me in his lap. I would wiggle away, but I'm so tired. He holds me against his chest for a moment. It's warm but firm. Aleks has more give than Harpo does. Harpo is comforting, but it's not what I want right now. I want Aleks back. My thoughts swirl at his harsh reaction. Has he been thinking about making me leave this whole time? Harpo slides me into the bed. He pulls the covers around my shoulders and asks what I need.

"I want to sleep. Will you wake me in an hour?" I ask. My sleep schedule is already ridiculous. I'd rather not make it worse. I'll need to eat soon too. Harpo turns off the light and tries to slide off the bed. "Will you stay?" His presence is comforting, even if it's not what I want. "I have a Kindle in the drawer. You can read if you want." The light from a phone hurts my head, but the Kindle shouldn't bother me. Harpo keeps his arm on my back, gently rubbing until I fall asleep.

The door opens, and bright light rushes into the dark space. I wince at the sudden intrusion.

"Get the fuck back in there and make it right," Sapph swears at someone. Someone is shoved into the room, and the door is slammed shut. The night on the light stand is flicked on. The sudden lights and sounds make my head throb. I groan as Harpo jumps out of the bed.

"She wanted to sleep. I was just keeping her company." Nothing else is said as Harpo leaves the room quickly. So, Aleks must be in here. Anyone else would've said something. I keep my eyes shut to ward off the light and pain.

Shoes thud on the floor. Clothes rustle and then drop. The light is turned off, and I sigh a breath of relief. The dull throbbing in my head subsides. The covers are lifted, and a warm, firm body with just enough give slides in beside me. Aleks pulls me against his bare chest. I breathe in his scent. He smells like mint and vanilla; the leather scent is faint.

"I'm so sorry, Aleks," I whisper into his muscles. "I'm sorry for not listening, staying safe, and thinking I could help." He shushes me and squeezes me in his arms. I sniffle, fighting off tears that threaten to spill. I tip my head up to look at him. It's too dark to actually see him. Despite the mid-morning light, his black-out curtains work well. I bump his chin, and he hisses out a breath.

"Tyler punched me," he explains. "I shouldn't have stormed out the way I did. I was just scared." His words are soft. Instead of saying anything else, I tuck into his chest again. We lie together for a long time. We hold each other and listen to our breaths. I count his, then mine, then drift off to sleep in warmth and safety I haven't felt in a while.

I wake a few hours later with my back to Aleks. His arms are wrapped around my chest tightly. He must have thought I was leaving when I rolled over and held me to keep me close. I preen at that. Despite what he says, he doesn't actually want me to leave. We need to figure out a way to make this less dramatic. He can't tell me to go every time he gets upset.

Aleks thinks he is so unworthy. He's not. Sure, he's broken, but he's still decent at his core. I can't help but wonder what Richard told him for all those years. Aleks internalized whatever it was and believes it to be true. It saddens me that he doesn't see his own worth. He's the president of the club. Although, if memory serves, he doesn't think he earned that. He said the previous board was forced to put Aleks in the VP position to justify the close contact with him.

I snuggle into Aleks's arms more, trying to push those thoughts from my mind. If I focus on his trauma for too long, I'll be the one to break. A long exhale is released into my hair. I feel the long, stiff shaft rub against my lower back. I wiggle my ass against it unabashedly. Aleks groans, and his hands tighten around my chest. One hand sits on my ribs. He strokes the underside of my breast with his thumb. It's a nice touch, but it's not what I want now.

I can't move my arms because Aleks has them pinned. My hips are free, though. I grind against him, eliciting a long moan. His lips are on my shoulder, kissing gently. For as rough and depraved as our relationship started, he has turned into a big softie lately. I secretly love it. I love seeing such a large man be so gentle. I wiggle one arm free and reach back to grab his length. His hand grabs my breast and squeezes so hard he may rip the thing off. His hips thrust into my back and prevent me from getting to him.

I groan, frustrated I can't get what I want. His hand leaves my breast to grip my forearm, effectively stopping me from grabbing him. His other hand slides down my body, leaving a trail of heat and want. I grab his forearm with my hands for something to hold onto. His hand plunges into my sweats and straight down my underwear. He is wasting no time in his endeavor. He slides one finger through my pussy. I'm glad he didn't dive in. While I want this, I'm not wet enough yet.

He circles my clit several times, causing my eyes to flutter. I grind against him, forcing my ass against his cock while simultaneously putting his finger harder against my clit. He drags his teeth along my shoulder. Not biting, just changing the sensation. I begin to hump his hand. I can't control it and don't feel an ounce of shame. This man does something to me that I can't control. Every touch drives me crazy.

Aleks continues this for a couple of moments until my panties and his fingers are soaked. All I can think about is getting his dick inside me. I hike my leg over his hips, giving him full access. Then it hits me. Unless we're doing anal, which Aleks is staunchly against, he's not getting very deep in this position, and that absolutely will not do. I wiggle to turn around. It's an awkward turn because Aleks doesn't expect it.

Once I am facing him, I grab his cock. His long, hard, glorious cock. I want to be buried with this cock. Ideally in my mouth, but I'll take it wherever, literally. I just want to be sure I get to spend eternity with this dick. I briefly wonder if I can put that in my will. A bit of precum at his tip brings me back to reality. I'll deal with eternity later. Right now, I need bliss.

I switch my hands on his penis and use my free hand to shimmy my sweats down. He does nothing to help. His arms are around my back, gently tracing circles, not giving a care in this world that I want to ravage him wholly. Once I free my leg, I kick it over his hips. I line his tip up with my entrance. I'm too high and have to shuffle down to get him inside me. I sheath his dick in my wanting pussy. Aleks groans at the tightness and presses a kiss to the top of my head.

I grind against him, letting the rough patch of hair rub against my clit. I clench around him then he takes over. His hand grabs my hips, and he thrusts inside me. I press the heel of my foot into his ass to encourage him to go faster. He doesn't need the encouragement. He fucks me fast and hard, just the way I like it. His hand grips my hip almost brutally. It could leave a bruise. I love the roughness.

We settle into a pace of frenzied thrusts and groans. It doesn't take long for either of us to hit that cliff. "Don't stop. I'm going to come," I mutter into his chest. The height difference keeps me lower than him. I could probably shift and pull him down to kiss, but that would throw off our rhythm. Nobody wants that. He pumps a couple of more times, and my orgasm crashes through me. I tighten around his cock, moaning in pleasure.

It's a light, breezy orgasm that makes me smile. I never knew I could have so many different orgasms. Sapph elicits earth-shattering orgasms when we play with pain. Aleks gives soul-crushingly beautiful orgasms. Then there's this one. So calm and peaceful and perfect. As my body calms down, I sigh into his chest contentedly. I can already feel his cum mixing with my own fluids on my legs.

He pulls back slowly and sits on the edge of the bed. His arms are on his knees, and his head is in his hands. Seriously, his thoughts are dangerous. What would lead him to this kind of sorrow after wake-up sex? I wait to see if he will get a rag to help me clean up. When he doesn't, I commit to sitting up. It's all going to spill out onto the bedsheets, but we can just wash them today.

"Aleks," I say softly before wrapping my arm around his back. I rest my head on his shoulder. He glances at me but doesn't say anything. I trail my fingers up and down his bicep, tracing the lines of his tattoos.

"I don't know how to forgive you for not listening in the restaurant," Aleks tells me. I sit for a moment to process what he is saying. His hurt is palpable, but my own is still present. He tried to make me leave. He wanted me gone.

"I'm not ready to forgive you for telling me to leave." He turns his head to me before dropping it into his hands. We've really created a fucked up situation. "We should talk about this." He nods, but neither of us moves. My fingers continue their trail over his ink.

"Did I ever tell you," I start, keeping my eyes on his arm, but I can feel his gaze on me, "that this is my favorite tattoo?" He has a tattoo of a woman on his bicep. She's gorgeous and powerful, staring out with an alluring gaze. I trace her lips, eyes, and hair. He stays silent, not offering any information about his tattoos. I didn't expect him to, but I love talking about tattoos. Not that I have any of my own. Wesley might have actually killed me if he saw one. I could get one now.

"Do you want coffee?" Aleks's question breaks my thoughts.

"Yeah, I need to eat, too."

He nods and walks to the bathroom. I follow him, and we clean up quickly. Before we leave the room, I strip the bed. Aleks watches for a moment, caught off guard by my side task. He grabs fresh sheets when he realizes what I am doing and helps me put them on. We walk through the halls silently. He leads me to the kitchen through the rooms instead of the restaurant. I can't help but wonder what it looks like. They cleaned it up, but it was on the verge of being destroyed when I blacked out.

In the kitchen, we find Shirley fussing around. She gives us coffee, and Aleks tells her she doesn't need to do all this. She assures him she wants to. Joe sustained a gunshot wound on his arm. It's not life-threatening and only required a few stitches. It just skimmed his arm, but Shirley is flustered and is staying here to help. Staying busy helps her cope with what happened. I offer to check in on him later, but she tells me that isn't necessary. Doc is still around to check in on people. I want to meet him soon. I was taken to the hospital before he showed up, but he does care for everyone else. I want to get some tips from him to help with that stuff.

I eat some toast and a banana. I'm not super hungry, but I need something. When I'm done, Aleks says we should go to his office to talk. I follow him with my steaming mug of coffee. I blow on it gently until we exit the kitchen. The kitchen exits at the end of the hallway closest to the restaurant. Aleks's office is just across the hall, but I freeze.

It's destroyed. Lights are missing, and holes and patchwork are scattered across the wall and floor. A massive stack of tables and chairs are in the corner. Those look to be in good condition. Another pile is clearly destroyed furniture. My heart aches as my breath hitches. Bullet holes decorate several of the booths. The floor is clear of debris and blood. The club worked hard last night to clean up this place after the fight.

I can't stop the tears that stream down my face over the destruction. How did it get this bad? What the hell was I thinking? I couldn't have helped at all in this situation. I've seen victims of shootouts. I did some training in Pittsburgh. People were brought into the ER with multiple wounds from guns or knives. I only saw them in the ER. I never went to the scene of the crime. Witnessing the aftermath of this, this level of desecration is overwhelming. More tears slide down my face, and I wipe them away.

"Come on," Aleks says gently at my elbow. He's sympathetic. I wonder how this makes him feel, seeing this beautiful, safe place decimated. I look at him, but he is already walking into his office. I take a final glance around the bar. All the alcohol is stored below the bar instead of on the wall behind it. Did they plan for something like this? They also have reinforced tabletops, so they must have.

Aleks sits at his desk. I pause beside the couch. If I go to him, I will cave and cry in his arms, and nothing will change. We will repeat this cycle. We'll hurt each other, push each other away, suffer, and then come back together to repeat it. It has to change now. I love him as he is and understand why he wanted to push me away, but we can't keep hurting each other.

I grab a tissue from the table and sit on the couch. I blot my eyes, drying the tears. I take a sip of coffee and refuse to look at Aleks. He won't start this conversation, but I need to gather my thoughts. I take a deep breath. I take another drink of my coffee in hopes it will give me strength. It's a futile attempt.

"I'm so sorry," I start and finally look up at Aleks. He stares at me stoically. "I underestimated the level of the threat to your club. To you." It suddenly occurs to me that Aleks and Tyler were at the front of that fight. I could have lost both of them. Sapph, too. I haven't heard about any of our men dying. Many received gunshot wounds and a variety of minor injuries, but no one gave me a final tally. "I know you don't trust my decisions about my own safety. I don't blame you. I made a stupid fucking choice." I pause to take a deep breath. Do I tell him it won't happen again? Does that sound too cliché?

"Will you listen next time we tell you to leave?" Hurt lines his question. I nod, and silence falls around us.

"I need something from you, though." He raises his eyebrows at my statement. While he may have issues believing I'll listen, I also have issues knowing when to listen. "I need you to talk to me more. Tell me things. Not the club business," I add to his incredulous look. "I had no idea things would get that bad," I motion toward the dining room. "When you choked me," I try to suppress my rising emotions: anger, hurt, fear, "I didn't know you were in a bad space. We could have worked through it without shit going sideways." That night was a fucking shit show. It makes for a great story now, but holy hell, I have no intention of repeating that.

"We worked through it after Catherine and Jo first showed up. We can do that every time." I meet his stare. He is neutral while I try to show every emotion in my face. I don't want him to have any doubts about how I feel. "I will give you everything. Everything, Aleks, but I don't know what you need. Tell me what you need," I plead. I want this to work so badly. I stop talking; everything I wanted to say is out now.

"I need a blow job."

I huff out a laugh, stunned by his statement. "What?"

"The other day," he sounds like he has never spoken. He's probably never asked for what he needs. He looks uncomfortable and won't meet my gaze, but he doesn't stop talking. "You did something to me. It silenced everything for me. I've never felt that." I let his words sink in. I could tell he was different after that, but I didn't realize how impactful it was for him.

I give him a smile and hold my hand out for him. I flick my fingers, and he rises, understanding my silent demand. I tug him onto the couch beside me and kiss his cheek lightly.

"Thank you for telling me," I whisper against his cheek and trail my hand down his chest. I stop at the hem of his jeans and tug his shirt to touch his skin. "I can give you a blow job every day," I kiss his jaw. Thankfully, it's the other side Tyler bruised. I don't have to worry about hurting him from this side. He grabs my hand and holds me still.

"I don't want one every day," he pauses, clearly torn about whether to continue. I've never met a man who didn't want one every day, but I've never met a man as broken as Aleks. He takes a deep breath and releases it heavily. He's committing to tell me. I suppress the urge to wiggle with delight that he will finally let me in, even if only a tiny glimpse. "I don't... I can't... They forced..." he stops talking with that, and I can fill in the rest. I press my cheek against his shoulder.

"You have trauma around oral?" His cheek rests against my head, and he nods. "Can you tell me when one would be helpful for you?"

"I'll try," he whispers. I squeeze his body tightly but don't resume my intentions to suck him. "Now would be good." His voice is barely audible. I wouldn't have heard it if I weren't against his chest. I give a slight chuckle and kiss his shoulder. I slip off the couch and in between his legs. I kneel between his feet and rub my hands up and down his legs.

He watches intently as my fingers creep toward the button on his jeans. I can see his member hardening in his pants. He wants this, needs this. I wasn't kidding when I said I would give this man everything. I unfasten the pants and tug the zipper down. I slip my fingers between the fabric to search out the cock that is inside when the door opens.

"Goddammit, Harpo," I yell and drop my head onto Aleks's thigh. I keep my hand in his pants, though. I'm going to start charging Harpo for all these shows he's getting. He's a creep like Aleks, just unintentionally. Though, I doubt his intentions at this point. He has access to all the cameras, right? Is he stalking us?

"Hey, Aleks. What the fuck, Vic? Seriously?" Oh, that's not Harpo. I jump up and twist to see Tyler with his back to us. He's still ranting when someone else pops in the door.

"You called for me, oh." There's Harpo. See? He's stalking us. His cheeks go beet red, and I grin at him.

"Yeah, 'oh'," Tyler grumbles. Aleks grabs my hips and pulls me down onto his lap. He barks out a one-word response to both of them. Tyler sighs and glances over his shoulder before turning to face us. He crosses his arms over his shoulders, clearly unimpressed with our antics. It's a little on me for not locking the door. They didn't knock, so it's on them too.

"We need more money for the crematorium, and the guys want to know what to do." Aleks nods his head toward the safe in the corner. Tyler glares at us as he walks over, only breaking it to enter the code.

"I was going to help," Harpo says, raising his hands innocently. I don't have to turn around to know Aleks is scowling at him. After finding Harpo in our bed last night and being reminded of how often he walks in on us, Aleks isn't going to be warm and welcoming. The thought of Aleks being warm and welcoming makes me smile.

"Is the paint and supplies order ready?" Harpo nods at Aleks's question. "Take some guys to pick it up and have them get started with that. We'll order new furniture later." Harpo nods and walks out. Tyler leaves the room with a bag, presumably holding money for the crematorium. Tyler makes a point to lock the door before he slams it.

Aleks pulls me against his chest and buries his head in my shoulder. I hold his arms, thinking about how sideways this talk has gone.

"Can we put a bell on Harpo to know when he is coming?"

Chapter Twenty-Four

VIC

THE CLUB IS GOING on a group ride today. Shirley planned a picnic at a nearby state park. The club reserved most of the camping spots so they won't bother too many people with the bikes. I can't for the life of me figure out why Aleks thinks he isn't a good guy. What person in an outlaw biker gang would think to book campsites to not bother other people?

I wait by Aleks's bike as everything is finalized. People chat animatedly. After the attack last week, the club really needs a break like this. Getting out on their bikes will be good for them. Plus, contractors are working on the restaurant; we need to be out of the way. The timing is perfect.

We finally get on the bikes to leave. I wrap my arms tightly around Aleks, no longer worried about making him uncomfortable. He would be with anyone else but not me. I hold onto his hips as he leads the way out of the parking lot. Tyler is by our side, with everyone else behind us. Shirley left earlier to get set up before we arrive.

Aleks leads the long group bikers and Sapph onto the interstate. They weave in and out of traffic for a while before riding on back roads to the park. Some men break off from the formation on the interstate and dart around cars playfully.

Aleks remains steady, but Tyler takes off with Lacey. Sapph pulls up beside us and waves wildly. I giggle and wave back. I've gotten more confident on the bike and will take one hand off Aleks. Only one hand. I'm not that confident yet.

When we exit the interstate, everyone falls back into formation except Sapph. She doesn't have an official spot since she isn't an official member. She rides in front of Tyler and Aleks, making her the leader of the pack. Aleks's chest rumbles with laughter, and his head shakes. He's amused by her antics. I wonder if the other men will be.

In my most recent perusal of the internet, I stumbled across a video where a man and woman were getting freaky on a bike. Granted, their motorcycle was parked, and she sat facing him. That doesn't matter because my hand is mere inches away from my favorite appendage of Aleks. With Tyler on our right, I slip my left hand lower. I don't know if Tyler could see if he looks over, but he caught me with my head in Aleks's lap a few days ago. This isn't any worse.

I slide my palm down until I find his cock and wrap my fingers over it. His stomach tenses under my other hand, but Aleks makes no effort to stop me. I press hard into his jeans to get the pressure just right. Too soft, and he won't feel it. My efforts pay off as he starts to harden beneath my touch. To his credit, Aleks shows no response other than his growing dick.

The road widens briefly, and Sapph falls back to ride beside us. Aleks grabs my wrist, but I don't stop. Sapph glances over, looks down where our hands are, then tips her head back in laughter. I can't hear her, but I can imagine the joyous sound. She gives a thumbs-up and takes her spot in front of the group again. I glance over to Tyler, but he is watching the road ahead.

Aleks puts his hand back on his handlebars, and I take that as an invitation. It's not, but I don't care. I unzip his pants and slip my fingers inside. As my tips brush over the silky length, Aleks's fingers wrap around my wrist. My fingers pause, not wrapping around his penis like I want. Instead, I slide my other hand under his shirt. I trace his muscles, sliding my fingers up and down his abs. He hisses out a breath and releases my wrist.

I slide my fingers in a little further. I'm getting close to the full extent of my reach. I have short arms, and he has a huge cock. I can't reach the tip, even stuffed in his jeans like it is. I wrap my fingers around the middle and squeeze tightly. His breathing increases, but his bike doesn't waver. With my fingers holding the underside of his dick, I use my thumb to stroke on the upperside. His chest rumbles with a word, I assume my name or nickname, but I can't hear it.

I trail my fingers over until my grip is reversed. With my thumb on the underside, I slide it up and press against the base. On his stomach, I drag my nails over his skin. His muscles tense again. I love the effect I have on him. I grip his base firmly and twist my hand. I still can't get a great grip to stroke him, but it doesn't matter. A bit of precum leaves a wet spot further down his jeans.

My panties are growing wet. I want to hump Aleks but am terrified to move on the bike. Gods, I could use some pressure on my clit. Instead, I wrap my middle finger and thumb around his base and squeeze tightly. I make little strokes near the base, working what I can. I pull my thumb back and slip my fingers lower to rub against his sack. It's a tight space, but I make do.

Aleks motions to Tyler. Once he has his attention, Aleks makes a few signals with his hands. I've picked up on a couple of signs from previous rides. My best guess is that Aleks told Tyler he's pulling off, and the club should ride ahead. That's what happens, anyway. Tyler pulls up beside Sapph, and Aleks turns down a road. During the turn, I inadvertently grip his cock to hold on. I'm not sure if he likes that or not because he exhales heavily. He drives for another moment then turns into a wooded grove.

Short palm-looking trees block most of the view. He tugs my hand from his cock and pushes me off his bike. He lowers the kickstand and pulls his helmet off deftly. It drops carefully to the ground then his hands are yanking my helmet off, and his lips crash into mine as my helmet softly thuds beside his.

"Now would be a good time to fuck me against a tree," I huff out when I break the kiss. "Or over your bike." His eyes flare with intense lust. I've hit a desire, whether he knew about it or not. His hands grip me roughly, one behind my knee, the other on my back. I love working him into a desperate frenzy. He tugs me into his lap, so I sit on the gas tank.

He tugs at the waist of my jeans roughly. He's in such a rush he's fumbling with the buttons. I help him get my pants undone, and then they are shoved to my knees. My boots prevent them from going any lower. With one hand on my body, he tugs his cock out of his jeans. I'm in an awkward position: back on the gas tank, grabbing at anything to hold onto, legs bound by my jeans and over Aleks's shoulder. It must be quite the fucking sight.

"You better be fucking wet because I'm slamming in," he growls, then does just that. He's not usually overly rough with me. It's taken some effort to get him to the point where he does things like forcing me to bend or slam into me. It's so damn worth it. I cry out as he sinks to the hilt in one go. I'm glad I'm so wet; he slid in smoothly and deeply.

With my jeans around my knees, I can't wrap my legs around him like usual. This is apparently pleasing to Aleks because he freezes inside me as his breathing grows more erratic. I let him adjust to the new tightness for a moment, then wiggle my ass. I'm sure it's great for him, but I want some movement. He finally pulls out and slams back in. He sets a brutal pace, and I won't last long like this. I doubt he will, either.

As good as his thrusting feels, I feel on edge, like I'll tumble off this bike at any moment. Aleks won't let me fall, but that doesn't alleviate my anxiety. I reach up and unzip one boot. He watches my hand but keeps his brutal pace. I tug the boot off and toss it wildly to the side. The jeans are pushed off my foot, and I wrap my legs around him. With this new freedom, I'm able to sit up more, changing the position of his cock inside me. We both groan at the new sensation.

I lean up, and our lips crash together in a frenzied kiss. I'm wrapped around him like a bear on a tree, and he thrusts up into me like a desperate man. His hands are on my ass, my back, my head, my neck. I've really done something to him because he is never this handsy. I love it. The desperation, the brutality, the primal need in him. His tongue forces its way into my mouth, searching desperately.

"Fuck, Aleks," I mutter, "I'm going to come." He is close, too. I can feel his stomach tensing, but he may be closer than I am. I reach between us with the intent of rubbing my clit to get off with him. He flicks my hand away, then his is there. He presses his thumb directly against my clit so hard I combust instantly. I cry out, tipping back onto the gas tank. My body twists and clenches with my orgasm. It's so glorious I don't even care about being unsteady on his bike. His dick empties inside me; small jerks fill my pussy.

He leans forward as his body settles down. His head presses against mine as we breathe raggedly. After a moment, when our breathing starts to settle, he grabs my back and ass and swings off his bike. Once standing, his dick slips out of me, leaving a trail of our combined release down my thighs. He wraps his arms around my back and leans down to hold me tightly. Between the Texas heat and our warm bodies, it's almost overwhelming. I don't say anything and give him the closeness he needs now. He finally straightens to his full height.

"I have some wipes, but I don't have anywhere to put them before we get to a trashcan," he explains. I'm thankful he didn't suggest throwing them on the ground. See? Good guy. He just also tortures and murders people. No big deal.

"There're bathrooms at the shelter, right? I'll clean up there," I slide my panties up, wishing I had brought a backup pair. I hadn't exactly planned to get fucked on his bike, not really. I button my jeans as he straightens out his. When we're done, he wraps his hand around the side of my neck and pulls me into a kiss. It's not a brutal kiss like before. It feels appreciative. I put my foot on his boot, so I'm not standing on leaves and sticks. I don't like being in socks in the woods.

I wrap my arms around him and return the kiss. I appreciate that we have moved past just forehead kisses. Now, forehead kisses give me butterflies. He pulls back from the kiss and opens his mouth. Then he closes it. Then he opens it again. He finally speaks.

"I love you." I don't think he has said that since Wes was here.

"I love you, too," I beam up at him. He kisses my forehead, and his thumb strokes my cheek. He opens his mouth to speak again. I give him time to get the words out. I take in his beautiful face. His blonde hair is braided back. He does that every time we ride to keep the ends from hitting me. Another good guy check. We'll forgive his Tony Montana moment in the restaurant last week.

"I've always wanted to do that," he finally says softly, breaking my trance. He nods his head toward his bike, and I grin.

"Glad I could fulfill your fantasy."

He huffs a laugh and grabs our helmets. He holds mine out to me, but I just stare at it. Now that we have stepped away from each other, I have my foot propped on my booted foot. I nibble on my lip because I don't know where my boot went. I tossed it wildly in the moment.

"Have you seen my boot?" I ask, pointing to my foot. He looks down, confused at my question, and then chuckles. He spots the boot, grabs it, and walks over to me. He kneels down and holds it open for me to step into. Gods, seeing this man on his knees in front of me does things it really shouldn't. My stomach is on a roller coaster. He slips my boot on as I hold onto his shoulder. His fingers work deftly to secure the laces that were loosened by the toss. It hit a tree branch and tugged some of them.

Despite the proper fucking and orgasm I just had, my core still tightens. Aleks's fingers move so precisely that I can't help but imagine what else he can do with them. When my boot is secured, he places my foot down gently then kisses my stomach. He pauses, kneeling at my feet, looking up at me. I stroke his cheek gently and realize I am madly in love with this man. He stands and kisses me gently. I melt into his arms, but he keeps the kiss brief.

We climb on the bike, but he grabs my hands and puts them higher on his chest, well away from my favorite appendage. I laugh as I squeeze him tightly. I'm not going to do that again today. Eventually, yes. Today, no. The club is going question our absence. We don't need to make it worse by staying gone longer.

We pull up to the shelter, where everyone is already partying. A few guys set up some tents in the club's camping spaces. Aleks has a strict no drinking and driving policy. The guys who choose to drink have to stay overnight. We're not in that category, and I'm thankful for that. I have no desire to sleep in this heat with the bugs. His policy is a good guy attribute, for sure. We won't mention the time he slammed me against the wall by the neck while he tried to kill his abuser for the second time.

With Aleks behind me, I join Tyler, Sapph, Lacey, and Harpo. Sapph gives a shit-eating grin; she's about to start something.

"So, where did you two go?" Sapph's voice is playful. Tyler glances at us and then groans. Harpo walks away, heading in Shirley's direction.

"Aleks was just showing me some of the palms," I answer smoothly. It's not a lie; we did see some of the plants.

"I bet you got some palms," Sapph says teasingly with an exaggerated wink. Tyler punches her in the shoulder.

"That's my baby sister, perv. I don't wanna hear about that."

The laughter is exhilarating. After our week, it's nice to relax and not worry about things. We spend the afternoon chatting, eating, and just hanging out. It's perfect. The only thing that would make it better is if it weren't hotter than Satan's ass. I would have worn a dress or at least shorts, but I don't like riding the bike in those clothes. It's not comfortable to me.

Just before dusk, we start cleaning up and prepare to leave. The guys staying behind settle in their camps while everything else is packed into Shirley's SUV. I stand by Aleks's bike, waiting for him to walk over. He finally does, and I hold his helmet out to him.

"Did you say anything to Harpo?" I ask before he puts it on. He gives me a curious look and shakes his head. "I think he's been avoiding me. Whenever I join a group he's with, he leaves quickly." Aleks glances around and spots Harpo on his bike.

"Want me to say something?" Aleks asks.

"No, I was just curious if you had. I thought maybe you did after you found him in our room." Aleks shakes his head again, and I pull on my helmet to end the conversation. It's not like Harpo and I were great friends, but I thought we could at least be around each other, especially after the movies and when he stayed with me while I slept. Maybe I misread things. Perhaps he was only spending time with me because he felt obligated to. I try not to let that thought get me down. I still have tons of friends here. Rio and Sapph, Lucy and Shirley. I even consider Lacey a friend now. She's cool to hang out with, and she and Tyler are adorable. So much better than him and Destiny.

Aleks and the board are on a conference call with Catherine about their first shipment. It will be tomorrow, and they are finalizing all the details. I'm nervous about it. They have done runs for the cartel since I've been here, but they don't tell me about those. They just leave for a few hours. This one is different.

I know more about this venture than any of the club's other businesses. This one involves the mafia. I don't know how different it will be to work with the mafia versus the cartel. Maybe it's no different. Catherine assured them the two groups won't cause any problems for the club. Apparently, she has ties to both. She's the ultimate crime boss. Mafia, mobs, cartels—she and Jo do it all.

The restaurant is looking much better. It's an entirely different Dionysus. They are still waiting for some tables and chairs, but the walls have been repaired and painted. The dining room is now a soft green. Plants sit on shelves, and the Edison lights have returned. It's brighter than it was before, but it feels more welcoming, less dark. I'm excited to see the finished space. They have the reopening scheduled for next week.

"Hey! Guess what I just got?" Sapph walks up to me with a long, thin package. My concerned look draws a laugh from Sapph. I'm worried it's a ridiculously long dildo. The box has to be close to three feet in length. It's not thick, but I don't know if I could handle anything long. "It's not what you think," she says before leaning in to whisper, "It's even better than that."

With a wink, she turns to head to her room. My mind reels for a moment before I hop down and follow her. A few bikers eye me as I follow her, but I barely notice. I need to know what's in the box. She tosses the box on her bed in her room after locking the door.

"What's in the box, Sapph?" I ask. "What's in the box?" I cry out in my best Brad Pitt imitation. She chuckles at my terrible impression. I am really not good at that stuff. She offers me a pair of scissors, and I practically bounce to the bed. Even if this is a 3-foot dildo, I'm still excited to try it out. Maybe it's some rope. We haven't used rope much. Would it ship in a long, skinny box like this?

I slice through the tape as my blood heats inside me. Tingles zip through my body, settling heavily in my core. The smooth rip of the tape heightens my excitement. I pull the cardboard aside, tug the packing paper, and lift the item.

It's a long, thin black bag with something hard inside. I glance at Sapph, who has a calm expression on her face. She is waiting to see my reaction. I tug the cord on one end of the bag to open it. A thin rod slides into my hand. One end has purple leather braided around it to form a handle. It's a cane that looks like bamboo, but I'm no wood expert. A small piece of paper falls from the bag, explaining where the rattan came from and how it's custom-made. The back side says it is purely a collector item; injuries due to improper use are not the maker's fault.

Sapph pulls the cane from my shaking hands. I can't hide the nervousness, the excitement, the overwhelming sense of adventure. She waves the cane through the air, slicing through with an audible whoosh. Those tingles from earlier? Yeah, they're on my ass now. I nibble on my lip as I watch her test out her new toy. She looks like a natural.

"I want to lay you on the bed," Sapph says, stepping directly before me, "then I'm going to play with you." Her voice is sensual and deep; those tingles move so fast that Flash would be jealous. They sit comfortably in my core, and I want everything she offers. A soft thwack hits the side of my thigh just above my knee, causing me to jump. The shock sends waves of desire through my body.

"Little bird," she croons, "you are wearing too many clothes."

With the grace of a newborn giraffe, I stumble out of my clothes, topple on the bed, and grunt unceremoniously as I attempt to get my shorts off. I seriously just need to stay in dresses all the time. Maybe just a robe. Maybe I'll just stay naked. Between Aleks and Sapph, I am constantly removing clothes. It's far too much effort.

"How are you feeling?"

"Good," I rush out, then quickly amend, "green."

"Good," Sapph steps behind me and kisses the side of my neck. I didn't think my body could get any hotter, but I am burning up. The cane lightly touches the side of my thigh, and the tip trails up my skin. Goosebumps cover my entire body. I close my eyes and lean back into Sapph, savoring her warmth.

"Get on your stomach," she motions toward the bed with her head. I climb on as Sapph tosses a pillow onto the center and guides me over it. With my ass in the air, she binds my hands together and secures them to the straps on her headboard. She repeats the process with my feet. "We've played several times," she says as if she has planned this monologue. "I'll ease you in because the cane feels different, but I'm not going easy on you, little bird." I wiggle my ass with anticipation. Yes, I want that so bad. Everything she has done to me this far has felt amazing. I want more. I want it all.

A quick smack rips a gasp from me. My skin stings where she hit me, but it isn't awful. It fades nearly as quickly as it happened. Sapph runs her fingers along my flesh, and I fight the urge to moan at her smooth touch. The variety of sensations I get with Sapph is unlike anything I have ever felt. I never quite know what to expect or how I will react in the moment, but at the end of the scene, I always enjoy it.

Another thwack hits my thighs in the spot where my ass ends. I jerk to get away from her but groan at the feeling. I can't see what Sapph is doing. Her back is to my face, and the cane is too close to my body for me to see what she is doing with it. I don't know much about cane lengths, but I almost wish it was longer. Almost.

Four smacks land in quick succession, and then her hand slides between my legs. I release a tense breath as the pain fades quickly. Those hits were harder than the previous ones and will only get harder from here. Her fingers slide over my wet slit, and I groan under her touch. I inhale deeply and let her touch soothe the ache.

The cane hits my ass twice, my upper thighs three times, then an especially hard hit to the crease between my ass and thighs. I cry out this time. The pain is intense: more intense than I thought it would be. The real kicker is the sound. The slice of the air and the smack against my skin sounds so loud in the small room. Sapph's warm palm caresses my ass. I take several deep breaths.

"Color?"

Her hands don't stop sliding over my skin. She doesn't slip between my legs like I want, but her touch is soothing.

"Green," I answer, but is that really true? Am I enjoying this? I like her hands on me. I long for her hands to trail higher, but do I want more of the cane? Before I can fully consider my feelings, the cane swats me five times. I yell out, only to be met with two of the hardest hits yet. Her fingers are on my cunt instantly. She really knows how to mix pain with pleasure. But is this the right pain for me?

I moan as she circles my clit. Her hand slides away, leaving a trail of moisture along my thigh. My body responds well to this, even if my mind isn't. I lose track of how often the rattan cane touches my skin. All I can hear is the contact. Smack. Smack. Smack. Pop. Pop. Pop.

I don't register the pain. The sounds overwhelm me. Smack. Another shot. Pop. The screams. Thwack. Suddenly, I'm no longer in her bed. I'm in Dionysus. The Long Horn Devils are in the restaurant. Aleks and Tyler are crouched behind a table. Pop. Pop. Pop. Scream. I'm losing everything. Despair swirls inside of me. I can't breathe. Everyone is out of reach. Blood pools around the floor. My body aches. An intense pain fills my head. My ass is on fire. A single color fills my mind.

"RED!"

The word escapes my lips subconsciously. Before I'm fully back in the present, Sapph's hands are on me. I'm freed of the restraints and rolled onto my sides. Tears stream down my face as Sapph wraps her body around mine. She holds me tight as I sob into her chest. Her room slowly appears in my vision. I take a deep, shaky breath as my body finally calms down. Sapph rubs her hands over my back then I hear her whispers. She sounds sad and broken as she apologizes profusely.

I pull back and look up at her face. Her eyes are watery with unshed tears. I stroke her cheek gently and lift for a soft kiss. She doesn't return it but doesn't push me away either. I rest on the bed in her arms, registering the fuzzy blanket that has been pulled over us. I'm safe here. I'm not alone. My thighs sting, but I'm still whole. Sapph breathes out deeply.

"Where'd you go?" Her voice is soft against the top of my head.

"The bar when we were attacked," I whisper against her chest. "The sounds," I mumble, unable to finish the thought. Her chest stutters with a broken breath. "Are you okay?" I ask, concern for her growing. She kisses my forehead. I'm clearly not in the right headspace because the forehead kiss doesn't bother me at all.

"I've had a few women safe word out," Sapph starts slowly. "It happens. We all learn our limits at some point, but this," she pulls me into a tight hug. One of my arms is pinned between my body and hers. I wrap the other around her back. We lay like that for several minutes. She never finishes her thought.

Her hands caress my back, shoulders, and thighs. The tension slowly ebbs from my body, making way for a different sensation. The heat in my core was never addressed; it didn't abate completely in my stress. Her touches aren't meant to arouse, but my skin doesn't recognize that. A hot woman has me in her arms, naked in her bed, and her hands are stroking my body.

"Sapph," I whisper a question into her collarbone. I want to kiss her. I want to alleviate this ache, but whatever happened was intense for both of us. She may not want that. In response, her leg presses between mine, spreading my core for her. My lips connect with her skin, unable to fight the urge. My fingers twitch, flicking the side of her breast. I try to grab her, but my hand is pinned awkwardly.

"You sure, little bird?" Her voice is filled with hesitation. I press my teeth against her skin, not in a bite, but to offer a different sensation. I grind my cunt against her thigh, and an idea pops in my mind.

"Yes," I say slowly, working up the courage to ask for what I want. I always feel so hesitant with Sapph. I can tell Aleks I want him to fuck me against the wall any day, but asking Sapph feels so different. I suck air into my lungs, hoping it's laced with confidence.

"Can we, have you ever," I stumble over my words, unsure how to ask for what I want.

"Out with it, bird."

"Scissor," I spit out and bury my face in her neck quickly. It feels like one of those things girls do in porn but probably don't enjoy much in real life. I've never been close enough to a lesbian to ask if it's something they want. Sapph's laugh is joyful but not the least bit judgmental. "Is that something you like?" I ask meekly.

"It's not my favorite, but it's not the worst thing either." Her smile is electric when I finally lift my gaze. She kisses me gently then rolls me onto my back, careful not to press my legs into the bed. She climbs off the bed to remove the rest of her clothes. She already stripped off her jeans and shirt, leaving her in her panties and bra. Once those are gone, she climbs back on the bed and straddles one of my legs.

She lifts my ankle to her mouth and kisses it gently. The warmth of her pussy hovers over my thigh. She isn't sitting on my leg; I can't feel her cunt on my skin. Her hands slide up and down my thigh, as her hips roll over my other one as if she can't be still. Her wet labia graze the top of my thigh, and I moan with anticipation.

"If this starts to hurt," she says, pausing all her touches, "tell me immediately. It won't be as intense at the cane. You don't have to use the colors. I'll be gentle with your legs, but I can only do so much." I nod in response. My thighs sting, but it's not the end of the world. The warmth emanating from my cunt eases that ache.

Slowly, Sapph inches closer to my body. She tugs my leg, shifting me so my hips are angled more toward her center. Then her clit hits mine. I cry out to the gods in thanks for that magical little bundle of nerves. Sapph holds onto my leg, securing my foot against her shoulder. At least it isn't awkwardly propped against her pec like it is with Aleks. Before my mind can spiral with comparisons, Sapph moves.

She grinds over my clit, rubbing back and forth. I watch our bodies rub together. My pale skin meets her golden skin. She moves over me like a goddess, rocking with the movement of the sea. Her wetness mixes with my own, creating a pool of arousal between us.

The angle is odd. I shift to get better contact, which only makes me more desperate. My hips thrust in response, causing us to get out of sync. Her hand lands on my lower abdomen to hold me still. I try; I really do, but I need more. I groan when I realize I can't get constant contact. It's like dry humping. It's fun, but I feel empty. This is not a position that works for me.

"It's not enough," I gasp out as my hips thrust under her hand. Sapph chuckles, presses her finger against my clit, and shifts her hips to hit a different angle. It's better, but I still feel hollow. I drop my head back onto the pillow and bring my arm to cover my eyes. I try to enjoy the sensation, but I need to be filled. "I need more," I beg.

Sapph leans down to kiss me gently and then rises from the bed. Despite my desire for more, I feel cold and empty with her gone. I move my arm to watch her. She walks to the dresser and opens the top drawer. Her ass is glorious. Soft but strong. A single freckle stands out on her left cheek, and I itch to kiss it. She turns back to me with a huge double-ended dildo and a bottle of lube. This is more like it.

She climbs back on the bed and straddles me. She holds the lube out to pour some into my hands. I cup them for her, and she squirts the cool gel in my palms. I rub them together gently so as not to drop any on my stomach. I'm unsuccessful, and a glob falls onto my stomach. I giggle as Sapph slides the long dildo through my hands. I work it like I would a cock, twisting my hands and gliding up and down.

Sapph rubs the drop of lube around my stomach. It makes my skin shine. The sight is so erotic that I don't mind the mess. When Sapph is satisfied with the dildo, she pulls it from me and lines it up with my entrance. She slides it in quickly. Between my own wetness and the lube, there's no resistance. She pumps a couple of times, then holds it in place. I watch as she angles the other end up and lines it with her cunt. Then she slides down to meet my opening.

A groan escapes me at the sight. I prop up on my elbows to see where we meet, connected by a long pink dildo. I have seen erotic images before, but nothing could have prepared me to see her attached to me this way. My pussy clenches around the silicone cock. When Sapph rocks against me, I nearly combust. I take several deep breaths to slow my orgasm. I don't wanna be a three-pump chump.

As Sapph moves, the dildo shifts inside me. I can't stop the orgasm. It crashes through me like a tidal wave. I cry out in ecstasy while my body rolls into Sapph's. Her hips shift faster over my cunt. I push up on my elbows to kiss her. The new angle shifts the toy inside me. My eyes go wide as my second orgasm builds so quickly. I grab her back with one hand to hold the position.

Sapph drops onto her ass to give me more room to sit. The new position gives me more control over my movements. I meet her thrusts, and our clits connect erratically. The dildo pounds against my g spot, and I yell through my second orgasm. My head drops toward Sapph as she grabs my shoulders. Before I realize what is happening, she is on her back, and I am in the position she had just moments ago.

Her thigh is over my shoulder, and I straddle her other leg. I thought the second orgasm would be the end, but I was so wrong. I rock against her, pulling out and slamming in. Her breasts jostle from my thrusts, and my mouth waters. I push her leg down over my thigh and lean in to suck a nipple into my mouth. Her breast jiggles against my mouth as I take as much in as I can. I pull off her breast but graze my teeth against her nipple. She hisses in response.

"Touch yourself," she instructs as her hand slips between her legs. "Come with me," she demands. Don't need to tell me twice. Shifting my weight to one hand, I rub my clit in the circle furiously. My breathing is rapid as I near my third orgasm. I'm tingling and almost over-sensitive. Our bodies slamming into each other is engrained in my mind.

Sapph shifts her hips, thrusting the dildo into a new angle. I explode at the pressure against the back of my pussy. A burst of liquid shoots from my opening, drowning Sapph's. Her eyes widen before glossing over with her own orgasm. We rock through the waves of ecstasy coursing through our bodies. I lean down to kiss her passionately.

Our bodies are calm in a tangle of limbs and fluids. We chuckle as we try to unwind and remove the toy. I whimper as she slides it out of my body. I collapse on the bed, only to have my thigh land on a huge wet spot. I glance down at it, feeling my cheeks heat with embarrassment. Sapph climbs in beside me, wrapping her sweaty body around mine. She follows my gaze to the large, dark spot.

"That was fucking hot," she mutters against my lips.

CHAPTER TWENTY-FIVE

ALEKS

VIC CAME TO MY room late last night, thoroughly sated. She fell asleep quickly on my chest. I held her all night as she slept. My mind reeled with details of our first run with the mafia, but I did manage a few hours of sleep. The romance novels were wrong; I've only had one or two nights of solid sleep since she arrived. I wouldn't trade it for anything. She's my girl.

We now have a round table in the restaurant. I conceded on the booth with the remodel and found a large table. If Vic keeps bringing people to sit with us, we need a bigger space. This morning, it's just the five of us: Vic, Sapph, Tyler, Lacey, and me. Harpo hasn't sat with us lately. Vic has noticed his absence but doesn't push him. She won't let me talk to him about it. I respect her wishes despite wanting to berate him for upsetting her.

Sapph has been cranky all morning, and her mood surprised me. Given how relaxed Vic is, I'm surprised by the difference in Sapph. I assumed Vic's joy was linked to whatever she and Sapph did last night, but maybe I'm wrong. It's possible something else happened after Vic left her. Sapph isn't normally this moody.

Tyler says something to Sapph, and she snaps out a retort.

"I'm not crazy. I've just been in a very bad mood for 40 years!" She crosses her arms violently over her chest, citing Steel Magnolias. It's one of her favorite movies. The angrier she gets, the more likely she is to make obscure movie references no one around her will understand.

"Sapph, you're only 34," Tyler points out.

"I got a six-year head start," she sneers.

"Maybe we should find you a new girl. Clearly, Vic isn't cutting it for you," Tyler says far more calmly than he should. He's adjusted to Vic being with both of us and will joke about it from time to time. He still likes to overreact to kissing and PDA. Sapph glares at him. I've seen her kill people with a simple flick of her wrist. The look on her face says Tyler is next.

"You are evil and must be destroyed."

Yep, she's going to kill him. Tyler is strong and can handle himself, but my money is on Sapph. He's a dead man, especially since she still speaks in quotes. Before he can dig a deeper grave, I speak up.

"You good?"

Sapph turns her glare to me. It doesn't abate; the murderous rage is focused on me.

"Sapph?" Vic's voice is soft and laced with concern. Sapph looks at her and softens her expression instantly. She seems sad now. What the fuck is happening with all my friends? Sapph is on a rampage. Harpo has been avoiding us. Tyler is making jokes about his little sister's sex life. I don't understand anything.

"I'm fine," Sapph says and rises from the table. "When do we leave?" She glances at me with a hardened look. Something is definitely going on with her. I have never seen her like this. I glance at my watch and tell her we have an hour. Before I can say anything else, she storms off toward the rooms.

"Should I go check on her?" Vic asks.

"No," I shake my head, "leave her." Maybe she'll calm down if she has time to clear her head. Vic scoots her chair closer to mine. I wrap my arm around her back and hold her close. She is tense now. Sapph's reaction doesn't help the day ahead of us.

This is the first run we are doing for the mafia. It will make or break this contract. If things go well, we will solidify our place with them. If it doesn't, I have no idea what will happen. Catherine assured us they wouldn't retaliate or try to take us out, but I don't have high hopes. I'll deal with whatever; I hope it doesn't happen in Dionysus. I don't want to remodel again or risk Vic.

A few of the guys start bringing our gear out. Guns, ammo, vests, and our Bluetooth helmets are laid out on tables for us to grab. Tyler and I rise to make our way over. Vic catches my hand and reaches out to hug me. She grabs the collar of my shirt and tugs me toward her. I willingly lean down as she kisses me deeply.

"Stay safe," she whispers, then makes her way to the rooms. She has a bunch of medical equipment ready in case things go wrong. Once we all make it back, because we will, she'll bandage up anyone that needs it. Hopefully, that won't be necessary.

The men load up their gear, and we do final checks on our communications. Harpo assists with that but will stay behind to watch security systems. I don't want him to come with us. He is a top-notch hacker and will be more helpful keeping an eye on things virtually.

In the parking lot, Sapph is already on her bike. I nod at her, and she nods back. She's never let her attitude affect a mission before. I have complete confidence she won't today, but it does little to stop my worry for her safety. We mount our bikes and ride out. Our goal today is to protect the truck while it drives to its next location. We will ride along with the truck. A few men will meet the truck closer to its origination point. Some of us will meet it outside of San Antonio. The rest will lead the truck from the other side of the city north toward Kansas.

It's different than our runs with the cartel. With the cartel, we move the product. Providing protection is different. In the future, we will provide a warehouse for the truck to process the drugs and leave some here. The extra steps of processing and protecting make this endeavor longer and riskier. I feel confident that we have enough plans and exits in place, but this is an illegal business with people we don't know well. Anything could happen.

We ride quietly in our formation. No one chatters over our connection. Everyone tries to let the roar of our bikes settle our nerves. Sapph stays near the back of the pack with our gunner. She's usually playful on our rides, but this isn't a regular ride. We cruise down the roads of San Antonio until we arrive at the location. The men who met them at the origination point have been with them for several hours. Nothing has gone awry so far.

Seven other people are with me to protect the load through San Antonio. Tyler and I ride with Tony Tiger and Tiny Rick, two older members who have been around longer than me, will protect the rear. Sapph, Rio, Monster, and Pitch will lead, watching for any threat that will approach. Every stint of the route will include 8 members in this formation. With this setup, up to six of us can fend off an attack while the other two cover the truck. With Harpo on surveillance, we can reroute if needed.

We sit on a bridge, watching for the truck to pass us. When the first two guys cruise by, Sapph and Pitch take the on-ramp to replace them, followed by Rio and Monster. Tiny Rick and Tony Tiger take the spot just behind the truck as Tyler and I fall in line at the tail end. The other men peel off and head back to the club. Their part of the run is over now.

We don't expect to be attacked within city limits. Most of the attacks on these shipments have happened outside of the city. This stint is for consistency and extra security. We can't rule out an attack in San Antonio. Drug dealers aren't known for their level-headedness. Since the first part of the trip went smoothly, I take a calming breath. I know we aren't in the clear, but I'm relieved the first part went well.

"We've got a couple of riders that just joined us," Sapph announces. "Probably nothing, but I'm keeping an eye on it."

I'm not crazy about the sound of that, but nothing I can do now. The truck is moving at a steady pace. We haven't seen any cops; nothing is out of place. This could just be a typical ride for us. It isn't, not even close to one. Stress has every muscle tense. Every new venture has me on edge. It could take months for me to relax into a routine and truly feel comfortable. The money is worth it, though. That's what I tell myself.

"Shit, they're crowding me. I'm pulling away," Sapph says. Her voice is level, but it has a frantic edge.

This was our plan. Should we be attacked, the riders on the edge would lead them away. We've all had experience with defensive driving, whether in practice or real life. We can't risk being unprepared for an attack on our bikes. So, we practice riding. Sapph will know what to do. I trust her completely. I take another deep breath in a weak attempt to soothe my anxiety. I'm positive Vic would try to beat me if I let something happen to Sapph.

"Pitch, go with her," I call out.

"Sure, Pres," he responds. I don't like the tone of his voice, but now isn't the time to worry about that.

"Fuck," Sapph announces, "they've got guns. I'm taking the next exit."

Holy shit. Well, this is why we were hired. The threat is real. I hope Sapph grabbed a bulletproof vest before we left. I didn't see what she grabbed, but hopefully, her sour mood didn't prevent her from making safe choices.

"Go with them, Monster. Rio," I instruct, "you got this?"

"Yeah, I'm good," Rio responds. "Three bikers are following Sapph off the exit. I didn't see any others."

I don't really know how to feel about that. I'm relieved there aren't others, but three guys following Sapph? That doesn't feel good. Pitch and Monster are with her; she's not outnumbered. We ride silently for several minutes. I pass the exit Sapph used as anxiety gnaws at my insides.

"I need backup! They're shooting at me!" Sapph screams into the intercom. My already tense body stiffens even more. Where are Pitch and Monster? Why are they shooting at Sapph? The truck is still on the interstate. Are there more people waiting to attack the rest of us? I scan the area, looking for any signs of a threat.

"We lost her," Monster answers my unasked question with more indifference than he should feel about her being attacked alone.

"Harpo, get us directions," I say to him. He listens to everything for this exact purpose. He'll be able to track Sapph and guide us to her. "I'm going to find her. Tyler, ride with Rio. Watch for anything."

Tyler and I switch lanes and speed up. He falls in beside Rio while I take the next exit. Harpo is giving directions to me, Pitch, and Monster. I follow every turn at speeds that push the limits. I hear gun shots ring out before I spot Sapph. She is off her bike, crouched behind a rock, returning fire to the three bikers across the street. They are squatting behind their bikes, shooting at her, waiting for her to run out of ammo.

"Where's your bike, Sapph?"

"Got hit in the shoulder," she answers breathlessly. "Can't fucking steer."

Fuck. Where the fuck are Pitch and Monster? I tell her I'm coming in as I speed up to her location. I slow down enough for her to clamber on then speed off. I fire at the attackers, hitting two of them. The third wisely ducks down and doesn't follow me. Sapph leans against me as I race back to the club. Only one arm holds onto my waist; the other is pressed between our bodies. I'm thankful she didn't have any qualms about my touch aversion. While I don't like this, it doesn't bother me. I can handle this to get her safe.

We make it back to the club where Vic and Harpo are waiting at the doors. Vic and a few others guide Sapph inside so Vic can help her. Tyler and the rest of the men on my run turn into the parking lot then, with Pitch and Monster just behind. Before I can approach them, Harpo gets my attention.

"You need to see this, Mor."

I follow him into my office where he sets his laptop on my desk. He clicks through screens of messages arranging a hit. A long string of messages I don't have the patience to read.

"What is this?" I huff.

"A text chain between Monster, Pitch, and some other guys. I haven't pinned down who they are yet. Seems to be some random guys they knew. Pitch arranged a hit on Sapph during this route, expecting us to think it was an attack on the mafia."

That mother fucker.

"Get everyone in church."

My teeth grind together as Harpo rushes out of the room. Anger burns every inch of my body. They put out a hit on someone within the club. Technically, Sapph isn't patched in, but she has been here longer than Pitch and Monster. Monster was patched in a year ago and hasn't given us any reason to doubt him. Pitch has always been a shithead, but he does the job and doesn't cause any serious problems.

I rip off my cut as Tyler walks in. My clothes are sticky from Sapph's blood. I yank the hoodie over my head, then the shirt, but it rips. I tear it off and toss it in the trash. Rage flows through my veins, and I want to kill them. I want to kill them for attacking Sapph. I want to kill them for attacking within the club. I just want to fucking kill them.

"Harpo told me," Tyler says, anger lining his words. "What are you going to do?"

I pull on a new shirt and take in the state of my cut. It's soaked. If I put it back on, I will still be covered in blood. I settle on carrying it until I have time to clean it. I don't have that time now. I don't even have time to consider what I will do. Instead, I stalk past Tyler and into the meeting room where every member of the club, minus the eight with the truck, are waiting for me.

I drop my cut on the table, take my seat and bang the gavel so hard I feel it up my arm. I glare at Pitch and Monster. Monster stares at the ground, unwilling to meet my gaze. Maybe he didn't orchestrate this. Maybe he had little to do with it, but he knew. And that's too much. Pitch, the fucking asshole, has the audacity to appear innocent. Vic occasionally mentions the audacity of mediocre white men.

I didn't understand the meaning of it until now. I stare into the face of a mediocre white man that has a death wish.

With a deep breath, I pull the stoicism straight out of my ass because I don't feel it at all.

"Explain why Sapph's blood is on my cut," I glare at Pitch. He shrugs nonchalantly.

"She got shot. You saved her. You're the hero we all deserve." If there wasn't a table between us, he would be dead. Unable to speak, I nod at Harpo. Without instructions, he connects to the TV in the room and shows the text threads planning this attack. Pitch finally looks guilty, but not enough to soothe me. I want him trembling with fear. Harpo explains to the club what he found. When he is done, everyone glances around uncomfortably. We haven't had attacks within the club like this. There have been fights and squabbles over girls or some shit, but nothing of this caliber. They fully intended to kill Sapph.

"Explain," I seethe. My voice is low and menacing, matching my emotions inside. Pitch looks up at me, glances quickly at Monster, who still has his head bowed, then back to me.

"She's fucking your old lady. We all hear them, in her room screaming when you're out."

"And that means you get to put a fucking hit out on her?" Pitch doesn't say anything, just stares with his goddamned audacity.

"You stupid fuck sack," I spit at him. Tyler curses under his breath. A few men shift in their chairs around the room. Those who have been around for a while are shocked by my reaction. If I acknowledged some indiscretion in the past, I would stare and then walk away. Most insults aren't worth my time. But these guys nearly killed one of my best friends. I've beaten men for trying to attack Tyler or one of my other men.

"What they do," I speak slowly, each word dripping with malice, "is none of your business." I stand from my chair and take a step toward Pitch. Everyone else sucks in a breath as I stalk toward him. Members step out of the way, giving me the space to walk easily.

"She's a fucking whore and trying to steal your woman," Pitch says. His words are angry, but a hint of desperation flicks just under the surface. I don't say anything else. I grab the back of Pitch's neck and slam his head against the table. His nose cracks with a sickening sound. He screams, then falls to the floor, clutching his face.

"Sapph and I have an agreement," I glare at all my men. "If you ever think a member of this group is doing something worth death, you bring it to me." My voice is low and heated. I grab the gavel and stand at the head of the table. I glance at Tyler and nod. We've spoken about holding another vote to change the bylaws. We planned to wait but now seems like a good time.

"I, uh, make a motion to change our bylaws and patch Sapph in," Tyler says.

"Second," Rio shouts from further in the room without hesitation.

"Motion to change the bylaws and patch in Sapph," I bark, uncaring about proper procedure and language. "All in favor," I raise my hand and look at my men. Every one of them raises their hand except for Pitch. I kick him where he is still curled on the floor. He whines but raises his hand. I storm back to my spot at the end of the table.

"It's unanimous. Bylaws are changed, and Sapph will be patched in." I bang the gavel on the table. The sound slices through the room. "Take these two to the closet. Sapph can decide what to do with them later." I kick Pitch in the shin for good measure as I leave the room to find Vic and Sapph. I'm still livid. Rustling and grunts sound behind me as the two men are drug to the basement.

I look for Vic and Sapph but can't find them. They couldn't have gone far. Sapph needed medical attention. I can't find them anywhere. Tyler runs up to me with his phone extended.

"Did you see Vic's messages?"

"No," I pull out my phone to check. A few missed calls and many text notifications pop up. I scroll through the texts quickly. Vic had to take Sapph to the hospital. Her injuries were too severe for Vic to fix on her own. Another message explains that Sapph was taken back for surgery and that Vic is in the waiting room. Fuck, this is worse than I thought.

Chapter Twenty-Six

VIC

THIS IS BAD. THIS is so fucking bad.

Sapph's shoulder is wrecked. I don't have the capabilities to repair it, let alone the equipment I need. The bullet is embedded in the bone. I cleaned the area, put a bandage on it, and drove her to the hospital. I wanted to tell Aleks and Tyler but couldn't interrupt their meeting. Sapph didn't tell me what happened. I'm not sure she was lucid enough to. She was struggling to stay focused and awake. She lost a lot of blood.

She is in surgery now, and I'm sitting in the waiting room, trying not to have a panic attack. I don't think the injury is life-threatening, but she bled so much. Doors at the end of the hall swoosh open, and several sets of heavy footsteps pound down the hallway. Aleks walks through the door first. I'm on my feet and running into his arms before anyone else can enter.

I can't stop the wave of tears when he wraps his arms around me. The stress of the day and fear for Sapph's safety is overwhelming. Aleks sidesteps so the others can come into the waiting room. I'm not sure who is here, but it doesn't matter now. Aleks holds my head and back as I sob into his chest. The past couple of weeks have been more stressful than I care for. Things would get bad when I was with Wes, but never this many incidents this close together. I can see why Aleks wanted me to leave. I won't leave, but I understand it. Is this number of attacks normal for them?

I calm down after a few moments. Tyler pulls me into a hug when Aleks releases me. A fresh wave of tears falls at the comfort I get from my brother. I went for so long without seeing him. We were so close when we were little. We've been close since then, just not physically. I don't cry as long this time. When I step back, Rio offers some tissues but doesn't try to hug me. I would probably keep crying if he did.

Now that the tears have shed, I feel a bit better. Rio hands a bag to me, explaining Harpo sent it for me. I open the bag to find clothes for Sapph and me, my favorite cookies, and a bag of candy. Harpo is so thoughtful. I ask why he didn't come. Tyler tells me he is working with Catherine to sort things out after this clusterfuck.

I take the clean clothes to the bathroom. I look like a wreck. I'm covered in Sapph's blood with wrinkled clothes. My eyes are red and puffy and tear streaks cut down my face. I remove my clothes and do my best to clean off the blood off my skin. I won't be able to get it all until I can shower, but I get enough off. Anxiety spreads through my veins at the amount of blood on me. I don't know how long ago she was shot, but it was a long time for her to still have been bleeding on me like that. I take several deep breaths to soothe the fear as I put my dirty clothes in the bag and cover them with several paper towels before placing Sapph's clean clothes on top.

I join the three men on the couches. They look like shit, too. Rio and Tyler are covered in dust and grime from the road. Their hair is flattened from their helmets, and exhaustion is written on their faces. Aleks is still covered in blood on one side, Sapph's blood. He had her on his bike for the ride back. I can't help but wonder if he had any issues with her being that close to him. He hasn't been more willing to touch anyone since I showed up. I don't know if that will ever change.

I watch the three of them, taking in how they look and act. Despite their exhaustion, they are jittery and chatty. The adrenaline hasn't completely worn off. They will all crash hard tonight. I will, too. The thought occurs to me that I should stay here with Sapph instead of going home. Sleeping in a hospital room is not ideal, but I'm not leaving Sapph alone.

Tyler tells me what happened with Pitch and Monster. My hands ball into fists, and my teeth grind together. The anger boils inside me. Aside from what I did to Wes, I'm not a violent person. Pouring alcohol on someone's cuts isn't entirely violent, though. I didn't do it in the name of cleaning his wounds, but compared to how he got those cuts, it could hardly be considered violent. After hearing what happened, I want to do some genuinely violent things to those men.

"Are you Runi's girlfriend?" A young nurse walks up to the group as she addresses me. It takes me a moment to realize she is talking about Sapph. It's rare someone uses her real name. I stand quickly and tell her I am. I spare a quick glance at Aleks. I should have mentioned that, but I haven't had a chance. In the chaos of everything, I forgot I told the nurses I'm her girlfriend.

"She's out of surgery now," the nurse explains. "You'll be able to see her in a few minutes once she's awake. The surgery went well. She should regain full use of her shoulder in a few months with physical therapy." I sigh a relieved breath. Gods, I was so worried about that. "We did have to give her blood. She'll stay here for a few days while we monitor her, but we expect her to fully recover." I nearly sob again at hearing that. The nurse leaves after promising to return once Sapph is in her room.

I drop into the chair behind me and place my head in my hands. I'm all cried out at this point, but relief shudders through me. Aleks rubs my back as Tyler and Rio discuss the good news. They send messages to let others know. I lift my gaze to find Aleks staring at me.

"You know," he starts in a low voice, "she told the nurses she was your girlfriend when she took you to the ER."

"Are you upset?" I ask, worry replacing that relief I just felt. Our arrangement was that Sapph and I would just be friends with benefits. We haven't discussed changing that.

"No," Aleks shakes his head. "It's just interesting." I offer a sad smile and lean into his side.

I must doze off against him because I start awake when the nurse comes to get us. She tells us only two can go back for now. Tyler and Rio decide to go back to the club. Since Sapph is doing well, they'll visit her later, giving her time to rest. Aleks walks with me as we follow the nurse back to Sapph's room.

Sapph is hooked up to several machines, and her shoulder is bandaged and in a stabilizing brace. I know what people look like after surgery. I've seen people connected to more machines than her. I knew what to expect when I walked in here. I still didn't prepare for the pang in my chest seeing her like this. My eyes swell with tears, but I will them not to fall.

Sapph turns her head and offers a weak smile when we enter. I kiss her cheek and take in the meds they have her on. It's been a while since I've been in a hospital, not counting my recent stay, but I still remember everything from when I worked as a nurse. Aleks takes a seat in the corner, stoic as always.

"How do you feel?" I ask softly. I know she doesn't feel great, but I need her to say something so I can gauge her mood.

"Like he threw me on a bike and nearly killed me," her lips turn up in an almost smile. Aleks snorts behind me.

"I didn't throw you. You jumped," his voice holds a hint of amusement. I can't help but smile. She's doing well enough to joke, and that's a good sign.

"What about Pitch and Monster?" Sapph asks seriously. I take a step to the side so she can see Aleks better. While they told me what happened, I wasn't there and don't want to mess up the details.

"They're in the closet. You'll decide what happens," he pauses, considering something. "Pitch was the mastermind. He thought you were trying to steal her from me."

"I could only be so lucky," Sapph says with a laugh, but it doesn't sound like a joke. I take her hand and squeeze it. She shifts over in the bed, and I crawl in beside her. I make sure I'm not on any of her lines as I snuggle in gently. Her entire body will be sore. Hopefully, she's on enough painkillers she isn't uncomfortable. Sapph rubs my back soothingly, which is ridiculous since she's the one that needs comforting.

"I don't want to decide," she says after a while. She looks to Aleks, then me. "You pick, little bird."

Aleks sucks in a breath at her words. He hasn't heard her use that nickname with me. He didn't know she also calls me that. Sapph glances at Aleks, misunderstanding his reaction.

"It impacts her as much as it did either of us. Why shouldn't she make that call?"

Aleks's expression is unreadable. He could be thinking so many different things right now. He didn't know about her nickname for me. He has tried so hard to keep me out of the club business. There's no way he would be okay with this. He stares for a long moment, then finally nods to Sapph. I'm surprised he agreed so readily.

"You should go back to the club and get some rest," Sapph says with a kiss to the top of my head. Aleks stands in the corner, clearly ready to go.

"No, I'll stay with you." Sapph just shakes her head and gives me a slight push.

"Go get some rest. Come back in the morning with good coffee for me."

"You sure?" I ask with a wrinkled nose. Sapph nods and pushes me again. I climb down from the bed and give her a quick kiss. Aleks practically drags me out of the hospital room. I don't want to leave her alone tonight. I want to stay by her side, offer her comfort, and care for her. Instead, I amble, holding Aleks's hand as he leads me to the bike.

The roar of the wind helps silence my thoughts as I hold onto Aleks's body. Today has been overwhelming. How did things change so quickly? And now I'm responsible for choosing a punishment for the two men that endangered my...

I'm not really sure what to call her. She's not officially my girlfriend. We need another discussion before we can claim that title. Fuck buddy feels too casual for what we have. Friend doesn't feel like enough.

My nerves ramp up as we enter the garage. I bite my lip as we climb off the bike and store our helmets. I don't know what to do. I don't want to go to bed, not yet. I won't be able to sleep. Aleks takes my hand and pulls me toward the rooms. When we get to the second floor, I stop. He looks back at me. Staring up at him, I can see the exhaustion in the corner of his eyes. The events of the day have worn him down.

"I'm not ready for bed."

He gives a slight nod in acknowledgment. "Want to go to the backyard?" I nod and turn in that direction. The backyard is surprisingly empty for as early as it is tonight. Everyone must be in bed or getting drunk in the bar. I spot Harpo by the pool and walk over to him. I thank him for the clothes and snacks. He is smoking and offers the joint to me. I take it and collapse next to him.

I take a long pull and blow it out slowly. Aleks sits on the chair across from us. I take another hit and offer it to him. Aleks takes the joint as Harpo asks how she is. I explain what the nurse said and how she was when we saw her. The joint is passed around several more times as we sit quietly. The effects hit me, altering my vision and relaxing my shoulders.

I drop my suddenly weighty head onto Harpo's shoulder. I feel him tense, but I'm too tired to really care. Aleks watches me, but his expression is unreadable. I can't try to figure him out right now. I stare at the stars in the night sky, feeling incredibly small and insignificant. The stars are beautiful. It's a clear night, but the light pollution keeps all the stars from coming through. The few that are bright enough to shine through are lovely, though.

"Sapph asked me to deal with Pitch and Monster," I say suddenly.

"What do you want to do?" Harpo asks.

"I don't know. I've never done anything like that. I'm a nurse; I help heal people," I explain.

"Want to know what I would do?" I nod against his shoulder, curious for ideas. I let my eyes close as I try to envision what he would do.

"I would take them out to the middle of nowhere, dump them, fire at them blindly, then leave," his casual tone makes me giggle. It's tough to stop once I get started. Harpo chuckles with me. Even Aleks has a lift to the corner of his lips. Once I settle down, I have questions.

"But wouldn't they come back and rat you out?" Harpo's shoulder shrugs against me.

"It's possible."

His answer doesn't give me much confidence in his plan. It's not a terrible idea: a bit of tit for tat. The three of us sit quietly for a while. Thoughts pop into my head and then fade as quickly as they appear. I give up on trying to find a solution for the men. I'll do that later. Instead, I absorb the heat from Harpo's body and the hot summer air of San Antonio at night. I think I am finally acclimating to the weather. Maybe. Sort of. Okay, fine. I'm not at all, but I don't mind it while I'm high.

Aleks eventually drags me inside. We shower together and crawl into bed. We're both too exhausted to do anything more than cuddle. I snuggle against his chest, inhaling his clean scent. I kiss his chest and slide up so my face is level with his.

"I love you, you know," I tell him gently. His lips find mine in a soft kiss. It quickly becomes possessive, but before it can become anything else, Aleks pulls back.

"Sleep, bird," he whispers as my eyes lose the battle to stay open.

Chapter Twenty-Seven

ALEKS

I WAKE UP IN Vic's arms. At some point in the night, I turned over and became the little spoon. One of her arms is tucked under my head, the other over my ribs. She has a leg thrown over my waist, and the entire length of her body is pressed against mine. She feels more like a monkey than a big spoon, but it doesn't change my feelings. I feel warm, loved, and safe. These aren't feelings I ever get. It's strange and almost unsettling to have her behind me.

Last night was weird for me. I wasn't surprised when Vic told the hospital she was Sapph's girlfriend. I expected that much. When Sapph called her "little bird," I was shocked. I haven't asked if she knew I call her "bird." If that wasn't enough to throw me off, seeing her cuddle with Harpo was. I had forgotten about him being in my bed with her until she rested her head on his shoulder. I wasn't angry, just confused. Something is clearly going on between Vic and Harpo, but I can't tell what. I don't know what to expect of Vic. The solution is a conversation, but that sounds miserable.

When I agreed to this arrangement with Sapph, I thought it was just that. I wasn't expecting an entire relationship for any of us. I haven't dated anyone, only had a couple of fuck buddies in the last few years. I want to date Vic, but she doesn't want to settle down with one person. Does she want a polyamorous relationship with Sapph and Harpo? Will there be more people in the future? What does that mean for me?

After breakfast, Vic and I go to the hospital. I take a car since we need to stop for coffee. It is weird driving a car instead of my bike. I can't remember the last time I drove a regular vehicle. Vic is happier this morning than last night. She orders coffee and does her happy dance after her first sip. She's adorable in a way I never expected for a girlfriend of mine.

When we get to her room, Sapph is already awake but not as happy as Vic. We give her the coffee and some flowers Vic picked out for her. Vic pulls a chair to the edge of the bed and chats about unimportant topics. Sapph is oddly quiet all morning. We have lunch; nurses come in to check on Sapph and adjust meds as needed. Vic chatters away about anything she can think of. She is trying to boost Sapph's mood, but it's not working.

It's close to dinner time when silence settles in the room. Several other members have stopped by throughout the day, but it's just the three of us. Sapph speaks up, breaking the quiet.

"They are discharging me tomorrow."

"That's good," Vic grins. "I'll let Shirley know, and she can whip up some of your favorite foods. Have they said if it will be morning or afternoon?" Vic pulls out her phone to start making plans.

"I'm not going back to the club," Sapph speaks firmly. I'm shocked by her announcement. It sounds final, as if her mind is set.

"Oh," Vic starts, crestfallen. "Okay, are you going to stay with a friend? I can grab some things from your room for you." Sapph shakes her head.

"No, I'm going to the airport." Vic's back straightens. This is a new development. She didn't have any trips planned that I knew of. She usually lets me know when she plans to leave. When she doesn't elaborate, Vic questions her.

"Why are you going to the airport? That's probably not a great idea after surgery."

"I'll be fine," Sapph's words are harsh, and Vic flinches. Sapph's expression softens, realizing how she hurt Vic. "I need to get away for a while. I'm going to see my grandparents." She's mentioned her grandparents before. She was close to one of her grandmothers, but she hasn't seen them in a long time. They don't live close by, but I don't remember where.

"Where?" Vic's word is so soft I almost don't hear it.

"India," Sapph replies, equally quiet. Vic sucks in a small breath. I rise to stand behind her. I hold Vic's shoulders, pulling her back against me. Our height difference is staggering when I'm standing, and she is sitting. I squeeze her shoulders, but she doesn't react to me. Sapph finally makes eye contact with Vic, who I'm positive is crying by now. Sapph glances at me, then explains.

"My grandmother was just put on hospice. I haven't seen her in years. She is my biggest supporter, and I need to go see her." Her eyes grow red as tears slip down. "Plus," she adds angrily, "I can't go back to that fucking club. They put out a hit on me." Vic chokes and leans over the bed. Sapph rubs the back of her head as her shoulders shake.

I haven't told Sapph we held the vote to patch her in. It hasn't come up and slipped my mind with everything else. I could tell her now, but I don't want that lingering over her. I won't use it to make her stay where she is uncomfortable. She clearly needs a break, and I don't blame her.

"How long will you be gone?" I ask, reaching out to rub Vic's back. She turns her head to look up at Sapph. Sapph shrugs one shoulder.

"I don't know. I found a good physical therapist I can work with. Maybe a few months. Maybe longer." She looks down at Vic sadly. "We can still call every day. The time difference will put us waking up and going to sleep around the same time." Sapph strokes her finger over Vic's cheek. Vic nods but doesn't move to sit up.

"Okay," Vic whispers. "We can bring you a bag of your things tomorrow before you leave."

Sapph shakes her head and then motions to something behind us. On the couch is a small weekend bag I haven't noticed. "Harpo brought me some things this morning. I'm going straight to the airport once I'm discharged. I already have my flight booked." Vic gasps, sitting up straight. She wipes her cheeks in a feeble attempt to stop the tears.

"Can I see you in the morning?"

"I think we should say our goodbyes tonight," Sapph shakes her head. I can feel Vic fighting her tears under my hands. She is trying to be strong and supportive for Sapph, but it's a struggle for her. She wants to keep Sapph here. I do, too, but Sapph has left enough that I am confident she'll return. Eventually. Hopefully.

A nurse walks into the room but quickly turns and says she'll be back later once she sees Vic. I squeeze Vic's shoulders before speaking to Sapph. "We're here if you need anything. I expect you to come back." Sapph nods to me.

"You'll have to turn the water off to my shower," she jokes. I laugh, remembering when Vic told me their shower was broken a few months ago. I hold my fist to Sapph, doing our usual no-contact fist bump. I offer her a sad smile, then lean down to Vic. I kiss her head and whisper that I'll wait in the hallway.

I lean against the wall and check my phone while Vic says goodbye. Catherine sent a message earlier today that I didn't check. She explained that the mafia doesn't realize the attack was internal. They believe it was an attack on their shipment, the exact reason we were hired. It's best they think that way. Knowing the truth would make us look weak and likely cost us the job.

She agrees we shouldn't tell them the reality of the situation then asks about Sapph's condition. I debate telling her Sapph is leaving. My thoughts war with a response before I finally tell Catherine she is doing fine. Once I send that message, Vic walks out of the room.

Her eyes are red but dry. Her cheeks are puffy, but she looks angry. She barely acknowledges me as she walks to the parking deck where the car is. In the car, she sits with her arms crossed and lips straight. I don't know what to say or do to comfort her. We ride silently for a while before she speaks.

"I want to see the messages." She doesn't need to elaborate. I know what she wants. I don't want her to see them. Pitch was a piece of shit before all of this, and it shows in his messages. He very clearly laid out why he wanted the hit on Sapph. She doesn't need to read that. At my hesitation, she holds her hand out expectantly. I take a deep breath and pull my phone out to drop in her hand.

She unlocks my phone, knowing the code from all the times we sat together and scrolled Reddit. Things were easier then, I think. But they weren't really. We were lying to Tyler. She was still scared of Wesley. She had no money and didn't like taking mine. Things are a bit more life-threatening now, but no less complicated. She types messages on my phone. She shuts off the screen and drops the phone into the console. She doesn't say anything else.

At the club, she climbs out of the car and stalks inside. I've never seen her stay this quiet for this long. Concern grows in my gut for her state of mind. I follow her like a lost puppy dog. I don't know what else to do, but I won't leave her alone. She goes straight to the closet in the basement. Tyler and Harpo are just outside the door, waiting for her. A small part of me is surprised, but the fear continues to spread.

Vic doesn't even stop to greet the two men. She pushes past them and into the white room. Pitch and Monster are chained to chairs in the middle of the room. Each has cuts and bruises on the exposed skin and likely more on the covered areas. Once inside, Vic stands in front of them without speaking. Tyler and I stand on either side of her. Harpo clicks the door shut behind him before joining us.

I can now see why people say I'm frightening. I never considered myself to be particularly scary. I'm just me, but watching Vic stand silently in front of people she's angry with, I get it. The silence is terrifying. How will this pan out?

"Even if," Vics voice cuts through the silence in a chilling tone. Pitch and Monster look up at her. Pitch is indifferent, but Monster is terrified, as he should be. Vic starts again, "Even if Sapph was trying to steal me from Aleks, how does that warrant death?"

"We don't steal from each other," Pitch hisses between swollen lips.

"Ha!" Vic yells loudly, humorlessly. Her hands ball into fists, then release, then curl in again. She's on edge but isn't sure what to do. I won't take this from her, but damn, I want to. I don't want her to go this dark. She's sweet and light and happy, not this terrifying little monster in front of me.

"She steals an old lady, so you steal her life? Is that how things go?" Vic asks Pitch. He stays silent. Her face rises with a wickedness I've never seen. A menacing smile spreads across her cheeks. She is terrifying and so fucking hot. Why is it so arousing to see her like this? I adjust my pants, praying I don't get a hardon in front of Tyler while his little sister tortures men. That would be awkward.

Vic walks to the corner where all the supplies are. She glances over them, then starts repeating "knives" in a sing song manner. It's downright petrifying. Monster is tense, staring at the ground. Pitch glares between Tyler, Harpo, and me, trying to look intimidating. The bar for intimidation is really high with Vic acting this way. Pitch falls short naturally, and being tied to a chair doesn't help either.

"Do you have any forceps?" Vic calls, looking at me then Harpo and Tyler. I shrug. While I'm sure there may be some in here, I always use fists. I don't grab anything from the corner. I'm glad Vic isn't using her fists, but the curiosity might kill me. My anxiety over her mental state is long forgotten by now. Watching her move around the room in her Daisy Duke shorts and t-shirt like she owns the place is doing unspeakable things to my cock.

"Um, yeah," Harpo starts when he realizes Tyler and I don't know. "In the drawer," he points, but eventually walks over to show her. They stand shoulder to shoulder, speaking quietly. Their voices are soft enough that we can only pick up a few words, despite the silence in the rest of the room. An odd feeling strikes me as Harpo grabs something from a high shelf to hand to Vic. It's not jealousy, not even anything like it. They work well together. They're good friends. Before I can consider that feeling any further, Vic asks about music and connects her phone.

Britney Spears blares through the speakers, sending a jolt through the room. Vic adjusts the volume and giggles. That's definitely a first for this room. No one giggles in here. She has this Harley Quinn vibe right now. She's hot, adorable, and utterly terrifying. She walks to the middle of the room where Harpo has placed a table. She drops her instruments with a loud metallic clattering and claps her hands.

"Alright, boys," she says cheerfully. "Let's get this party started." The song changes to the song by the Black Eyed Peas and I can't help but wonder if that was intentional. "Sapph tried to steal me, you tried to steal her life. Both of you were unsuccessful, I might add. Though, Sapph never actually tried to steal me. Sharing is caring, my friend. But I digress." Vic turns to the table. Her voice is back to her normal, cheerful tone, but it's not right. There's an evil undercurrent to it. She's in a different headspace than normal.

"Stealing, stealing," she swoons as she snaps on some nitrile gloves. With a pop of the last glove, she turns to face Pitch with a scalpel and forceps in her hand. "Now, I'm going to steal your voice. Tyler, will you hold his head please?" Fear widens Pitch's pupils. Tyler strolls over and grips Pitch's head. "Don't twist," she instructs, "I want his tongue, not his life."

Pitch bites his lips together in an attempt to stop her. She just laughs and shoves the forceps between them. Pitch grunts and fights as Vic works to grab his tongue between the forceps. She is focused solely on the task at hand. The song changes to Adele and I wonder how many people have been tortured to Adele. The number has to be pretty low, right?

Vic finally gets his tongue and yanks it out. She makes the first slice and blood pours from his mouth. She doesn't hesitate. Pitch's screams turn to garbled whimpers. Tears stream down his face as Tyler loosens his hold ever so slightly. When Vic is done, she tosses the forceps with the tongue on the ground. It splatters sickeningly as the metal clatters against the hard floor. She grabs another pair of forceps and walks toward Monster.

"Can Harpo hold me?" he asks meekly. Vic is stunned, but simply nods. Harpo walks over as Monster takes a deep breath. He holds his tongue out for Vic, and she freezes.

"You aren't going to fight me?"

"No, we tried to kill her. It's the least we deserve," Monster explains, holding his tongue out again. Vic stares, warring with herself over his response. I stand straighter, ready to approach her. Whether she'll need support or someone to do this for her is to be determined.

"Why did you do it?" she asks gently. Monster shakes his head, looking down at the ground.

"I didn't want to be involved. I like Sapph. It was weird that she would try to steal you, but Pitch included me in the messages. I was as guilty as him at that point."

"You could have told us. We could have stopped it." Vic sounds hurt and broken again. I take a step toward her, but her focus is on Monster. He takes another breath and meets her gaze.

"I know." He sticks his tongue out, closes his eyes, and waits for his punishment. She looks to Harpo, then me, and over to Tyler. Monster peeks an eye open, assessing the situation. "I'm guilty, Vic. Do it." She glances back at me with a question in her eyes. I don't know what that question is. Does she want me to do it? I haven't done it before, but I will. Does she want to do something else? Does she want to let him go? I'm not okay with that, but I'm sure we can work something out.

Vic walks to me and holds her arms wide. "Hug me," she whispers as she leans into my chest. I wrap my arms around her body, but she keeps her hands out. They are covered with blood and saliva and she is holding the forceps and scalpel. "Is she coming back?" I squeeze Vic tightly. I know what she is asking, but I can't say that Sapph will come back. She always has, but she has never left like this before. When I don't answer, Vic pulls away with a nod.

She stands in front of Monster, who still has his tongue out and eyes closed tight. Vic stares for a moment, then stabs the scalpel into his chest. He screams with pain as Harpo grabs his shoulders to hold him upright.

"Oh," Vic says calmly, back to her terrifying persona, "I think I went too deep with that one. Do we have a medical kit in here?" Tyler laughs from his spot across the room.

"No, Vic. We don't have a fucking medical kit in here. We're the fucking bad guys. We don't take care of people." Vic cuts along the patch on Monster's cut. It bleeds as she drags the scalpel through his cut, shirt, and skin beneath.

"Well, I'm not a fucking bad guy, Tyler," Vic sasses as she slices through the bottom part of the tag. She is removing the tag with the club name on it, inch by inch. Blood covers his chest as he whimpers in Harpo's arms. "Will you go get it from our room? It's in the closet. I don't want him to die." Tyler laughs loudly as he leaves the room.

The song changes to Miley Cyrus just as Vic finishes removing the patch. She tosses it on the floor beside the tongue in the forceps. She takes a sidestep and cuts into his name tape. Monster isn't fighting, only twitching occasionally with the pain. She isn't cutting as deep as the initial cut. She sings along to her playlist as she makes quick work of the name tape. It clatters on the floor with a wet sound as she moves to the back.

"Hold him forward," she tells Harpo. Then she slices through his back, removing the large logo patch in the back. Monster openly weeps as she cuts through all the layers to remove the patch he once earned. I had never considered removing patches. We always take the cut, but we take the whole cut, not just the patch. He'll be left with a scar where these were though. It's a devious plan.

Tyler returns with the kit and whistles at her work. He drops the kit on the table with a loud thud and checks on Pitch. He's fading in and out of consciousness. Vic notices and asks Tyler to remove his patches before he is unconscious. Tyler cheers and grabs a large knife, opting for it over the scalpel Vic uses. I hold Pitch's shoulders while Tyler cuts. Pitch doesn't fight, barely has the energy to hold himself up at this point.

"I never considered cutting patches," Tyler glances up at me. "We should do this more often." The devious glint in his eyes matches his sister's. I forget how similar they can be at times. It's almost eerie. When the patches are removed and on the floor, Vic puts a few stitches in the deeper cuts and Pitches tongue, insisting she doesn't want them to bleed to death.

When she is done, she begins cleaning up. The three of us help her, making quick work of the process. She has stopped singing, despite one of her favorite songs by P!nk playing. She takes in the two men in the chairs. Pitch is unconscious. Monster sits weakly in the chair. Both men are covered in blood and bruises with exposed, broken skin glistening where their patches were. She glances between the three of us as many emotions flicker through her eyes.

"I'm done with them. You can do what you want now," she says to no one in particular.

"I'll get them out of here. Dropped off somewhere to fend for themselves," Tyler answers.

"Good," she thinks momentarily before asking, "Is anyone in the backyard?" Harpo digs out his phone to check. I keep my eyes on her, unsure of where she is going with this. She has astonished me with every new move today. A thrill runs through me as guesses fill my mind at what she's thinking.

"It's actually empty," Harpo explains, turning his phone to show her the security feed.

"Can you lock the doors to keep everyone out for an hour?" Harpo nods and presses a few buttons on his phone.

"I'm gonna fuck him in the pool. Give us an hour before you unlock it?" She pauses, then adds, "Or come out there."

Jesus fucking Christ. Tyler groans and my dick jerks, hardening quickly in my jeans. I adjust my stance, trying to make extra room. I did not expect the evening to go like this, but I'll be damned if I'm going to complain about it. Harpo blushes but assures her he will do that. Vic grabs my hand and leads me to the backyard without another word.

Once we are in, the door locks behind us. Vic sheds her clothes as she walks to the pool. By the time she makes it to the edge, she is completely naked. I'm frozen by the door when she dives into the water. Her ass soars through the air, and my mouth goes dry. The splash of the water breaks my spell. I go to the edge and sit in a chair to remove my boots. Vic resurfaces, props her elbows on the edge, and watches as I remove my socks and shoes. I stand and unzip my pants, letting my cock jut out straight. She bites her lip, eyes filled with unadulterated lust.

Vic pulls herself out of the water and crawls toward me. My cock leaks as water slides down her body. I tug my shirt over my head as she kneels at my feet. Her hands stay on her thighs as she wraps her lips around my dick. I groan and keep my eyes on her. She stares up at me, giving me exactly what I need to make this experience enjoyable. She hasn't done this since the ice cream social. I've wanted it, but we haven't done it. We were interrupted several times, and it hasn't happened.

She takes me to the back of her throat and hums. I groan at the sensation. My eyes roll back in my head. I could come just from that. She leans away, then dives back into the pool. I don't know what this girl is doing tonight, but I follow her. I dive in behind her and follow her to the edge. She props her elbows on the pool's edge as I rise to meet her.

"Fuck me, Aleks," she commands.

I've never fucked in a pool before, but that doesn't stop me from sliding up to her. Her legs wrap around me, lining up my cock with her entrance perfectly. I slide in but have nothing to grip onto. I can't thrust with my normal rhythm. It feels awkward instead of pleasurable. She rolls her hips a few times but quickly comes to the same realization. Because we are in the deep end, we don't have a good way to thrust deeply. She releases her legs then shifts to the side.

"Up here," she tips her head behind toward the poolside. I climb out, and she's on me faster than I expected. She shoves me on my back and drops down on my cock quickly. We both moan at the feeling. I grab her hips as she bounces on me.

My knees are bent over the edge with my feet in the water. She rides me violently, seeking her release.

"Make me come on your cock, Aleks," she demands. My hand finds her clit as she changes the motion of her hips. I moan at the new direction. "Don't come inside me," she grunts between thrusts. I'm confused; she's never told me not to come before. After a moment, she curses and grabs my shoulders.

"Sit up. This surface hurts my fucking knees." I do as told while she shifts with me. Once I'm sitting, she grinds on me. I return my fingers to her clit, working hard circles over the nub. She's in the mood for violent sex. It's not generally in my comfort zone, but I'll give this woman anything. Within moments, she is clenching around my dick. Her walls tighten, her head tips back, then her whole body shivers with her orgasm. It takes every ounce of self-control not to nut inside her. She slows her movements, then slides off me into the water. I watch as she resurfaces to grab my thighs.

"Slide down," she says softly, more like her normal voice. I scoot to the pool's edge, trying not to drag my tight balls on the rough surface. Once I'm at the edge, she sucks my whole length into her mouth. I groan, understanding why she told me not to come. She bobs a few times before my balls tighten. My release is so close. She hums around my cock, and I lose it. The first few spurts hit her tongue then she sucks harder. My stomach clenches as she tries to suck my soul out of my dick. My eyes roll into the back of my head as pleasure courses through every cell in my body.

My orgasm lasts forever, jutting into her mouth as she licks and sucks. My cock finally softens, but Vic doesn't remove her mouth. She changes to soft licks and kisses. A ticklish feeling courses through my body, causing me to push her away from my oversensitive dick with a laugh. She grins up at me. I want to burn that image into my mind. I want this face to be the last thing I see when I die. I stroke her cheek gently, then push her back into the pool.

I slip into the pool in front of her. She wraps herself around me like a little monkey. Her lips are on mine instantly. I can taste both of us blended on her tongue. I kiss her deeply as I hold onto the edge of the pool. She pulls away from the kiss but stays wrapped around my body.

I realize my demons have been silent for days now. I've been emotional: angry, scared, nervous. But I didn't lose myself. Richard and his bullshit crossed my mind but didn't overwhelm me. I have finally found some peace in this fucking hell hole. Vic is my peace.

CHAPTER TWENTY-EIGHT

ALEKS

I FINISH A PHONE call with Catherine. The run with the mafia is tonight. Eight of us will ride out I 35 toward Corpus Christi. The mafia shipment is arriving in that port today. We will ride back around the truck until we hit San Antonio. We'll swap out with another group of eight. They will follow the truck to Waco then come back to the club. This stretch has had the highest number of attacks according to Catherine. I don't question the rest of the route the shipment will take.

Other motorcycle clubs have attacked the trucks in hopes of stealing the product, and the cartels have attacked a few times in attempts to thwart their competition. Occasionally, the law will get involved. That is where Harpo will come in with his tracking. He has been working with Rio so we can have more than one guy tracking these runs for us. It's a good move, but I have a nagging feeling I can't quite place. Harpo has worked for me for nearly eight years without backup.

I walk into my bedroom in search of Vic. I freeze when she walks out of the bathroom. She is wearing wide-legged trousers with a red button-down tucked in. The top few buttons are undone and showcase a necklace Sapph bought her.

Her hair is down and curled at the ends. She has on more makeup than I have seen her wear.

"Will you run up to my room? I have a pair of black booties I want to wear in there, but I need to leave soon," she explains as she walks back into the bathroom. She has an interview today. Part of me doesn't want to get the boots in hopes she will stay, but I do as asked and get the boots for her.

"You don't have to get a job," I tell her as I hand the boots over. She only mentioned the interview in passing, never giving me a chance to discuss it with her. "We will pay for everything you need." I don't need to mention that we have been paying for everything for the last several months.

"I know," she says while pulling the boots on. "It's not about the money." She stands in front of me, stepping into my space. "I need to get out of here more often. I love you guys but can only do so much here."

"You can help with our injuries. There's always something for you to do," I try again. If she's always working, I won't get to see her as much. I don't want her to leave.

"There's not enough, and you know that. I can count on one hand the number of times I've been needed." Her arms slide around my waist. I reluctantly wrap mine around her back. She stares up at me from my chest. "It's only part time, two or three days a week. I'll still see you all the time."

I don't say anything else and squeeze her tightly. I don't understand the need for a regular job, but I've never had one. Since I was a teen, I've consistently earned money through the club. Even with the businesses I own, I'm mostly an investor. I have people running the businesses for me. I don't work steady hours; it suits me well.

"I love you and your beautiful face, but I need something else to do. Besides," she pulls away to walk to the door, "I should do something with that expensive ass education I got." She slings her bag over her shoulder and glances up at me with a questioning look. "Wish me luck?"

I step up to her, gently grab her chin with the side of my index finger and thumb and lift her face to me. "You don't need it," I tell her softly, leaning in for a kiss. She pulls back before I can kiss her.

"You'll ruin my lipstick," Vic says softly then points to her head. "Just give me a forehead kiss." My lips turn up in a playful smile.

"I thought you didn't like forehead kisses," I question.

"Only when I don't get passionate, tongue fucking kisses," she responds playfully. I kiss her forehead and watch her leave our room.

I walk to Harpo's room and knock on the door. He calls me in, and I settle on his couch. This time, his monitors are on, showing maps, screens of code, and websites with information I can't process. He finishes typing something and then spins in his chair to face me. I learned a while back that he needs to finish whatever he is working on, so I wait patiently until he addresses me.

"We ready for tonight?" I ask when his attention is on me. He nods in response.

"Yeah, Rio will take point after the switchover. I'll be here to help, but he'll run it alone."

That's good to hear. I'm glad Rio is doing well. If Harpo has confidence in him, I do too. I don't know much about this stuff. I can gather essential information on someone, but Harpo goes far beyond that.

"I have another question for you," I start slowly. Harpo tips his head for me to continue. "I want to take Vic out somewhere. She's tired of being here all the time. But that's not my area of expertise," I explain, hoping he understands.

"You want to take her on a date?" He gets it.

"Yeah, but not like dinner. Somewhere else."

"Hmm," he pauses, thinking of a response. "The fair is in town. She might like that." That's a good idea. I've never been to the fair, either. It wasn't something I ever thought to do. My entire life is this club. "You might consider taking a car," he says cautiously. "It's hot, and she isn't fully acclimated to the heat. A car might be better since she won't wear shorts on the bike." As much as I despise cars, he does have a point. Vic refuses to ride in anything but long sleeves and pants on the bike. I don't blame her, but I haven't laid down a motorcycle since I learned to ride. I don't push the issue with her.

It strikes me how in tune Harpo is with Vic. They're close to each other and spend time together when they can. Harpo has been flighty lately. He'll spend time with her, then bail earlier than expected. Or he'll avoid her for several days. She notices every time but has stopped bringing it up. It's strange to see him act like this. He has always been consistent.

"Thanks. Everything good with you?"

"Yep," his response is almost too fast. It toes the line between a normal response and a rushed one. I don't push it, though. If he needs to tell me something, I'm sure he will. I nod to him and leave the room.

I don't know what to do for the first time in a long time. Vic isn't here. Sapph isn't here. Everything is squared away with the club. Tyler is spending the afternoon with Lacey before our run tonight. What did I do before Vic came into my life? I try to think back to before she showed up. I drank, moped, and worked out. That was all I did. I can't drink today since I have the run in a couple of hours. I don't want to mope, surprisingly. Things are going well; I don't need to sit and wallow. Working out does sound good.

I change and head to the gym. I pull on my headphones and start up some music. Despite Vic getting her phone a few months ago, she still uses mine for music. So, when Britney Spears blares through my headphones, I'm not surprised. At this point, I'm comfortable working out to Britney Spears. It has a good beat and keeps my mood up. The only downside is I occasionally pop a boner remembering the first time Vic worked out with me. Other than that, it's great.

I don't see Vic before we leave for the run. She came back from the interview while I was in the gym. She didn't interrupt me, and I worry the interview didn't go well. I would be surprised if it didn't. Vic has an excellent resume, all the paperwork she needs, and a fantastic personality. And I don't just believe that because I love her. She is genuinely great with others as long as she isn't torturing them. Even then, she still has good bedside manners.

Harpo helped Vic get everything she needed squared away before her interview. She has her driver's and nursing licenses. She changed her address, and the divorce is settled. Wes tried to fight it, but the papers were solid. The only thing for him to do now is payout. We aren't surprised he hasn't done that yet. She doesn't need the money; it's the principle of the matter at this point.

Tyler, six other guys, and I mount our bikes and ride off. I texted Vic before we left, but she didn't respond. I push her from my mind so I can stay focused on the task ahead. The ride out to the meeting spot is quiet. We didn't expect any issues during this part. After we meet the truck and leave, things will be dangerous. We pull into the warehouse to meet the drivers and park our bikes. We walk over to two guys standing beside a truck smoking cigarettes.

"You Mor?" One of the men ask. I nod as I stop in front of them.

"Clint," Tyler speaks up.

"I'm Emilio," the first guy informs us. "That's Lonnie. You guys ready to ride?"

"Yeah," I answer. "We'll have two in front of you, two behind. Two others will be further ahead and behind, watching for trouble. Catherine gave you the radio?" They wave a device in front of me. Since we don't have direct contact with the drivers yet, Catherine is still our go-between. We hope to cut her out within a few months, but we must build trust first. We had Catherine give them a radio to connect to our Bluetooth helmets. We need accessible communication in case things go wrong. Without saying anything else, we mount our bikes and head out.

Tyler and I take the lead to watch for anything. We scan for cops, bikes, and SUVs that look suspicious. The guys closest to the truck will dart in and out of traffic. They'll stay close to the truck but not close enough to look out of place. Their job is to ensure no one pops up from the side or cover us if we need to run someone off. They will stay with the truck at all costs. The two in the back watch for anyone coming up from behind. If we miss someone that tries to approach after we pass, they will be the guys to deal with that.

The ride is surprisingly smooth. We are lucky tonight that this ride goes well. Not all of them will, but for a first ride, we couldn't ask for a better trip. We discussed how to handle the swap. The drivers didn't want to make more stops than necessary. We found a gas station just outside of the city. Each group of two bikers will meet their respective replacements at a different location to take over while the truck refuels.

Tyler and I meet up with our guys. We swap helmets so the new crew is on the same wavelength as the drivers. We give a brief rundown of how the night has gone. Then the two drivers take off. We wait and watch as two more bikers pass, then the truck with the two bikers behind. We watch for another moment until the final two guys follow the convoy. Once everyone has passed, Tyler and I ride off to meet up with our men.

We ride back to the club together. Since we don't have our Bluetooth helmets, the ride is peaceful. There's something different about riding at night. The air is cooler, so it doesn't feel like riding through a heater. Fewer cars take up space on the road. We can cruise faster than we would during the day. Night rides can be relaxing.

At the club, I check in with Harpo and Rio. Things are going well. Rio looks a bit nervous but is doing well according to Harpo. With everything settled, I head to my room to change into something cooler. I expect to find Vic in the backyard, dancing or swimming. I'm surprised when I see her in a tiny lace thong and matching bra on the bed.

Vic clicks off the TV and tosses the remote aside.

"How was your run?"

"Good," I answer simply. "How was your interview?" I step over to the bed to remove my clothes. She rises on her knees, unzips my hoodie, and pushes my cut aside.

"Good," she teases. "They have a few more interviews and will let me know by next week." I hang my cut on the wall as Vic pushes my hoodie to the ground. Her hands slide against my stomach to lift my shirt over my head.

"I thought you would be out back tonight," I speak softly as Vic runs her fingers over my chest.

"Maybe later. We should celebrate now." Vic leans in to lick my nipple, then wraps her lips around it.

"How do you want to celebrate?" My voice is deep and husky from the arousal. I place my hands lightly on her hips as she moves to my other nipple.

"You could make love to me," she says playfully. I tip her chin and lean down until my lips meet hers.

"Is that what you want?" I brush a soft kiss over her lips. Her hands grip my waist.

"No," she mumbles.

"Tell me what you want."

"I want you to fuck me from behind and pull my hair," her voice is deep and sensual as she explains exactly what she wants. "I want you to come on my back, then take me in the shower and finger fuck me against the wall. Then, we'll go to the backyard where I'll sit in your lap while you hold me, and we smoke and watch all our friends have fun." Her fingers trail my stomach as she talks. They make deft work of unbuttoning my pants and wrapping around my cock.

"Goddamn," I whisper. "You're insatiable."

I toe my boots off and spin Vic around. She drops to her elbows with her ass up to me. I take a moment to appreciate the view. This is the position I took with girls before Vic. I haven't had her like this for fear of treating her like the others. I rub my hand over the globe of her ass realizing how stupid that was. Vic is nothing like them and this would never be so emotionless.

My fingers slide down her slit to find her soaking wet. She's probably been in here thinking about this for hours. She has a tendency to tease herself into near orgasms. I have a feeling that's what she's done tonight. I pull the thong to the side and rub my dick up and down her wet opening, coating my hard length in her arousal. She moans at the motion.

I notch the tip just inside her and grab her hips. She wiggles, trying to get me further inside her, but I don't budge. She shakes and thrusts, growing more desperate by the second.

"Aleks, please," she whimpers. Her movements grow more violent, and I tighten my grip in response. She groans at my rough grasp, and her pussy clenches around me. She's so desperate.

"I need you, Aleks," she begs with her face buried against the bed. That's all I need to hear. I slam inside her and she groans loudly. I keep one hand on her waist to hold her steady and wrap her hair around my other. Her back arches as she leans into the pull. She cries out, muttering a string of curses and pleas. I pound her from behind ruthlessly.

On instinct, I thrust her head down to the bed. I lean over her, releasing my grip on her hip to support my weight on the bed. My hand stays on the back of her shoulders as I pound inside her. My balls slap against Vic's clit, drawing out short, broken moans. For a moment, my mind flashes to the times I've been in this position. Vic whimpers and I remember all the noises I suppressed so as not to give Richard the pleasure.

"Aleks," her soft voice breaks my thoughts. "Please make me come. I want to come before you come on me. Please," her breathy words bring me back to the present. I lean back from her and wrap my arm around her body. I flick her clit several times, and she cries out with her release. Her tight walls clenching around my cock keep me in the present. She chants my name through her orgasm and that is what pushes me over the edge.

I remember to pull out and finish on her back at the last minute. The white liquid spurts over her back, covering her lacy thong and smooth skin. A couple of jets shoot up to land on her bra, and some make it to the ends of her hair. She whimpers as the smell of my semen fills the area. I collapse on my back beside her. She immediately climbs over me, straddling my body as she peppers kisses on my face and neck.

"You're perfect, Aleks," she mutters between kisses. "I love you. You're beautiful. Thank you. You're wonderful." I've never needed praise, but damn if it doesn't have my heart squeezing. Without thinking, I wrap my arms around her to hug her, only to rub my hands through warm, sticky semen. She giggles as she realizes what I just did.

"I believe I was promised a shower," she reminds me as she rests her head against my chest.

"Yeah, it's in your hair, too," I explain. Vic chuckles as she continues trailing kisses over my skin. I scoop her up and go to the bathroom to give her exactly what she requested.

CHAPTER TWENTY-NINE

VIC

IT'S BEEN A WEEK since Pitch and Monster were left on the side of the road outside San Antonio. We haven't heard anything from them. Curiosity spikes occasionally over what happened to Pitch, but it's always brief. I don't really care. He may live; he may die. Part of me feels bad for Monster but not Pitch. I have to live daily with only a call or two from my best friend. Pitch is to blame for that. Death would be too good for him.

I never thought I would be able to torture someone. Even after everything Wes did to me, I didn't know I would be capable of inflicting pain. I couldn't beat someone the way the guys do. I would hurt myself in the process. Physical violence isn't the only way to hurt someone, though. I enjoyed coming up with creative ways to hurt people who hurt me and mine. My experience is limited to Wes, Pitch, and Monster. Part of me wants to do it again, but at the same time, I don't. I don't want to follow that darkness, no matter how fun it is.

I'm chowing down on breakfast at our round table. I bounced with joy when I saw Aleks replaced the booth. Now, I get to sit between Aleks and Tyler. It was going to be Sapph, but that's not happening. Harpo is sitting with us today. I love it when he is here. He's such a great friend. I haven't had many male friends, so it's really nice to have one. He doesn't always want to be around us. He's introverted and needs time alone. That's fine with me. I enjoy the time we do get together.

"Bird," Aleks says softly, leaning close to me. I glance up at him as I sip on my creamy iced coffee. "Harpo told me about a fair. You want to go to it?" My eyes light up with excitement. I've been to a fair once or twice. Usually, it was for visibility for Wes. He would meet with constituents and show that he's a "regular guy" and "just like them." I never got to go on any rides or eat the foods I wanted. We walked around a space crowded with people and greasy food while trying to look friendly and happy. It was miserable. Aleks won't make me do that, and that's exciting.

I nod enthusiastically, glance at Harpo, and ask if he's going. He shakes his head and explains he has work to do. My face drops, but I'm not surprised. He hasn't gone out with me since we saw Top Gun. I wish he would. Maybe I'll invite him somewhere soon. Now isn't the time to push that issue. He has things to do, and I have funnel cake and perilous rides waiting for me.

I finish breakfast quickly and rush to the room to change clothes. I wear shorts around the club because Satan's ass is jealous of how hot it is down here. Some days, I regret moving from Pennsylvania to Texas in late spring. I should have gone in November. It's late summer now, and I still haven't acclimated. How does one acclimate to the bottomless pits of hell? I step out of my shorts as Aleks closes the door to the room.

"I'm going to take the car today," he tells me. My eyebrows shoot up in surprise. He hates taking the car. I wasn't even sure he could drive one until he took me to the hospital.

"Really?" I stand there with my shorts around my ankles, my ass hanging out. He chuckles as he walks by and pinches my ass. I tug my shorts back up and change into a tank top while he changes into sneakers. I pull on comfy shoes and kiss his cheek before heading to the garage. I turn on the radio and jam out as we ride. I haven't felt this good in a long time. I'm not passing up a minute of enjoying this.

Once inside the fair, Aleks asks what I want to do. I lace my fingers through his and start walking. I don't know what I want to do; I'll figure it out when I see it. I point to all the different things I find interesting. We arrive at a barrel racing show and sit in the stands to watch. I cheer on the riders as Aleks sits quietly beside me. I'm not surprised he's so quiet, but how does one remain that quiet at such an exciting event?

After the races are over, we walk around. I find a funnel cake stand and get one with all the toppings. Every single one. We find a bench to sit on as we chow down the sugary goodness. I giggle as Aleks gets some powdered sugar on his face, then his cut. We walk around more, just strolling through all the vendors and booths. We walk through one of the barns, but the animal smell is potent. While it's not as bad as some places, it's still not somewhere I want to linger. They do an excellent job keeping it clean, but the hot air doesn't help.

Once we are back in the fresh air, we go to the games and rides. We play a few games but don't win anything. I complain about how they are rigged as Aleks tries to win the largest toy for me. I'm not upset when he doesn't. I have no desire to carry that around. I convince Aleks to go on the Ferris wheel with me. He's very skeptical but agrees. I love the view from the top. Aleks gives me a sweet kiss while we are stopped.

"I love you," I whisper to him.

"Love you, too," he says back, but something flashes through his eyes that I can't identify.

"What are you thinking?" I question.

"I never thought I would get this."

My heart breaks into a thousand pieces at his response. I snuggle closer to him, clinging as hard as I can. He deserves to be this happy. I really hope he is. He seems to be, but I don't have a good baseline to judge him. I should ask Tyler later. Or maybe Harpo. He would know.

After the Ferris wheel, we decide to leave. It's getting hot and crowded. Aleks drives us away from the fair but not back to the club. He turns into a forest and parks in a secluded area. He has a blanket and snacks for us. It's not a complete picnic, but we hang out alone. Outside of our room, we never get to hang out without other people around us.

He spreads the blanket on the ground beside a tree. He leans back against it and pulls me into his lap. We snack as we discuss the likelihood of Aleks opening a coffee shop. He already has several businesses and has said he doesn't want to open more. I'm almost positive I can convince him to open one just so I can get my favorite drinks made for me. It's all in jest, and he knows that. It's a fun, hypothetical, meaningless conversation.

My phone vibrates on the blanket. I check it to find Sapph video calling me. I answer and hold the phone so Aleks and I are in view.

"Hello, Sapph," I greet. She responds, but she looks a bit sad. Her grandmother passed a couple of days ago. Sapph got to spend time with her, but it wasn't enough. I ask how the services went.

"It was fine," she sighs. "I just need a distraction now."

"We can do that," I start. Aleks lifts me and stands up. I watch as he walks to the car but turn my attention back to Sapph. "I got the nursing job!"

"That's awesome, little bird. Tell me about it."

"I'll be working two days at an urgent care clinic. It'll be nice to return to some chaos without throwing myself in full-time." I tell her more as Aleks walks back with a stand in his hand. I got the call yesterday about the job and haven't had a chance to tell her. I give her more details about the hospital as Aleks sets up the tripod. He has more stuff in that car than I realized. I wonder if it's all his. The car belongs to the club; it's not his personal vehicle.

Aleks takes the phone from me and secures it in the tripod. He lifts me up, takes his spot, and pulls me back into his lap. I'm telling Sapph about the fair when Aleks rubs his hand over my shoulder. It's a sensual touch, not something he ever does in front of other people. I don't know if a video call with Sapph truly counts as being in front of other people, but she can see what he is doing. With the tripod's new angle, our torsos are in view.

As I tell Sapph about the funnel cake, Aleks slides the strap of my tank top off my shoulder. I gasp and say his name, but he presses his lips against my skin. What is he doing? I glance at the phone to find Sapph focused on us. Before I can say anything else, Aleks tugs my top down, exposing my breasts. I inhale quickly, covering myself with my hand.

"What are you doing?" I hiss at him. He pauses and glances between me and Sapph.

"Giving her a distraction," he says matter-of-factly.

"Yes," Sapph says, "I want this distraction."

I scan the area around us. It's deserted and doesn't look like many people know about it. I slowly lower my arm. Aleks's hand returns to my breast. He gives a quick squeeze and then pinches my nipple between his fingers. My core tingles with excitement. I've never had phone sex before. I've never had a threesome, if this can be considered one.

Aleks shifts his legs, adjusting me to the center of the screen. He parts my legs over his thighs. I still have my clothes on, and everything is covered except for the one breast. I feel exposed, and that makes my cunt moist. I didn't think being watched would be such a turn-on, but it is. Aleks tugs down my other strap. My tank top gathers beneath my exposed breasts as he fiddles with my nipples.

He is pinching them instead of grabbing them. He's giving Sapph a good show. I'm surprised he's capable of such actions. I didn't think he would be willing to share in any form. He struggled with my arrangement with Sapph, but here we are. His lips are on my neck, and I arch back into him. My breasts are forced forward as I whine under his touch. I close my eyes and tilt my head to give him better access.

"Is she already wet?" Sapph's voice is breathy. Aleks's hand leaves my breast and slides down my body. Instead of going in my shorts, he slides over my thighs and slips in through the leg. His fingers slide over my soaking opening. I bite my lip as I look at Sapph on the phone. Her gaze is intense with flushed cheeks.

"I'm so wet," I answer when I realize Aleks won't say anything. Aleks nibbles on my ear, causing me to roll my hips into his fingers. They brush against my opening again. My concerns about being on the phone, Sapph being involved, and being in a public space fade away. I want more.

"Show me," Sapph demands. I look up in time to see her take her shirt off. She tries to rip it off but struggles to get it over her cast. She growls but manages to remove it and toss it aside. I wish I could see her breasts, but she hasn't moved to change the angle of the phone. Aleks's hand withdraws from my cunt to unbutton my pants. He pushes them over my hips as I press up on my heels. I kick the pants to the end of the blanket and settle back on his lap. My feet are positioned on the outside of his thighs with my core wide open. It's visible on the screen.

"Can I tell you what to do?" Sapph asks tentatively. Aleks flicks his fingers through my opening as Sapph watches. He nods behind me. His long hair drops over my shoulder. I reach behind me to push it out of the way. "Wrap one hand over her breast," Sapph instructs and Aleks complies. "Put one finger inside her."

I whimper as Aleks slides one single finger inside me. Only one, just as told. I hate it so much. It's such a teasing move. I can't get off with one. She knows that. Sapph knows I want to be stuffed and fucked. But that doesn't matter to her. She's not going to give me what I want.

"Sapph, please," I beg.

"Oh, you wanna beg?" Sapph croons. "Take it out and spread her open for me." Aleks pulls his finger from me as I fight back a whimper. His fingers pin my labia aside so I am on complete display for Sapph. "Fuck, you are so wet." A slight breeze blows over my open core, and I roll my hips.

"Sapph, don't tease me. I need to be fucked."

"Oh, you wanna tell me what to do?" She asks sardonically. "Smack her pussy for trying to tell us what to do." Aleks hesitates for the first time. I feel him tense behind me.

"Aleks, you don't..." I'm interrupted by his hand tapping my open pussy. I almost wouldn't have felt it if I hadn't noticed him release me. It wasn't a smack in any sense of the word. I shift against him, biting my lip, needing more touch.

"I said smack, not wave at it," Sapph demands. Aleks tenses again but doesn't hesitate. The contact is harder than last time but still softer than Sapph's warm-up hits. I grab Aleks's arms, which are wrapped around me, and roll my hips, opening them up more.

"Hit me hard, Aleks," I beg softly. "Punish me for speaking out. Make me feel good." He inhales deeply against my neck. I'm so distracted by his breath that when his hand lands harder on my exposed pussy, I gasp.

"That's it," Sapph whispers. "Give our little bird two fingers to show her she's a good girl." Aleks slips two fingers inside me and strokes. I whimper as shivers roll through my body. Sapph says something to him, but I can't make out the words. His hand grabs my breast while his fingers work my soaking core. I roll my hips into him, completely lost in his touch.

I hear Sapph's words this time, but it doesn't register until Aleks nips my shoulders. I grind on his fingers inside me, aching for more. I roll my hips and feel his hard cock under me. I shift back and forth so my ass rubs his cock. He hisses into my ear, then his hand hits my wet pussy harder than last time. The sound of his hand slapping my wet skin leaves me writhing against him.

"Sapph," I mumble, "please, I need more." I whimper as Aleks squeezes my breast with a brutality I'm not used to from him. "Can he fill me so I can come for you? I want to come on his cock, Sapph."

"Yes," Sapph shifts around on the screen. "Put your dick inside her. I'll be right back." Sapph disappears from the screen as I lean forward. Aleks is unbuckling his pants with a quick finesse. I shift onto my knees and then slide back until I am above him. Before I sink down, he grabs my leg to stop me. I twist so I am partially facing him.

"Are you okay with this?" I ask but am distracted when I see his hand stroking his long dick. My mouth waters with desire. I almost miss the nod before he tells me to grab the phone. I pull it off the tripod and offer it to him.

"Put it on the ground."

I place it on the blanket between our legs and glance back at him. He has a devious smirk on his face as I realize he is going to have me bend over the phone. Sapph isn't back on screen yet, but she will love that angle. I turn back and kiss him deeply. His fingers reach up to tickle my pussy. I curse at the feeling of multiple fingers quickly grazing my slick core. He hooks one finger inside me and pulls me backward. I adjust on my hands and knees and slide back to meet his cock. As I start to sink on him, Sapph returns on screen.

"Jesus fucking Christ," she mutters. "Ride him, little bird. Ride him," I bounce on Aleks's cock as I stare down at the phone. Sapph found a tripod or some sort of stand for her phone. She sits against the wall with a dildo thrusting inside her. My tits bounce on screen then Aleks's hand slides over and pinches my nipple. I groan and grind over him. In this position, my clit gets no stimulation. I prefer clitoral stimulation during sex. With everything going on, I'm so fucking close already.

I mutter 'fuck' several times while Aleks tweaks my nipple. I whimper as my movements become more erratic, seeking the release I need so much. Aleks slips his other hand around slowly. I realize where he is going and grab the phone. I angle it just in time for Sapph to see Aleks flick my clit. I barely hold the phone as my orgasm crashes through me.

Liquid squirts out of my body as I scream. A powerful orgasm rips me in half. I nearly sob as Aleks flexes inside me with his own release. Sapph's eyes widen as she watches me squirt on the blanket beneath us. Aleks's semen leaks from my pussy around his cock.

"Holy fuck," Sapph mumbles before her own orgasm crashes through her. I watch her pussy quiver as aftershocks roll through mine. Aleks's arms band around me just before I crash onto the ground. He scoops me up and twists me into his lap. His lips press against my forehead. He takes the phone I forgot about from my hand and props it on my knees. Sapph has a hazy, content look on her face.

"If I would have known that's how you would distract me, I would have called sooner." We all laugh at her statement.

"That's my go-to distraction," I mutter against Aleks's chest. Sapph perks up in response to some noise on her end.

"Shit, I think my parents are up," she stares off-screen.

"What the fuck, Sapph?" I tease. "Do you always have phone sex in your parents' house?" She glances at me with a devious grin.

"It's not the first time and won't be the last if I have any say in it," she explains. "It was definitely the best." I blush and snuggle into Aleks more. I could definitely get used to having both of them, but I shouldn't. I don't know when Sapph will be back. Aleks may not be willing to do this more than once and probably wouldn't if she's here.

"Gotta go. Talk soon." Sapph disconnects before we can respond. I toss the phone to the side and wrap my arms around Aleks. He holds me back just as tightly.

"Thank you," I mumble into his chest. He tips my chin up, a motion I love more and more each time he does. He gives a gentle kiss.

"Anything for my bird."

If my insides weren't already liquid, that would do it.

CHAPTER THIRTY

ALEKS

I think I'm coming home soon.

It's about time.

I'm thinking by Thanksgiving. Anything going on then?

Vic's birthday is next week.

Perfect.

I can hear the devious plans Sapph is dreaming up. Thanksgiving is in two weeks. Sapph has been gone for close to two months. Vic has been here for over six. Having Sapph back will be amazing. The video calls are fun, but it's not the same. We haven't had phone sex again. Vic and Sapph have, but I wasn't around for that. While it was a fun activity, I'm not upset about missing out on it. I enjoy having Vic to myself.

I text with Sapph for several more minutes, making plans for her return. Vic leans over to me to peek at my phone.

"Who are you texting" She asks incredulously. "You don't even text me like that." She all but whines the last part. Why would I text her when she is sitting beside me?

"Catherine," I lie.

It could be the truth. Catherine is arriving today. She and Jo are coming in for a check-in. Things have been going smoothly with the mafia. We've had several more runs with them. We fought off a couple of attempts. One attempt to attract the truck was by a rival cartel, not the one we work for. It was bloody, but we were successful. After that, the mafia increased the number of runs we go on. The club is rolling in money. We've started renovating some of the members' rooms and are considering expanding the club.

Vic rolls her eyes at me. She knows I'm lying. I don't think she suspects Sapph is coming home. We want it to be a surprise for her. Sapph has several plans. I only hope she doesn't disappear with Vic for several days. I expect at least 24 hours of them being locked up in Sapph's room. Hopefully, it won't be longer than that. I haven't been away from Vic for more than a few hours and prefer to keep it that way. She is my peace, my heart, my everything.

My life isn't one of those cheesy romance novels. I still sleep like shit. I hate being touched by anyone but Vic. It's not like she magically cured me. I jump when she touches me unannounced. I haven't choked her, but I can't say I haven't come close. We haven't kissed in the rain since I picked her up from jail. I don't think kissing outside the jail is romantic, but Sapph reads some weird romance. Who knows? Maybe people are into that.

"I need to get ready for work," Vic tells no one in particular as she rises from the table. She kisses my cheek and rounds the table. Harpo walks up, and Vic wraps her arms around him. She has been trying harder to get him to hang out with her more. She really wants him to be her friend. He tries, but there is more going on with him than I know. He hasn't said anything but has been so off the last couple of months.

He wishes her a good day as she saunters off. She loves working again. She tells me some fascinating stories. She takes precautions not to share private details that could get her in trouble. And even if she did, who would I honestly tell? The demons in my head don't break any HIPAA laws.

Harpo sits at the end of the table to discuss the meeting with Tyler and me. We don't have much that hasn't already been said. We just rehash what we know to make sure everything is fresh. Tyler is still dating Lacey. They are surprisingly good together. I always thought Lacey was a patch chaser, wanting the highest-ranking member she could get. While Tyler is that person in this club, she hasn't tried to use that to her advantage. She likes being around him. She and Vic get along well, even going shopping a few times.

Catherine arrives with Jo, and we greet them at the door. A prospect helps them get their stuff into their room. Once they freshen up, they meet us in my office. It has been such a long time since they were first in here. Things are so different now.

"They want to do a processing run this week," Catherine starts, always straight to business.

"The warehouse is set up and ready to go. We finished the remodel a couple of weeks ago. Everything works and is in place," Tyler explains.

"Good. We'll let them know, but Harpo already has the details for us to go over," Catherine turns to him.

Harpo leads the conversation. He explains that we'll meet the truck like we usually do. Instead of the trade-off, we will lead them to my warehouse. This is one of the properties in my name, not the clubs. I'm not positive how that happened. It belonged to Richard, who left it to me in his will. He really had some sick sense of humor. Or torture. The warehouse was quickly updated to serve our needs for the mafia. They'll bring in their shipments, including clothes for Aphrodite, my boutique. A few women will show up to process the drugs, and then my men will guide the truck back through San Antonio toward Waco.

When it's time for the run, Tyler and I head out with our six men. We meet the truck and guide them to the warehouse. We don't run into any problems on the way. We had some a couple of weeks ago, but it's been quiet since then. It won't last, but I'm glad for the simplicity tonight. Catherine is already waiting at the warehouse when the truck backs in.

A crew of men unloads the truck. I stand to the side with Catherine and watch the process. Jo chats with my men off to the side. She is wearing a knit cap tonight to cover her rainbow-colored hair. She has at least five different colors in her hair that I can see. I haven't seen her with that many before. It's pretty but very bright. It makes her easy to spot in a crowd and more recognizable in illegal activities. She hides it well, though.

Tyler is joking around with Jo when a group of women enter the warehouse. I'm surprised to find they know exactly what to do. The only thing they are unsure about is which room to go into. Tyler guides them then returns to Jo to goof off. It's nice to see them building a good relationship. It's always good to have established relations. Catherine and I stand quietly, neither needing to talk or joke around. Our phones ding with a message from Harpo that things are all clear and Rio is taking over.

"Harpo tells me you are having some issues in Chicago," I speak to Catherine, both a question and a statement.

"Not issues like here," she nods to the truck leaving the warehouse. A new one will arrive shortly to drive the drugs north. "The capo there is shady. I want to get better eyes on him before I renew his business contracts." Harpo has been working on research for her on that project. Rio has taken over all the club's security. Harpo does any digging or hacking we need, but it doesn't come up frequently.

The next truck arrives around the same time as the members who will replace us. The women come out of the room they were working in. The mafia's men walk into the room and bring the drugs out. They load bags of drugs in various sizes into the clothing crates, then the truck. After everything is packed, we drive back to the club while the other group rides with the shipment. By the time we get back, it's late. I go to my room and find Vic passed out after her shift.

The following day, I am doing paperwork in my office when I hear Jo yell at Vic. The bar doesn't open until this afternoon. Only members and prospects are in the dining area. It's quiet in the early morning. I step into the hallway to watch Vic. I'll never get tired of watching her. I lean against the wall, out of the way enough that they won't notice my presence.

Jo is at the bar with Harpo by her side. Vic settles at the seat between the two. I can just make out their conversation.

"You're polyamorous, right?" Jo asks Vic.

"Yeah," Vic answers with a slight shrug.

"What is your ideal number of partners?" I've not spent much time with Jo, but she has never been one to hold back on personal questions.

"Um, I don't know. I think I'm maxed out now with Aleks and Sapph. Maybe if Sapph weren't coming back," she hesitates briefly. "I'm holding out hope it'll be soon. But I think two may be all I can manage. It's a lot, especially with the club." Jo nods solemnly. Harpo's shoulders drop, and he turns to face the bar instead of Vic.

"Vic!" Tyler yells in a sing-song voice across the bar. She offers a gentle smile to Jo then hops down and makes her way to her brother, yelling his name in response. Tyler has always been a happy-go-lucky guy, but Vic takes him to a different level. I'm glad they were able to reconnect after all the time between us. I'm also happy he didn't kill me when he realized I was fucking her.

Jo rubs Harpo's back and offers an apology to him. There is a correlation between his mood and Vic's answer. I'm going to get answers from him.

"Harpo," I call out. He turns to look at me, trying to hide his forlorn expression. I nod to my office for him to follow. I take my seat, and he settles across from my desk. I don't exactly know how to ask what just happened. Before I can come up with an answer, he speaks.

"I'm going to Chicago. I'm leaving in a couple of days." That's just before Vic's birthday, and Sapph returns.

"Why?"

"Catherine needs my help up there. Diego, the capo for Catherine, is getting into some shit. She needs a guy on the inside." Catherine never said anything to me about wanting Harpo to go to Chicago.

"How long will you be there?" I ask. I don't want to lose Harpo. He has left for short stints with Catherine, but something tells me this won't be a brief stint.

"A few months, at least. Depends on how long it takes Diego to trust me." He doesn't sound excited about this trip. Not that I blame him. Traveling from San Antonio to Chicago in November is quite the change.

"Does it have anything to do with Vic?" I venture to ask. His eyes snap to mine then dart away quickly. That's all the answer I need. It does have something to do with her.

"I..." he pauses, then looks at me. "I fell in love with her. I'm not going to tell her. I just need to get away to clear my head."

"Fuck," I mutter. I get that Vic is amazing, but I didn't expect all my friends to literally fall in love with her. "Jesus Christ, I asked you for dating advice. She's always hanging on you." Harpo is saddened by my words. "I'm sorry, man," I apologize. "I never suspected that was the case. I shouldn't have asked you for all the help with her. That was unfair." I feel like shit. If I had suspected he was in love with her, I wouldn't have asked for fucking dating advice. Fuck, I'm an asshole. He waves his hand in the air.

"I'm glad you didn't know. I'm also glad the advice helped."

"You should tell her," I say. She may not love him back or be able to, but she would want to know. He shakes his head.

"I don't want her to feel bad or try to change her feelings," he looks up at me. "I didn't want to tell you because I don't want you to feel bad. It's my problem to deal with." Part of me wants to call him out for running from the problem, but it might be the best solution. Without telling Vic, she won't stop trying to spend time with him. He's not wrong that she will feel bad to realize their feelings aren't equal. She genuinely sees Harpo as a good friend. He is, but it has to suck being in love with a friend that can't return those feelings.

"Do you want to leave quietly? I'll cover your absence after you're gone." He looks up at me and nods.

"Yeah, that would be great."

Harpo left a week ago with Catherine and Jo. The mafia runs are going smoothly, and they didn't need to stay any longer. Vic did not take Harpo's quiet leaving well, especially since I couldn't explain the real reason why. She texts him frequently, though I try to do my best to stop her. I apologized to Harpo this morning for her texts. He replied that he doesn't mind and appreciates them. Vic is mostly sending him videos and memes. I hope it's harmless enough.

We're sitting at the table in the restaurant. It's closed all day. Sapph will be here any minute. Shirley is preparing a barbecue for tonight. The only way I can keep Sapph from disappearing with Vic for several days is to force them to be with the club. We'll have a party tonight and patch Sapph in. She never had a cut before. She wore a leather jacket, but it didn't have any patches on it. Tonight, I get to officially patch her in. I've worked out the details with the board, but not the rest of the club. I didn't trust them to keep it a secret.

Walking in now

I check Sapph's text and glance at Vic. She's in a heated debate with Lacey over who the better artist is: Britney Spears or Taylor Swift. My vote is Britney Spears, but I'm a bit biased. The front doors open as Vic makes some comment about

Britney still being relevant today. She is so invested in the conversation that she doesn't notice Sapph walk in.

"I'm back, bitches!" Sapph announces loudly for everyone to hear.

Vic's head whips up. The second her eyes land on Sapph, she scrambles out of her seat. She bumps into mine and several others as she beelines as fast as she can for Sapph. She squeals, catching Sapph's attention. Sapph spots her just as Vic leaps into the air. Sapph holds her arms out to catch her, but both women collapse on the floor.

They are laughing, crying, and kissing. I walk over to them, glad the restaurant is closed. Their actions would probably get the cops called for public indecency. I give them another minute until Vic starts practically dry-humping her. I grab Vic and lift her off Sapph. Tyler helps Sapph up and gives her a quick hug before Vic can attack her again. Sapph gives me a nod but turns back to Vic.

"My little bird," she croons as she steps in again. Sapph cups Vic's cheek and pulls her in for a deep kiss. It almost feels inappropriate to stand this close while they make out like that. I don't blame them. I would do the same thing, but it feels odd to just stand here.

"Okay," I state firmly. "Shirley is grilling tonight. You have a few hours until you need to be in the backyard. Go to your room." I nod over my shoulder as they break apart and look at me. Vic has tears streaming down her flushed cheeks, but she looks so happy.

"Did you know?" Vic asks me.

"Who do you think planned it all?" Sapph answers. I would think Vic is mad if I didn't know any better. She punches my arm lightly, but Sapph tugs her away. They run off toward their room, giggling and conspiring. I return to our table with Tyler and Lacey with a grin.

"I don't know how you do that, man," Tyler says, glancing at the two and then at me.

"What?"

"Let your girl go off with someone else, knowing they are gonna fuck." I shrug in response.

"It was going to be me or Sapph. I wouldn't win that challenge."

"Good point," Tyler says, and Lacey smacks him.

"You can't say that," she admonishes. "You're supposed to be on his side." Tyler huffs a laugh.

"Look, I love Aleks like a brother, but he is fucked up. Besides. Sapph is into some kinky shit. Aren't women supposed to be better partners?" He glances at me thoughtfully. "Don't lesbians get married on the second date? Shit, they would probably be married, living on a commune with thirty-two fucking animals. And I'd have to drive ten hours into bumfuck nowhere to find their off-the-grid farm." He laughs playfully. "So, thanks for letting my sister fuck both of you." I join his laughter at that hypothetical situation. I am glad that didn't happen.

I'm in my office, putting the final touches on the paperwork to officially make Sapph a member. She won't need to sign it today, but I want it ready for when she does. A knock on my door draws my attention. I look up to see Sapph walking into the room. I collect the papers and tuck them out of sight in a drawer. Don't want to ruin that surprise.

She collapses in the seat across from me. Her cheeks are still flushed from whatever she and Vic did. Her hair is wet, thrown over her shoulder. She looks relaxed and happy. I'm just glad that she is back.

"I want to talk with you about something," she says, leaning forward to rest her elbows on her knees. I expected this conversation. I didn't realize it would happen this soon after she returned. It's only been a few hours since she walked through the doors. I nod for her to continue.

"I want to ask Vic to be my girlfriend," she says calmly, then quickly adds, "but I don't want that to change your relationship. I don't want her to be monogamous with me when she has you." I'm thankful she added that last bit. I didn't expect her to try to take Vic from me, but she could.

"You should tell her tonight," I say. Sapph could ask, but we all know Vic's answer. "You should also tell the club while you're at it." The last thing we want is to repeat what happened during our trial run. It's not my place to disclose Sapph and Vic's relationship, but I will if it puts my members in danger.

Sapph nods her head thoughtfully. "Yeah, that's a good point." She leans back in her seat, eyeing me suspiciously. "You don't mind?" I huff a laugh and shake my head.

"I expected this before you ever left," I debate adding more. Still, I don't want to spoil anything in their relationship. They both love each other, but I don't know if they have told the other yet. I won't ruin that if they haven't.

"Thanks," she says softly. I don't always get to see Sapph's softer side. It's a nice change once in a while. "Want to walk up together? Vic will meet us up there."

I join her, and we walk silently to the backyard. Most of the club is already there. Music is playing; some people are swimming or dancing. Shirley has the grill going, and it smells incredible. Vic is on a lounger chatting with Lacey. They are probably still arguing over Britney Spears and Taylor Swift. I nudge Sapph's shoulder and point to Vic. Sapph glances down to where I just touched her and back to me. I shrug and walk off toward the bar.

I still don't like being touched by anyone but Vic. I can manage small touches occasionally. I don't like to, but I can. Sapph walks over to Vic as I go to the bar. Lucy is serving everyone despite being told she doesn't need to. She likes the work, so I don't fight her on it. She passes me a beer and the bag I stored there.

Lacey walks to Tyler's side when Sapph sits with Vic. They chat quietly for a moment, and then Vic's eyes widen. She glances at me for approval, and I nod.

She doesn't need my permission to date Sapph, but she wants to know it won't upset me. I give them a few minutes to hug and celebrate together before I join Tyler. He whistles loudly, drawing the attention of everyone in the club.

"We are gathered here, in holy matrimony, to celebrate…" Tyler huffs when Lacey slaps his stomach to stop his speech. No one is getting married; he's just being dramatic.

"Sapph," I call out and wave her over. She looks like a deer caught in headlights. We've never singled her out like this before. "You've been a part of this club for years, and it's time we made it official." I pull the cut out of the bag and hold it up for her. Her eyes go even wider than they already were. "We changed the bylaws after the stunt Pitch pulled. You're a full member now."

I hold the cut open as she slides her arm through. Her shoulder is healed with nearly full range of motion back. She adjusts the cut and glances around with wonder in her eyes. Vic stands by her side when someone from the crowd yells, "Speech!" Sapph huffs and turns to face the club.

"You mother fuckers should have done this years ago!" Sapph yells at everyone. She throws her arm around Vic's shoulders and pulls her in close. "Vic is also my fucking girlfriend now. So don't get any hair-brained ideas about me trying to steal her from Aleks. It's the twenty-first century; she can date both of us!"

The club cheers as Sapph plants a massive kiss on Vic's lips. Vic's cheeks turn red. They break the kiss as everyone turns back to dancing, swimming, or whatever they were doing before. Vic pulls away from Sapph, who starts chatting with other members and showing off her cut. Vic walks to me and wraps her arm around my waist. I glance down at her with a smile on my face.

"You're exquisite," she whispers.

I lean down and kiss my girlfriend's forehead.

Epilogue

VIC

Today marks a year since I showed up at Dionysus on a hunch that it was the bar owned by the Steel Warriors. It's hard to believe how much has changed in that year. I'm not the same woman I was then. None of us are, really.

Aleks has relaxed so much since I first showed up. He still lives up to his tag name, but he smiles more than those first couple of months. He's secure in our relationship, friendly with his club members, and occasionally cracks a joke. He tolerates Sapph being physically closer to him. He's not comfortable, but he tolerates it. Which is perfect for me because I love being squished between the two. I don't get it often, but I love it when we make a Vic sandwich.

Tyler proposed to Lacey last week. I haven't cried that hard in a long time. I'm so happy for him. They are perfect together. I love Lacey, even though she thinks Taylor Swift is better than Britney. I won't ever forgive her for that transgression. She's a few years younger than me and didn't grow up with Britney, but I still won't forgive her.

Rio has been excellent with security since Harpo left. His sudden departure sent me into a tailspin. Aleks tried to help but couldn't do much. I was still so raw from Aleks pushing me away and Sapph leaving after her accident. I couldn't accept Harpo leaving, too. It took me a couple of weeks to get back to normal. I still text Harpo occasionally. He is working with one of Catherine's capos in Chicago. He seems happy, but I miss him. I haven't fully processed the shift in our relationship.

"Here, let me help," Sapph finally offers. She bought me this strappy lingerie set to wear tonight. She's taking Aleks and me to a dungeon party her friend is hosting. I'm surprised she convinced Aleks to go. I don't know how she managed that. The lingerie is gorgeous but difficult to get into. She shifts the straps, and I realize this will not cover anything except my cunt. Even that has a hole for easy access. It's the most exposed I will be in front of other people.

"Little bird," Sapph groans as her fingers graze my pussy while she adjusts a loop. "You aren't supposed to be this wet already." Her fingers stay on my opening, sliding up and down. I breathe through the sensation. I've been learning to enjoy the touch instead of rushing to the orgasm. It's no easy task because I want that release. But the build-up is half the fun, so I will enjoy it.

She finally pulls away and sucks my taste off her fingers. My stomach does a flip, and I step over to kiss her. My taste on her lips makes me wetter. She takes a whole step back and grabs my dress. Her plan isn't to fuck me now, but I wouldn't be opposed to a quickie. Instead, she holds the yellow bodycon dress out to me. I slip it over my head and then tug it down. The outline of the lingerie is visible beneath the material. Very little is left to the imagination in this outfit.

"Perfect," Sapph kisses the tips of her fingers and waves them in the air in a chef's kiss. I chuckle at her antics as she helps me into a pair of six-inch heeled boots. I've never worn any this high and am terrified of falling. I hope she or Aleks will catch me. We meet Aleks in the garage next to one of the cars. His eyes go wide when he sees me. I'm pretty sure he stops breathing.

I step up to him and plant my hands on his chest. Despite the high heels, I'm still a few inches shorter than him. I'm closer than before, though. I kiss him gently. His hands grab my ass, then quickly slide up higher. He's used to holding my waist and miscalculated how tall I am now. I pull back to smile at him.

"Get in the back with her," Sapph commands. "I'm driving."

Aleks rolls his eyes, causing me to giggle. We climb in the back, and I settle in the middle, leaning against him. He keeps his hand respectively on my knee. My skin tingles beneath his touch. I want him to slide up higher. Sapph has a plan tonight, and it doesn't seem like Aleks will sway from it. For being an outlaw, he sure can be a stickler about plans.

We pull up to a house in a nice neighborhood. It has a huge yard, and the neighboring homes are barely visible. The driveway is empty. I expected more cars for a party. Maybe they parked further down the road? Sapph parks and guides us into the house with a bag slung over her shoulder. She rushes to the door, but the sidewalk is made of rocks. Aleks lets me hold his arm while I walk. I can manage flat surfaces fine, but this dramatically slows me down.

"Come on!" Sapph shouts once the door is open. I roll my eyes this time as Aleks and I slowly enter the house. Inside, I take in the modern suburbia décor and the silence.

"Sapph, you said this is a party. Where is everyone?" I implore.

"I never said party. I said dungeon. Come on," she grabs my arm and tugs me downstairs. Aleks follows behind me as we enter the basement. Sapph flicks the light on, shrouding the space in soft white light. She was not kidding about this being a dungeon. A St Andrew's Cross stands in one corner. Benches and chairs fill the other corner with one of the wave-shaped cushions along a side wall. Floggers, whips, and canes are hung near the cross. Rope hangs above the benches and chairs. LED lights are strung on the walls, and Sapph flicks them on, then lowers the other lights. The purple light creates a sexy feel.

"Why are you still in that dress?" With Sapph's command, Aleks walks over and grabs the hem of my dress. He slides it up my body. I raise my hands with my eyes focused on his face. He bites his lip as he peels the fabric away. He releases a deep breath as I stand before him in my lingerie. He steps in to kiss me, but Sapph calls out to us before he gets the chance.

"Over here," I find her standing beside one of the benches with a flogger in hand. This is my favorite. I walk over to her quickly, losing track of Aleks. She stands behind me and whispers how sexy I am into my ear. She pushes me forward so my chest lands on the bench. She pulls my arms over the edge and secures them to the bench. With these boots, I'm bent at a 90-degree angle.

The flogger lands on my ass, tingling my heated skin. I moan and turn my head to find Aleks. While he doesn't comment on my activities with Sapph, he hasn't shown interest in being involved. I can't see him. Another hit from the flogger distracts me from his presence. She hits a few more times then the licks become constant. She has two floggers and is spinning both against my ass. I groan loudly as my pussy clenches with the pain. Gods, it feels so good.

"She's making too much noise," Sapph says conversationally. "Fill her mouth."

For a moment, I can't remember who she's talking to. Then Aleks appears in front of me. I tip my head back to look at him, but the angle is too hard. I can't see him. Instead, I watch as he unzips his pants and pulls his cock out. I'm not surprised to see it's soft. He strokes it a couple of times to no avail.

"Sapph," I try to turn to look at her. "Let me have my arms." It's silent momentarily, and I can't tell what is happening. Then Aleks releases my arms from their bindings. While he is bent over, I trace my free hand over his stubbled cheek. Once my other hand is free, I cup his face and pull him in for a kiss. The floggers strike me again, and I groan.

"When I said, 'fill her mouth,' I didn't mean with your tongue."

Aleks stands in front of me. I grab his waist and take his cock into my mouth. I keep one hand on his stomach while the other cups his balls. I suck and lick the soft skin with my tongue. Sapph takes up flogging again, and I groan over his dick. He jerks inside me, hardening under my ministrations. Aleks slides his hands over my cheeks. Despite freeing my hands, I can't look up at him from this position.

My skin stings from the soft leather of the floggers. Aleks is completely hard in my mouth. I love the taste of him. Sapph stops flogging me and bends over my body. She whispers about what a good girl I am. My mind swirls in the haze of sensations and pleasure. She pulls me up; spit dribbles down my chin when Aleks's cock slips out of my mouth. She lifts my thigh and positions my boot against the bench I was leaning on.

"These boots need to be removed," Sapph tells Aleks. With his eyes on me, he unzips the boot and slides my foot out. The sight is so damn erotic I have to bite my lip to suppress a moan. When the boot is gone, he tosses my sock and cups my calf. He kisses my shin, and Sapph guides my leg down and shifts my weight. They repeat the process with the other boot.

I am putty in their hands. I can feel myself slipping into sub space. They guide me to the St Andrew's cross. Aleks secures my hands to the top of the cross. Sapph kneels in front of me. I fucking love it when they kneel before me. I may be the sub in this scene, but looking down at them is heavenly. She spreads my legs and straps each one to the cross.

Aleks grabs my chin and pulls my attention to him. His lips are on mine, and I moan against him. My fingers itch to grab his cock and stroke it. Sapph opens the hole in the crotch of my lingerie then her tongue is on my pussy. She licks my cunt as Aleks invades my mouth. Having both of them like this sends me writhing. My arms jerk to be released so I can touch them. It's pure torture that I can't. Sapph's tongue flicks my clit, and I'm about to come.

Then both of them step away, and I cry out. I was so close, and she stopped it all. I try to pull away from the cross to get them, but I can't. Aleks has tucked his cock back in his pants, but it's no less hard. His eyes are glazed and stuck on me. Sapph is digging in the bag she brought. She walks back to me.

"Do you know what I learned recently?" I believe she is asking Aleks, but neither of us responds before she answers her question. "Our little bird loves it when we kneel in front of her. Why don't you have a taste? She's so wet."

Aleks doesn't need more than that. He's on his knees with his tongue in my cunt instantly. I whimper at the sight. I really do love them on their knees. The way they worship me turns me into mush. I tug my hands against the chains, angry I can't run my fingers through his hair. He left it down today, and it's so soft and luxurious.

My ass is spread apart, and Sapph's tongue licks my back entrance. She doesn't stay there long because the position is weird with the cross. Her tongue is replaced by a lubed finger. Aleks continues working my clit but has pulled back from my opening. Sapph must be too close for his comfort. Doesn't matter to me. The feelings are glorious. Sapph's finger is teasing my ass. Aleks is licking my clit. I'm going to come in no time.

My pussy clenches with my impending orgasm, and Aleks steps back. I grunt at the loss and stare at him in confusion. He stands and kisses me deeply. I sigh against him at my taste on his stubble. Sapph gets a second finger inside me, and I groan. Aleks pulls back and walks to the bag. My head is swimming, not processing everything that is happening. He passes something to Sapph then his hands massage my breasts. I close my eyes, savoring the touch. Even if they won't let me come, I will enjoy every second.

A plug slips inside my ass. It's not overly large and feels like heaven. Sapph taps it a few times. I moan and nibble on my lip. Aleks's lips wrap around my nipple. My hand pulls again to hold his head. It's less frustrating that I can't touch him this time, but I'm still unhappy about it. Aleks moves to the other breast, and then a clamp is secured to the one he just had his mouth on. I moan loudly at the sensation. Once both nipples have clamps on them, the plug vibrates in my ass.

"Sapph," I beg, "please. I need to come. I can't handle it." The sensations are almost overwhelming. My body is on edge. My orgasm is so close it nearly hurts. A slight breeze could get me off at this point.

"Oh, little bird," she laughs. "We get to come first. Watch Aleks."

He stands in front of me with his cock in his hand. I'm reminded of the first time we were together. He masturbated in the shower in front of me. But I got to masturbate then, too. This is just wholly unfair. I watch as he strokes himself. His chest rises and falls.

"Aleks, please," I whisper. I don't know what I'm begging for. My release? His release? He steps in and kisses me. I roll my hips against him. He groans as my stomach rubs against his cock. "Will you come inside me?" I whisper in his ear. I could come just from his tip pushing in. His breathing is heavy and ragged as he rests his head against my shoulder. I nibble on the shell of his ear. My cunt tingles with desire.

Moisture leaks down my thighs as the plug vibrates at different intervals. I moan when it kicks up high. I hump the air, hoping for anything to get me off. Aleks steps back; his eyes are hooded as he looks up at me. He closes them tight as the first spurt of his release hits my stomach. I look down to watch the white jets land on the lingerie straps and my skin. I love watching him come on me as much as I love watching him kneel before me. His lips crash into mine with the end of his orgasm. Despite knowing it won't help, I tug my hands, wishing they were free.

"My turn. Stand behind her," Sapph chants.

Aleks tucks his softening cock away as he rounds the cross. His lips are on my neck, and I tip my head to give him better access. Sapph drags a chair over, plops down, then whips out a vibrator. I watch as she rubs circles over her clit then slides it in and out. Aleks nips my neck as his hand slips around my body unnoticed. When he tugs the chain between the nipple clamps, my pussy clenches hard. It's almost enough to send me over the edge. Almost.

"You're so fucking beautiful." Sapph slips the vibrator out and rubs it over her clit. She prefers clitoral stimulation to get off.

"If you let me out, I could do that for you," I whimper. She laughs sardonically as Aleks tugs the chain harder. I cry out. My body wants to collapse over, but I can't with the restraints. "I need to come!" I yell, and both of them chuckle. They fucking chuckle.

"Give me a color," Sapph demands, slipping the vibrator inside her cunt.

"Green!" I cry. "I'm fucking green, but I need to come," I whine in response.

Sapph pulls the vibrator from her and walks to me. Aleks stands up straight, but his hands stay on my sides. "Open," she tells me. I open my mouth, and she slips the vibrator in. I moan at her taste coating the toy. Aleks pulls on the chain, tugging my nipples roughly. My entire body clenches, and my moan changes to whimpers as pain mixes with desperation.

"Hands off," Sapph tells Aleks as she pulls the vibrator from my mouth. "Eyes on me," she instructs as she returns to her chair. She wastes no time in circling her clit with the vibrating toy. I watch with hooded eyes as her body clenches. Moisture gathers between her lips, just beneath the toy. She moans loudly as her orgasm rolls through her. Her scent fills the room. I find myself jealous of the air that gets to absorb her orgasm while I'm forced to watch from a distance.

The plug has been still in my ass. It's not until Sapph looks at me with a wicked grin that I realize it was intentional. The toy kicks into high gear along with Aleks and Sapph. They move around me quickly, but I can't process what is happening. My eyes close as I'm manhandled. My hips thrust against Aleks and Sapph, whoever is closest to me. I'm so close. I'm almost there.

I'm placed on the floor in Aleks's lap. I'm facing him, and his shirt is gone. I collapse against his chest, remembering the sticky semen on my stomach. I don't even care that we are a sticky mess. My body was already slick with sweat and my own arousal. I grind my hips against him, knowing the jeans he's still wearing will be enough to get me off. He grabs my hips to stop me. I try to force my hips against his grip, but he's stronger than me.

Sapph is at my back. She takes one of my hips and slides the vibrator coated in her fluids inside me. I groan at having two toys, both vibrating. She shoves me into Aleks by pressing her body into my back. The Vic sandwich pushes me over the edge. My entire body convulses. My vision is white. My skin feels nothing and everything. So much fluid drips down my legs that I almost worry that I've peed on Aleks. It's not pee, though.

Aleks grabs my hair and pulls me back to kiss me. I can't make my lips work. My eyes flutter as my body jerks. Soon, the vibrating toys become too much. My moans change to whimpers. Sapph stops the toys and removes the vibrator first, then the plug. I sigh contentedly and collapse against Aleks. I have no control over any part of my body.

Aleks holds me tight while Sapph cleans everything. I can hear her wiping the furniture and toys. She comes back to me and works on removing the lingerie. It's not an easy process, and I protest every movement I have to make. Sapph gently wipes down my body. Aleks positions me so I don't have to move my muscles.

"Sorry about your pants," Sapph says softly. "I didn't expect that, and I don't have other clothes for you." Aleks chuckles, the sound rumbling through his chest. I swoon and nuzzle against him.

"That's how you celebrate an anniversary," I mumble playfully. Aleks pinches my side but can't suppress his laughter. This is how I want to celebrate everything from here on out: an orgasm in a Vic sandwich. I sigh contentedly as Sapph settles beside us and rubs my arm. A year ago, I thought my extensive knowledge of motorcycle clubs from Sons of Anarchy and the four romance novels I read would help me survive in this world. Nothing could have prepared me for falling in love with my brother's two best friends and the challenges we have faced. Coming here was the best decision I ever made.

IF YOU ENJOYED BROKEN GOD, BE SURE TO CHECK OUT THE REST OF MY BOOKS AT

APRILGAISFORD.COM

PS STAY TUNED FOR HARPO'S BOOK, SECRET GOD, IN 2025.

Also By

Hidden Gods Series

A series of dark romance ranging from sapphic mafia, FFM motorcycle club, MMF mafia, and more.

Corrupt Goddess

Hidden God

Secret God (coming 2025)

Sweet Briar Series

A completed why choose fairy tale series about a cursed princess who must find her true love. Spicy, queer, and magical.

CURSES AND THUNDER

FATE AND LIGHTNING
340

ROOMMATES

A queer why choose romance about a guy down on his luck taken in by three roommates.

About the Author

April is a non-binary parent living in Minnesota. They are an avid reader, with a special interest in smut. They love collecting random things, such as coffee mugs, posters, graphic tees, scrunchies, and more. They love long romantic trips around Target and buying new books to add to their emotional support pile.

Acknowledgements

I need to give a huge shout out to Karan at Haven Books! She was a wealth of information. I should also apologize for all the nights I went to writer's group and spent the time asking questions instead of writing. Thanks for that!

Also, thanks to Ben, Stephanie, Emily, Caitlin, Kandace, Nicole. You all are excellent sounding boards! lol much love!